SELA

SELA

BOOK TWO OF THE LELAND DRAGONS SERIES

BY JACKIE GAMBER

SECOND EDITION

Published by Big Imagine 2023

ISBN: 978-1-7360238-3-9

Library of Congress Control Number: 2012934357

©2012, 2023 by Jackie Gamber

Cover art ©2023 by Ellen Kjiersten Gamber

Sela is a work of fiction. Names, characters, places, and incidents are the product of the author's imagination or used fictitiously.

First edition published 2012.

All rights reserved. Published in Atlanta, GA, USA.

Cover Art by
Interior Design by
Ellen Kjiersten Gamber

Written by
Jackie Gamber

To Michael Fletcher
For sharing my passport to new worlds
From my Sela to yours, with love

SELA

CHAPTER ONE

Sela's art was dead inside, just like her hope.

But she tried. She huddled on her bed, enwrapped in a quilt, and tilted her painting canvas toward the crack of morning light stabbing through her thatch ceiling. Not that more light made any difference. The blobs and swishes of oily pigments remained blobs and swishes, and refused to pull themselves into the sunset landscape she'd been trying to capture for days. Weeks. Years.

As a young dragon, she'd loved dipping her claw into colors and urging them into smooth elm leaves, or into dappled hawk feathers, or sun-glittered dragonflies. Whether on canvas, or smooth river stones, or simply scribbling in the rocky soil around the Leland Mountains, her art had been effortless. Vibrant and alive. Almost lifting away to become the thing she'd created.

But her hands were human now. After all the years since that day, her limbs still felt foreign and detached, as though they belonged to someone else. Trying to paint, she couldn't wrap her fingers comfortably around the brushes. She couldn't feel the weight of the pigments, smell the subtle differences in color mixtures. Her art felt foreign and detached, as well, and came out onto canvas as lifeless as her spirit.

She slipped her bare feet to the timbers that were her bedroom floor and crossed quietly toward the corner. She set the painting against the wall, backside out, the way she set her every failed attempt. Her canvases lined several feet of the wall or were stacked askew and coated in thatch dust. All of them backside up, or out. All of them abandoned.

Save one.

She knelt and tugged at a loose wall plank. Behind it awaited her first and only try at a portrait. It, too, was scrabbled and unfinished, and a poor replica of her father's majestic face. His red scales appeared dry, his horned crown faded. Where she'd tried to capture the sinewy lines of his neck, the painting cut off abruptly. She'd given up.

But his eyes, brown and hollow, haunted her. They were the single feature she'd managed just right. Yes, they were distant. Cool. Empty. But it's exactly how she felt each time she looked into his gaze.

When Sela became human, her father's eyes changed. He loved her, like her mother did; she knew that. But he'd stopped being proud of her. Ever since that day.

She heard a creak of a footstep on the stairs outside

her bedroom, and hastily replaced the portrait, and the wooden plank. Then she threw herself back into bed.

"Sela, you awake?"

Orman Thistleby poked his head around the lace curtain door to her bedroom.

She pulled her quilt over her head. "No."

"Hah!" Orman's hands tugged at the quilt. "No lazy bones today! Much to do, up you go."

"I'm up. I'm up," she muttered.

"Don't see your feet on the floor." Cold fingertips poked at her bare feet.

She squealed and wrenched so hard she tumbled to the floor. She lay cocooned in her quilt, her face pressed to her dusty braided rug. "I wonder if anyone starts their morning so brutally."

Orman crouched, resting his elbows on his knobby knees. His gray eyes, surrounded by crags and wrinkles, found her face. They were bright, like his smile. "I'd guess most folks get up when the sun tells them to."

She pushed up to her knees, tugging at the quilt, straining to free herself. "That must make me unlike most folks."

"That," said Orman, pinching at the edge of the quilt near her shoulder. It dropped away in a puddle of patchwork around her legs, freeing her. He rose, tugging her to her feet. "That," he repeated, "...is the understatement of the millennium, Sela Redheart." He patted her cheek, and then turned, hobbling toward the doorway. "Breakfast is burning. Get yourself around, or you'll miss it."

"I might not get to eat it, but if it's burned, I certainly won't miss it." She playfully tossed a crocheted pillow at his back, but it stopped just short of his spine and dropped to the floor.

Cheater.

"As much a cheater as a young lady who throws pillows at an old man while his back is turned." Orman disappeared behind her doorway curtain.

She hurried after him. She really was hungry, and breakfast didn't smell burned at all. She hiked up the skirt of her sleeping gown, and started down the rickety stairs that led into the cottage below. Her feet just touched the brushed dirt floor of the main chamber, when Orman, already at the fireplace in the kitchen nook, held up his hand.

"What is—?"

Orman scowled, and waved her back toward her room.

A knock rattled the front door, startling her. She clutched the handrail and leaned toward the window, trying to get a peek. "Who is it, Uncle Orman?"

"Get back," he said, and pointed upstairs again. "Stay in your room until I say." He scuffled toward the door.

"But—"

The knocking became pounding. Orman had to throw himself against the door and grip the latch to keep it from shuddering open. "To your room!"

Sela frowned. Here was the first visitor they'd ever had to their little home in all the years she'd been living with Orman, and now he was sending her upstairs to hide like a child.

"Sela," Orman said through clenched teeth. His knuckles were white where he held the latch.

"I'm going." She spun on the stairs, and hurried toward her room. But she stayed by the doorway, and pressed her ear close to her curtain to listen.

"Give an old man time to reach the door," Orman called out over the relentless hammering. She heard the latch give way, and the creak of the opening door.

"This is the home of Orman Thistleby," said a deep male voice.

"Yes," Orman snapped. "I know. If you attacked my door just to tell me that, it was a waste of audacity."

"You've failed to respond to the census issued by Venur Moras Shornmar."

"What do you take me for, you upstart? Venur Shornmar died eight months ago."

Sela slowly and carefully pushed aside the curtain to peek downstairs. Orman was trying to shut the door, but a massive boot blocked it. The boot surged forward, forcing the door open. Orman stepped back, scowling up at a man who emerged through the doorway.

"Venur Moras Shornmar the *Second*," said the man. His chin was covered with blonde stubble. His sandy hair was shaved close against his neck, but his bangs were long, and slashed across his angry eyes. He wore a tailored coat with shiny buttons near the shoulders, and a swatch of purple cloth crossed from his left shoulder to his right hip. He slapped a rolled parchment to Orman's shoulder. "The census is not optional."

Orman thrust up his hands, knocking the man's hand away. "Bah! My porridge is burning!" Orman shuffled toward the fireplace, and stuck a poker through the handle of an iron pot hanging over the flames. He set the pot onto the hearth. "Look what you've done! It's pig food now."

"You'll be pig food if you ignore this again, old man." He threw the rolled parchment to the table. "All of Leland's women will appear before the Venur, including your niece."

Orman stretched to his full height. His gray beard wagged against his chest as he lifted his chin. "Who offends my family's honor? I have no niece."

The man narrowed his eyes. "The town speaks of a girl who lives with you who has reached the age of maturity."

Orman pointed his crooked finger into the man's face. "There is no girl under my roof who has reached any such of age of any such determination!"

The man waved a hand. "It's not my job to argue about it. You've got one week. If you don't respond, you'll be breaking the law, and your niece will appear before the Venur anyway." The man yanked open the door. "As witness at your trial." He strode outside.

Orman slammed the door behind him.

Sela rushed down the steps. "Orman! Why did you lie to him?"

Orman scowled down at the steaming pot of porridge. He poked a wooden spoon into the sticky depths. "Who's lying? I don't have any brothers and sisters, so how can I have a niece?"

"You know he means me. Townspeople have heard me call you Uncle Orman."

"They wouldn't have if you'd learn to keep your silence. Bring me a bowl."

Sela plucked a clay bowl from their wooden table, and carried it to him. "Careful, it's got a chip." He took it with a nod, and scooped a glob of dark porridge into it. "Why did you tell him I don't live with you?"

Orman returned the bowl to her hands, the clay warmed from the hot breakfast. "I never said that. I told him there was no girl here who'd reached any sort of determined age." He bunched his wrinkled face. "Do you know how old you are, exactly, in human years?"

Sela carried her breakfast to the table. "No. I guess not." She dabbed her finger at a blackened lump in her bowl.

Orman patted her arm, and then drooped onto the bench beside her. "Dragons and humans age differently, my dear. Maybe in human years, you are as old as you look."

She stared into her porridge. "Makes me wonder if I'll be young all over again if I ever change back." Then she stiffened. "I mean, *when*. When I change back."

"Yes, when. We'll sort out what happened somehow."

She and Orman and her parents had been trying to figure that out for years, and none of them were any closer to the truth.

She touched her fingers to the curled parchment on the table. "So what are you going to do about the census?"

"What census?" Orman shoveled a spoonful of porridge into his mouth.

"That man said you'd be breaking the law if you don't respond."

Orman wagged his spoon at her, porridge splattering to the table. "Never you mind about that. Are you finished?"

She looked at the bowl full of pale rivulets and scorched lumps. She decided she wasn't as hungry as she thought. "Yes." Instead of eating, she began to unfurl the census parchment.

Orman snatched it away and pointed it at her. "Then hurry and dress. Your father gets grumpy when we're late." He shambled into the kitchen nook and tossed the parchment into the fireplace, where it caught near the front corner and began to smoke. "I'll saddle Nimrod." And then he stepped outside.

Chapter Two

Bannon Raley trudged toward Simson town square, hitching his canvas pack of parchments higher onto his shoulder. He stopped at the edge of a fountain to scrape the mud from his boots, and when that didn't clean it all, he stomped his foot against a granite rock. Chickens squawked in alarm, and ran off in all directions away from him.

He slumped onto the fountain wall. He would have liked to cup a handful of water over the back of his sticky neck, but the days of refreshment from this fountain were long gone. Fissures crackled her basin, and her center column reached up with a gnarled, empty fist.

In fact, the whole rumpled village of Simson seemed achingly tired. Stone huts squatted around the fountain, tipping haphazard straw roofs in some sort of obsolete greeting. Arbor oaks and sweeping willow trees drooped toward the sloppy roads. Even the flies were even silent as they circled, too weary to bother buzzing.

He knew how they felt. He was tired, too. He'd had

to leave his horse at the town stable, because Simson streets were too narrow to navigate on horseback. Having tromped around the city most of the day had left his feet aching, and his spine slick from the heat.

"You finished?" asked a voice behind him. He turned to find Sway Burnam, his fellow guard, sauntering toward him. His broad face was pink from sun. The canvas bag over his shoulder was full of parchments, too.

"For now," Bannon said. "I think the old man on the farm outside of town is going to ignore it completely."

"You know how many I had to stand and wait on to be filled out?" Sway dropped his bag and slouched beside Bannon on the fountain wall. "What's wrong with this town? Can't they read?"

"I don't know. Maybe they've been minding their own business so long they forgot they're a part of Leland. Half of them didn't even know Moras died." Bannon slid his hand through his damp hair and looked toward the path from where he'd come. "That old man knew, though. Something odd about that one."

"What, just one? You should have seen the barmy goats I talked to. Plenty of them up and offered their daughters to send back with me right now." Sway shook his head, and plunged his hands into a side pack for a water bladder. "Crossed my mind to take one. Pretty little curls, all wrapped around her head." He tipped up the bladder and gulped. Water trickled onto his chin and clung to dark stubble.

"I'm sure your wife would understand."

Sway wiped his sleeve across his mouth and smiled. "Was her I was thinking of, with her coming due any second now. She could use a helper."

Bannon took the bladder and laughed. "I'm half-tempted to talk you into it, just to watch a pregnant woman batter a grown man with a frying pan."

Sway puffed his chest, and thumped his fist against it. "I could take her." Then he rubbed his chest, and winced. "Ow."

Bannon laughed again, and held the bladder to his mouth to drink. The water was warm, but sloshed against the back of his dry throat, and he felt better. He stood. "Let's get the horses. We might make it halfway by morning."

"You want to go now?" Sway pushed the water bladder back into his side pack. "The tavern's just around the corner. I can't see us making much progress in the dark, anyway."

"I want to go now. Come on, old man."

"Bannon. For pity's sake. One drink."

"I've never seen you take just one drink."

Sway smiled. "So a drink and a half, then."

Bannon held up his hand to insist, but just then, Sway's eyes locked onto something over Bannon's left shoulder. Sway's eyebrows shot up. Bannon turned to see what caught his friend's eye.

A boy was approaching. No, on second look, it was a young woman wearing dark trousers and a pale tunic that hung past her knees. In the two days travel to Simson and the day of business he'd spent walking the town, no one had as much as raised a chin in greeting, let alone spoken. Bannon watched the young woman come closer, curious.

"Well, now," said Sway, moving past Bannon to intercept. "About time we met a friendly face," he said to the girl. "With all the closed doors you people live behind, a man might think this is a ghost town."

The young woman paused. Her hands were behind her back, and Bannon's reflexes went on alert. He stepped up beside Sway, but with a closer look at the girl's face, he saw her green eyes weren't hostile, only nervous. Emerald green eyes. Set in a delicate face circled by a dark braid that wound her head like a wreath. A crown, maybe, by the way she lifted her chin and looked down her nose at Sway, despite the man being a full head and shoulders taller than she.

"Now don't be like that," said Sway. "You didn't come all this way to be unfriendly, did you, Miss?" His thick hand reached out to stroke that dark braid.

The young woman's eyes flitted to Bannon. She seemed to know him, though he was sure he'd never seen her before. He would have remembered those eyes.

"I want to talk to your friend," she said, with a voice smoother and younger than he was expecting. Her words were for Sway, but her eyes were still on Bannon, and he got the distinct feeling she was expecting him to do something about Sway's unwelcome touch.

"Uh, Sway. Chum. Why don't you head into the tavern, and I'll meet up."

Sway stepped back. "Eh, it figures. Girl doesn't

know a real man when she sees one."

"Maybe you smell married."

Sway laughed, and punched Bannon's arm. "No such thing, my friend. You can take away a man's freedom, but you can never shackle his spirit. That's where his smell comes from, you know. His spirit." He thumped his chest, and then strode off past the fountain.

"And here I thought it came from his armpits," murmured the woman.

They shared a smile. It was such a minor thing. Just a small, warm grin. But it slapped Bannon with surprise, because he couldn't remember sharing such a thing before with anyone, and surely not with someone he'd just met. He felt suddenly as awkward as though he'd just kissed her flat on the mouth. Maybe she sensed it, too, because she lowered her gaze and shifted her feet. And cleared her throat.

"Do I know you?" he asked.

She shook her head, eyes looking toward the ground. Both hands were still behind her back.

"But you wanted to talk to me."

She nodded. She took a breath. "What will happen to my...um, to people who don't turn in the census you're asking for?"

"They'll be arrested."

Her face darted up. "But why?"

"Because they'll have broken the law."

"But why is it breaking the law?"

Bannon shifted his pack against his shoulder. "Because your Venur has said so."

"Is that who you work for?"

"Not exactly. He's borrowing me. Leland hasn't had much of its own guard force for a long time."

"Why not?"

"You ask a lot of questions." Bannon meant to sound irritated, but he smiled again, despite himself.

"I get that from my mother, I think." She smiled again, too.

The moment turned awkward once more, and, this time, *he* cleared his throat. "So, uh…was there anything else?"

She nodded, and her face turned solemn. Her hands came around from behind her back, and he realized what she'd been holding all along wasn't a weapon, but one of the rolled parchments, burned at the edges. "I don't want my uncle to be arrested." Her face wrinkled up, and he was afraid she might cry.

"You're doing the right thing," he said, taking the parchment. Their eyes met. And he saw that, though there was pain behind her eyes, they held no tears. "Do you get those from your mother, too?" he asked.

"What?" She tipped her head.

"Your eyes."

At first, her face tightened in fear. Then she blinked and smiled, and her cheeks filled so brightly with red she must have felt it, because she touched her fingertips to them.

Either she didn't get out much, or Bannon was better at delivering a line than he thought he was. She didn't answer, and he wasn't sure what he was supposed to do next, because he'd never made a woman blush before, so he unrolled the parchment and pretended to review it. Bits of scorched edge crumbled against his fingertips.

"Orman Thistleby?" he suddenly asked, realizing. "You're that old man's niece who doesn't exist."

"He didn't exactly lie."

"Oh? You're a ghost, then?"

She took a step back.

"Says here your name's Sella."

"Sela. See-la," she corrected.

"No last name. No age."

"Do I have to have that part?"

"Well, it's the point of filling one out. Half-answered is the same thing as not answered."

"Can't you just turn it in anyway? Maybe I couldn't read it."

Bannon frowned. "First the old man, and now you."

"I have to go. Please don't tell Orman about this."

"Why not?"

"I have to go, or he'll know what I've done." She turned to hurry away. "He probably already knows." She took several quick steps, then paused. "What's your name?"

"I'm Bannon. Bannon Raley."

She smiled and nodded. She turned to run.

"Sela what?" Bannon called. "Thistleby?"

"No!" She waved over her shoulder. "Just Sela!" She turned a corner, and was gone.

"Now, see, a real man wouldn't have let her get

away so easily," said Sway from behind.

Bannon shoved the census into his pack. "I thought you were drinking."

"I was. I'm done."

"Already?" Bannon turned to look at his friend. "You're slipping. I've seen you drink places dry."

Sway scowled. "I did drink the place dry. If a man isn't going to stock like a tavern, shouldn't hang a tavern sign over the door. Come on." He shouldered his own pack, and trudged off toward the stable.

Bannon would have laughed, but felt a twinge of disappointment, instead. He'd never admit it out loud, but he preferred traveling with Sway when the man had a few drinks in him. Just a few. A jovial Sway moved his horse faster, and waxed poetic and talkative, and freed up Bannon to slip into a quiet rhythm that made time and travel pass quickly. Now the two days would last forever.

They retrieved their horses, checked their saddlebags, and were on their way out of town as the high afternoon sun turned downright sizzling. The road, so muddy this morning, was already baking dry, and the air was thick with humidity.

"I like a dry heat," said Sway, beginning his list of complaints.

"Mm-hmm," said Bannon.

"Air's too thick. Slow going."

"Mm-hmm," said Bannon.

"And now we've got to follow behind an old man and a boy with a fat ass."

"What?" Bannon sat up straighter, and looked ahead. Sure enough, just far enough away to be a dark silhouette, a rickety old man led a fat, swayback donkey along the road. Atop the donkey sat a delicate rider. "That's no boy." He dug his heels against his mount's ribs to catch them.

"Afternoon," he said, as he sauntered his mount past Orman Thistleby and his niece.

Emerald eyes shifted and settled on his face. The rider smiled, a little, and opened her mouth, but the old man shot a warning look, so she just pressed her mouth closed and looked off toward the trees.

"On your way with you," said the old man, his gray beard rumpled against his tunic.

Sway and his horse caught up to them just then, and he sidled up. "Oh," he said, leaning toward the young woman. "Well, hey—"

"We'll be leaving you to your travels, then. Safe journey." Bannon gave Sway a hard look. "Let's go."

Sway didn't speak, but his fuzzy brows arched. He lunged on with his mount.

The old man looked suspiciously at Sway's back, then to the woman, then to Bannon. Bannon just smiled. He wasn't ready to leave just yet, but for the woman's sake, he knew he should. As though they'd never before spoken.

Even as he continued on, rocking with the trot of his horse, he felt her eyes burn into his shoulder blades. It was those eyes he'd wanted another glimpse of, just to see if they were really as green and piercing as he'd remembered them.

They were.

He glanced over his shoulder to see if she really was still watching him. If she was, he couldn't tell, because the old man had led the donkey off the road as was disappearing into the trees. "What the…?"

"What?" Sway swiveled in his saddle.

"Where are they going?"

"I don't know. Let them be, that old buzzard gives me the creeps. And what was all that with the looks between you and the girl? Too hot out for all that nonsense." Sway dragged his forearm across his forehead.

"There's nothing in those trees but more trees. What do you think they're doing?" Bannon turned his horse.

"I thought you wanted to get halfway by tomorrow."

"I do. We will." Still, Bannon nudged his horse toward the place off the road where the man and the girl disappeared. He could hear the trudging of the portly donkey through the scrub, and hushed talking between the two. Just as he was thinking it was none of his business, and was tugging the reins to turn back, a bright flash erupted in the trees, followed by a sprinkle of shimmering dust that floated down and became obscured by the woods. "Sway! Did you see that?"

"Huh?" Sway looked up from where he was hunched in his saddle. His mount plucked a patch of grass from the side of the road and lazily chewed.

Bannon slid off his horse and crept into the trees.

He found the donkey nosing the bark of knobby willow. It flicked an ear as he approached, but didn't bother to look at him. There were no sparkles in the air, on the leaves, or flickering on the underbrush. There was, however, an expanse of smooth slate deep in the ground as though someone had dug deep to find it. In the center of this slate laid an orange stone as big as his fist. At first, he stared. Then he stepped down onto the slate, and knelt to touch the stone. It was warm.

"Bannon, you lummox, where'd you go?" Sway broke the limbs off a short tree as he lumbered near, then drew up short. He let out a low whistle. "Would you look at that? Biggest chunk of crystal I ever laid my eyes on. That'll get me a new roof and a pretty little something for the missus." He stepped onto the slate beside Bannon.

"We'd better leave it."

"Are you mad? Someone doesn't want to part with it, they shouldn't have left it for any fool who happened by to find it." Sway crouched and grabbed, but the crystal didn't budge. "Stuck," he groaned, trying to wrench it free.

"Just leave it. Come on." Bannon nudged Sway with the toe of his boot.

"I'm not leaving without this rock."

"Oh, yes you are," said the donkey.

Both men startled. Bannon hopped back and off the slate, staring at the beast that disinterestedly settled onto his belly and drew up his legs.

Bannon nudged Sway's arm. "Come on," he said

again.

"Right behind you."

Neither man spoke as they climbed back onto their mounts and trotted off toward the horizon. Sway was guiding his horse plenty fast. Maybe the two days wouldn't last forever, after all.

§

"What in blazes was that all about?" Orman sputtered, gripping the clear crystal around his neck, his knuckles bulging as he waved them near Sela's face.

"What are you talking about?" she asked, arms crossing.

"That soldier from this morning just happens to pass us on the road, looking as though he knows you from somewhere, and then just happens to stumble onto our crystal, and just *happens* to almost manage to steal it!"

"What? How is that my doing?"

"I had to use the carnsarned donkey to scare them off. Now they'll be suspicious." Orman reached into the collar of his brown tunic and slowly withdrew his withered staff. He planted it into the ground and pushed off in a huff. The crystal at the top, gripped in place by twisted, carved fingers, glowed white-hot. Sela knew Uncle Orman was angry, and she knew better than to provoke him just now. Still. It wasn't really her fault.

She followed him along the veiled and winding path through the thick beech and pine trees of Mount

Gore. It had been almost six months since her last visit, but it felt like yesterday. Pine branches tickled her shoulders as she passed, washing her with their heady scent. Slices of sunbeams warmed her face as she passed through them, and her boots landed softly on thick layers of needles and underbrush.

She loved this place, this mountain where she'd been born. Where her father still ruled as Herald of the Reds on the Dragon Council. Where now she had to sneak on hidden paths to Mount Gore Manor, instead of boldly soaring on the red, glittering wings she'd been born with.

Still, she'd rather walk her way around the mountain than to never come at all.

She caught up with Orman, who was picking his way around a jumble of stones that must have broken loose since their last visit. His walking stick crystal was nearly clear again. "I don't know why those soldiers followed us, Uncle Orman."

Orman paused. "Sela Redheart, I'll never understand why you think you can get away with lying to me."

The sadness of his voice surprised her. She was speechless as she stared at his wrinkled face, but only for a moment. "Maybe you were in such a hurry that you gave us away."

He pursed his lips, searching her eyes. "Maybe." Then he continued his way up the path toward the clearing where her father would be waiting. "That crystal is our only way back. I'm too carnsarned old to make it the traditional way."

"And too carnsarned stubborn to come up with a less dramatic sort of transportation," said a resonant voice in dragonspeak.

Sela nudged past Orman and broke into a run. "Father!"

She couldn't yet see him over the crest of the path, until he poked his snout above the edge. Then she swerved to meet him, and more of him became visible. First his full head, then his strong neck, and then the tips of his wide, crimson wings. She threw herself at his throat and hugged tightly.

Kallon Redheart laughed, and she felt the rumble of it all the way to her toes. He dragged her into the clearing, her feet bouncing along the ground, and she giggled. "Where is Mother?"

"Awaiting you impatiently at the manor. We've sent the staff on holiday, and she's stayed up all night making sweet biscuits and blackberry jam."

"With her own two hands?" Sela asked, and was immediately sorry. Of course her mother had no hands. It was a slip of the tongue. "I mean—"

"I know what you mean," said her father. He bent his forelegs, jerked suddenly to his right, and swung Sela onto his shoulder blades. "She claims to remember the recipe from when she was your age," he said.

Sela landed with an 'oomph', and circled her arms around his neck. "Mother remembers all sorts of interesting things, doesn't she?"

"And thank the stars for that," said Orman, leading

them across the clearing. "I'll take biscuits and jam over muskrat consommé any day. Most dragons don't understand the human palate!"

Her father was silent, save for the stepping of his feet against the soft ground, and Sela wondered if she'd let slip another uncomfortable thought. Her mother had once been a human too, after all, and so she and Sela shared an experience no one else could appreciate. Dragon tastes, desires, instincts, all tumbled together in their minds with the perplexity of their human memories. She tried not to keep reminding her father how other-creature she'd become, as if she could hide such a thing from him.

But he'd loved her mother before she was a dragon, all those years ago. Accepted her. Why couldn't he bring himself to accept his human child?

"The mountains aren't safe," said her father, his wide head swinging toward Orman. "I nearly sent word to cancel this visit, but her mother insisted I not."

"And I had hoped to extend this one, Kallon," said Orman.

"Extend?"

"Even Simson isn't safe anymore. Word of the census has reached to the farthest corners, and your daughter will be discovered." He looked over his shoulder, met her eyes with his tired, craggy stare. "If she hasn't been, already."

At that, she looked away. She watched the pinewood treetops stagger as her father pressed through them, the clearing long behind them. Birds leapt from their rocking nests, scolding her in their flight.

It's not my fault, she wanted to say to them. But they wouldn't likely listen, or care, any more than Orman.

"Mount Gore may be compromised," said her father. "We'll have to discuss other options."

She'd been hearing that since she first turned human. How Mount Gore couldn't be her home anymore; how, for reasons no one would discuss openly, her "condition" put her and other Leland Dragons in danger.

She knew she should care about the situation and the safety of her Dragonkind, but she was tired of being something that needed options. A complication to her parents. A difficulty for her uncle. She just wanted to come home, once and for all, and to stay here.

To belong again.

"Sela?" called a voice through the trees. Her mother's voice was breathy, excited. She must have smelled her coming. Sela never was able to play hide and seek from her when she used to play those sorts of games. Her mother would pretend Sela was lost, but no matter how well she covered herself with leaves, or buried herself into the earth, or flew up into the boughs of the highest oak tree, her mother would find her. Her jeweled head tilted, her green eyes glittering, her mother would grin and say "My, you really had me that time."

Sela always knew she hadn't fooled her.

Her mother plunged into the trees, parting them so Sela could see the mouth of Gore Manor just behind. Her mother's ruby wings swept forward, hugging both her father and herself, and she cried out, "Oh, I've missed you!"

"I've missed you too, Mother," said Sela, muffled beneath leathery appendages.

If she only knew how much.

Her mother's wings withdrew, and she crooked her neck to smile into Sela's face. She looked deep into her eyes, straight into them the way her father never could. She touched the curve of her claw to Sela's cheek.

"I know," she said.

Then she stepped back and held out her forelegs. "Slide off your father, and let's get you fed and watered. Then you know what we'll do next?"

Sela's heart skipped. She was afraid to suggest it, in case she was wrong. She turned onto her belly, slithered down her father's shoulder to his leg, and then to the ground. She faced her mother hopefully.

"We will fly," she said.

Sela drew in a breath.

"Riza," said her father. "I really don't think—"

"Nonsense," said her mother. "I can take her safely down the mountain."

"Riza," said her father again.

Her mother took her shoulders, guided her around gently toward the manor. "Our daughter isn't only here to visit, Kallon," she said. "She is here to remember."

Chapter Three

Drell coiled his serpentine tail and relaxed against the sky. He drew in his legs and spiraled downward, lazily flapping his wings, watching tiny sandstorms erupt from the endless desert below him. He veered and drifted a few feet from the sand's surface, creating ripples of miniature dunes. This late in the day, the sun was too hot and the desert too scorching to land, but Drell was content to kiss at the sands with his movements, watching the grains shift and retreat beneath his shadow.

Ironic, he often thought, that his midnight-black form produced his only twin; a dragon shape as dark and solitary as he. His Kind called him Shadow, meant to be affectionate, but it was a constant reminder of his aloneness. Rage Desert dragons were the color of their sun-bleached surroundings; of tawny, marbled browns and pale corals, patterned uniquely from tribe to tribe. No desert dragon was the color of coal. No desert dragon had ever been.

Drell was a borrowed offspring.

The Ambercrest tribe that shared their home and their way of life gave him a sense of connection, in a way. But his visits from Vaya Brownwing kept him from feeling completely alone. She would appear unexpectedly, bringing him sweet fruits from the mountains, or a cask of cool water from Ares River. And they would fly, and she would share stories of her life in Leland, and sometimes, more often in the past few months, she would even lead him into the mountains. Late at night, or early in the day. Teaching him of the trees, the meadow, and the dragon village to which he was forbidden to go.

He was her secret in some way. A way that had always been implied but never discussed. She made no reference to their relation, and he called her by her given name, Vaya, but in time, he'd come to realize their bond had to be more than friendship.

They shared the same golden eyes.

He sensed the Leland Mountains to be his true home, and he dreamed of someday returning there, to live among the Dragonkind that, for now, remained a mystery.

"You linger too long," said Tay Ambercrest, swooping above. Drell had been so engulfed by his thoughts that he hadn't even sensed the dragon coming. "The heat will roast you inside your own skin."

"I am thirsty." Drell veered and inclined to where Tay hovered, his honey-dappled wings slowly beating. Drell admired the slender dragon against the desert landscape, as he often did. At certain angles, his dragon brethren seemed to disappear, camouflaged entirely by the distant rocky border, the blanched sky, the sweeping, mottled sands.

"At this time of day, even heavy thoughts are too much a burden," said Tay, smiling at his own humor. Then he sobered. "And I smell a brewing storm."

Even the desert dragons feared the sand funnels that gave the desert its name. Grains rose up like tentacles, frenzied and growling, and sank into the sea of sand, only to reappear yards away, angrily spewing. The granules of a Rage storm could flay the scales from a dragon in matter of moments. Sudden squalls were certain death.

Drell didn't hesitate. He continued to incline, up and away from the threat of being caught by a funnel. "Of all the skills I have learned, I've yet to recognize the scent of a storm."

"Not all Esra dragons do," said Tay. "Those of us that have seen one and lived to tell about it have had the memory scalded into our brains."

Drell paused, allowing Tay to swerve beside him. "You've never told me about that."

"Haven't I?"

When Tay failed to elaborate, Drell didn't press. He'd learned to respect Tay's privacy concerning certain things, and this, apparently, would be one of them. Tay was the closest thing Drell had to a father, and although he didn't call him by the title, Tay had earned all the veneration of one.

"You were searching again," Tay said quietly.

"No. Not this time."

Their beating wings fell into shared rhythm. Beneath them, their shadows collided, appearing as a great, misshapen beast against the passing sand.

"You have nothing to prove," said Tay. "You are our Kind. As much to the others as to Lena and me."

"I know," said Drell. And yet, he was drawn, again and again, toward the heart of Rage Desert. To the sanctuary ruins, chewed and swallowed long ago by the angry sands.

The ruins were said to be the cradle of the dragon race, the place from which all magic began, and where dragons first formed from the bones of the earth. In a time when water flowed to nourish the land, the land in turn became feed for its first creatures. Green, swaying fronds and succulent vines once flourished.

Until the sands came, brought as a curse for transgressions long forgotten. The earth belched its innards, dry as death, and choked off the water. Dragons were forced into the sky, out of the arms of mother earth, to fend for themselves.

And day after day, year after year, century after century, the violent, punishing sands continued to feast.

According to Tay, what was once considered history has become mere legend, and Esra dragons didn't even believe a ruined sanctuary existed. To them, the sand has always been.

Drell didn't believe it, either. Not really. But, still. He was often drawn to the desert to search. Because few Esra dragons could withstand the brutality of their desert, and to find the center, and the lost ruins, would take a kind of fortitude like no dragon before him.

If Drell the Shadow was successful where no other desert dragon had been, perhaps he would really, finally, feel like one of them.

"You have nothing to prove," said Tay.

And Drell replied, again. "I know."

CHAPTER FOUR

Venur Vorham Riddess arched back into his carved wooden chair and stretched his arms above his head, releasing a loud, satisfying yawn. Then he scratched his fingers into his wiry black hair, and drew them down his face, massaging blood into his numbed cheeks.

"You could do with a cup of tea," said Fane Whitetail, Vorham's milky-pale advisor. The dragon's shoulders were hunched, his neck awkwardly twisted. Whitetail's wings were curled beneath him, wrapped like a sausage, so crammed he was into Vorham's study.

"And you could do with my knocking down a wall for a bigger office."

Whitetail smiled. "Yes. I did wonder why your eminence insisted on meeting here. It is fortunate I am of slender build."

Slender. The dragon was downright scrawny. Runt-like. Vorham had often mentally compared his white-washed advisor to the blonde Meedes Steed residing in his stable. He did so again now. And again, he was certain the stately horse outsized Whitetail by a hand or two. But it wasn't Whitetail's strength or aggression Vorham had come to appreciate over the years of the dragon's service. It was Whitetail's uncanny ability to insinuate himself into any group and to retrieve the kind of information only a trusted ally should be able to discover.

Vorham was ever amazed at Whitetail's talents. And ever on guard against them.

Vorham pushed from his desk and stood. He shuffled parchments together, pushed them into a stack, and held them toward Whitetail's hovering face. "After all these years, this is all we have. Marriage to a Leland citizen. It's so desperate."

"Or clever."

Vorham threw the parchments to the floor of his study, and marched across cobbled stones to stare at the portrait of his father, Ebouard Riddess, hung between two candle sconces. "Desperate and provincial."

He heard Whitetail gathering the parchments behind him. "Or clever," he said again. "Your father would approve."

Vorham regarded his father's portrait, the man's dark eyes peering out from a face of mahogany. It wasn't his father's skin alone that matched the wood, but his aged layers of wisdom, the carved edge to his smile. He'd been the kind of Venur, and the kind of man, a son could look up to. High moral standards. True to his word.

Severe. Inflexible. Out-moded.

He would indeed approve of Vorham's plan to expand Esra's borders into Leland. To combine the two provinces into a vast property by marriage. Leland's oldest Venur, Moras Shornmar, who had outlived two wives and three sons, had finally died in his sleep eight months ago. His only surviving son, born late in life and mentally inept, had inherited a province full of buried riches, and no acuity for how to manage it.

And so Vorham, by way of cunning Whitetail, offered to marry a Leland citizen; female and of age. The junior Shornmar couldn't offer a family member, having none, so the next legal course was to offer Vorham's choice of the province. In a matter of weeks, Vorham would have himself a wife, a dim-witted brother-in-land, and, finally, the assets of Leland Province. Legal. Moral. Provincial. Indeed, his father would approve.

Which is exactly why Vorham hated the plan.

"Besides which," said Vorham, stonily eyeing his father's portrait, although he was talking to Whitetail. "Marrying a Leland woman does not avail those mountains." Those mountains rich with crystal ore. Raw, dense, and just waiting to be mined. "Waiting to be *mine*," he corrected aloud.

"Redheart cannot control them much longer," said Whitetail. "His grip on his land and his Dragonkind has been tenuous, at best, since taking his place on the Dragon Council. He leads little more than a rabble; dragons are scattered across the province like chaff."

"It is an accident of birth, you know," said Vorham. He turned his back to the portrait. "That I should be of the family who claimed the land to the West. Family who saw those mountains as unyielding and impenetrable as the raging desert below them. A family who could not have been more wrong."

"They could not have claimed them, even if they had wanted to," said Whitetail. "The mountains have always belonged to the dragons."

"My father would say it's Esra's fate to one day be taken by Rage Desert." Vorham withdrew the parchments from Whitetail's grasp. "But desert or no," said Vorham, shuffling the sheets without looking at them, "I made a swipe for those mountains before, and I will do it again. Esra and Leland will become one, and the mountains among them, and I will live to possess them." He circled his desk once more, settled into his chair, and laid the parchments before him. "Let the desert take the rest. I will have those mountains."

Whitetail lowered his snout, bowing as gracefully as he could in the cramped space. "You are as close as you have ever been to having them," said his advisor.

"I have been this close before."

"Your brother-in-law has no way of interfering this time."

Vorham smiled, dryly. "You know, I just realized that soon I'll have two brothers-in-law, Jastin Armitage *and* Moras Shornmar, and both of them diminished in the brain. I must be getting soft as I age. Benevolent."

"How so, venerable ruler?"

"First, allowing them into my family. Second, keeping them. Well, Shornmar isn't a family member yet, but I will have to keep him for some time before I'll be able to do anything about that.

"But Jastin? Surely he could meet with some sort of accident. A man of his age. Engaging in all kinds of risky behaviors."

"He took down a dragon just six months ago," said Whitetail. "His vigor for killing them has flared disastrously in the years since the Leland thunderstorm."

Vorham nodded. "Yes. I just wish he would concentrate his efforts on those mountain dragons."

Whitetail remained silent, and Vorham looked up to find his expression stoic. "Present company excepted, of course, my friend."

"Of course," said Whitetail, his gaze cool on Vorham's face.

Vorham sat back in his chair, studying the white dragon. He'd often wondered at the thoughts in the creature's brain; how he felt about watching his dragon brethren slaughtered by the ministrations of humans such as himself. Men of means and power, slaying mighty beasts of Whitetail's ilk. And not just watching, but being a part of it. Joining forces.

If Whitetail had feelings at all.

"Is it difficult to hear me talk so casually of killing your kind?" he asked.

"You do not limit your casual talk of killing to dragons, your high eminence," said Whitetail, lowering his snout again. "It is a rare man of means and power who has arisen to his station without some due violence."

"Yes. A rare man." Vorham's eyes traveled to his father's portrait again.

"Besides which," continued Whitetail. "It is but an accident of birth that I am of a tribe of scales and wings. A tribe who saw humans as unyielding and impenetrable as the raging desert around them. A family who couldn't have been more wrong."

Riddess returned his gaze to the dragon. "Well said."

"Thank you, honorable Venur," said Whitetail, pressing his snout to the floor. "You are most generous to allow me to verbalize freely."

"And speaking of unyielding and impenetrable," said Vorham, spreading out the parchments across his desk once more. The parchments containing the latest information from the Leland census; eligible ladies, names and family members, cities and ages. His gaze focused on a particular parchment that appeared scorched around the edge. "How do I make a proper show of this?"

Whitetail arched his neck to peer at the parchments, as well. "I imagine the maidens might take better to the idea if it is presented as a prize."

"How do you mean?"

"If they feel they are competing with others for marriage to a Venur, they will want to win. Perhaps let them collect at a focal point in Leland, so they can size each other up, so to speak. Then have a selection of ten or so women, and call them finalists, and treat them to a visit here for several days, where you present them with all the best food, wine, and pageantry befitting a Venuress."

"Really lay it on thick," said Vorham.

"Yes, in a manner of speaking."

"But I can't marry them all."

"No. After a set amount of days, you make the final selection with pomp and ceremony. The rest of the women will be returned home, disappointed. And your wife will feel as though she captured a treasure."

Vorham sat back against his chair and crossed his arms. "It would be much easier to just send one woman here and get on with the whole thing."

"Indeed," said Whitetail, turning away and carefully easing toward the study door. "But think of appearances."

"Yes," said Vorham, turning his gaze again to his father's portrait. "I must always think of appearances."

The painting had gone crooked against the stone wall. "I haven't visited him in some time."

"Three months," said Whitetail.

Vorham scowled over his shoulder. "Did you mark a calendar?"

"It is my duty to keep track of details."

"Yes," said Vorham. Another one of the Whitetail's talents to be on guard against. "But it's not as though he knows the difference."

"I was making no judgment, Venur," said Whitetail, shuffling toward the office door, hunched and crooked like a snow-carved gargoyle. "Do you wish to visit him now?"

"Any changes since last time?"

"None, as far as I can tell. But I'm no expert in these matters."

Vorham laughed. "Don't underestimate yourself." He rose and stepped into the hallway, making his way toward a back staircase.

To this day, Vorham suspected. How could he not? Years ago, Whitetail had sworn an oath that Vorham's father would die within hours of their pact, but he didn't. The Venur collapsed after the spring maple feast, as Whitetail said he would. But there the man lingered, in that place between waking and sleeping. Just enough breath to stay alive, but as limp and unresponsive as a corpse.

For days, and then weeks, Vorham allowed physicians and healers. For appearances. As a grieving son searching for answers. Eventually, his father, as stubborn in death as he was in life, outlasted even the healers' perseverance. Nothing could rouse the leader. Nothing could put him out of Vorham's misery.

Whitetail seemed as puzzled as everyone, and Vorham couldn't see any profit to Whitetail keeping the elder Riddess at the brink all these years. But Vorham suspected.

How could he not?

Upon reaching the blank, stony wall at the base of the discreet stairway, Vorham touched his hand to a pale slab of granite near his hip. A doorknob appeared against his palm. Then the stone façade dissolved away from his hand, receding like an unraveling blanket, to reveal the door to his father's room behind the magical ward.

Appearances, again. Years ago, when Whitetail created the ward, it was at Vorham's insistence that his father be respected. Protected.

What Vorham really wanted was to get on with the plans he'd made. Step into Venurship and let the citizens move on. Forget. Surely it would only be a matter of time before the legalities of death and inheritance would make all things legitimate.

And still, time wore on. And so did his father.

Vorham pushed open the door. A lacy cobweb stretched, and then snapped, dragging sticky threads across his cheek. He swiped at them, stepping quietly into the gloomy space. He stalked quietly to his father's deathbed.

Avara, his father's caretaker, dozed beside the bed in a velvet chair, her loose, wavy tresses caught in the carved spindles behind her head. Gray, shining hairs tracked through her mane, and faint stains of age spots scattered over the back of her hand, where it rested against the open pages of a leather book.

She'd been a younger woman when she first accepted this post.

In contrast, his father lay unchanged. His broad forehead and chestnut complexion were unmarred by time. His black hair remained close-cropped. No stubble sprouted on his chin. His arms were thick, strong, and his pristine, tailored waistcoat rose and fell with the heaving motions of his deep breath.

"Ebouard Riddess," whispered Vorham, as he'd whispered so often for the past years. "Why won't you die?"

CHAPTER FIVE

Jastin Armitage crouched on the roof of his two-room home in South Morlan, tugging at rotten planks. A neat pile of clay shingles lay in waiting to his left. The sun was high and relentless. He tugged his cotton tunic over his head, knocking loose sweat droplets that had collected at the tips of his dark hair. He mopped the cloth across his brow, and scrubbed it down his beard and throat.

Then he paused and turned his face toward his bare shoulder, listening. From far down the dirt road came the hollow thunder of horse hooves and the rattling of a speeding carriage.

Few in Esra Province could spare the luxury of horses and coach, save for the Meedes stables to the south, where some of the finest mounts off all neighboring provinces were bred. And his greedy, braggart of a brother-in-law, the Venur at Riddess castle. No one from Meedes would be coming from the north on this dusty, abandoned path to Jastin's solitary home.

That left only one conclusion.

He groaned.

The carriage crested a rise in the road, and confirmed his annoyance. The carriage was painted a garish gold, with ebony and purple banners convulsing in the wind at each corner like bruised, manic pigeons. It neared, and slowed, with the driver—also dressed in purple and black-slapping reins and "Ho"-ing the horses into a cadence.

Jastin tossed his damp tunic to the roof tiles and swung himself over the edge. He dangled, and then dropped the last few feet to the ground. No bother with the ladder. He was eager to greet the visitor and see him off as quickly as possible.

But when he reached the opening coach door, it wasn't Vorham Riddess who emerged. A second man, dressed in the purple and black of Riddess Castle, ducked forward and came to stand on the top wooden step. "An invitation to a dragonchase in honor of your upcoming birthday, m'lord." The man offered an unsealed letter.

"My what?" Jastin took the letter, smearing mildewed sawdust and perspiration onto the parchment.

"Your forty-second birthday."

"How does Vorham know how old I am?" Jastin himself had lost track of his age, or had at least tried to, and certainly hadn't bothered to celebrate it in a long time.

The man shrugged delicately. "I'm afraid I wasn't given that information. Your return reply is requested at your earliest convenience."

Jastin unfolded the invitation and scowled at the elaborate script. A dragonchase in his honor. A holiday at the castle. He hadn't seen his brother-in-law in years, and suddenly this? And an enticing dragonchase to ensure Jastin's interest. He tasted manipulation at the back of his throat, and spat at the ground, trying to rid himself of the sting.

But the only way to find out what Vorham was up to was to stride into the moldy castle and ask. "I'll be there," he said to the messenger. "I won't write. Just tell him I'll be there."

"Excellent." The man nodded.

Jastin tucked the invitation into the waistline of his trousers. "You want a drink of water or something?"

The messenger glanced to the coach driver.

Jastin hitched his thumb over his shoulder. "I've got a well in back. Help yourselves."

"Sounds great to me," said the driver, and he climbed down, tying off the horses to the hitching post beside the road.

"Thank you," said the messenger.

The two men fell into step behind Jastin, and he led them past his single-story house, along the in-laid stone path that wound behind it, past his stable, his cedar storage shed, and finally to the small well he'd dug himself. He lugged a bucket up from the depths, and cool, crystalline water sloshed over the bucket to the dry earth, darkening it. He rinsed each hand in turn by spilling more water over the edge, and then scooped handfuls of the refreshing liquid to his mouth.

He offered the bucket toward the men, who arched their brows. The messenger glanced from the well, to the house, to the shed.

"No servants," said Jastin. "No wife. No children to bring a cup. You can get one yourself from my shed, if you want."

"Yes. Thank you." The messenger removed his cap, smoothed his thinning hair across his damp scalp, and replaced the cap. Then he cautiously made his way to the door of Jastin's shed.

Jastin watched him, and wondered what the man thought was going to leap out at him from the haphazard shrubberies. He looked back to the driver.

The coach driver smiled and shrugged, and plunged his hands into the well water. "Got a bald spot on your roof, there," he said.

"Yeah."

"Going to fix it before the rain?"

"That's the plan," said Jastin.

Just then, a clatter erupted. It was the clang of falling tools, and the high-pitched snap of dried bone against bone. Jastin winced, and turned to find the messenger standing just inside his shed, with a metal cup in one hand, and a shriveled, curling dragon claw in the other. Jastin's metal spears and arrows, garden hoe, and shovel were toppled around the man like a fence. Jastin's collection of dragon trophies—scales, teeth, claws—were strewn on top of the pile. The messenger was wincing, too.

"Apologies," he said. "I seem to have dislodged your items."

"It would seem," said Jastin, striding toward him.

"You have so many," the man continued. "I only meant to touch the one."

"That's from a Green," said Jastin. He reached for the man's elbow and guided him outside. "Greens lose their color as they wither, looking more like a Brown. But there's no glitter, like with a Brown. That's how you tell the difference."

"I see."

"Why don't you keep that one?"

The man brightened. "Really? You wouldn't miss it? My son would love to see this."

Jastin pushed a loose arrow into the shed with the toe of his boot, and then closed the door. He'd deal with the mess later. "As you said, I have so many. Take it with my compliments."

"Well!" said the man, looking to his companion with shining eyes. "Well, I say. Much obliged, Mr. Armitage."

"Not at all." He continued to steer the man away from the shed and toward the well. "I do have to get back to my repairs, gentleman. Please take your time to refresh here and then see yourselves off, if you don't mind."

"Yes, yes," said the messenger distractedly, offering his treasure for the driver to inspect.

"It's a Green, he says?"

"That's what the man says. Ever touched one, Mo?"

"Can't say as I have. Look at the size of the thing."

Jastin left them to admire the dragon claw, and smiled vaguely to himself as he climbed the ladder once more to his roof. He'd only spread his trophy collection to the shed because he'd run out of room in his house. He figured he had enough dragon parts to cobble together a small tribe of them.

Never satisfying, though, the kills. None of them Red. None of them Gold.

Never satisfying.

He was just nailing in the last wooden slat, and was reaching to start on replacing the tiles when he finally heard Vorham's men at the carriage. He turned to regard them, waved when the driver clucked the horses to action, and then watched until the last of the trail dust settled back onto the road after them.

Then he reached for the invitation still wadded into his waistline. He unfolded it, and slowly read it one more time.

Chapter Six

Sela thrust out her arms and closed her eyes. Wind rippled against her cheeks, sent stray hairs snapping like whips against her ears. "Faster, Mother!"

She felt the rumble of her mother's laughter travel up through her legs. She squeezed them more tightly against her mother's slender neck, nearly able to clasp her feet together beneath her ruby throat. She bucked a little with each serpentine arch of her mother's spine, but was unafraid. She was in the sky, where she was meant to live. To breathe.

She flew, as she was born to do.

"Faster," she cried again. She fought against the force that tried to pin her arms back, to wrestle her spindly arms to her sides. And she imagined. In her mind, her arms sprouted leathery flaps. Her flesh stretched and filled in, bending into shape, tapering gracefully to slender tips. She leaned forward, opened her mouth, and let the airstream peel back her mask of human teeth to reveal fangs; to scour away her facial skin to expose glittering scales; to twist up her snapping hair into sharp, bony ridges. She was as much a dragon now as she had ever been. She was sure of it.

She opened her eyes and looked down at her hands. Her pale, goosepimply human hands.

"That's enough," she suddenly said.

Her mother slowed, and tipped her face toward Sela. "Already? Are you sure?"

She had gone flying with her mother every day for the last five days. Every trip into the sky had been exhilarating, as long as Sela closed her eyes and pretended. She tried to dredge up whatever power within her was there, tried to manifest the change she desired so deeply. But each flight ended in disappointment, and today's pain from it was more than she could take. "I'm sure. Please."

Her mother spiraled toward the ground.

She alighted so softly, Sela barely felt it. She hesitated a moment, unprepared to touch her feet to the ground. Resenting the ground. Hating it.

Then she slid off, and her bare toes buried into the sandy mountain path. She stared down at them. She wiggled them.

"You have the toes I had when I was your age," said her mother.

Sela uplifted her gaze to her mother's majestic face. She'd forgotten, again, that her mother had been human, too. Once upon a time. She wondered now what she'd been like, then. Before she could fly.

"I don't want them," she said.

"I know."

"I didn't choose them."

Her mother settled onto the ground on her belly, and tucked her feet beneath her like a self-assured feline. "You must have."

Sela shook her head. "No. I don't know. Maybe. But I didn't mean to. Whatever happened then, I didn't mean to. I was afraid."

"Afraid?" Her mother lifted her chin and deepened her green gaze on Sela's face. "You've never said that before. What else do you remember?"

"I don't know. Nothing." She took two steps toward the trees and stared up at their lacy tips. "The woods. The voices."

"Voices that frightened you."

Sela nodded. Trying to piece together what bits of memory she had about that day was like trying to fit tattered, unraveled yarns together in the dark. What was real, what was imagination? How had she manifested a power within herself she didn't even know she had? "I was a fledgling. I was hiding from you for fun. Then I was hiding for real. And I didn't really understand how I'd changed until you found me."

Her mother laid her paw against her back. "I knew you by your eyes."

Sela turned to face her mother, feeling tears burning at the edges of her sight. "Here, on the mountain with you and Father, is the closest thing I have to being who I'm supposed to be. Why I can't I just stay?"

"I'd like that very much. I miss you."

"Then can't you talk to Father? Get him to agree to keep me?"

Her mother looked away now to the trees. "I have, Sela. Believe me." When she looked back into Sela's face, Sela saw that tears had welled in her mother's eyes, too.

"But he doesn't want me anymore. I've disappointed him."

Her mother stiffened. "Whatever makes you think that?"

"He can't stand that I'm not a dragon. That I somehow chose to be something he isn't!"

"Sela!" Her mother rose up to her feet, her nostrils flaring. "When I met your father, I was as human as you are now. I wasn't a disappointment to him, I was his friend. And he even came to love me."

"But *you* changed to please him."

Her mother narrowed her eyes. Not in an angry way, but in that slow and preoccupied way as she did when she was deeply pondering. "I didn't change to please him. I changed to please myself. As it so happens, becoming my true self meant your father and I could be together. We could create you."

"But you created me to be a dragon." Sela turned away again, and dug her toes into the sand. "When will I get to be my true self again?"

She felt her mother's warm breath against the back of her neck as she exhaled slowly. "I wish I had an answer for you. Maybe if you strive for change to please yourself—"

"Staying here with you and Father would please

me."

Her mother reached both paws to her shoulders and gently turned her. "That would please me, too. But your father believes it is dangerous here—"

"More dangerous than out there?"

"...and more than just concern about Blackclaw, this mountain is a place of Dragonkind. I didn't understand when I was in your place, either, though your father tried to explain it to me. The very fabric of this place is woven of magic. Those who belong here thrive. Those who don't, cannot."

Sela belonged here. She knew it down to the tips of her sandy toes. She was strong here, stronger than any other place. And she was happy here. She thrived.

"I know you feel that way," said her mother. "And in some ways, you're very, very right." She rested her forepaws on the ground and narrowed her eyes again. "But you are what you are now, Sela. And I believe too much in destiny to consider it coincidence."

"Destiny?" Sela asked.

"You have a purpose, my child. And whatever it is, it cannot be found here, hidden in the shelter of Mount Gore."

Sela took one step backward, slowly. "You don't want me here, either?"

"That's not what I mean, and you know it." Her mother shook her head, and paused a long moment, regarding Sela's face. Then she spoke again. "I was pulled away from my home to my calling. And I don't want to hold you so tightly you can't be drawn away to yours."

"But I don't want a calling," said Sela. "I just want to be home."

Her mother smiled. "Well. We'll talk to your father at dinner."

§

Orman followed Kallon's slithering tail through the underbrush, ducking snapped birch branches and clumsily hopping over knuckles of elm roots. "What happened to using the trail?" he asked. "Some of us don't maneuver so well anymore."

"If someone sees you, they'll know Sela is here, too," Kallon rumbled quietly. His tail disappeared between two wide elm stumps, and a chipmunk peered out over the edge of the one on the left.

"Bah," said Orman. "There is such a thing as being too careful." He hadn't had to do this much of his own walking in a long time. Maybe ever. At least not since he mastered wistful crystal travel. Bits of orange stone were scattered here and there in clever places all over Leland, zipping him across miles and back without so much as losing his breath. The headaches were a nuisance, but he'd grown used to them. And remembering the hiding places was easy. He had a mindful crystal for that.

Too bad he hadn't thought to bring a wistful stone along with him. Meant he'd have to tramp on foot again in the future to take care of that. "Bah," he said again. He'd take the path next time, consequences be damned.

Then the bothersome undergrowth turned soft like

woven rugs beneath his tired feet. Craggy birch trunks gave way to wide-spaced maples with arching branches that fanned his warmed face. Wren Meadow.

Orman sensed the magic even before he stepped fully in. It coursed through the leaves, through the roots, through to the open grass to the north of Ares River. It pulsed as a heartbeat, strengthening his tired bones, and reminding him why he was drawn to his own mountaintop here.

He stepped through the trees, toward the edge of the stream, and gazed up the nearest mountainside being blissfully pummeled by cascading water. The top had been sheared off decades ago, before Kallon's grandfather had led the Reds, and it had softened to a lumpy plateau. Today it offered a view of the vibrant azure sky.

His favorite home. Mount Krag.

Kallon spoke from several feet behind him. "You miss it."

"Think of how my crystals would shine, all that water, all that power back in the mountains."

"You regret your choice," said Kallon. "You've sacrificed in ways a father should be able to do."

Orman turned to face Kallon, who was crouched beside the river. One wing sagged into the water, pooling it. His muzzle was low, his claw drawing circles in a patch of nearby mud.

"That's your own voice in your head. Don't mistake it for mine," said Orman.

Kallon pushed to his feet and lumbered along the

gentle river to its bend, and followed it east. Orman, feeling fitter and more able than he could remember, caught up to his side. Then they both slowed, and stopped altogether before a stone archway, into which had been carved "Libremen en Leland". Leland Library.

When Riza and Kallon had first discussed the scroll library, Orman had pictured a grand, old museum of a building, with wonderfully dusty corners and stained glass windows for devout study. But of course he'd been thinking as a blasted human again.

Riza's design was much simpler, and much more serviceable to her dragonkind. A single arch marked the slab of land left open to the sun, or the stars, and turned all of Wren Meadow into a lush and welcoming learning center. Granite mounds rose here and there, naturally sculpted to mimic the nearby mountains, with hollowed passages for holding scrolls. Not the original scrolls, naturally. But meticulous copies.

Orman helped, when he could, but had shown Riza the lettering techniques with ink and crystalline dust to protect the scrolls from aging in the open air. Designed to last lifetimes.

"She's been busy," said Orman. He passed under the arch. Kallon went around it. Orman stopped again, and couldn't help but smile, a little, at sheer number of mounds and scrolls tucked into them. "How many?" he asked.

"Nearly one hundred shelves. And she still collects so many scrolls they're filling our resting room, and the hallway to the Great Room." Kallon sat back onto his haunches and wrapped his wings against his forelegs. "She's only just returned from Buethal Province—"

"Buethal?" Orman asked. "From across the sea?"

"Is there another Buethal?" Kallon breathed out sharply, his nostrils flaring. "She's only just returned, and plans to go back."

Even Orman was surprised at Riza's determination. Knowing at the same time, he shouldn't be. "She needs purpose. It's good she's found it."

"Since her child has been taken from her, you mean."

Orman scowled, and wished he had his walking staff to rap Kallon across the nose. "If I'd meant it, I'd have said it."

"She's away more than she's home. When she's here, she pores over parchments as though she's trying to memorize the whole dragon history since creation. She spends more time looking at her scrolls than she does at me."

"With your mug, do you blame her?"

Kallon shook his head. "It's not my face. I've failed my own fledgling; I've failed her, too. She can't stand being here without Sela. She can't stand being here with me."

Orman crossed his arms. "Are you mistaking your head voices for hers now?"

"I'm not mistaking it." Kallon rose to his feet and leaned toward the nearest granite shelf, nudged it with his nose. For a moment, Orman thought he might blast flame at it and scorch every parchment inside.

Orman hadn't thought to protect the scrolls against that.

But Kallon only grumbled something, and laid one jeweled paw on the shelf's apex. "I don't know what I'm doing."

"It's never stopped you before."

"I'm serious, Orman."

"Well, so am I."

"You know he's been seen. Riza heard talk two weeks ago on a flight into Esra."

"You mean Blackclaw?" Orman asked. "She's sure?"

"She's sure of the talk. Last we heard, he'd surfaced somewhere in Kayal, south of the cliffs."

"You think he's closing in?"

Kallon shrugged one shoulder. He gazed out across the meadow, his pink tongue playing at the edge of a fang.

"And so he's going to come here and what, Kallon? Challenge you to duel? Oust you as Council Leader? That doesn't strike you as more than a little foolhardy?"

"No," said Kallon suddenly. Growling. "What's foolhardy is sitting here waiting for him. Expecting him. While everyone I love is coming and going across his path like oblivious little kutterbugs."

Orman pulled back his shoulders. "This beast of him in your mind isn't real. You've created it. You defeated him once, you've already—"

"I didn't defeat him, Orman, he killed me. You conveniently forget that part, but it's the truth. And then he *left*. I didn't capture him. I didn't overthrow him. He left."

"In shame."

"What difference does that make? Shame only fuels him. It feeds his anger, and makes his decisions for him."

"See there, I think you're talking about yourself again."

Kallon reared back, pulled his paw from the shelf, and blasted a snort of sulfuric breath into Orman's face. "I've seen what that dragon is capable of, and I will not underestimate him. Sela is vulnerable now. She would have been weak had she remained a dragon, but now she's completely helpless." He turned, took a step into more open space, and thrust out his wings. "By harming her, he destroys me. And then all Leland Dragons are susceptible. If I have to ban Sela from this mountain I will."

"Kallon," Orman began to say.

"I won't let him get near her, and I don't need to hear whatever you have to say."

His wings lofted, and he rose sharply. Without another word, he soared off across the meadow, over the treetops, and banked toward Mount Gore.

And, blast it all. He didn't even have the decency to take Orman with him and save him the walk back.

§

In the afternoon, Sela carefully picked her way through the trees and underbrush. Her backpack bounced against her spine. Her rope sandals dug into the sides of her feet, her toes gripping instinctively for purchase. Heavy rains had slickened the pine needles and decaying litter, submerging some patches of ground altogether. Climbing her way around Mount Gore was more complicated than flying. But she was determined.

She had only a short time before her absence was noticed. The thought nudged at her, but hurrying didn't help. Trying to rush only made her hands clumsy and her feet more unsteady.

She paused at a rock outcrop, where the trees parted and she could see out across the Leland Mountains, and their marbled spires. She'd been told stories of the days when the mountains were crumbling. The days before her father took his place as the Herald of the Reds on the Dragon Council. But there was no sign of weariness now. Each knuckled mountaintop pushed at the sky, daring it to resist. Deep valleys were thick with fir trees and jack pines and sweeping elms, like an emerald afghan laid out beneath a king's feet.

She breathed in the sight of it, memorized the scent of it. But as fulfilling as the scene was, it was not the only thing what she came to find. She turned onto her belly and lowered herself over the outcropping to the mottled stone landing below it.

Her perfect hiding place. Her perfect painting place.

It had been years since she'd returned. Years since she'd had the courage.

She opened her pack and withdrew her weaselhair paintbrushes. She dragged the soft hairs over the lines on her palm, and listened to the bustle of flying creatures in the treetops, and the slither of crawling creatures among the loose rocks cascaded down the mountainside. To her left was a smooth expanse of what must have been a path. Dabbled now with patchy growth and pebbles, it nevertheless carved itself subtly around and down, toward another smooth outcropping several feet below. She hadn't remembered that.

She replaced her brushes in her pack and inched out from her hiding place and into the open, testing the traction of her sandals on the path before shifting her full weight to her feet. Confident she wouldn't slip, she swung her pack against her spine and carefully continued, following the sandpaper trail for several yards, back and forth across the scrubby slope. At the next ledge, she peered over. Another landing, like her hiding place, with more trail leading down and away.

She laid herself again onto her belly, and swung her legs over the side.

Just then she felt the passing of a cool shadow above. She dropped quickly and scrabbled into hiding. Had they discovered her missing already? She'd thought she'd at least have enough time to discover where the trail led before her father would come searching. She peered out, up into the sky.

From below, she recognized the smooth, scaled belly of a flying dragon, but it wasn't her father. Nor was it her mother. The wing expanse was nearly the right size, but the smooth appendages were slender, with stippled copper tips. The dragon banked and curled around to pass over again, and Sela caught sight of her profile and auburn back. Vaya Brownwing. Sela almost shouted and waved, before she remembered she wasn't supposed to be seen here.

And then a second dragon came soundlessly into view. With scales as black and gleaming as burnished onyx.

Blackclaw! Sela nearly did call out, then, in warning. But in that same moment, she also recognized the black dragon as too small and too fledgling to be the monster her father had always described to her. There was no time to shout anyway, because Vaya pointed toward the treeline, and gestured and roared. The black dragon veered suddenly and dove into the forest and out of sight.

And then her father really was flying down the mountain. His shadow passed over Sela's peering face, but she didn't dare move, lest she call attention. He swung up and over, and circled Vaya, who paddled the air with her mighty paws, treading in place.

As they spoke, Sela's looked toward where the young dragon had been. Directly in front of her. At the place where the trail led into the trees.

She wanted to make a run for the trail. But her father was there, hovering, his leathery wings languidly churning the air. His voice rattled the stones beneath her knees, and he glared at her. "You realize, you have been seen."

She didn't bother replying as she crawled out to meet him. His enormous paw clasped loosely around her waist and hoisted her up and over the mountain trail.

She twisted, trying to look backward. She pushed against her father's knuckles to stretch up, and she saw Vaya still lingering in the sky, her face taut and questioning.

Sela pushed a strand of tickling hair from her eyes, and then looked down again at the trail. Vaya's shoulders drew up with an alarmed breath. But Sela gave a single shake of her head. She knew better than to form words in her thoughts, because to think *I won't say anything* in the presence of her father was the same as blurting it aloud. So she did what she could. She smiled.

Vaya's face relaxed. And then the brown dragon smiled, too.

And then for the rest of the journey from mountainside to Gore Manor, enclosed in her father's stern grasp, Sela tried to think about anything—*anything*—but the mysterious young dragon hidden in the trees below.

CHAPTER SEVEN

J astin Armitage emerged from the treeline just outside Riddess Castle, and paused his chestnut mount, Blade, to let him chew at a scrap of purple alfalfa flowers wrapped around the trunk of one of the Venur's sugar maples. He patted Blade's neck, allowing his faithful friend a moment of refreshment.

He decided to take a sip of water, himself. He turned in his saddle to collect a water bladder, just as a twig snapped in the scrub pines behind him. Instead of retrieving the water bladder, he covertly laid his hand on his sword hilt at his hip.

"So you did go back for him, after all," said Layce Phelcher, his brother-in-law's wizard. She was wearing man's trousers, several sizes too big, rolled up at the ankles, and rolled down at her waist, making her look pinched into the linen material like a mole in a potato sack. Her black hair dangled loose and wild to her waist, obscuring all but the intricately-beaded sleeves of her tunic. When she reached up to stroke Blade's back leg, she jangled. He saw no crystals, but she must have been wearing them somewhere. She was a walking wind chime.

"He's beautiful," she said. "He hasn't aged a day." She smiled up at Jastin, and blinked at him with her blue, blue eyes.

"Neither have you, Layce," he said honestly. "Are you ever going to grow a gray hair?"

"Doesn't seem enough to go around," she said, pointing at his own dark hair where it met his beard. "You're hoarding it all." She laughed. "Maybe you ought to try a bite of that alfalfa."

"I'll keep that in mind." He nudged his heels into Blade's flanks to rouse the horse from his snack. "Are you going toward the castle, or away? Do you want a ride?"

"I'm going toward it, but I'll walk. I'm not needed for a while. But of course I can't spend all my time waiting here in the woods."

"Of course," he said absently, and took hold of the reins.

"I'm glad you're finally here."

That made him pause again. He quirked a brow, regarding her where she stood near his right leg.

"It means the circle is coming round. Things are going to get interesting again." She walked to Blade's muzzle and grasped at his bridle, turning the horse's face to look into his eyes. "Do you know how boring it is to be a wizard liaison between a self-absorbed Venur and his non-existent dragon vassals? I'm so happy to see you. Even if you had to bring along *that* fellow on your back."

"Look, do you mind?" Jastin gave the reins a tug to dislodge Layce's hands. "Even if you're not in a hurry to get there, I am."

"Liar." She did release the bridle, but rubbed her knuckles against Blade's forehead. To Jastin's dismay, his mount nudged his face against her hand, enjoying it. "You don't want to be here anymore than I do. You just can't stand not knowing what Riddess is up to."

"Are you still talking to my horse?"

"You tell me." She lifted Blade's nose and peered toward his throat. "I could talk through him, if you'd prefer."

"What are you...?" Jastin stiffened in alarm, and then swung over Blade's side and landed his booted feet onto the ground. "Tell me you're just trying to get my goat, Layce." He followed her gaze with his own, searching Blade's neck for a dangling crystal amulet. He saw nothing.

"I don't have any use for a goat, yours or anyone else's," she said. "Although, on second thought, ram's horn dust can be a spell accelerant with some crystals. I wonder if goat's horn would be a decent substitute."

He passed his hand over Blade's damp hide. He'd searched the horse repeatedly in the months after he'd found him in Leland Mountains, after Layce had tried a communication trick with a hidden crystal. He'd found nothing. After bathing the horse and inspecting equine orifices he'd never admit to aloud, he'd concluded that Blade had lost the communication crystal in the mountains, or that Layce had never actually planted one in the first place.

"Oh, I did, it's right there," she said, pointing. "I guessed it was removed a long time ago. If I had any idea it was still on the old gelding…"

"He's a stallion, Layce."

"That could have been some fun, eh, boy?" She grinned, and dug her knuckles more actively against Blade's forehead. Blade rumbled a soft whinny.

Jastin ignored Blade's betrayal. He couldn't blame him. Layce just had a way of getting under the skin. She was doing it now, to Jastin, too. There was no green amulet dangling from any part of the horse, and there likely never was.

"Our minds are as easily fooled as our eyes," Layce said. "Sometimes, what we're protecting is all on the inside."

Did the woman ever make sense? Jastin released a low breath, and gathered Blade's reins. He gave the horse a quick pull, knocking away Layce's hand. "We'll just be off now."

"Suit yourself." She stuck out her hand to grip the side of Blade's saddle.

"What are you doing?"

"Taking the ride you offered."

"But you said you'd walk."

Layce lifted her bare and dirtied foot into the stirrup. "Because you were going to ride. But now you're going to walk, so I'll take the seat." With a grunt, she hoisted up and over, and dropped onto the saddle. Her black hair swirled around her face and neck, and then settled about her shoulders, absorbing her beneath an ebony shawl. "Because you still haven't asked me."

"Asked you what?"

"Well, I don't know, do I? Haven't even formed it in your mind, yet, or I'd have answered you by now."

Jastin closed his eyes and gave his head a slight shake, before he pushed off to lead Blade around another sugar maple. Every conversation with Layce was an acrobatic competition. He knew better than to expect a straight answer from her concerning anything, let alone information as vital as discovering his brother-in-law's plans.

"Oh, there it is," said Layce. "Vorham wants you dead."

He drew up short. "He what?"

"This walk is going to take a very long time if each step is following by a long pause."

"Layce. Did you just say Vorham brought me here to have me killed?"

"No. But I did say he wants you dead." She gazed out over the sugar maple grove, and pursed her lips. "So it makes sense to lure you here with a dragonchase. Bring you into range, so to speak."

Jastin walked again, guiding Blade between two swaying maple trees. He was doused in cool shade beneath the limbs, just as he was saturated with doubts as to whether he should go on. He hadn't imagined Vorham having the fortitude for an outright attack. But Vorham was younger, and driven. He had help being cunning. And soldiers to be his muscle. But why, after all this time, would Vorham strike now?

"Maybe he thinks all your years of solitude have worn away your edge," said Layce.

Jastin glanced over his shoulder at her. "I've always been alone."

She arched her brows so high he thought they might take flight right off her forehead. "How would your wife like to hear you say that?"

Jastin stopped so abruptly Blade rammed his nose against his spine. He spun to face her, holding Blade's bridle steady so he could glare directly into her eyes. "You go too far, Layce."

She tipped her head, studying him. For a moment she seemed genuinely surprised. "What, did you forget?"

He ground his teeth against each other, willing himself to stay calm. He hadn't forgotten he was once married. Married to Vorham's young sister, a woman who was too good for him, but chose him anyway. Jastin Armitage. Captain of the Venur's army. A brute of a soldier who knew nothing about how to treat a woman's heart.

He'd paid dearly for his misguided venture into romance. What was once a breathless rush of confused wonder had begun to stale the moment he'd slipped his ring around her finger. She'd married him, yes, but she'd never really been his. He didn't know how to hold onto her, any more than he knew how to contain the rushing waters of Ares River.

"She was taken from you before she had a chance to leave you," said Layce.

Jastin yanked at the reins and wordlessly continued on.

"I was wondering how long you were going to pause this time," said Layce. "We've hardly gone two yards."

"I despise when you do that."

"Keep track of our travel, you mean? Not that there's been much to measure. As I say, we've gone only a few yards all morning."

"I despise when you hear what I'm thinking," he said, his voice flat with irritation.

"Oh, that. I think what you mean is how you hate that I *can* do it, not really that I am doing it. Because you aren't able. So I have the advantage."

"No, I hate that you do it." He slipped on a patch of wet grass, and his boot wedged beneath a tree root.

"You hate that I do it with you," she pressed. "You wouldn't mind if it were someone else. In fact, my knowing what your brother-in-law is thinking is very fortunate for you just now."

Jastin tried to tug his boot free, but the tree root held it firm. He kicked at it with his other foot. He bent and wrestled his hands around it.

"And you've certainly benefited in the past from it, as much as you will in the coming days."

He heard her feet quietly hit the ground. And then she was beside him, touching a speckled blue crystal to the root. He recoiled. If there was one thing he hated more than Layce's constant jabbering and relentless mind reading, it was her wildly unrestrained use of magic.

"No!" He pushed at her hand, but the tree root crumpled and withdrew, freeing him. "I'm not a child," he roared, offended at her help. "I've managed to grow this old without your ways, you know. I don't need to read thoughts. I don't need to use crystals." He snatched at Blade's reins, and stalked around another maple tree before marching resolutely toward the castle.

A moment later she was beside him, curling her leather-soft and wrinkled hand around Blade's reins, just above Jastin's clenched fist. "He doesn't like when you force him."

Exasperated, Jastin swiveled to release a snarl into her face. At the same time, he realized he was cutting the tips of his fingernails into the palm of his hand. He released his grip on Blade's reins.

Layce gently tugged his horse forward, and Blade loped into a smooth rhythm.

"You constantly jabber, too, you know," she said over her shoulder. "In your head. Everyone does. It's deafening, sometimes." She turned around, switched the reins to her right hand, and walked backwards a few steps. "As my thoughts form, I speak them. It's only fair."

She turned back to the front, switched the reins again, and led *his* mount, *his* faithful chestnut stallion, across the expanse of prairie grass toward Riddess Castle.

She called over her shoulder, "Are you coming or not?"

He briefly closed his eyes, took a deep and calming

breath, and stepped forward to join her.

"Good," she said. "Because I need your help."

He nearly stumbled again. "*My* help?"

"I could handle the girl on my own, but the girl *and* him? I'm not sure I can manage."

"What girl?"

"What do you mean, what girl? The bride, of course."

Jastin wondered again why he even tried to keep up with Layce's verbal circles. "The bride. Right."

"Right," Layce echoed. She offered over Blade's reins. "Meet me at my chamber as soon as you're able. We've got a lot of work to do."

§

Kallon blew sparks across the two candelabra in the Great Hall, igniting the wicks of their beeswax candles. He then pushed their stems with his paw, centering them in the expansive room. The flames cast weak light, making the meeting more ominous that it should have been, but the gloomy atmosphere matched perfectly to his mood, at least.

He settled onto his haunches, awaiting Riza, who was saying goodnight to their daughter in her room around the corner. Orman waited, as well, seated on the slab of a marble table, his legs folded. The table, used to feed a roomful of hungry dragons, dwarfed the wizard, and in the dancing light from the candelabra, Orman looked more a child than a wrinkled old man.

"There are no easy answers," said Orman.

"I have been wondering if there are answers at all," Kallon replied.

Orman rested his elbows on the insides of his knees. "Your father often had the expression you've got, when he worried about you."

Kallon swung his head to find the woven tapestry depicting his father's noble profile on the carved wall. He dragged a candelabrum closer, illuminating the scales in the artwork that glittered as real as Kallon's own crimson face. "Maybe he would tell me what to do."

He heard Riza's measured footsteps, and glanced across the room, where she entered. Flamelight lit her snout, and then her eyes, and then the jeweled spiral of horns that encircled her crown. Her gait was slow, the tilt of her head weighted by sadness.

His broken heart sank heavily against his ribs.

"I always wished I could have met him," said Riza, her gaze on the tapestry. "And now I wish Sela would have known him."

"He would have liked that. To see Kallon as a father," said Orman.

"He would have been a far better role model," said Kallon, swiveling to study the artwork again. "Maybe if Sela had known him, she wouldn't have…"

"What, Kallon?" Riza placed her front feet on the marble, beside Orman, and looked down her snout at Kallon. "Maybe she wouldn't have what?"

Kallon shook his head. "We're not here to discuss what's already happened," he said.

"Maybe we should be. It's long past due."

"It won't change whatever happened that made her decide—"

"Decide?" Riza swept over the table like a ruby wave, and descended to the floor in front of him. "Why are you so fixated on that word? How many times must she explain she didn't decide anything?"

Kallon shook his head again. "We need to talk about what to do *now*. I'm not going to be baited into—"

"Baited?"

"Riza, please," said Kallon. "You and I can argue later, but right now this is about Sela, and I need your help deciding what to do."

Riza clenched her jaw, and glared momentarily at the floor. But then she firmly sat. "In that case, I suggest we let her stay. She has been begging to move back home for months."

"Impossible," said Kallon. "She was spotted again today. She refuses to stay within a perimeter, and can't be trusted to keep to the trees. I found her creeping toward Wing Valley, and if I hadn't stopped her when I did, she would have kept going. Straight into the village."

"You see what I deal with," said Orman.

"Well. Perhaps you should leash her," said Riza.

"I've thought of that, believe me," said Orman.

Riza cast a dark look toward Orman, and even the crusty old wizard flinched. "She's a creature of the wilds, like her father. And his father. Just because she looks human doesn't mean her wanderings can be tamed out of her because they're inconvenient."

"Not inconvenient, Riza," said Kallon, moving toward her. "Dangerous. You don't seem to understand."

"Now that's where you're wrong," she said, lifting her chin. "I believe I'm the only one in this room, in this realm, that truly, deeply understands."

There was a moment of silence between the three. Then Orman spoke. "No one is suggesting she be tamed, carnsarnitall. But she doesn't listen, no matter what we try."

"I agree with Orman," said Kallon.

Orman crossed his arms and regarded Kallon as though he wasn't sure if his agreement was a good sign or not.

"If she would only do as we ask," Kallon began to say.

"If she would only hide in a cave and stop being herself, you mean," said Riza. "If only she would turn away from the world, and cuddle up into a ball of flesh, tucked against some rocks."

Kallon felt heat rise into his throat. He was tired of explaining himself, weary from sounding unreasonable. The situation was only temporary, but he could never seem to make Riza understand. She saw him as weak and timid, but he was only pragmatic. Caution was best. "Only for now," he said, reaching a paw toward Riza's shoulder. "Don't you see? Just until—"

Riza turned her shoulder to avoid his touch. "Just until *you* feel safe, Kallon. Which is how you judge your every move." She turned, and began a slow walk toward the open arch in the mountainside manor. "But you can't control your daughter's every move. And you can't control me." She paused, and turned her delicately scaled face to regard him again. "I take back what I said about Sela meeting your father. I'm glad he's not here to see how you're handling this."

Kallon's heart retracted. He watched her saunter through the arch and into the night. While her tail tip slithered down Gore Manor's carved steps, and her wings burst from her back, he stared mutely. Then, she leapt powerfully and took to the sky, the sweep of her wings battering wind into invisible waves. And as she disappeared from view, the air from his lungs went with her.

§

Sela listened in the hallway, and then peered around the stone-carved wall and through the manor entrance to see her mother glide silently into the stars. She shuddered, although the night air was warm. Then she turned, and made her way back down the hallway toward her room.

She had been a problem for so long, she'd almost become accustomed to it. Or, at least, she'd been trying. But now, she realized she was problem *between* her parents, too. A wedge, instead of the bond that should be.

So it was time to let go. She had become human for reasons she didn't understand, but she could at least comprehend she wasn't changing back. Maybe she never would. And hanging on to childish dreams, and to the Leland memories that came with them, only tightened the noose around her heart, and drove her parents further apart.

It was time to grow up.

In her room, she changed from her sleeping gown into her baggy trousers and tunic, and tightened her rope belt around her waistline. She tucked wisps of hair into her braid, tidying it as best she could, and rewrapped it around her head and pinned it into place. She rubbed at her eyes, which stung with moisture, and then slid her backpack over her arm.

Then she blew a kiss to the air, and bid the mountains, and her family, goodbye.

§

"Riza didn't mean that," said Orman. "She's just upset."

Kallon regarded the old man, feeling as wrinkled and fatigued as Orman looked. "She's upset. It's why she meant it." Kallon strode forward in the Great Hall, and moved to stand in the archway, looking up at the sky. He could barely make out Riza's twisting shape as she blotted out the stars with her flight.

Orman came to stand beside Kallon, and rested his cool palm against Kallon's foreleg. "She hasn't gone far, you see? She's just flying off her frustrations. She'll be back soon."

Kallon wasn't so sure. Riza's flying had taken her

across villages, provinces, and even the sea. Sometimes, he awoke to find her already gone, with only a scrawled note. But surely she wouldn't leave without saying goodbye to Sela.

Once Sela and Orman returned to Simson, though, he couldn't be sure of anything Riza might do. "I'm losing her, Orman," he said.

"Yes," said the wizard, quietly. "And you're just standing here, watching her go."

"But she doesn't want me to follow. What can I do?"

Orman stepped through the arch and stood for a time on the carved marble landing of the manor. "Well, you've tried an awful lot of *not* doing anything. How's that going?"

Kallon rumbled in frustration. Apparently Orman wasn't going to be of any help. But what was Kallon thinking? He knew less about Riza's heart than ever, and so how could one frail old man, wizard or otherwise, have any advice?

No, chasing down Riza would only turn into another argument, and he would be pushing her away, not drawing her back.

"Your silence is doing the same thing," said Orman.

Kallon rumbled again. He ground his teeth. And then, he blew out a sharp, heated breath. Not because Orman was wrong, but because he was right. He hated that.

Without a word, Kallon lifted his wings and dove upward. The sky was warm, and starlight enwrapped him with a familiar grip. He tried to relax against it, but his recent flights had been more about watching and alertness than about pleasure lately, and it was difficult for him to switch out of the habit. Besides, he still didn't know what he would say to Riza when he caught up to her, and he was nowhere near being able to loosen up with that challenge wedged between his shoulder blades.

A moment later, he felt the brush of shifting air, and heard the soft, leathery whisper of Riza's wings. She passed over him, curled around to face him in the sky, and then languidly paddled her wings to carry herself backward. Her green eyes were made dark by the night, and by the tightness of her jeweled face. She regarded him in silence. In expectation.

"You're stronger than I am," he heard himself say.

She blinked. Her face softened. "That isn't true."

"It is, and we both know it."

She paused in mid-air, and then lunged beneath him, circled back again, and hovered above. "You've always been stronger than you think."

He rolled to his back, his wings pulling smoothly up and out, backstroking, while he watched her from below. "You defeated him, Riza. Not me."

She lowered her head, arching her graceful neck, to look him in the face. "We all did. You, me, the council, and the tribes. We ousted him as a community. The way it's supposed to be done."

"But I would have died. You sacrificed—"

"And so did you. You flew into the boundary to save me."

He continued to backstroke against the sea of stars,

regarding her face, and remembering when he'd lost her, all those years ago. He'd touched her cold lips, he'd seen her human face pale with death. Now in his mind, he placed that lifeless mask over her dragon face, but it shook him violently. His rhythm disrupted, and his wings clambered. He dropped like a stone.

Riza's four legs shot down to catch him, and in that moment of balance, he steadied. Then, claws intertwined, Riza relaxed into a barrel roll, and they spun, controlled and twirling, toward the treetops.

Just as they brushed the tips of the tallest pines, they released one another and banked up and out, away just a few feet, and then closed in to fly side by side, their wingtips caressing with each powerful stride.

"You're a lovely dancer," said Riza, into the wind.

Kallon smiled, because he still didn't really understand the phrase, no matter how many times she said it. It was why she enjoyed teasing him with it. Then she slowed, and concentrated her green gaze on his profile. "You flew into the unknown to save me, Kallon. All I ask is you do the same for our child."

But Sela *was* the unknown, to Kallon. He didn't know how to save her.

"Yes, you do," said Riza.

"You are stronger than me," said Kallon again.

Riza turned her gaze to the horizon, and released a breath so quiet, Kallon could barely tell the difference between it, and the wind in his ears. "*We* are strong," she said. "We'll go together."

"To find Blackclaw?" he asked, his ribcage

tightening.

"Once and for all."

He took her paw in his, and an image of Riza's death mask rose again behind his eyes. He shuddered, and suspected she could feel the trembling of his digits, but she didn't comment. Kallon breathed in deeply through his nostrils, and closed his eyes, trying to settle the hammering of his heart. "Once and for all," he said.

§

Bannon Raley and his latest fellow guard, Hamos Lynch, led their mounts toward the door of the huddled little cottage, set beside a muddy stable, beside a muddy field, just south of the tired old town of Simson.

"You're right," said Hamos, withdrawing a handkerchief to swipe at the dampness on his brown face. "You remembered the way just fine. Even in the dusk."

"It's only been a few days." In fact, it had been ten days exactly. After returning to Riddess Castle with Sway, he'd had barely enough time to eat a meal of barley cakes and ale, when he discovered his Venur was gathering more men to loan to Leland. Word was out that Leland's maidens were to gather at Shornmar Castle for a selection celebration, and the number of participants were expected to overwhelm Shornmar's dried out and meager guard forces.

Bannon immediately volunteered to return.

It wasn't just for the chance to see the girl again,

he told himself. Bannon grew restless if he lingered too long in one place. His barracks room in Riddess Castle was spare and quiet, and he liked it that way. But the bare stone walls became tomblike and suffocating if he didn't stretch his legs on the long, traveling assignments he asked for. Outside, in the forest and the fresh air, he was really at home.

So when he'd arrived with Hamos at Shornmar Castle, and discovered soldiers were needed to gather some delinquent bride-elects, including one Sela Thistleby, he didn't even unsaddle his mount.

Not just for a chance to see the girl, he swore to himself. He'd said it so many times in his head while he traveled toward Simson it was becoming a mantra.

"I don't think anyone's home," said Hamos. He tucked his handkerchief into his back pocket and then swung off his russet horse to land both feet in crusty mud.

Standing there with his coffee-brown horse behind him, his coffee-brown face wrinkled in frustration, and coffee-brown sludge slapped against his boots, Hamos seemed lost in the evening scenery, with only the purple shirt and black trousers of his uniform hovering like some kind of soldier ghost. "Think they skipped out?" he asked, almost startling Bannon.

"Last I saw them, they were heading out of town, but they turned in the census the same morning, so I'd guess they're coming back."

Hamos mulled this over, pressing his lips together, and then he spat toward his feet. "Let's see if they left a note." He winked, and tied off his mount at the rickety gate of the mule pen.

"You don't think we should just—?"

Bannon swung his leg off his blonde mount, Breeze, just as he heard the splintering of a wooden door. He wrapped his horse's reins around a pen post, and then strode across the stone-littered yard to meet Hamos.

Inside, Bannon took a closer look at the place than he had the first time he'd been there. The main room was small, with wide beams in the ceiling, and dried herbs hung upside down against the windows of the near wall. A plank table was set with clay dishes, a hurricane oil lamp, and one wilted cornflower in a clay vase. To the right was the kitchen alcove. The fireplace was cool and sooty. Copper and iron pots clung to stone walls. And Hamos had the wooden door of the food cupboard open, rummaging among the shelves.

"Find a note in there?" asked Bannon.

"Cornmeal," he said, scowling. "Lots of it. And one cinnamon stick." He shook his head in disappointment, but slid the spicy twig into his shirt pocket. "You check upstairs. I'll see what's in the next room."

Bannon had almost missed the set of stairs, hidden in a corner of darkness. "Find me a match," he said. "Losing daylight in here."

Hamos offered him a tapered fireplace match, and he carried it to the hurricane lamp on the table. He struck it against the wooden table, and held the flare of light to the lamp wick. The wick caught flame, and threw shadows at the walls, the ceiling. Suddenly, the little cottage seemed even smaller. And somehow, unwelcome. As Bannon placed the glass chimney into place on the lamp, he had the distinct feeling he ought to turn right around and walk back out. He even felt invisible hands touching his shoulders, pushing him backward.

"Hamos?" he asked.

Hamos had made his way to a door near the base of the stairs, where he paused, and regarded Bannon with upraised brows.

"You feel that?"

Hamos squinted, tipped his head. "Feel what?"

"Maybe you shouldn't go in there."

Hamos snorted a laugh, and pushed open the door. The frame was so short, he had to duck. And then he disappeared into the blackness on the other side of the wall.

No horrible screams of pain or fright erupted, so Bannon dislodged his hesitation with a lifting of his shoulders, and he climbed the unsteady stairs.

The light from his lamp found a doorway of lace, and he pushed it aside to enter a small chamber built haphazardly into the space between the kitchen alcove and the thatched roof. He swung the lamp forward to reveal a bed, swallowed by a patchwork quilt gone ragged at the edges. Beside the bed was a squat nightstand with another lamp, so he crossed the floor, knelt, and touched wicks to light the second.

Gathering starlight twinkled through the thatch and rough-hewn planks of the ceiling, and combined with the lamplight to suffuse the bedroom with a rich glow. But there was little to see; only a wardrobe stood against the wall at the foot of the bed. A wardrobe with two pairs of boy's trousers and a small blue tunic. Was this even the girl's room? The girl's house? Maybe he hadn't remembered correctly after all.

He spotted a wooden box on a low shelf in the wardrobe, and opened it to find small pots of paint and furry brushes. And then pale and dusty squares of… something…caught his eye from the left. He replaced the box, closed the wardrobe door, and carried his lamp as he crossed the floor. He knelt again, and touched the fabric squares.

Painted canvases. So many, they lined the wall, stacked in disarray. He searched them, turning them out to inspect them. But they were all, every one of them, coated in dusty fingerprints and unfinished.

"Find anything interesting?" asked Hamos, standing suddenly in the doorway.

"I don't think so. Just a bed. Boy's clothes. And these."

"Yeah, me either. Just a bed downstairs, and an empty trunk. Looks to me like they've packed up and aren't coming back anytime soon."

"Maybe," said Bannon, replacing a canvas to its place atop a grimy column. "But I'd just as soon know for sure before we turn in their names."

Hamos shrugged one shoulder. "No sense heading back in the dark, anyway. Come morning, though, I'm gone." He descended the stairs, and called over his shoulder, "I'll see to the horses."

Bannon nodded. He'd decide in the morning if he'd join Hamos, or wait. As irritating as that bizarre old man was, he hated to cause undue trouble. For the woman's sake, if nothing else.

The woman. Sela. Whom he began to think of a ghost.

CHAPTER EIGHT

In Kallon's sleeping chamber in Mount Gore Manor, sudden dawn leered in through a carved window, and poked at his eyelids, teasing them open. He lazily stretched on his bedroll, and then inched his snout toward Riza to breathe in her warm, sleepy scent. Her eyes were open, too, and she smiled.

Suddenly Orman's voice was a clap of thunder in the hallway. "Kallon."

Riza was on her feet instantly. "Sela," she said.

Kallon reached the doorway first, followed so closely by Riza he could feel her heartbeat against his rump. He drew up when he spotted Orman, standing outside his guest room door.

"She's gone," said Riza.

"Took my wistful crystal," said Orman. "She's got a strong head start."

Kallon tensed, his shoulders taut and his wings cramping against his impulse to fly. To search. "Where do we look?"

"You won't. I will."

"But—"

"You've got other important business," said Orman. "Just as important."

"I told her I'd run away to find my destiny," whispered Riza, one paw over her eyes. "I told her I'd run *away*."

Kallon turned, rested his chin on her snout. "This isn't your fault," he said. "It's mine. I pushed her away."

"Where would she go? I hate to think she's alone, believing this is her only choice."

"Me, too," said Kallon, closing his eyes. Still nuzzling Riza, as much to comfort himself. "I wouldn't want this. I would never want this."

Orman stepped between them, and reached up to capture each of their chins in his rickety hands. He gave them a tug, and looked back and forth between their gazes. "When you've finished lollygagging," he said, "we can get on with what needs doing." He released them, and crossed his spindly arms. "You've entrusted her to me all these years. You still can."

Kallon touched his knuckles to Riza's cheek, and she blinked slowly. Her eyes brimmed with wetness, but she nodded. "I trust Orman. And we need, more than ever, to find Blackclaw and put an end to all this."

"We'll put an end to all this," said Kallon.

"It's settled then," said Orman. "Now. If you two could drop me off before you go, I'd be much obliged. It's a long walk to Simson. And I might just catch up."

§

Bannon sat fully dressed on Sela's bed. He'd tried to sleep, but the girl's scent—fallen pine needles—lingered on the woven sheets and the tattered quilt. It taunted him, invaded his dreams. Her green eyes seemed to stare at him from a distance, although he couldn't see her, exactly, through his mind's fog and shadow. Sometime in the night, when he'd awoken fitfully to a strange sound like a distant thunderstorm, he gave up on sleep and simply sat up, watching for dawn.

At least he knew for certain he'd remembered the house, and that this was the girl's room, after all.

As yellow daylight began its slow creep through the window, Bannon's eyes adjusted. The room appeared much as it did the night before; spare, dusty, and abandoned. Soon Hamos would rouse, and declare his intent to leave. But if they returned to Riddess Castle without her, she and her uncle would be accused of evasion and very possibly declared criminals.

And he felt, somehow, as though it would be his fault.

He'd bullied the old man. He'd told the girl the census was only information. And then he filled in the parts she'd left out, and turned it in.

But he was only doing his job. His *job*, he reminded himself. He'd bullied plenty of Leland citizens into turning in the census. He'd told all the maidens it was only information. He'd even helped some of them fill in missing parts, as well.

But none of the others had eyes the color of dew-dampened meadow grass. None of them had the scent of the forest. Only this one girl, as mysterious as the clouds and as just as elusive—

His own thoughts cut suddenly when he noticed a dislodged wall plank, just beneath the window, as though someone had pulled it away but hadn't seated it fully back into the wall.

Not someone. The girl.

He sat forward, and eased his feet to the floor to go investigate. But then the front door creaked, and he heard soft footsteps below. He veered toward the stairs, instead, just as Hamos's booted steps thumped loudly, followed by a frightened gasp.

He took the stairs two at a time, and found the girl on the front stoop; her fingers pressed to the splintered wood around the door's lock, with her mouth agape, eyes staring at a shirtless and disheveled Hamos. Her legs tensed like a jackrabbit about to escape.

"Sela," Bannon called. "Don't be afraid."

Her gaze shot toward him, nearly pinning him to the last stair. He held up his empty hands. "We're not here to hurt you. We've been waiting for you."

"It's about time you showed up," said Hamos. He scratched at his wide, brown chest, and then stepped backward into the room from whence he emerged.

The girl studied Bannon's purple sash, his black trousers, his scuffed boots. Then her eyes returned to his face, and narrowed thoughtfully. "You're that guard."

"Yes," said Bannon, distracted by his pleasure that

she remembered him.

"Why are you here?"

"Because of the census," he said. "For the bride selection. You didn't appear at Riddess Castle—"

"What bride selection?" she asked.

He hesitated. Then he moved forward a step, passing the room where Hamos grunted and fumbled with the shirt-and-sash layering of his uniform. "Didn't your uncle explain the census to you?"

She stared at him in silence.

"Venurs Riddess and Shornmar want to unite the provinces by marriage. But your Venur doesn't have an heir, so he's collected the names of volunteers."

"I didn't put my name into anything like that."

Bannon cleared his throat. "Maybe 'volunteer' isn't the right word. The census…" His words faded, and so did the color in her face. Her eyes closed briefly, and her grip tightened on the door. He leaned forward, prepared to catch her, should she faint, but she spoke quietly.

"I understand now."

When her eyes opened again, they were filled with sadness. Bannon's breath caught, and he fumbled a moment for words. "So you'll need to…we're here to…"

"I'll go with you," she said. "I just want to collect my things."

Hamos joined them in the room, fidgeting with his purple sash at his waist, where it had come unstitched. "We've waited long enough. There's nothing here worth gathering. We already checked."

"Hamos, for pity's sake," said Bannon.

Hamos groaned. He rubbed at his belly. "I'm tired of dried meat and cornbread, Bannon. I want a hot meal and warm soak."

"And you'll have it, as soon as we reach the castle. Five minutes won't make any difference to your stomach."

Hamos grumbled quietly, but only walked toward the door, still trying to affix his sash to his waistline. He paused, gave the girl a pointed look, and then trudged past her when she eased out of the way. Outside, he called, "Five minutes!"

The girl didn't wait to be told again. She brushed past Bannon, perfuming him with her woodland scent, and slipped off a backpack from her shoulders as she hurried up the stairs. When she reached the top, he slowly followed and came to stand, awaiting her just outside the lace-draped doorway.

"I'm coming," she said.

Moments later, she ducked back through the lace, her backpack in place and looking awkwardly angled. At least she was quick. He glanced back into the room as she descended the stairs, and saw the wooden plank beneath the window, the one that had previously been ajar, was meticulously pressed back into place and undetectable as ever having been disturbed.

§

Outside, Sela led Nimrod, Orman's donkey, to the corral outside the stable. She pushed at his rump, forcing him within the fence, while he peered over his shoulder to eye her. Accusingly. But she didn't speak, for fear Orman's voice would chastise, or shout, or otherwise betray her in front of the soldier saddling the horses.

Besides, she needed to believe Orman hadn't tracked her yet, wasn't watching her. Or she might lose all determination to leave.

She watched the dark-skinned soldier tighten the cinch on a brunette mare. He scratched at stubble on his throat, and wiggled the saddle to make sure it was tight. He must have sensed her, because he spoke without looking at her. "You don't want to be a Venuress?"

"What do you mean?"

He lifted his left foot into a stirrup. "Girls were gathering at the castle before we left. Excited. Loud. Dressed up in their mothers' ball gowns." He cast a glance over his shoulder before he hoisted up, leathers creaking, into the saddle.

Sela smoothed her palms over her rumpled trousers. "My mother doesn't own a ball gown."

"Too hard to ride in a dress, anyway," said the second soldier, coming up behind her. "And you'll need to leave the donkey."

"Yes, I was..." she began to say, but sucked in a sharp breath, instead. Beginning with her ankles, and then her knees, and then her hips, she lost all feeling.

"What the-?" asked the soldier. He grabbed at Sela's waist, but his fingers passed through her as though she was an illusion. He gaped, and tried again, his hands clawing at air.

Sela slowly backed away, but she was disoriented, failing to sense the ground beneath her feet. She felt at first as though she was floating, and then as if she was falling.

Run, came a sudden thought.

She tried. She spun, and found herself encased in donkey flesh. She was passing through the animal; she was a part of it. It swished its tail, and she felt the tickle of it somewhere inside her knees. She cried out.

And then it stopped. Her body filled in, and she smelled donkey and felt the sun's warmth baking its withers. The animal brayed, and twitched, and then Sela shot forward and hit the ground on her hands and knees. She tried to reorient, looking up at the soldiers and their horses.

The near soldier knelt beside her, his sandy bangs rumpled against his furrowed brow. "What just…?"

"I'm better," she said, pushing to her feet. Her first step made her woozy. She caught her balance with her hand on the donkey's saddle. And she released a breath, grateful to feel substantial again. "I'm all right."

The soldier hesitantly put out his hand to touch her arm, and then, feeling it solid, he steadied her.

"Sela?" the soldier asked. "What just—?"

"I'm not sure," she said. "I think someone thinks they're helping." She couldn't exactly glare at Orman without seeing him, so she tried a mental one. In case he was still there, somewhere.

She blinked slowly, and her senses gathered. She looked from the man's hand on her arm, to his face, which was lined with shadow and concern…not anger. "Your name is Bannon, isn't it?"

His expression softened. "Yes."

She nodded. "I'll ride with you?"

He smiled faintly. "Or with Hamos."

She glanced left, where Hamos sat on his mount. His eyes were flat with suspicion, and he openly scowled. She looked back to Bannon. "I'll go with you," she said.

His smile widened. "And you're meeting Hamos on a good day."

Bannon whistled through his teeth, and his pale horse drew near. Her mane was white as sheep's fleece, and was braided into a rope.

"Up you go," said Bannon, lifting her. She swung into the saddle.

Bannon pulled himself up and into place behind the saddle. He reached his arms around her to clasp the reins.

"I wish I'd understood the census when I gave it to you," she said quietly.

"Would you have turned it in?"

"I don't know," she said. Probably not. But if she hadn't, she would have nowhere to go from here. She'd have run from Leland, and been left with few choices. Further south, into the unknown? West, toward mysterious and dangerous Murk Forest? She hadn't thought far enough ahead to decide to *where* she was running.

He pulled the horse to his right and guided it toward the road. Hamos and his mount fell in behind.

She looked back to the little hut, her second home, and to Nimrod, who lipped muddy grass into his teeth, his reins dangling.

It had been hard enough to say goodbye to the mountains. This exodus ground salt into her wound. She watched behind them as Bannon's horse carried them along the path, her home growing smaller and smaller. She felt her heart shrink along with it.

Eventually, when her neck ached from stretching, and her shoulders cramped from leaning, she turned her upper body to face ahead. "After I'm not chosen, what happens next?"

"You're so certain?" asked Bannon.

She was. She didn't agree to travel with them because she had the slightest hope of becoming a bride. She just needed time. To think. To plan. To hide, until she knew what next to do. "How can Shornmar make this agreement with Riddess if it's against our will, anyway?"

"He's your Venur," said Hamos, riding his horse beside them, and then past them, with an irritated huff.

"He's not my Venur," she murmured, repeating the phrase Orman had so often said in their years in Simson. Sela was the daughter of Kallon Redheart, Herald of the Reds and Leader of the Dragon Council. She was heir to the council seat and the Leland Mountains. She didn't need to be a Venuress to rule; in the eyes of dragons, she already would.

At that thought, she startled. She was heir to the council seat. The Leland Mountains.

Orman hadn't only been trying to protect her from the public because of the census! In human land laws, if she married the Esra Venur, her heritage could become his property!

She pressed her hands to her sickened stomach.

"How long will this take?" she asked. Until she'd been turned away from Shornmar castle officially, her fear of the worst would be scratching at her insides.

"We can cut through the trees and be there by nightfall," said Bannon. She felt his voice rumble against the back of her neck.

"Then what happens?"

"What do you mean?"

"How does the selection happen? When will I be released?"

"Oh." He shifted. "I don't know. I don't know anything about that part," said Bannon.

The tightness in her stomach grew worse. She coughed, feeling her breath bound up behind her tongue. "I think I'm going to be sick," she murmured.

Bannon reined up his horse, and it jolted to a stop.

"Don't let her off," said Hamos, ahead of them. He turned his mare, eyeing Sela. "She'll bolt."

She hadn't thought of using it as a trick until Hamos suggested it. Now she was alert, and she surreptitiously glanced around them. They'd just passed into the thin outer edge of Simson Woods, and she recognized the dip in the terrain just to their left. The nameless creek would be a few yards to the south, and her childhood play spot, the fir tent, if it was still there, would be a long jog beyond that.

But then what would she do? She didn't have much of a gap on Orman, who was undoubtedly tracking her. On her own, she'd be found before she could catch her breath. And if she didn't appear at the castle once and for all, would the guards go after Orman? She sat, genuinely ill from indecision. It was the crux of her pain; she often talked herself out of her instincts and instead followed her judgments. Or was it the other way around? But the results were the same. She was trouble to the ones she loved.

And how did she know Orman was even looking for her? It was just as likely that he'd finally wearied of her, and decided to let her face her consequences alone.

Hush you say, came a voice into her mind.

She startled, and looked sharply over her shoulder at Bannon. His eyebrows rose up. But of course it wasn't his voice. She looked around his shoulder toward the trees. She couldn't see Orman, but she sensed him.

Bannon jerked the horse into motion. "If you're better, then," he said.

"Yes," she said. "Let's hurry."

The horse nosed its way onto a trodden and faintly damp path. Its rhythm evened out, and their pace quickened. "Now you're in a rush?" asked Bannon.

"I just want to get this over with," she said. And she needed more space from Orman. His crotchety old voice in her mind was more of a relief than she wanted him to know. Regrets hovered at the edge of her mind, threatening to spill. And she couldn't afford that. Not now. She'd made up her mind to separate herself from her kin, and she would go through with it. One way or another, she would figure this out on her own.

"Something odd about your old uncle," Bannon said.

"My uncle?" She swiveled her waist, searching the path behind them. Surely Orman wasn't close enough to be whispering to Bannon? Nimrod was as crotchety as Orman, and he hated trees and damp paths. He couldn't have caught up already.

"You passed right through that donkey as if you were a ghost."

"I was just feeling faint, that's all. I haven't eaten this morning."

"You passed right through. I think your uncle doesn't want you to come with us."

She searched Bannon's gaze. Was there a faint burgundy glow behind his hazel eyes? "Don't listen to him, Bannon."

"You need to get off this horse."

"And what would that accomplish?" she said loudly. "I have this under control. I've made my decision."

"You haven't made a smart one," said Bannon. "You're impulsive and angry right now."

"I'm not angry," she said. She straightened her spine, looking forward. "I'm trying to do what my family wants of me. I'm accepting my place."

"Not like this," said Bannon.

"What choice do I have?"

"You could get off this horse right now." Bannon

jerked the horse to another stop.

Hamos was watching them over his shoulder, his suspicious eyes turned downright hostile. He drew up his mount, circled her around, and brought her to a stand on the path. "What are you doing, Bannon?"

"It's not his fault," she tried to say.

"Bannon Raley," said Hamos. "What are you doing?"

"Look," said Sela, even louder than before. "There is no point in causing more interest than I already have. I know my uncle thinks I am making a mistake by going to the castle with you, but I don't stand even a tiny chance of being noticed, let alone chosen."

"Agreed," said Hamos.

"So I can either go along with this and be eventually sent on to resume my life," she continued, "Or I can run right now and raise up all kinds of attention."

Hamos nodded, looking from her face to Bannon's, his eyes dark with shadows. "What's happening here?"

"I'm…trying to help Bannon understand."

"Bannon doesn't need to understand," said Hamos. "He's got a job to do, and a guard of his rank ought not to let a woman interfere with that."

"I'm not trying to interfere," she said weakly. She glanced over her shoulder at Bannon's face, studying his eyes. He was blinking, but slowly they came to a focus.

"Are you getting sick again?" he asked.

"No," she said. "Are you?"

Bannon looked at Hamos, opened his mouth to speak, then didn't. He shook his head. "I don't think so, but I have one splitting headache."

§

Someone was interfering with Orman's magic. He felt it when he'd tried to diffuse Sela at the corral, and then again when he was trying to reach her mind. It had taken all his strength just to manage what he could from such a distance. But his magic's failure to linger wasn't weakness.

Another wizard was sticking their nose into Orman's business, confound it.

"So help me, Nimrod," he said to his disinterested donkey as he fed him a bucket of barley, preparing the beast, and himself, for a long, non-wistful crystal journey. "I'll get that stubborn girl back home, and deal with that busybody wizard while I'm at it."

How to deal with him, Orman wasn't sure. He'd figure that out as he went. But the concern that really stuck in his craw was that he was dealing with another wizard at all. Sela was headed straight into a kind of trouble Orman had been trying to avoid for years. But now, someone else knew, too, and was fighting magic with magic to keep Sela going.

And that was a kind of trouble even Orman hadn't thought of.

CHAPTER NINE

Sela could see flameshine from a bonfire in the distance. The evening had descended slowly, biding its time, settling hesitantly around them like moths upon their shoulders. But the night couldn't be postponed forever, no matter how desperately Sela wished it. They crested a hill on the path, and Shornmar castle loomed before them, its hulking stone shoulders blotting stars from the dark sky.

The bonfire, its flames as high as the castle wall, lit the faces of soldiers who collected at Shornmar gate. A covered wagon clattered into view and wobbled to a stop, the horses shying nervously at the column of fire.

Sela knew just how the horses felt.

"We'll take you to the gate. From there, you'll be escorted inside."

Sela could already feel the heat of the bonfire. "What happens then?"

"I don't know."

Sela watched the distant wagon door open. Two

elegant figures descended. Their satin gowns and slippers caught the flicker of fire and turned their garments into starglow. Their gloved hands touched at their upswept hair, tidying the rows of beads—also shining—woven into their tresses.

They looked as though they wanted to be a Venuress.

"I'll walk to the gate," she said.

Bannon slid off the back of the horse and came aside to offer his hand. "Give your name to the guard, and he'll take care of you from there."

"All right." She gripped his hand, swung her leg, and dropped to her feet on the ground. It felt good to stand again, and she rubbed her palms at her numb backside. "So. That guard there. At that gate."

Bannon nodded, regarding her silently.

"Right." She looked toward the gate. Her heart fluttered, and she couldn't get her feet to approach the castle.

"There are a lot of women," said Bannon. "You can try keeping your eyes toward the ground."

"My eyes?"

"Eyes as green as the Fell Lake basin. If you look directly at anyone, they'll get you noticed."

"Oh." Her gaze did dip toward her boots, then, and to her chagrin, she smiled. Not how she wanted to react, at all, but at least her discomfort got her feet moving again. She gave the horse's shoulder a sound pat, murmured goodbye, and hurried toward the gate.

Her steps grew steady as she passed the bonfire,

which made her wince from the heat. She passed a crowd of soldiers, which made her wince from the stench. And she spotted the two girls, glittering like butterfly wings, speaking to a guard with a parchment. She approached.

"...by way of Reacher's Pass," said the one with ebony hair. "We thought we might not arrive at all, and so you can imagine our relief."

The guard, his face taut and splashed with firelight, waved them aside, and lifted his chin to call out to Sela, "Boy, get over here. I sent for your mother but she ain't... oh, eh. Who are you?"

"I'm here for the census. My name is Sela."

"Census?" The guard squinted up his eyes and leaned closer. "Aye, yeah. I thought you were Binamen."

"No, I'm Sela."

"Aye, yeah," he said, consulting his parchment. "Last of the last, you are."

"Yes. I'm sorry."

"And there's the woman now. I only fetched for you half an hour ago!" The guard shook his fist at an approaching woman, whose dress and frock were rumpled, as was her face, and Sela wondered if she'd been roused out of bed.

"I came as soon as I got word," said the woman, her voice as sleep-crumpled as the rest of her. She turned her back to the man and bowed creakily. "Come ladies, I'll show you to your rooms. The others have prepared for bed, so you'll need to keep quiet. Beauty rest, you know."

"Of course," said the dark-haired girl, bending at the knees to scoop up a small cloth satchel. "I'm so glad we didn't miss the choosing. I feared we were too late."

"Only just made it," said the woman. She lifted her skirts away from her dirtied boots and drowsily led them through the gate, past the last of the milling crowd, and then into complete silence.

Here, within the outer walls of the castle, the crowd noise beyond the stones was completely dampened. She could sense movements and the tossing waves of bonfire shadows just at the top of the wall, but as they walked closer to the castle, the night sounds swelled in her ears.

"I'm Gladdis," said the younger girl.

"Oh. I'm Sela."

"You look my age," said Gladdis. "About seventeen?"

"Do I really?"

Gladdis smiled, and pointed to Sela's braided coif. "I like your hair."

"You look like a boy," said the older girl.

"That's Emlee," said Gladdis. "She's my older sister. And she's also why we are arriving so tardy." Gladdis leaned toward Sela and lowered her voice. "She took too long deciding on her trousseau, and then too long to pack it, and then insisted on stopping too frequently to repair her hairstyle."

"I didn't know I was supposed to be here until today."

Gladdis looked surprised, or confused, but didn't comment. She politely nodded.

"Come along," said their drowsy escort, guiding them through a flower garden. Sela could make out the skeletal frames of unlit torches here and there throughout the landscaping, but the group made do with moonlight.

Upon reaching the massive stone arch that opened to the entryway, however, bright torchlight flared like daylight. Gladdis and Emlee lit a-glitter again, their beads and ribbons casting spidery radiance against walls and windows.

Sela glanced down at her tunic and trousers, dusted from travel. She touched her wind-mussed braid, withdrew her hand to examine the thin line of grime beneath her jagged fingernails.

She'd be turned loose soon enough.

She wanted to ask what came next, but they were all hurriedly led through an enormous room that could have fit Sela's entire house inside it, and toward a marble staircase. Painted portraits lined the wall, hung to follow the curve of the massive banister. Among the faces was a landscape painting of soft pinks and greens, portraying a countryside dotted with wildflowers. She slowed her pace, studying the artwork.

"You'll reside in the room across from the staircase," said the woman. "Rest well. The choosing ceremony begins at high dawn."

Sela watched the woman and the two sisters as they swept onto the top step, crossed the hallway, and then opened a carved wooden door. They spoke quietly among themselves, not noticing Sela wasn't following.

When she heard the door close behind them, she looked back to the painting again.

"The Garden Glade," said a voice behind her.

She turned, startled. A figure was pressed against the shadows of the wall at the base of the stairs. "Pardon?" she called.

The figure emerged into light. He smiled shyly, his head cocked aside, before he pressed his hand to his cheek and looked away. His frame was a man's; broad shoulders and solid legs, but his face was round, cherubic, like a child's. "I go there every day, if Lestir lets me," he said.

Sela moved one step lower, studying him cautiously. He wore a well-kept sleeping gown and fur slippers. He smelled of lavender and muslin, and was as shiny clean as the butterfly sisters, but was hunched with the humble posture of a stable boy.

"You go to the glade in the painting?" she asked.

He nodded. He peered around his fingers at her face. "It looks just like it. I made it."

"The painting, you mean? You made it?"

He nodded again. He hopped onto the lowest step, and then pressed past her and touched his fingertips to the stippled oils on the canvas. "I do this with the brush, and it makes flowers."

"Who taught you how?"

He shrugged both shoulders and shook his head. "Nobody teaches me, I'm an idiot."

"I don't think an idiot could paint those flowers so well."

"I am. Up here." He tapped his forehead. "I can't learn anything. That's what Lestir says. So I don't learn. I just do."

Sela looked back at the painting. "Well, it's beautiful. I haven't been able to do anything like this in a long time."

"You like it?"

"Yes," she said, her gaze tracing the arc of green grasses in the oils. "I like it very much."

"You take it," he said, suddenly pulling the frame from the wall.

"No!" she cried. "Oh…no, I couldn't."

He pressed the painting to her chest, his blue eyes bright. "I can make another one!"

She grasped at the edges of the gilded frame to push it away, but he was looking directly into her face, with the excitement and joy of a little boy. How could she disappoint him? So instead, she hugged the gift to herself and smiled. "Thank you. It's very nice of you."

"You are nice," he said. "Pretty girl. You're a nice girl." He tapped his soft fingertips against her cheek. "In my next picture, I'll make flowers like your eyes."

Sela grinned, because his delight was contagious, and because she wasn't sure what else to do. "They're green," she said.

"Pretty green," he said. "Meadow grass. Pine trees. Like the glade. Oh!" He pressed his hands to his face. "I forgot. I talk too much. I'm supposed to be in bed."

"I'm supposed to be in bed, too," she said.

"Me too." He peeled his hands from his face and

shrugged, fingers splayed. "Sleep well." He hopped down the stairs, both feet at once, and when he reached the landing, he hopped right out of his slippers. He bent, tucked each slipper beneath each arm, and walked barefoot across the stone tile floor. Just before he disappeared into another room, he waved.

Sela waved back to the oddly charming boy-man, whoever he was, as best she could while holding the large painting. He was already gone.

§

Riza Redheart glided silently through low clouds dusky with tomorrow's rain. She banked just over Wing Valley, studying the torch flames that danced along the edges of the main road in the dragon village, like mischievous pixies frolicking on the banks of a dry river. Save one. One torch, near the herbalist shed, was snuffed, sending a string of gray and curling smoke toward the night sky.

The village road was empty, but she lowered cautiously, sniffing for dragon scent. Most were too faint to consider a risk, except for the heady musk-and-cinnamon scent she'd come searching for. Vaya Brownwing.

She followed the aroma trail beyond the unlit torch and into the dark shelter of oak and maple trees to the east. There, she landed, tucked in her wings, and tiptoed across craggy slabs of mountain granite that were nibbled at the edges by moss and lichen.

"I've warned him to stay put," said Vaya from the shadows. She emerged, then, into moonlight, her golden eyes solemn. "But he loves to fly. To explore. He doesn't see the danger of his ways."

"My child is as wild-hearted as yours," said Riza. "But I can hardly condemn her for it. It is exactly that call from the sky that brought me to this mountain. Brought me into the wild." Riza settled to her haunches and drew her tail around her feet. "She's out there now, chasing her destiny. Or running from it. I don't know which."

"I saw her here, on the mountain, just a few days ago."

Riza nodded. "A visit."

"A visit from a fledgling that shouldn't have to be kept hidden from home," said Vaya. She eased closer, and laid her bronze-brown paw over Riza's.

They lingered in silence for a time, sharing each other's grief without voicing it, and understanding each other's pain without thinking it.

Then Vaya withdrew her paw. "She saw him that day. Drell. We'd been flying, and she saw him."

Riza lifted her chin. "You're sure?"

Vaya nodded. "She seemed to understand the secret. And I wondered if…"

"If I've finally broken my promise to you, after all these years?" Riza released a spark of breath. "No. I've told no one about your son."

"I am not ashamed of him," said Vaya. "He's brave and headstrong, but kind. Respectful." She closed her eyes briefly, seeming to wither, but then she opened them again and leveled them steadily on Riza's gaze. "He is not his father. He isn't."

"I believe you," said Riza.

"My father would not be so benevolent. And neither would your mate."

Riza couldn't speak for Hale Brownwing, Vaya's father, but Vaya was right about Kallon. He would never think of Drell as anything but the son of his mortal enemy, Fordon Blackclaw, and therefore an enemy himself. "Vaya, in the coming days, our secret is going to be even harder to keep," she said.

Vaya drew up, her breath stilled, her eyes frightened.

"Kallon and I are leaving the mountain come morning. I don't know how long we'll be gone. I don't know where our travels will take us—"

"You are hunting him. Blackclaw."

"Yes." This time, it was Riza who placed her paw over Vaya's claws. "His memory grows as a poison in this place. Fear of his return is as powerful as though he were still here, threatening our future."

"I know," said Vaya. "Dragons are speaking aloud what they once only murmured. That Kallon came to leadership too young, and his fear of Blackclaw cripples him."

"I suspected as much," said Riza. Admittedly, she had come to wonder just how true that statement was, herself.

"But our Kind will be glad to see him take action,"

Vaya added. "To see him be the leader you and I know he is capable of being."

She regarded Vaya's eyes, turned glittering by the moon, and searched them for answers; did Vaya still have feelings for Kallon, the last of the Reds who was to be her mate? Did she resent Riza for bearing Kallon the heir that should have been theirs? Once, Vaya hated Riza... or so she'd said. Now, was their friendship based on something real, or only their shared misery and a long-held secret?

Vaya blinked slowly, her gaze revealing nothing but the cloaked sadness Riza had always known it to carry.

"Kallon will ask your father to lead in his absence. He is there, speaking with him now." Riza didn't have to mention the irony.

Vaya nodded. "Father has been studying the situation as well. He has heard of dissent in the north, and claims it rings of Blackclaw's influence."

"We will investigate there, and following the trail of sightings. But I don't know how we'll avoid Esra for long. Too many rumors of a black dragon already haunt the desert."

"Yes. I see." Vaya paced two steps, withdrawing her paw from Riza's grasp, and stared up at the stars. "You should start there, while we're able to prepare. I'll speak with Drell and his..." She swallowed hard against the next word, "...tribe. We'll send Drell into the Morlan Caves until Kallon is satisfied the rumors are no threat."

"Well done," said Riza.

Vaya curled her graceful neck to peer at Riza over

her shoulder. "I do not enjoy that you must lie to him on my behalf."

Riza generally rationalized that she wasn't lying; only avoiding the information. But Vaya's words stung, anyway, in the hidden place where her conscience knew the truth. "Perhaps one day, I'll no longer need to."

Perhaps, said Vaya, into Riza's mind. *But not today.* Then she lofted, her leathery wings reaching into the treetops, pushing away, and then reaching once more beyond them, into the open sky. She hovered, searching the distance, and then veered southwest, across the mountain and into the stars.

CHAPTER TEN

Sela watched from a window as the gray morning crept across Shornmar courtyard and silently climbed the castle's stone walls. Faint light peered in, and lit the room with anticipation. Girls stirred behind her, whispering excitedly. Satin bedcovers rustled as the visitors, four to the bed, set their bare feet on the wooden floor.

She was glad for the movement, reminding her she wasn't alone, although it did little to relieve the dark emptiness weighing at her heart the way the hulking brocade curtains smothered the window.

The past few days had swept her feet along as though she'd been jogging down a steep hill, forced to keep moving or fall. But in the night, among the soft breathing of strangers in an unfamiliar room in a foreign village, she reached the bottom. No longer running, she was now lost.

"Have you been standing there all night?" asked Gladdis, coming to stand beside Sela. She wore a crisp, cotton nightdress, and her hair was a river of marigold yellow along her spine. She peered out the window into the courtyard below.

"I slept a little."

"In your clothing." Gladdis kept her gaze toward the window, but commented, "And you haven't even taken down your hair."

Sela ran her hands around the braid enwreathing her head. She felt a crackle, and withdrew a bit of crispy elm leaf that must have been there since her visit to Mount Gore.

Gladdis watched her, and took the dry leaf. "Do you brush your hair?"

"Of course." She brushed her hair whenever it needed it. Or at least, whenever she thought of it. Admittedly, it wasn't very often. She hadn't been trained in calling attention to herself; her human years had been the kind where she tried to remain unnoticed. She hadn't much use for self care beyond the basics. Not that it was any of Gladdis's business. She almost became offended, but finding Gladdis smiling at her with a kind of amazement, Sela reconsidered.

"So many of us," said Gladdis, "bathed in milk, and tailored our clothes from our mothers' wedding gowns. We dug at our fingernails and scrubbed at our faces, and have tried to trade our clumsy milk maid rearing for ladylike graces. To appear something we aren't."

A giggle sounded behind them, and they both turned to see a girl with auburn hair twirling in the center of the room, a jade-green velvet dress pressed against herself. Other girls ooohed and squealed, and Gladdis's sister, Emlee, madly tore open her carpet bag to show off her own special outfit.

"Well," said Gladdis. "Some of us have to try harder than others, I suppose."

"But, trying for what?" asked Sela.

"Are you serious?" Gladdis turned to look her squarely in the face. "This is our chance to become a Venuress. A woman of real means, with the power to make a difference."

"What kind of difference?"

Gladdis blinked slowly, studying Sela. "Where are you from?"

Sela lifted her chin. "I'm from Leland. The same as you."

"You may be from Leland, but you're not the same as me." She shook her head. "I don't mean to offend you. I'm just not sure what to make of you. It's as though you don't even *want* this."

"I don't. I just want to go home," said Sela, hearing the words from her mouth before she could even think them. "But, I can't."

"None of us can, until this is over." She looked at the girls who were busy with waking and yawning, and talking.

"Even once this is over," said Sela, following Gladdis's gaze to watch the others, as well, feeling vaguely envious of their excitement. "I'll have to find somewhere else to go."

Gladdis tipped her head. "Your home must be

something special, if it's better than living as an Esra Venuress."

Sela's belly suddenly seized with homesickness. To her horror, tears welled. "Yes," she managed to croak. "Very special."

Gladdis regarded her silently. Patiently. Then she tucked the dry, crumbling piece of elm leaf into her own hair, behind her ear. "My home in Cresvell isn't special at all, but if you need somewhere to go, you can come with me."

"Really?"

Gladdis nodded. "I know Emlee will be chosen. And I wouldn't want to go all the way home alone."

Just then, a knock sounded at the immense oak door. "Ladies, it is time to rise." The door creaked open, and the face of the woman from last night peered in, refreshed and pleasantly coiffed. "Dressmaids are in the room next door, and will be arriving soon to help you prepare. Breakfast in the drawing room. And then we will gather you outside for the choosing."

Sela released a long breath. With the choosing today, she wouldn't have to spend another night in this cavernous fortress.

Emlee and the others broke into chatter, voices over top of voices. They burst into activity, withdrawing clothing and jewelry and toilet items from their luggage.

"If you want," said Gladdis, "I could help you brush your hair."

"No, but thank you. How about I help you with yours?"

"All right," said Gladdis. She smiled again. "Let's hurry. The sooner this is over with, the sooner we can be sisters."

Sela paused, feeling her own smile push away the lingering fears at the back of her mind. "And you can tell me all about Cresvell."

§

Bannon Raley leaned back against the cool castle stones. He watched the parade of women, like festooned cranes, bobbing and preening among the lilacs and roses of Shornmar Courtyard. Dresses of yellow swirled against skirts and hats of scarlet, or blue, or shimmering white, gathering into a graceful semi-circle, awaiting the opening of the big show.

He'd managed to avoid bird-wrangling duty, but he couldn't help but watch from a distance. The experience was surreal, in a way. Women gathering to be selected for marriage, as though Venur Riddess was some sort of prize? What he knew of his Venur was hardly enough to judge the man as a husband, but then again, lands and riches might be reason enough to become Riddess's wife.

A trumpet sounded, and the flock broke out in twittering. Officials in Leland colors of red and gold stood on a platform, waving their gloved hands and speaking in tones Bannon couldn't hear. An Esra soldier, in purple and black, escorted a woman in a sky-blue dress to the platform. She was smiling, and waving manically to the others as she passed. Apparently, she'd been chosen.

Another woman was peeled away from the flock and escorted forward. Behind her, an elbow shoved, and Bannon caught a flash of movement. Then he heard a voice.

"I didn't steal it!"

He pushed from the wall and craned his neck, trying to get a look into the colorful, dizzying crowd.

"I don't mind giving it back, I'm just trying to tell you I didn't steal it!"

Then she stumbled out from the crowd, still dressed like a boy, and fell to her knees beside the branches of a lilac bush. Her backpack skidded from her spine and hit the ground to her right.

"Sela?" Bannon called.

She upturned her face, blinking. Then two Shornmar soldiers were beside her, pulling her to her feet. The one to her left held a painting cut from its frame. He lifted it above his head. "How far did you think you would get?"

"If you would just let me explain."

Bannon crossed the grass in only a few steps. "What's going on?"

Behind them, another horn sounded. Faces, one by one, began to turn, and excited clatter was replaced by hushed murmurs.

"Please," said Sela, her face pale. "Last night, I met a man who told me he painted that picture. And he gave it to me. Honestly." She clutched at Bannon's sleeve. "Tell them you know me. And that I didn't steal it."

How could he say that? Maybe she *was* a thief. A huckster of some kind. Maybe she was even really a boy. He studied her, realizing he couldn't say he knew her. He really didn't.

She must have read suspicion on his face, because her expression tightened. She turned to the guard on her left. "Let me describe him. He was wearing a very nice robe and fur slippers. He said he'd taught himself to paint. He looked like a sort of man and child at the same... wait! There he is, right there!"

She pointed toward the platform, and all faces, of guards, colorful cranes, and officials, swerved to follow her gesture.

The man to whom she pointed was startled at the sudden attention. He smiled, and then pressed his hands over his eyes. The feather of his woven hat drooped. His brass chain jangled against his meticulous tunic.

"Venur Shornmar?" asked Bannon. "He gave you the painting?"

"That's the Venur?" asked Sela, turning wide, frightened eyes to him.

"Come on, let's go," said one of her guards, and dragged her away from the lilac. She scrambled to hold on to her backpack.

"Aren't you even going to ask the man?" asked Bannon.

"I'm not going to bother the Venur with this thief," said the guard.

"Wait! Wait," said Sela, her voice rising in pitch.

"Wait!" echoed the voice of the Venur. He waved

his hands, and hopped with his feet together, one, two, three, down the platform steps. "Wait for me!"

The guard drew to a stop, and quietly groaned. The second guard exchanged a look with him.

"Venur Shornmar," said Bannon, as the man closed distance. "This girl claims—"

"I can make another one!" The Venur leaped toward the upraised painting, snatched it from the guard, and pressed it to Sela's belly.

Sela grasped the canvas. "They think I stole it."

"No, no, no. No, no." The Venur shook his head so adamantly, his cloth hat went askew. "Come with me. You watch with me." Shornmar took Sela's elbow, and then slid his hand to her fingers. She rolled the canvas with one hand, slipped it over her shoulder and into her pack, and then took his hand.

"Come watch with me." Shornmar swung their hands as he led her toward the platform.

Sela gave Bannon a hesitant smile over her shoulder, and then lifted that shoulder in a small shrug. Bannon watched her go, and smiled a little, himself.

The two guards muttered to each other, something like "dimwit," and returned to herding the giggling flock.

§

The morning dragged on endlessly. Sela shifted her weight from one leg to other. She wiggled her ankles, trying to release cramps in her feet, tired from standing. She was wedged between two Shornmar officials whose crimson tunics were damp beneath their armpits. Chosen girls huddled together, their skirts gone limp, their expressions weary. What began as excitement for them had turned them as miserable-looking as Sela felt.

And the other girls, the ones in the courtyard that had been passed over, weren't bearing up much better. Sela finally caught sight of Gladdis, who yawned behind her gloved hand.

Then, finally, a horn sounded. A voice boomed from somewhere in the center of the platform, "Venur Shornmar thanks you for your cooperation. The choosing is concluded."

Disappointment rippled through the crowd in the courtyard. Sela understood, but didn't share it. She wished she was down there, now, herself, and nearest to the front gate, so she could be running already to freedom.

Four horse carriages clambered into the courtyard, along a cobblestone path. "The chosen will be escorted to Esra Province, to Riddess Castle," said the voice from the platform. "A picnic lunch will be served upon reaching the river pass. Our guests who will not be traveling today will return to Shornmar Castle, to await plans for their return home."

And it was over. Sela breathed for possibly the first time all morning, and moved to make her way toward the platform steps. But a trail of girls was already sweeping down and over the grass and into the carriages, so she waited.

And then a strong arm gripped her shoulder.

"Move along, move along," said the voice that had been announcing all morning. Sela looked over to find a squat man with a lanky, yellowed beard guiding her down the steps. "Don't crowd into the carriages, ladies. You, and you..." and he nudged Sela toward the final carriage, "... take that tasseled one, there."

"Oh, but I'm not—"

"Pretty girl," said the child-man of a Venur, suddenly at her side. "I'll help you." He slid her pack from her back and again took her hand.

"Wait," she said, resisting his pull. The crush of bodies from the platform swept her forward. "I'm not chosen!" She dug her toes into the courtyard grass. "I'm not supposed to go!"

"You go," said the Venur, tugging hard. "I'll make another picture."

"Stop!" Sela twisted, and tried to break from the crowd. But she felt suddenly weightless, and the ground disappeared from beneath her feet. "Uncle Orman?" she cried aloud. "Help!"

I *am helping, carnsarn it,* said his voice in her mind. *Stop fighting me!*

"I'm not fighting you," she hollered, because hands were around her waist, lifting her into the carriage, and she was slapping at the hands and pushing with her feet, and she'd forgotten she didn't have to talk to him aloud. "I'm fighting *them!*"

"Have a good time," said the Venur, his round face glistening beneath his crooked hat. He waved, and then set Sela's pack on the carriage floor, between the feet of a girl in a daffodil-yellow dress.

Sela was placed on the bench beside her, despite her desperate battle. The moment her backside touched the brocade seat, she felt solid again. Too solid. Heavy. So heavy she couldn't move. *Uncle Orman,* she said in her mind this time, because her mouth didn't work.

Hang on, child, he spoke back. *I'm coming.*

Her first realization was that even his head voice sounded worried. Her second was that the carriage was already moving, and, wherever he was coming from, he was too late.

§

Jastin felt a sting through his hands like a rope burn. Then the sting turned to sizzle. "How much longer?"

"Just concentrate," whispered Layce.

He tried, but his hands suddenly burst into pain as though they'd caught flame. He resisted the impulse to scream, but he yanked his hands from the glowing orb in the center of Layce's satiny bed. The pain evaporated, but he felt drenched with perspiration; across his brow, beneath his arms, around his waist. What had he let Layce talk him into doing?

Layce uncrossed her legs and stretched her feet toward her embroidered bed pillows. She relaxed back onto her arms, smiling, the rainbow of her crystal necklace quietly clattering. "It worked."

"What worked? Setting my hands on fire?"

"Oh, pish. That wasn't fire. Look, your hands are perfectly fine."

He looked. They were. But he was powerfully thirsty, and, just for a moment, Layce seemed cast in a kind of fog, softening her features and her smile. She was younger. Prettier. Delicate, strewn across her bed like a long-stemmed rose on a cushion. His gaze lingered on her blue, blue eyes.

But she scowled. "It's just an after-effect. Don't get any ideas." She pointed to the corner of her bedroom, past the piles of books and baskets of crystals that filled the available floor space. "There's some water in the pitcher on my desk. Take a nice, long drink."

He hated how she knew his mind, but even more so when she caught what he was thinking even before he had a chance to know himself. He rolled on her bed, onto his hip, and then dropped his feet to her floor and stood. "After effect of what? You swore I wouldn't do any magic."

"You didn't."

"So why do I feel as though I just spent two hours hauling hay bales into my loft?" He spotted her desk near a cobweb-filled corner, but the path from here to there was completely blocked by strewn books. He took one gingerly step over a 3-inch-thick tome.

"Because you're so stubborn."

"Because I'm what?"

"Stubborn. It's why I needed your help. You're one of the most stubborn—in fact, probably the *most* stubborn—person I've ever known."

"Besides you, you mean." He gave up trying to be careful, and took to scooting his boots along the floor, shoving lumpy stacks out of his way.

Layce hmphed. "I'm determined. There's a difference."

He finally reached the desk, but he faced a new dilemma. Her desk was stacked with more books, and scraps of gingham and leather, and broken candlesticks coated in dust. "You expect me to dig around under all that mess to find a drink of water?" He'd sooner slurp from Blade's trough.

"Suit yourself. It's the only way to shake the effect of the glamour so I'm not so alluring."

"Not the only way," he muttered. Conversation was working just fine. "And you still haven't told me how I helped." He turned to make his way back across the room, still scuffling his feet to clear a path, feeling weaker as he walked.

Layce placed her bare foot on the cannonball-sized orb on her bedspread, and rolled it around with her toes. "You wouldn't understand if I did."

"Try me."

"Let's just say I needed powerful resistance to pull off a spell, and you're the most opposing conduit I could ask for." She sat up then, and scratched her fingernail at the tip of her nose. "Except it tired even you, and I wasn't expecting that."

"And here I thought you knew everything." Jastin made his way to the door, although the effort of moving had sapped what energy he had left. He gripped the handle, barely feeling it against his palm.

"You're not going to get very far like that," said Layce. "You need water and a nap."

"I don't need a nap," he said. And then his legs gave out. He slumped to the floor.

"Jastin!" Layce scrambled across the floor and dropped to her knees beside him.

He was conscious, he was just too exhausted to move. Conscious, and angry. "What did you do to me?"

"It's not me. It's the wizard!"

She was confusing him again. Layce *was* a wizard.

"No, *her* wizard. The girl." Layce slipped a crystal from around her neck and laid it against his chest. Normally he would bat the thing away from him, but he couldn't raise his arms. He felt lighter, though, and less stiff.

Layce slid her hands beneath his arms and lifted him somehow. She eased him onto her bed and pushed him against her pillows. "I knew he was a wizard, because I could feel it. And he's strong. Better than me."

"Are you talking about a wizard or a girl?" The room tilted, and he clutched at the bed.

"Both, you oaf. The girl is with a wizard. And I… well. I may have underestimated him, a bit."

Jastin was having difficulty focusing on her face. Especially when she leaned down and squinted at him. "What does that mean?"

"It means you might be feeling poorly for a few days."

"A few days?" He tried to sit up, but he broke into

another sweat at the effort. Layce gave him a simple push, and he bounced onto his back.

"But don't worry. As soon as he arrives, I'm sure he'll put you right as rain."

"When he arrives?"

Layce laid her cool fingers against his brow. "The girl is coming, thanks to us," she said, smiling. "And as the girl goes, so goes the wizard."

He closed his eyes, and felt himself drawn toward sleep, although he resisted it. Not here. Not in Layce's bed. Not in his brother-in-law's castle. Not now.

"See? Stubborn," said Layce. "Sleep is best, for now. But he'll be here in plenty of time before your birthday. They're already on their way."

"Great."

"You'll know he's closer, anyway."

Jastin's eyes flew open, and he narrowed them on the fuzzy outline of her face. "What do you mean?"

"He's using your strength to track you, so as he gets closer, you'll get worse."

"Worse than now?" he asked, his voice a harsh whisper.

"I'm afraid so."

He closed his eyes again. The minute, the very second, he had his strength back he was going to use it to strangle her. "Can you find me that water pitcher now?" he asked.

"Oh. You must still be thirsty."

"No," he groaned, rolling to his side. "I'm going to be sick in it."

Chapter Eleven

Vorham Riddess stood on the top step of his castle's marble entrance. He watched his servants trimming hedges, tidying the grass slabs between his ivy-covered statuary. He tried to appear interested in the preparations for Jastin's birthday celebration, but he really took more pleasure in watching people work because they had no choice. He'd ordered them to.

It had been his favorite part of being raised as the son of a Venur, and became ever sweeter when he took control of Esra after his father. Not all servants indulged him his gratification, of course. The eldest, the men and women who'd been serving since his father's time, were already bent and humbled to their tasks, too worn and habit-formed to do anything but mindlessly obey. The younger servants, however, were different. Some of them. They carried stiffness in their shoulders and a silent sort of resistance to his orders. Oh, they obeyed, as well. But they didn't like it one bit.

His mute house servant, Leesa, traipsed by with a

flower basket.

"Where are you taking that?" he snapped.

She paused with her back turned, and slowly faced him. She curtsied, pinching her brown skirt and brown apron together as she dipped. He wasn't sure what her hair color was, her strands were always tucked up under her brown muslin coif, the head covering of all female house staff. But her eyes were the auburn of the Rage desert, and they swirled as fiercely as any sand storm, especially when he taunted her.

She nodded toward a stone pedestal at the far edge of the inner curtain wall.

"That's meant for the bridal reception this evening, not the birthday celebration."

She lifted her chin, her taupe skin blazing beneath the high afternoon sun. But she merely nodded again, and spun to return from the room she'd just exited.

Fane Whitetail crossed the courtyard to stand at the base of the stairs, curling his scaly white tail around the base of a water bearer statue. "Since when does the Venur of the castle bother himself with placement of floral decorations?"

"It's my mood," said Vorham. "All this infernal waiting, waiting, waiting."

"The procession is on schedule, honorable Venur," said Whitetail. "Your brides will arrive by nightfall."

"You make it sound as though I'll marry more than one. Heavens forbid. One peasant wife is enough."

Whitetail lowered his snout. "I assure you that after a meal and a rest, and a trousseau of finest garments from Esra's handpicked clothiers, none of your potentials will look like a peasant."

Vorham chuckled. "Potentials. I like the sound of that."

"A few more days patience, and all gears will whirr into motion, and no force in the province can stop it."

"Yes," said Vorham, saying it aloud to reassure himself. "A few more days." He watched Leesa return to the outside landing, but veer away from him to avoid eye contact. He smiled vaguely.

"How fares Jastin?" asked Whitetail, turning his serpentine head to watch Leesa as well.

"No improvement yet, although Layce swears he'll be well enough for the dragonchase." Vorham shook his head. "I've never known my brother-in-law to be ill a day in his life. I almost wonder if he isn't plotting."

"Retaliation for inviting him to a dragonchase?" Whitetail crookedly grinned. "Unprecedented."

"Jastin Armitage is a soldier at heart, which makes him wary. He suspects something. I would."

"Whether he does or not, I don't believe him capable of feigning the symptoms he's exhibiting. I've examined him myself," said Whitetail. "He's feverish and weak."

"Almost too easy," said Vorham, feeling his black mood lift a bit at the thought of the upcoming event. "His imminent accident couldn't have a more convincing prelude."

"Almost too easy," repeated Whitetail, offering again that crooked grin.

§

Orman Thistleby rode his donkey slowly, following the trail of horse-drawn carriages. His left hand upraised to dangle a topaz crystal toward the path. The crystal hummed softly, and drew him steadily, tugging him westward into Esra Province, and toward Riddess Castle.

Someone had trapped Sela with a resistance spell and locked her into that carriage just as sure as if they'd tied her up and tossed her in. Someone at the castle wanted her there. Either as a direct part of the land-bride farce that had overtaken the sensibilities of the entire land, or for some other blasted reason.

The more Orman tried to make sense of what happened, the more annoyed he became. The more annoyed he became, the harder he concentrated on zapping the daylights out of the trickster at the other end of his crystal.

But it wasn't just the frustration of being out-spelled that gnawed at his gizzards. He'd lost Sela.

He'd lost control.

He'd been trying to protect her, as he'd sworn he'd do. To keep her from the world, from being endangered. From being too human. It was why he didn't tell her what the census really was. He thought he'd been doing the right thing. It wasn't as though he'd ever been an uncle before! Children weren't crystals, to be ordered about. Although he tried. It was the only way he knew.

"I should have told her," he said to Nimrod. The

donkey didn't even bother to twitch an ear.

Too late, Orman realized he should have explained to her the census was part of this lottery. A game of chance that would expose Sela to a world of treachery she wasn't prepared for.

Orman had known Vorham Riddess since he was knee-high to a kutterbug, had seen him grow from a quiet mystery of a child into a greedy buzzard of a man. He'd witnessed the embarrassment he'd brought to his father, the violence he'd brought to his province. And now the bully claimed to be reaching out in aid to Leland at the passing of its own Venur? Aid? The man didn't know the meaning of the word.

And it was just as unbelievable that Vorham Riddess really wanted a wife. That lunkhead hated sharing.

The Venur once had a mother, and a sister. One disappeared, one was murdered, and when his father took ill and wasted away, Vorham Riddess stepped blithely into solitary power.

No, Orman knew a dangerous game was afoot, and his stubborn silence hadn't kept Sela from the scrimmage; it had pushed her straight into it.

"Confound it all, Nimrod," he said quietly, drooping in the worn saddle. "What does an old man like me know about raising fledglings?"

Just then, the crystal jerked in his hand, nearly tearing him from the donkey's back. He clutched at the saddle with his right hand, fighting to stay upright.

"That's it," he hollered in triumph. "We're close

now!" Close enough that Orman could peer at the surface of the crystal and expect the visage of the wizard he'd been tracking to swirl into view.

"Illuminate," he murmured. Sure enough, miniature clouds formed inside the bright shard, and, as they dissipated, Orman could see a man with his eyes closed in illness—it served him right!—dark hair strewn over a pillow, his dark beard frosted with silver gray...

Jastin Armitage! The snake! The snake in snake's clothing!

"I'll hang him for the bears!" Orman hollered. "I'll tie him to an anthill and smear his ears with honey!" He shook his fist. He pumped his feet. He thrashed angrily, and lost his balance. He swayed, and then plopped to the ground. "I'll sort his innards with a butter knife!"

Jastin Armitage was more a jackass than Nimrod. What in blazes was he doing casting a resistance spell over anyone, let alone Sela Redheart? The man didn't know a crystal from candy. How could he manage magic at all?

Then Orman sat up. Of course Jastin didn't know magic. But he could be used by someone else who did. Orman had been tracking the *vessel*, not the culprit!

But it didn't matter just now, because Jastin's image began to stir inside the crystal. His brows furrowed. His eyes opened. Blearily, Jastin stared back at Orman, and for a moment, their gazes locked.

"Confound it," muttered Orman. He threw the crystal to the ground and hastily buried it.

Jastin hadn't cast the spell, but the man knew

the wizard who did, and by letting Jastin see Orman through the crystal, now that wizard also knew Orman was coming.

Blast it all. Dadgum and confound it.

§

Jastin pressed the heels of his hands to his eyes, and then he pushed, sitting up. He was in Layce's bedroom, trapped between her bedsheets, which were soggy from his perspiration. Her velvet window shade was tucked aside into a crack in the wall, and afternoon light bathed him, glowing his damp skin. The light was warm, but not uncomfortable now, like it had been for the last… hours? Days?

He circled his fingers against his chest, between his pectorals, twisting black hairs into knots. Just there, a throbbing pain had been tormenting him. It was gone.

Layce emerged from a shadow and sat beside him on the bed. "Who did you see?"

"What?" He blinked wearily.

"As you awoke. You saw him, just before he broke contact."

"I don't know," said Jastin, irritated by her voice, her pestering. He slid his legs from under the blankets and set his bare feet on the floor. "How long have I been here? Where are my clothes?"

"Here." Layce tossed a nightshirt at his chest. "You'll want to bathe, I think, before you dress. Your things are in your usual room."

He tested his legs before he stood to his full height. He felt numb around the edges, as though he'd climbed Mount Gore. But he was plenty strong, and recovered. "I'm going to throttle that old goat."

"What old goat? Who did you see?" Layce slipped off the bed and jangled her way closer, reaching out to help slide the nightshirt over his head.

"I might have been hallucinating."

"You weren't. You recognized him."

Jastin pulled the cool linen over his face, and settled the garment onto his shoulders. He passed his hand over his beard, and then scrubbed his fingers into his whiskers for a good scratch. "I can't swear it, but I think I dreamed about Orman Thistleby."

Layce sucked in a sudden breath. "Orman Thistleby?" she whispered. "*The* Orman Thistleby?"

Jastin pushed past her, ready to hunt down his room, a bath, and a plate full of his brother-in-law's best roast. "I think there's only one."

"Oh, no," she moaned. "Oh, dear." She ran around her bed, expertly avoiding her piles of belongings, and threw herself at her wardrobe door. She yanked the door open, and cried, "Oh no!"

Jastin paused, growing alarmed, himself. "What's wrong?"

Layce pressed her hands to her cheeks, her skin as pale as the blonde wood of the wardrobe. "Orman Thistleby, coming here! Whatever am I going to wear?"

§

Sela climbed slowly from the carriage, stiff from travel. Exhausted from not only straining against whatever magic had been holding her prisoner, but from resisting the tears and sense of hopelessness that had been scratching at her resolve. As her feet touched mottled ground, finally, she felt her spirit as weak and unsteady as her balance.

She thought she'd had it all figured out. She didn't.

Horses snorted and rattled their reins as the three carriages emptied of passengers. Sela stood to the side, her hand braced against a footman's handle, and watched the other girls file quietly onto cobblestones, gather into small clusters, and then turn to gaze up at the massive fieldstone wall before them all.

"Riddess Castle," said a coachman.

The ground rumbled, and the girls broke into startled murmurs. The wall split open, spewing dust, and revealing an iron portcullis guarded by two purple-clad soldiers. Behind them, through the gate's metalwork, Sela saw the sweeping courtyard, massive marble steps, and above that, sky-piercing spires cloaked with ivy. The bastion was easily twice the size of Shornmar's castle, and the grounds, from what she could observe, expanded outward into knolls of velvety grass pinpricked by wild lilies and violets.

Sela pushed away from the carriage to shuffle closer. She wrapped her fingers around the gate's ironwork and stared through it at the tableau, her heartbeat knocking in her ears. Sandstone columns encircled the courtyard, decorated with etching of beetles and purple coneflowers. Coneflowers also filled triangular patches of earth, spilling their leaves onto the cobblestones around them. Beyond the coneflowers, fountains of blue-violet hydrangeas showered the meandering path to the steps of the main entrance.

She wanted to see this view as a painting, as a distant and imagined world, created simply from the mind's eye of an artist. A pretend rendering. A false front to a place that couldn't possibly be real.

It was no painting.

Next the portcullis shuddered, and creaked. Sela released it and hurried backward, into the cluster of girls that seemed to be holding a collective breath. Except Emlee, one of the butterfly sisters, who stepped right up to the rising gate, adjusted the drooping oxpheasant feather pinned to her cascading golden locks, and awaited an escort to the castle as though she already belonged.

"Follow me," said a voice, and Sela lifted to her tiptoes to peer over the heads of the girls. A dark-skinned woman, draped in a voluminous purple caftan dripping with ivy and purple and black ribbons, gestured the gate. Hydrangea petals dangled from her wiry, black ringlets. The woman seemed carved from the landscape itself. "I am Veshlie," said the woman. "I will introduce you to Riddess Castle."

Sela followed, and so did the other women, shuffling wearily. Lovely green and blue and yellow hems caught on the cobblestones, once-bright hair feathers and baubles withered. The bride-elects appeared less like festooned maidens, and more like ragdolls stuffed into crumpled linen napkins.

Except for Emlee. Her pearlescent blue eyes shimmered beneath the glaze of the settling Esra sun, and she used them to look around herself, scrutinizing the scenery, and, Sela guessed, to imagine her woman's touch on the decorating.

Sela took her time, letting the others fill in the path while she slowed and waited for last place. Then she felt a tug on her sleeve. "Sela!"

She turned, startled, to find Gladdis smiling brightly beside her.

"Gladdis! What are you doing here?" Sela almost threw her arms around the girl, but managed to only take her hand. "I thought you weren't selected."

"I wasn't, and neither were you," said Gladdis, "but here *you* are." She leaned in to whisper, "I saw you get caught up in the crowd, and put into a carriage, with that look of horror on your face. And so I thought, if one girl can get misplaced in the chaos, can't two girls?"

"You stowed away?"

"I told you I didn't want to go all the way home by myself." She pulled Sela's hand to catch them up to the others.

Sela resisted, just long enough to make Gladdis pause. Then she really did hug the girl, tightly. "I'm so glad you're here," she said into Gladdis's shoulder, wondering if it would be a good time to cry, yet.

Gladdis returned the hug, just as firmly. "Hopefully

Emlee will keep her mouth shut. I'll talk to her as soon as I get a chance." She broke the embrace and stepped back, wincing. "But first, I really, really to find a privy."

"Me, too," said Sela. "And I'm starving. All I can think about is Uncle Orman's oatmeal drizzled with honey."

They hurried past hydrangeas and up the marble steps, through the vestibule and into the reception chamber of the castle. Ahead of them, their guide was speaking to the girls as a group, but Sela drew to a stop, and looked around herself at the enormous, cave-like room. To the right, a secondary room abutted this one, separated only by tiled urns as tall as Sela, overflowing with ferns and greenery, gathered together with statuary and artfully arranged to funnel guests away from the walls. In the second room, a purple velvet banner hung from rough-hewn ceiling timbers, emblazoned with an orange circle which held the black silhouette of a sword behind a dragon head.

The Great Hall, she assumed. She inched closer to an urn, and peered around it. Cherrywood tables lined end to end, stained dark as pitch, in tidy rows facing the dais, a raised stone platform. Then Sela gasped. Mounted to the wall behind the dais was the head of a sand-colored dragon, with a sword stabbed clean through it, behind its left eye, and out through the jaw.

She looked back up to the banner. The sword wasn't *behind* the dragonhead. She lowered her gaze to the dragonhead on the wall. Its scales were mottled, pale, and a kind she'd never seen before. Its eyes were dull and coated with thick dust. But it was real. It had been, once.

What kind of sick mind would hang a dragon corpse on a wall as a trophy?

The clatter of plateware drew her eyes to a far corner of the Great Hall, near the stone archway of the kitchen and scullery. A lone man was seated at a table, digging his knife into a roasted and glistening slab of meat. His black hair was askew, and curled with moisture where it brushed the back of his neck, and the edges of his mouth within his dark beard shimmered from the fatty meat. His white tunic appeared rumpled but freshly clean.

Surely the Venur wouldn't be eating alone in the middle of the day. But this man was no hired hand. He wasn't wearing the colors.

The man hacked at chunk of meat, and raised it to his mouth, just as he spotted her watching him. He paused. He blinked. Then he dropped his knife, meat and all, to his plate, and wiped his hand across his mouth. He shot to his feet.

"Excuse me," she said, feeling her face go hot. Only minutes in this new place, and already she was drawing attention to herself, making trouble. She turned for a quick retreat.

"Stop," said the man.

She almost didn't. But his voice echoed, and bounced from the Great Hall into the reception chamber, and the other girls began to spin, one by one, toward the sound. Sela flinched, and turned back, an apology already on her lips. "Please forgive me, I didn't mean to intrude—"

"Who are you?" he asked, walking quickly toward her. He wore boots, but they were whisper soft. He drew in close—too close—examining her face. She saw the gray at his temples, then, and the gray of the whiskers in his black beard.

"My name is Sela," she said, easing back a step.

He closed the gap between them, and took her chin in his fingers. He stared at her eyes.

"Please," she said, recoiling, trying to break his grasp. He held firmly, wrenching her neck.

"Mr. Armitage?" called Veshlie. "Is something wrong?"

The man seemed to gather himself, and he released Sela's chin. Sela touched her fingers to her face where the pain still stung, and looked over her shoulder to their guide, who was drifting toward them like a purple wraith, her steely eyes on Sela.

"I was just looking," she said, her voice sounding pitiful, even to herself.

"Who is this girl?" The man pointed at Sela, demanding.

"Answer him," said Veshlie.

"I did. My name is Sela."

"She is a guest of your Venur, Mr. Armitage. She is a Leland maiden, chosen from the many." The woman laid her dark hands onto Sela's shoulders, and directed her to turn to the center of the room.

"Leland maiden," the man repeated.

"From Simson," Sela said, taking the opportunity to

duck behind Veshlie.

"No harm was meant, Mr. Armitage. We will leave you to your business." The woman pressed her hands to Sela's backpack and urged her forward. Then she whispered between her teeth, "I suggest you don't wander."

Sela rejoined the group, and Veshlie circled around them to lead them across the room, and toward a maze of hallways at the back of the reception room. "This way, please," she called out. "Now that Sela has found the Great Hall and kitchen for us, I'll show you to your quarters."

"Who is that man?" asked Gladdis, tugging again at Sela's sleeve.

Sela peered over her shoulder. He was still watching her, his face shadowed. "I don't know."

"It's as though he knows you," said Gladdis.

"I don't see how he could."

"He's frightening."

Sela nodded, and hurried to keep up with the others, trying to ignore the feel of his heavy gaze on her back.

§

In the chamber where she would spend the night, Sela ran her hands over the bumpy masonry and trailed her fingertips along the mud-and-lime mortar between stones. So like Mount Gore Manor, except without the mortar. The manor was carved directly into Mount

Gore, and all the walls were solid rock. Thinking of Leland, she closed her eyes, and felt suddenly drained.

"I'm so far from home," she said. "Just a few days ago, I was with my mother. My father. In the one place that makes me happy." She opened her eyes, and turned to lean back against the wall. "The one place I may never see again."

In the windowless room, a large woodcarved bed was set haphazardly in the center of the dusty floor. Its wool and featherdown blankets had been cast hurriedly into place, and a splintered nightstand was wedged beside the headboard. A single candle cast wavering light from the stand, filling the room with the scent of beeswax and singed cobwebs. A trunk in the corner served as the wardrobe—Veshlie had mentioned dinner gowns inside—but Sela thought it would make a nice seat.

Gladdis removed a hand mirror from her bag and tilted it toward the light, examining herself in the reflective glass, scowling. Then she laid the mirror onto the bed, and reached beneath her hair to untie her pale blue dress, pushing it to her waist. "Strangely, I don't miss my home at all. But I have nowhere else to go."

"Maybe you'll be the Venuress," said Sela. "And you won't go back."

Gladdis made a sound at the back of her throat, and pushed her dress completely to the floor to step out of it. She draped it across the foot of the bed, smoothed the soft fabric, and then tiptoed across the floor in her chemise and petticoat to peer into the trunk. "As long as

Emlee is here, I won't get a second look. I never have."

"I don't see why. You both have pretty eyes. The shape of your face. You could almost be twins, actually."

"It may seem that way to you," said Gladdis, holding open the lid of the trunk and rummaging inside it. "But Emlee has something special, something that draws men's eyes. Something I simply don't have."

Sela pushed away from the wall and circled around the foot of the bed. She dropped her backpack to the floor, grasped the candlestick, and carried the light toward Gladdis. "What does she have that's so special?"

Gladdis withdrew a lump of fabric from the trunk and straightened, regarding Sela. She shrugged deeply. "I don't know." Then she shook out the fabric, and it billowed out into an explosion of sparkles; a glimmering ruby dress that caught the candlelight and dazzled the room with tiny, glowing prisms.

"Oh," breathed Sela. She set the candlestick on the floor and reached for the dress. "It looks like my mother."

"I'll bet she's very beautiful," said Gladdis. "Let's see if it fits you."

"Oh, no," said Sela, hugging the dress to her chest. "No, I can't wear something like this." Still, she couldn't resist pressing the fabric to her cheek, and drawing in a deep breath, hoping to find her mother's scent of musk and faint nutmeg.

"But it's perfect. It's meant for you."

"No," Sela said again. "You wear it, Gladdis. I'll just wear what I've—"

A knock sounded on the door, and it opened. Veshlie leaned into the room. "Ladies," she said. "Sela and Gladdis. Are you finding what you need?"

"Yes, I think so," said Gladdis.

"I apologize for the condition of the room," said Veshlie. "It seems when we took the final count of our maiden guests, we had more than we'd anticipated, and so these quarters—"

"Oh, we don't mind," said Gladdis, nudging Sela with her elbow.

"No," said Sela. "Not at all. It's very nice."

"Well, we have plenty of provisions for all of you, there's no need to scrimp. If you'll please change for dinner, I'll gather you in one half hour."

"But I'm perfectly comfortable in what I'm wearing," said Sela.

Veshlie's brow tightened. She lifted her chin, and looked so fiercely down her nose that Sela actually shivered. "I insist. You will be meeting the Venur this evening."

"We'll be ready," said Gladdis, and nudged Sela again. "Thank you."

Veshlie nodded, eyed Sela a moment longer, and then retreated, closing the door.

"For someone who is trying not to be noticed, you're certainly making a lot of noise." Gladdis turned, picked up the candlestick, and replaced it on the night stand. "You should really think about this, Sela. All the other girls will be dressed in ball gowns, their cheeks pinched, their hair swept up into curls and ribbons, and you want to be the one wearing trousers." She pressed a fist to her hip. "I can't think of a better way to hide than to put on that red dress, brush out your hair, and blend in."

Sela groaned, but knew Gladdis was right. "You'll have to help me."

Gladdis returned to the trunk and reached inside it again. This time she withdrew a marigold-yellow dress of smooth taffeta, with a bodice of appliqué petals. She turned shining eyes to Sela. "My favorite color."

"It matches your hair perfectly!"

Gladdis sat onto the edge of the trunk, laying her dress onto her lap and thoughtfully studying it. "How could anyone know my favorite color? How could anyone know I was coming, when I didn't even know, myself?" Gladdis shook her head, and then stood. "Impossible. Veshlie even said they were caught off guard."

Sela lifted her own dress, and watched it dance with candlelight, flickering red sparks across Gladdis's face, her arms, and her yellow dress. "Perhaps *Veshlie* was caught off guard." She thought back to the odd tingle of magic at Shornmar Castle, and being pressed into a carriage against her will, despite Orman fighting to free her. An utterly foolish but insidious thought tickled against the back of her neck, and slithered beneath her skin. "Perhaps Veshlie was caught off guard," she said again. "But I think someone else knew exactly who was coming."

§

Layce Phelcher paced outside her chamber, her hands wringing against her abdomen. Jastin had never seen her so nervous, in all the years he'd known the woman. Nor had he seen her so lovely, wearing a gown of hydrangea blue that swayed in layers against her legs as she walked. Her creamy shoulders were bare, her mink-black hair upswept into waterfall of ringlets. He paused, watching her from afar, and nearly forgot his anger, and the reason he'd traipsed through the castle to find her.

She looked over at him, and breathed out suddenly. "Oh, Jastin. How do I look? He's going to be here any minute."

"Who?"

"Orman Thistleby. At the back gate. I'll need to meet him."

"Why?"

"Because it's locked, of course." She smoothed the dress at her slender waist. "My father talked about him so much. He admired him, all those years ago, before he disappeared into the mountains."

"Your father disappeared into the mountains?"

Layce drew her brows together. "Orman Thistleby did. After the death of Bren Redheart. Remember?"

Of course Jastin remembered the death of Bren Redheart. But he didn't pay much attention to wizards, or whatever happened to them after that. "Look, Layce, I know you're not telling me everything you know about what's going on here. First, you ask me to help you with something to do with Orman Thistleby... and yes, I remember who he is to those dragons. What I don't understand is why he's coming here, after all these years, and what it has to do with the girl in this castle who looks like—"

"Oh, there he is," said Layce. She stepped toward Jastin and took his hand. "Come with me, in case I can't think of anything to say."

Layce not have anything to say? Jastin would have laughed, except he was still reeling from the shock of seeing Riza Diantus's face on a girl in boys' clothing in this castle, miles away from Leland.

Riza Diantus. He hadn't thought of her name in so long he was surprised he remembered it. Remembered *her*. But outside the Great Hall, moments ago, he'd looked into eyes the green of fir trees, and, although that girl had called herself Sela, he knew he'd been looking into the eyes of Riza.

The girl who had reminded him where his heart was.

"Layce, I need to know—"

"I know you do. And you will. But first, you have to help me."

Jastin planted his feet, and when Layce tried to pull him through the hallway, her hand broke from his grasp. "I've done enough helping," he said.

She turned to face him, her gaze downcast. "This is different," she said.

Jastin crossed his arms. "Oh?"

She began to speak, hesitated, and then lifted her gaze to his face. "I don't have magic for this."

"For what?"

"For…" She pressed her lips into a flat line. "For…"

Jastin's arms unclenched, and he lowered them to his sides. He felt a smile itch at the corners of his mouth. "Are you telling me you've got feelings for that dried up willow root?"

"No!" She shook her head. "I've never even met him!" Now Layce was the one who crossed her arms. "Oh, don't look at me like that. I think I'd rather you scowl at me."

"I'm sorry," said Jastin, irritatingly amused, when he wanted to be angry with her, force some answers from her. "I just didn't think the old man had it in him." Jastin took her hand, then, and led her toward the carved stone steps leading up to the main level. "Once you meet him, you'll change your mind. He's a miserable crank who doesn't have the heart to share any feelings."

"Look who's talking," said Layce.

They climbed the steps, and on the main landing, turned right. The arching hallway to the back gate led them past the scullery door, the wine storage door, and the wooden ramp used by wagons and wheelbarrows to carry foodstuffs and supplies. Staff bustled from door to door, pinching Layce and Jastin against the rough stone walls, and tripping their feet.

Behind the kitchen, the heat from the brick ovens brought perspiration to Jastin's brow. The smell of broiling pheasant brought wetness to the back of his tongue. His stomach growled.

"Let us through," said Layce quietly. Two women in plain brown head wraps stepped aside, holding their bread baskets out of the way. A man in a muslin apron wiped his hands on the cloth, smearing char marks, and moved into the wine storage doorway.

"You didn't see us," Layce said, barely whispering it. As they passed, the staff fell back into step where they'd paused, and discussed their tasks as they hurried.

The crackle of magic provoked Jastin's nerves, and he hunched his shoulders as though he were protecting himself against the rain. But they made it finally through the hinged doors behind the kitchen, and into the open air of the back bailey, where they crept along the inner curtain wall toward the rusted, rarely-used iron gate on the east side. He hadn't skulked about his brother-in-law's castle in a long time. Hadn't skulked about anywhere, for that matter, and he resented the feel of it.

"Get used to it," said Layce. "This is just the beginning."

He opened his mouth to say something malicious, but Layce stopped suddenly, and jerked on his hand. "There he is."

Sure enough, the shriveled old coot, looking as wobbly and pale as Jastin remembered, stood boldly on the opposite side of the iron door in the wall, and waved an emerald crystal toward the padlock, his face and beard glowing oddly green in the light. "Orman Thistleby," Jastin called.

Orman kept his gaze trained on the padlock.

"When I get my hands on you, you slimy so-and-so, I'm going to wring out your innards."

"Don't!" Layce said suddenly. She hurried toward the door and held up her hands. Both men arched their brows, and blinked at her face. Layce shook her head. "No, I mean, do what you want with his innards, but don't break the lock. There are wards."

Orman squinched up one eye. "I know there are wards, young lady, but I haven't met one yet I can't outsmart."

"Oh," said Layce, smoothing her dress again near her waist. "I'm not that young." She giggled behind her hand, and cast a blushing look toward Jastin that completely contradicted her statement.

Both of Orman's eyes scrunched up. "Eh? Oh, I see now," he said. Then he looked from Layce to Jastin, and back. "Well are you two going to stand there jabbering at me, or are you going to let me in?"

Jastin moved toward the door, hand outreaching, but Layce put her fingers on his arm. "I'm sorry, Mr. Thistleby," she said. "We can't let you in."

"But you haven't called the guards, either, so what in the blazes are you doing here?"

"We came to warn you."

Orman turned a suspicious look to Jastin, and Jastin didn't blame him. He hadn't come to warn Orman about anything. He came to watch Layce go flustered over the old buzzard, but so far, she hadn't entertained him as much as he'd hoped.

"Warn me," said Orman. "After kidnapping my

niece, locking her up, locking me out, and fighting me every step of the way, now you're going to warn me? About what? Listening to two folks on a side of a gate I'm trying to get to, who think they're helping?"

"Your niece?" Jastin asked. "Your *niece?*"

"It isn't that I don't want to let you in," said Layce. "But there are wards on the gate, and wards in the yard, and wards on the castle that I didn't put there, and even I don't know my way around them."

"I believe that," said Orman. "You're wearing too many crystals all at once. A sure sign of a novice."

"A novice!" Layce drew up, and her blue eyes snapped. "I'll have you know I was trained by the best of the Esra wizards. The Phelcher name is synonymous with—"

"Phelcher," said Orman. "Den Phelcher of the Seraphim Spell?"

Layce's posture softened. "The very one."

"Your husband?"

Layce lowered her chin. "My father."

"Ah," said Orman. He regarded Layce, then, gone silent.

Jastin looked between them, and then stepped into the silence. "Your niece?" he repeated. "The girl with the face of Riza Diantus?"

"I don't know what you're talking about," said Orman. "Riza Redheart has her own face, which is attached to her own body, far away from this castle."

"Riza *Redheart?*" Jastin felt his voice pull away, dragged down a dark tunnel, echoing in his own ears.

And then he remembered. Not that she'd become a dragon, a filthy, stinking, hulking beast; of course he remembered that. But he remembered his anguish, and his pain. He gripped a protruding stone in the wall to steady himself.

Where that memory had come from, he didn't know. He thought he'd banished all but anger from his soul. He'd believed himself cured of being able to recall it, and so it had swept over him, and unfastened him when he wasn't expecting it. "Whatever you're up to, the both of you, I don't care," he said. Which was true. "Don't tell me anything about it. And don't ask for my help. Ever again."

He turned away from the wall, and walked steady steps across the bailey and toward the castle. With each step, he felt himself grow darker and darker inside. Stronger. Familiar. Comfortable.

Less curious about why his brother-in-law, Vorham, sent for him, and more eager to just kill himself a dragon.

CHAPTER TWELVE

Sela made her way anxiously toward the dais in the Great Hall, squeezing Gladdis's hand, and watching the bustle of stiff citizens in fur-lined tunics and gilt-edged gowns choosing and arguing over seats. Servants scuttled around the perimeter of the room, bowing and nodding, and pouring wine or setting out baskets of flour cakes soaked in butterfat. The other maidens, flitting like sequined moths, whispered behind gloved hands and hovered behind the open benches of the dais table.

The other girls, with their tresses uplifted in thick layers of braiding, or flowing delicately down their spines, or a mixture of both, appeared effortlessly feminine. They glided in their gowns of blue, or green, or pale pinks, gracefully gesturing, seeming more to dance than to simply point and communicate.

But Sela kept stepping on her hem. Her hair, unwound from its braid and left to sway against her bare shoulders, tickled her skin, making her brush constantly at the sensation, feeling it like annoying flies. She couldn't have felt more uncomfortable, and conspicuous, than if she'd been wrapped with fencing wire and dangled from the ceiling.

Except no one seemed to notice her. Which suited her just fine.

She and Gladdis were just reaching the steps of the raised dais platform, when she caught sight of the guard—Bannon, she remembered—entering from the back of the room. She watched him for a moment, awaiting eye contact, and then she gave a small wave.

He frowned briefly. Maybe he didn't remember her. But then his features lifted, and he smiled. He gave a nod.

"Ladies and gentlemen," announced a dark-skinned man in a sweeping purple vest that hung to the top of his black boots, and cut away to puddle onto the floor behind him. He stood at the front of the dais platform, arms lifted from his sides. "Venur Riddess welcomes you to this celebration of the union that is to come; between man and woman, boundary and boundary, and future to future. Please meet our most honored guests, the lovely Leland maidens from whom your Venuress will be chosen."

Polite applause rippled through the room, and the announcer waved his hands toward the long benches behind the table. The girls swept forward and alighted into their places. Sela and Gladdis hurried to sit, too, finding themselves at the end nearest the wall and farthest from the high-backed, velvety chair that had yet to be occupied.

"Please enjoy the meat and wine this evening, in honor of the upcoming ceremony," the announcer continued. "And join us for a continuation of celebration tomorrow, in honor of the birthday of Jastin Armitage, former captain of your Riddess Guard and brother-in-law to your esteemed Venur. A dragon hunt!"

More applause erupted, hearty this time, and someone across the room even shouted "We ride!" There was a whoop. Someone tossed a hat into the air.

Sela turned her gaze upward to the severed dragon head looming over the dais, and her stomach went sour. She was hungry, but she knew she wouldn't be able to take a bite.

"Allow me to present the man by whom all this is made possible." The announcer stepped back and gestured his left hand toward the velvet chair, in which a man was now seated. The man smiled, his teeth bright within a face the color of the inky tea-and-licorice concoction Orman made her drink when she had a stuffy nose. His eyes were dark, too, and small in his round face. He regarded the faces in the room with a sort of sterile, distant expression that made his smile seem more sinister than friendly.

"Venur Vorham Draven Riddess!" The announcer shouted the name, and made a dramatic flourish of a bow, backing away from the seated Venur, down the dais steps, and into the shadows.

Now the guests stood, and the applause ricocheted from the arching ceiling, rattled against the stone walls. Sela surreptitiously pressed one finger to her ear, plugging it, and tried not to wince.

One maiden stood to join the others in energetic clapping, her hands silent in satin gloves, but delicately cupped. Emlee. Torchlight found the buttons in her fair hair, and the shine in her steady gaze on the Venur's face. She smiled from her place directly beside his chair.

He looked at her then, gave an appreciative nod. As the applause withered to sporadic pops, the Venur glanced toward the benches, vaguely nodded again, and then spoke to Emlee. Sela thought she read his lips to say "Thank you. Please sit."

Dinner passed slowly. Achingly slowly. Sela pushed at the mound of beans and meat on her wooden plate, but she couldn't make herself put anything into her mouth, with that dragon carcass hovering just inches from her head. She watched guests empty bottles of wine, ask for more, and empty them again. Women cackled, men belted laughter. Gladdis was quiet, nibbling here and there at her food. Sela finally turned to her.

"I have to get out of here."

"Are you sick?" Her brow furrowed in concern.

"No. Not like you mean. Did you not even notice the dead dragon on the wall, right there?"

Gladdis lifted her gaze, and she wrinkled up her nose. "Of course I did. Smells funny."

"It's disgusting. I don't think the Venur would appreciate a decoration made from someone lopping off *his* head and stabbing a sword through it."

"It's just a dragon," said Gladdis.

"What's that supposed to mean?"

Gladdis studied Sela, her eyes thoughtful. "It means, you know. It's a trophy. A part of the Esra tradition."

"Tradition?"

"There's a dragon hunt tomorrow. Someone will probably take the trophy from that one, too."

"What?" Sela gasped, feeling heat rise into her throat.

"Leland used to do it, too, but we don't have very many dragons anymore."

"Is it any wonder?" Sela stood suddenly, now sick in exactly the way Gladdis had meant.

"Where are you going? What did I say?"

Sela leaned down to stare into Gladdis's pale eyes. "Imagine dragons rounding up humans. Your family. Calling it sport. Chopping off your heads and having feasts beneath your faces."

Gladdis cringed, and pulled back, her shoulders raising. "They wouldn't do that."

"Of course they wouldn't," said Sela.

"They don't think like that," said Gladdis. "They don't *think*. They're just beasts."

Sela wanted a vicious response to that, but anger seethed up behind her teeth and locked her jaw. She glowered at Gladdis. Then she turned abruptly, ran down the dais steps, winded her way through milling people, and hurried into a hallway, looking for a door, or a window, or someplace to catch a breath of air before she threw up whatever was roiling about in her very taut and very empty stomach.

The nearest hallway took her past the scullery, and the blistering heat of a bustling kitchen. The smell of roasted meat slapped at her nose, adding insult to her injured senses. She avoided that hallway and searched for another. She followed a line of torches toward a flat wall that turned sharply right.

There, she discovered a small alcove with doors made of colored glass, the archway above decorated with a garland of dried coneflowers. She touched her hand to a door, and pushed it slowly open.

"Prayers won't help," said a voice behind her, startling her.

She released the door and turned. "I'm sorry?" It was that bearded man. The one who seemed to dislike her from the moment they met.

"You've found the chapel, but prayers won't help."

She looked behind herself, at the doors, at the garland over the carved doorway. "The chapel?"

"Or maybe you were just snooping."

"I wanted some air." She regarded the man, trying to decide if she was afraid, or just annoyed. "Mr. Armitage, isn't it?"

He nodded, and took a step closer. "Jastin." He tipped his head, studying her with a kind of anticipation that made her wonder what reaction he'd been expecting. "And I know who you are. It isn't possible, I realize. But here you are. And I recognize you as though it was yesterday."

"I'm sorry, Mr. Armitage. I've never seen you—"

"Jastin." His jaw clenched. "It's Jastin."

"All right. Jastin." Her annoyance was evolving into a sort of fear, after all. "Whatever your name is, I've never seen you before, and I don't know how you could possibly know me." She pressed her shoulder to the wall and stepped around him.

He pressed his hand to the wall, blocked her with his arm.

She drew up with a sharp breath.

He leaned in tightly, and forced his face into the crook of her neck.

"Stop," she whispered.

"You smell like him," he said, and pulled back to search her face again.

"Like who?"

His lips parted, and she could see the tip of his tongue against the back of his teeth as his mouth worked to speak, struggling as though he could barely bring himself to form the words. Then he finally spat, "Kallon Redheart."

Her heart clenched.

"Who?" she tried to ask casually, but it was too late.

He smiled a sneering sort of grin, and she knew he'd finally gotten the reaction he'd been looking for.

"Is everything all right here?" asked a voice in the hallway. Jastin eased back and leveled a gaze on Bannon Raley, who rested his hand on the pommel of the sword at his hip, and gave Jastin the look right back.

"The lady and I are having civil conversation," said Jastin.

"Bannon," whispered Sela.

"I don't think it civil at all to have cornered one of the Leland maidens, chosen for the Venur, and without the company of an escort," said Bannon.

"I've cornered no one," said Jastin. "I'm familiar with protocol, being captain of the guard—"

"Former captain," said Bannon.

Jastin smiled, but it was a dark, threatening version of the expression. "We're friends, aren't we Riza? We're reliving old times."

"You've mistaken her for someone else, old man," said Bannon. "And you've mistaken me for someone who finds you intimidating. Be on your way."

"I'm not through here."

Bannon gripped the handle of his sword, and withdrew it, just an inch, so that the torchlight glittered against the steel. "Yes, sir. You are."

Jastin glared at Bannon. Turned the glare to Sela. She shrank back, her breath held, as it had been through the entire exchange. Then he pushed away from the wall and stalked back down the hallway, his footsteps swallowed by the sound of clattering iron pots and servant hubbub.

Sela finally released her breath. "Thank you, Bannon."

Bannon replaced his sword, watching down the hallway. "He should be glad it was me, and not one of the other guards who interrupted. I, at least, have some respect for who he used to be, but the others..." He shook his head, and turned his gaze to Sela. "To the others, he's a relic. A joke."

He didn't seem funny to Sela, with his face on her neck and his wide shoulders pressing her to the wall.

"He called you Riza."

"I know," she said, swallowing tightly. "He's been drinking, I think."

Bannon nodded. "I almost thought you were someone else, too. At first. Without your trousers."

Sela smiled. "I almost wore them underneath. But Gladdis wouldn't let me."

"Gladdis?"

"One of the other Leland girls. My friend." Although as she said it, she remembered their last conversation, and wondered if she could actually be a friend to anyone who considered the slaughter of dragons so indifferently.

"If you wanted the use of the chapel, you should have asked Veshlie. Or me. Just to prevent this sort of thing. There are few gentlemen around here."

"Yes, I wasn't thinking." And she hadn't really wanted the chapel, of course, but his point was well taken.

"If you'd like privacy, I'll wait outside, and then I can escort you back to the Great Hall."

"Oh." She looked at the glass doors, and then gently nudged at one. It swung easily open, but whatever lay on the other side was hidden in thick, impenetrable darkness. "I can just come back."

Just as she was reaching to close the door, light from the hallway caught a flash of gold from deep within the chapel. An eye.

She yelped, and hopped backward. "Did you see that?"

"Here," said Bannon, and he plucked a torch from a wall sconce, offering it.

She accepted it, but it was heavy and too hot, too close to her face. Even with both hands, she struggled to control it.

Bannon gave a snort of a laugh, and retrieved it. "Here," he said again. He gently nudged her aside, pushed open the second chapel door, and then, holding the torch away from her, nodded for her to enter.

She did. Slowly. Once inside, Bannon swung the torch to flare light into the room, and Sela instantly saw what had startled her. A dragon carving hung from the ceiling, with a wing span so wide the tips disappeared into the dark where the torch couldn't reach. Its scales appeared formed from gold, warm and burnished, and the sweeping arch of its neck lowered its face so that its eyes—as clear and richly brown as her own father's— stared directly into Sela's face.

"Oh," she breathed, and lifted her hand to touch it. But she couldn't reach. Not quite. "It seems closer than it is."

Bannon circled the room, lighting fat pillar candles and beeswax squares where they lined the walls, stacked on tables, or were fixed into the masonry. As he moved, swells of flamelight followed, illuminating the sheer size and depth of the chapel. Her father and mother could both fit easily into this space, with room to spare. "It's a cave!" she exclaimed.

"I'd think you were insulting the chapel, but you sound happy about that."

She crossed the pressed dirt floor to draw her hand over the carved wall. "I just mean it's so big. And it feels different. From the rest of the castle."

"It is, I suppose. Rarely used. Leftover from another time." Bannon slid the base of the torch into a tall sconce in the center of the room, positioned just below the gold dragon, so that the torch flame arched up and through the figure's open mouth, appearing to breathe directly from the dragon's face.

"At least that one isn't dead," she murmured.

"Hm?"

"This dragon seems almost, I don't know. A part of the worship."

"A part of the reverance, at least," said Bannon, crossing his arms and regarding the effigy.

"Not like the other dragon hanging in the Great Hall. The corpse as a trophy."

"Corpse?" Bannon raised a brow, studying her. "It's a banner as real to the Riddess family as the crest on their streamer. It announces them."

"As murderers." Sela lowered her hand from the wall to an unlit candle on a short table. She picked it up, examining the charred wick and the bumps of lingering wax from previous burnings.

"You believe it's murder to kill a dragon?" he asked.

Sela lowered her hands, and turned, very slowly, to face him, her eyes blinking. "What?"

"It isn't murder in Esra," he said, hesitantly, studying her reaction.

"What is wrong with this place? With the people of this castle? With the people of this province?" She threw the candle to the floor, and it snapped and bounced. She stomped toward the door.

Bannon stepped back, blocking her exit, his hands raised. "Wait."

"Get out of my way," she fumed between her teeth.

"Wait," he said again. "I'm only telling you what the law is. That it isn't a crime to kill a dragon."

"Tell that to his family."

Bannon lowered his hands. "What do you mean?"

She stared at him, her fists clenching. Her breath came in short, shallow huffs. She felt pressure inside her skull, and her vision grew blurry. Too upset for words, even if she knew the correct ones to argue with, she shook her head. "I have to get out of here," she said for the second time tonight. "Let me out."

"Tell me why you're so angry," he said, unmoving.

"You make me sick. All of you." She tried to push him out of the way, but he was a boulder, and she barely shifted his weight.

He gripped at her arms. "Sela."

"Don't you touch me!" She ripped herself from his grasp. "Don't you ever touch me. I don't know what made me think I could be one of you, blend into your kind as though I fit in." She pushed at him again, but he still resisted. "Let me out of here! I can't stay. I don't want to find my destiny if it means I have to pretend you don't make me sick!"

Bannon continued to study her, his hazel eyes dark with confusion. He did finally step aside, but he rested his palm on the nearest door, his lips parted to say something.

Sela didn't care to hear whatever it was. She pushed open the second door so hard it swung out and thudded into the wall, rattling its decorative glass.

"Don't go because of me," he said quickly. "I'll wait outside."

The sadness of his voice made her pause. She looked at him over her shoulder. His face was stoic, distant. But she was sure she'd heard heaviness in his tone.

"I didn't come here to pray," she said. "I was just looking for fresh air." And her need for it hadn't gone, it had multiplied.

"Oh." He backed up two full steps, and then turned to the back of the room, toward the deep shadows where candlelight hadn't penetrated. "It's here," he said. He passed beneath the dragon sculpture, his footfalls disappearing into darkness. A grinding, cranking sound erupted, and then moonlight pierced the shadows as a sliver that expanded into a bright square.

Sela hurried toward the window, now fully open, and stood before the open air. She closed her eyes, breathed in deeply. "I don't belong here," she said.

"I believe you."

She wasn't sure what he meant by agreeing so quickly, and she didn't think she cared, either, but she did open her eyes and scrutinize him.

"You're not like the other chosen. You're not like any woman I've met in Esra."

He turned his gaze to the dark sky through the window. His eyes tracked the movement of a fleckowl across the treetops, and then lifted to find the stars. By the way his gaze traveled evenly, Sela thought he must be counting them. "What sort of destiny were you looking for here?" he asked.

She hadn't meant to blurt that. Now that her anger had subsided, she was embarrassed at her outburst. Although she still meant it. "I shouldn't have said what I did."

"That we make you sick?"

She drew up her shoulders, feeling tightness crawl between her shoulder blades. "I was angry."

"I've never killed a dragon," said Bannon. He turned, and pressed his back to the wall beside the window, his shadowed eyes on her face. "I've never killed a living thing, not even a moss fly, except what I've needed for food."

"But you're a soldier."

He crossed his arms against his abdomen. "Esra hasn't seen war in generations. My job is to be ready for one, so I train. And I scout property lines. Deliver summons. Take orders for whatever menial task my Venur has in mind."

"Kidnap maidens to marry?"

He wrinkled his brow, and then smiled half-heartedly. "Everyone I know of came willingly. Even you."

She supposed that was true.

"Why did you?" he asked.

"Why did I what?"

"Come willingly."

"Maybe 'willingly' isn't the right word," she said.

He nodded, chewing at his bottom lip.

Sela watched him for a moment, studying the way the moonlight cast shadows in the creases of his face, beneath his nose and chin. Candlelight enhanced the color of his skin, competed with the moonlight to make his hazel eyes warm, and his tawny hair a soft frame around his features.

His gaze shifted to her face.

He'd caught her staring, but he didn't seem to mind. He remained silent and still, patiently regarding her, so she let her eyes wander down his throat, and to the cleft of his purple shirt. More shadows hinted at his collarbone and the faint swell of a pectoral muscle that looked firm and well-developed, from what she could tell beneath the loose fabric. That, with his wide shoulders, would seem to make him a strong flyer, if he had the wings for it...

Suddenly he was pressed against her, and his fingers were lifting her chin. "Sela," he whispered.

She startled, but she wasn't afraid. His scent was fresh rain mixed with clove. She breathed it in, watching his face, transfixed by the wonder of what was happening behind his eyes. Something sparked them, lighting them into warm cinders.

"Do I really make you sick?" he asked quietly.

Giving it some thought now, with the scent of him in her lungs, and feel of his hands gliding across her ribs to come to rest against her back, she decided that no, that's not how he was making her feel at all. She shook her head, and eased ever-so-gently forward.

He smiled then. Soft and secret, like the one they'd shared that first day they met. One hand lifted to trace his knuckles over her cheek, just in front of her ear, down to her jaw. Her eyes closed at the sensation, like moth flutters.

"Have you kissed a man?" he asked.

She shook her head again.

"May I be the first?"

Her eyes opened to find his face a hair's breadth from hers, the smolder of his gaze warming her skin. She understood then, why her pulse thrummed in her ears, why goosebumps raised beneath his touch. "Yes," she whispered.

Their lips touched, and parted gently. His hand cupped beneath her hair, guiding her head to tip, to deepen the kiss.

And within Sela, the knot that had formed around her broken heart eased open. She lifted her arms to embrace his neck, feeling the movement as a sprouting of green branches from a stunted sapling. Life coursed through her veins, enlightening her, reviving her. Against his mouth, she bloomed.

He broke the kiss, his eyes searching hers. And then, slowly, they shared another smile.

And she wished desperately that Orman was here so she could ask him what kind of baffling, wonderful magic had just happened.

She came to awareness, remembering the enormous chapel, the open window. Voices spoke distantly.

"Sela…" Bannon began to say.

The voices grew louder, and a flash of white blocked the moonlight, swallowing them into shadow. But just as quickly as it came, it passed. The outlying trees beyond the window swayed casually as though nothing had happened.

"Did you see that?" she asked. She went to the window, her fingers grasping the sill. She rose to her tiptoes to peer out. "It was a dragon."

"A what?"

"A dragon. A white one."

"Here?" asked Bannon, joining her at the window.

"They passed the window. They must be in the courtyard."

"Are you sure of the color?"

"I think so," said Sela. "They're lost or confused, or something. I have to warn them." She touched his arm. "Show me how to get out there."

Bannon leaned through the window, his chin lifted, staring out across the lawn. "What is he doing in the courtyard at this time of night? Something with the hunt, maybe."

"The hunt?" Sela had forgotten about it. She pushed away from the window, alarm skittering across her shoulders. "Then I really have to warn him!" She hurried to a wide wall in the chapel, just beyond a burning candelabrum, and swept away a dusty cobweb obscuring an immense, stone-carved door.

"I can show you the way to the courtyard," said Bannon, walking toward the glass doors they'd used to enter. "But I don't think we should—"

"Where does this lead?"

He paused. "Where does what lead?"

"This door, here." She dug her fingertip into the crack between door and wall, clearing dust and caked grime.

"That's just a wall."

"No it isn't. Look. It's made to appear as a wall, but there should be a mechanism somewhere to activate. We have a lot of doorways like this at... oh, there it is." Her finger caught on a latch embedded within the crack. She scratched at it, and twisted her finger. "It won't budge. Must be rusted over, or something."

Bannon came to stand beside her. He passed his hand across the stone, across the crack, and then regarded her with narrowed, thoughtful eyes. "I don't see anything. I don't feel anything."

"But it's right there. You're touching it."

"Why don't we just use the hallway behind the kitchen." He took her hand, eyed her briefly from the side of his face, and then led her through the swinging glass doors and into the hallway from where they'd come.

She wasn't sure if he doubted her senses, or doubted her sanity, but Sela knew an obscureway when she saw one. Classic dragon architecture. Why couldn't Bannon see it?

As they neared the kitchen area, he released her hand. Fewer servants occupied the kitchen, but several had moved into the scullery, and were plunging iron skillets and buckets into steaming water, or scrubbing at silver tableware, or yawning behind their hands, their eyes glazed and tired.

As she and Bannon hurried through, she glanced toward the Great Hall. She caught sight of two men strewn across a table, snoring, but heard the scrape and echo of other tables being pulled across the floor. There was a clatter of a drum, and the long, resonant tone of a stringed instrument. She was about to ask Bannon what was happening, but before she formed the question, he had tugged her through a narrow wooden door, and into the night.

Outside, she tried to make sense of where she was. Walls cut across expanses of smooth grass, abutted more walls, and turned sharp angles around the castle proper. Torches clung timidly here and there, but cast light too frail, feeding shadows instead of scattering them. The stable, the granary, and other outbuildings interspersed fieldstone partitions, with rooftops like the curved spines of bulky, sleeping beasts.

"To find the window from the dragon chapel, you can cross the inner bailey to the wall, and follow it left," said Bannon. "But I don't think you need to—"

"There he is!" Sela pointed to the moonlit sky, and to the swaying tail of a retreating dragon. A flash of milky white banked sharply, and then was gone. "Did you see him?"

"I'm not sure," said Bannon.

"Well, whatever he was doing here, at least he left now. He's safe."

"Oh?" asked a voice from the shadows. "Who is safe?"

She and Bannon turned toward the voice. As Sela's eyes adjusted, she saw a man pulling a door closed in a near wall, before he swept regally forward.

"Venur Riddess," said Bannon. He snapped his heels together and tightened into attention. "The maiden was asking for air, and I escorted her here."

The Venur came closer. Close enough for Sela to see his dark skin suffused with light from the kitchen windows. He was shorter than she was expecting, with his shoulders only slighter higher than Sela's. And he appeared older, more wrinkled than she'd thought before, but that might have been an effect of shadowplay.

"The maiden," said Riddess. His gaze felt heavy on Sela's face while he regarded her. Studied her. She felt trapped beneath it, and stood unmoving and silent, hoping her stillness would vaporize her, turn her imperceptible. "I thought I had met all of you," he said.

Sela glanced to Bannon.

"She visited the chapel after dinner, and then requested air," said Bannon.

"Ah. A pious woman." Riddess crossed his arms, and spun at the waist to look toward the sky, to the place where Sela had spotted the dragon. "But you saw something," he said. "Up there."

"We aren't sure what it was," said Bannon.

"We aren't?" Riddess looked between them, brought his gaze to rest again on Sela.

She thought thin, wispy thoughts. Of water. And air. And invisible things.

"Well, if we've had enough air for now," said Riddess, offering his elbow. "I'm sure the musicians are ready. And I need a maiden to dance with."

Sela felt her face go cold. She glanced again at Bannon, who nodded. She looked back to Riddess, who arched his brows, his eyes flat. Annoyed.

She took his arm.

§

Vorham Riddess was certain he'd seen all the maidens at dinner, and had personally spoken to each in turn, for protocol and manners. The guests seemed to find it appealing, the maidens had brightened at his attention, and the staff smiled. Yes, he'd met them all.

But this girl, this silent, anxious girl, he hadn't seen. Not at the dinner table, not in conversation after. She was a surprise.

He intensely disliked surprises.

He led her around the castle grounds, refusing to take the kitchen hallway at the back of the Great Room; that was for servants. As owner and Venur of Riddess Castle, he used the front door for a grand entrance, the way he'd used the front door as his exit. His business with Whitetail had been discreet, of course, but he made bold statement of his comings and goings in his own home. Let any servant or soldier dare to questions his movements.

This soldier, Bannon Raley, who walked with them into the castle, seemed stiffer and more formal than usual. Guilty of something. If the pair had strolled out for moonlight romance, that was one thing. If they'd followed Vorham, or caught sight of his conversation with Whitetail…well. He'd consider that a kind of questioning his movements. And that was an entirely different sort of issue.

Now that they'd reached the Great Room, dinner tables had been cleared and stacked out of sight. Servants with silver trays filtered through the guests along the walls, offering mugs of mead or snifters of brandy and red wine. Breadsticks dipped in chocolate and cinnamon were the delicate desserts passed around in woven baskets. The evening was far from over.

He led his mute dance partner to the center of the room, past the other maidens milling about in a corner. The woman called Emlee, whom he'd been considering as a first choice, clamped her pert mouth into a tight line. This pleased him. She was lovely and poised, and knew how to draw him into conversation, but had been aggressive with his time, and overly confident. She needed reminding that the choice of Venuress was his, and his alone. All choices would be his alone, both before the wedding, and after.

Oh, he would dance with Emlee tonight. Perhaps

even steal a private moment for a kiss. But first, he would put her in her place.

He gave a flourish of a bow to his dance partner, and opened his arms to embrace her in the waltz position. She drew in a sharp breath.

"I've never danced."

He smiled. "So you do have a voice."

She looked self-consciously about the room. Her eyes paused on the face of a maiden in a yellow dress—it matched her hair perfectly. What was her name again?—and she gave the girl a pleading look.

"What is your name, maiden?" he asked.

"Sela," she responded in a near whisper.

"Sela," he repeated, the name seeming somehow familiar. "Please take my hand."

She did, and he laid her fingers onto his shoulder. Then he upswept her other hand, her skin a pale glow within his dark fingers. He slowly twirled her toward a corner. "Follow my lead. And you can tell me what you were doing outside in my courtyard."

She stumbled across his foot. "I'm really not good at this at all."

Whether she meant dancing, or lying, he wasn't sure. He slowed his pace, and allowed her to catch her balance. "A waltz is in three steps. Watch my feet. One, two, three. You follow."

The girl stepped forward, scuffled against his toes, giggled nervously, and tried again. She was concentrating so hard on her movements he was never going to get answers from her as he wished. "Wait," he said, and paused them both. "Try this. Stand on my feet."

"What?" She widened her eyes. Eyes of emerald. He hadn't noticed them before.

"Stand on my feet. It's a good way to learn."

She glanced about the room again, and then gingerly stepped onto the toes of his shoes. He tightened his grasp around her waist, drawing her to press against him. She blinked those green eyes at him, startled, and although he'd only meant to keep her balanced, he decided he liked the advantage of power. What was she going to do? Tell him no?

He led her again into the steps of the waltz. "One, two, three," he whispered, turning her in a careful circle. He heard rippling murmurs in the crowd as he danced her toward one group of watchers, and then toward another, but he ignored the attention. His focus was on the girl, waiting for her to relax into the movement. After a few minutes, even though concentration still wrinkled her brow, he asked again, "What were you doing in my courtyard?"

"Wasn't I allowed to be there?" she asked.

Now he scuffed his toes. They bobbled a bit, and then recovered smoothly. "Of course," he finally said.

She remained silent. She was evading answers the same way she was evading the rhythm of the waltz. His frustration was growing, but he bit it back. "I asked you a direct question. As your Venur, I expect—"

"You're not my Venur," she said.

He rocked to a stop.

She looked into his face, her mouth parted in

surprise. "I mean…"

"I know what you mean," he said. He should have been angry. Offended. In any other case, he would have been. But she was right, strictly speaking. He looked back at her, and her plain, uninteresting face, and her disquieting green eyes, and tried to work through his confusing reaction. She awaited patiently, her small feet on his polished shoes, her slender waist pressed against his belly, her delicate hand entwined in his. The room shared her expectant pause, as though each guest, maiden, and servant bated their breath, watching the Venur inwardly shuffle through his emotions, searching for the one he would respond with.

He smiled. It was as much a surprise to him as the room, which released a collective breath, and to the girl, who arched her brows before hesitantly smiling back.

"Perhaps we've started off on the wrong foot," he said.

She laughed outright, making him realize he'd made a pun. He chuckled, to mask that he was unaccustomed with that sort of humor.

"You say your name is Sela?"

She nodded.

"Shall we try again?"

Her expression turned thoughtful. Then she nodded again.

He hesitated while the musicians masterfully transitioned into a new melody. Then he straightened his shoulders, adjusted his arm around her waist, and swept her into a gliding circle. "One, two, three," he said.

§

Layce Phelcher watched from the corner of the room nearest the kitchen. She liked the commotion that camouflaged her, the wafting scents that made her undetectable. And she liked the vantage point.

From here, she could see Jastin Armitage pouring cup after cup of red wine and sulking and staring suspiciously at Sela of the Red Dress.

She could see Bannon Raley, *refusing* cup after cup of red wine, and sulking and staring suspiciously at Venur Vorham Riddess.

She saw maidens wilt despairingly onto benches. Except for the girl in the yellow dress, who watched the dancing couple, her mouth agape. And the girl named Emlee, who balled her hands into fists at her sides, and stalked out of the Great Room and toward the chamber stairs.

She watched guests whisper behind their hands, or yawn behind them, or make faces of amusement at each other.

But what most captured her attention was Vorham's face, which still held a dusky smile as he waltzed Sela of the Red Dress from corner to corner, monopolizing the dance floor.

A *smile*.

She turned and crept her way through a throng of guests near the kitchen hallway, carrying a bronze goblet. A special one, which had never touched the lips of any being. Which she'd had secretly made by the Enwall family of Blaisvil, specifically for this evening. Into which she'd poured a mixture of honey and marmalade, plus four ounces of red wine. Within the mixture, she'd left a pale pink passion stone submerged for twelve hours. The spell had stipulated only eight, but she'd given it four extra hours for good measure.

Stepping past the kitchen and into the scullery, she now sighed wistfully into the goblet. She plucked the stone from the liquid, and tipped the goblet to let her sweet wine love potion pour out into a dishwater bucket. She plunged the goblet and the stone into the water and swirled them clean.

Her first attempt at a love potion, and she never even had the chance to use it.

Venur Riddess *smiled*.

§

Kallon swooped to a landing atop a rumpled expanse of sandstone at the edge of Rage Desert. He and Riza had just come from a collaborative meeting with the Esra Dragon Council, discussing the rumors of Blackclaw sightings in their area. Collaborative, so he thought.

Riza circled him, her wings rippling from desert heat. Even with the setting sun, the desert spat blistering fumes to obscure his vision and seize his lungs. Dunes capped and broke against each other like ocean waves, making the desert seem a writhing, breathing thing. A devouring thing.

Riza careened into place beside him, and gracefully sat, enfolding her wings around her legs.

"They're withholding something," said Kallon.

"The Esra Council?"

"They were evasive and unhelpful. Purposefully."

Riza shook her neck, dislodging a cascade of sand that had pooled within her horns, cast there by the harsh winds. "They are no more an ally to Blackclaw than you are. Why would they withhold something helpful?"

"I don't know, Riza. But I'm not convinced by their words that they *aren't* allied to him."

She narrowed her eyes. "That's harsh."

"Is it?" Kallon asked, studying her reaction. "You know as well as I do they were keeping a conspired secret."

"Many tribes have many reasons to keep secrets. It doesn't mean everything leads back to Blackclaw." She looked away, then, out across the shifting desert. The sunset reflected in her eyes, splashing them with orange and muted yellows. "At least, not in the way you mean."

"Then how do you mean?"

She blinked, dousing the sunset a moment, before it reignited her irises. "I am only saying there are good reasons to respect their privacy concerning certain affairs of their tribe that have nothing to do with our mission."

"Shouldn't it be for me to decide whether or not it pertains?"

She turned her desert gaze to him. "Do you have

the right to invade every layer of every heart?"

"Invade? I am only trying to get to the truth!"

"As far as Blackclaw sightings, I believe you have. Can you not be satisfied with that?"

Kallon rose to his feet, and stiffly drew back his wings, broadening his chest. "You believe? I am to take them at their word because you believe them?"

Riza stood, too, her nostrils flaring. "Can you not?"

Kallon regarded her, recognizing the anger he so often aroused in her. Recognizing the tilt of her chin, the raised scales along her spine. But for the first time, he saw something else in her eyes. Guilt.

He deflated. His wings drooped to the sandstone. Memories rushed through his mind, linking scene to scene, making sudden sense of all Riza's long trips away, her mysterious disappearances in the mountains, her cool responses to his nuzzling.

"I could," he finally managed to say, "…if I could be sure of your own honesty."

She recoiled. She touched her paw to her heart, her eyes wide and going dark with the setting sun.

"Do you keep secrets from me, Riza?" he asked.

She was silent for a long time, while the desert winds spat sand at their feet and bayed ominously in their ears. Then she spoke. "As much as anyone tied to old promises. Surely you keep things from me."

He shook his head. "Not intentionally. Never intentionally."

She looked away, but there were no ribbons of sunset reflected in her gaze now. Only shadows. And sadness. "Will we fly north through the night? Or find shelter?"

And then he heard it, as clearly as a twig is snapped from a dead branch. A crack. In his heart. And he felt it twinge, and then rupture, spilling pain against his ribs, overflowing through his skin, and his scales, oozing out to shower to the ground in tiny slices of agony and collect against his feet like so many particles of Rage sand.

Riza loved someone else.

§

Bannon stood against the wall of the barracks, staring up at the sky, and grinding his teeth together. Wisps of anger passed through his senses, blurring them, the way the gauzy cloud cover dimmed the stars.

He knew better. He did.

But the anger was there, all the same.

A hand on his shoulder pulled his mind into focus. Leesa Naren stood beside him, peering up into his face, smiling. But she spotted the darkness behind his eyes, because when their gazes met, she gently frowned.

He laid his hand over her fingers on his arm. "I thought she was different. The one named Sela."

Leesa nodded.

"Familiar and mysterious at the same time, somehow. From the moment we met. She has an understanding about things." He tapped his chest. "In here. She understands."

Leesa touched his chest, and then her own.

"Yes," said Bannon. "Like us." Then he drew up his shoulders. "Or not. I don't know. I acted too quickly on my feelings."

Leesa's brows raised, and even in the dark, he could read her surprise. Her face reflected his own inner confition.

They'd done well enough until now—he and Leesa had—in keeping to the edges of the castle household, watching from a distance, performing their duties. From the time they'd arrived and settled into Esra life, just three years ago, until now, it had been easier. Less complicated. Days unfolded in much the same thythm, morning to dusk, duty to free time. Whatever scandals and drama that had once plagued the province and her castle had faded to ghosts and tired rumors, and he'd never really discovered the Venur's history and his path to power.

But then, that wasn't why he'd come.

He and Leesa were here for a reason all their own.

"You're handling the commotion better than I am," he admitted to her. "So much has happened so fast; all the new people, the festivities, the constant noise and movement, coming and going..."

She tightened her grip on his arm, her face sobered. Tight with question.

"I know. A dragonchase, of all things." How he was going to manage that, he didn't know. He just didn't know.

She tugged at his sleeve. Then she removed her coif,

ran her fingers through her dark hair full of starshine, and nodded toward the woods on the other side of the castle wall, brows raised.

She knew him well. She was the closest thing he had to a sister. And she knew a long traipse in the Esra wilds was a tonic to his blood.

He would have gone, on a different night. "You go without me," he said. "I'm going to make rounds, and see what I can find out about tomorrow's hunt."

Just then, a voice called out. "Leesa? Is that you?"

Leesa startled. She hurriedly replaced her coif, and tucked those strands into hiding.

Veshlie walked closer, squinting. "Leesa? What are you doing out... oh, hello Bannon."

"Veshlie," he said, nodding.

She looked between them, suspicions racing behind her perceptive eyes, but she merely said Leesa's name again. And, "Cook Marl has asked for you to handle the pre-measures for morning. She won't leave the kitchen until you do."

Leesa turned to obey without so much as a glance.

She was definitely better at this than he was.

"Goodnight, Veshlie," he said.

Veshlie left without a glance, either.

Chapter Thirteen

Sela woke up hard to the sound of a dragon shout. Her eyes snapped open. Her heart pounded. She lay in the bed she shared with Gladdis, trying to catch her breath, trying to remember why her dream startled her the way it did.

The feeble gray morning leached beneath the door of their windowless room, fading the embroidered red and yellow roses of the bedspread. The candles had long gone cold. She shivered.

She sat up and knuckled at her eyes, dizzy and restless from her dream. The memory of her father's roar filled her with sadness. She missed her first home, and her second. Twice homesick.

Then dragon shout came again. She froze. She wasn't dreaming. That sound came through the walls. She slid off the bed, trying not to wake Gladdis, and tiptoed to the door of the room. She opened it a crack, and pressed her face against it. She didn't see anything. But she heard something.

Somewhere, a man shouted, "Get the wing! He's

knocked it loose!" Metal rattled; the grind of iron chains. Feet trampled and claws dug at soft earth. Another shout came. This time, with a voice filled with pain and fear. It begged, "Let me go!" in dragonspeak.

The hunt!

Sela gasped and threw open the door. She ran down the hallway, around a corner, and toward a curving banister. Her bare feet hardly touched the steps as she tore down them. Her flapping hair blinded her—she should have braided it back into place last night!—and she slapped it, pushing it out of her eyes. Then she stumbled, coming to a sudden stop.

She nearly collided into a servant woman with a basket of breads. "Excuse me," she panted.

The woman curtsied, averting her eyes.

Sela turned backwards, back to running as she called, "Did you hear a dragon?"

The servant peeked up. She blinked. She looked behind herself, then back to Sela.

"A dragon," Sela repeated. "Have you heard one around here?"

The woman nodded. She pointed toward the hallway that led to the courtyard.

Sela faced the way she ran, and called a "thank you!" over her shoulder.

Her feet thumped hard against stone. Her jaw rattled with each step, but she only ran faster. She swerved left around a corner, and then right. She drew up in the middle of a room with no windows, eerily similar to the one she and Gladdis were using as a bedchamber.

A dead end.

Frustrated, she returned back the way she came, repeating her path in reverse, memorizing the cracks in the stone walls, trying to make a map of them in her mind. She found her way back to the stairwell, circled slowly to get her bearings, and then shot off again in the direction the servant woman had pointed.

This time she turned right, and then left. Still, she found herself in same windowless room as before. Was this castle playing tricks on her? She turned back to retrace her steps with clenched teeth, as afraid for her sanity as she was for the dragon she was trying to find.

At the stairwell, she glared at the hallway from where she'd just come. She took one step. Nothing seemed unusual, so she took another. She heard shuffling feet behind her, and peeked over her shoulder. The servant woman stood on the landing, watching her with raised eyebrows.

Sela pointed down the hallway. "I keep going that way but I can't get out."

The woman frowned, but came down the last few steps and held out her hand. Sela took it, and walked for the third time down the gray corridor. "I swear the castle is doing this on purpose," Sela said.

The woman regarded her without expression.

Sela watched her while they walked. Getting a closer look, Sela realized the woman wasn't quite as old as she first assumed. What she thought to be age were lines of exhaustion around the servant's auburn eyes.

Her hair was completely hidden beneath a cloth wrap. Dust smudged her nose and throat. Dirt stained her smock, too, and the edge of her skirt that needed fresh hemming all around the edge.

"I didn't see you last night at the celebration," Sela said.

The woman shook her head.

They reached the windowless room, and the servant stopped. She pointed toward the wall, at the arched doorway that spilled morning dawn over the blotchy dirt floor.

Sela stared. "That wasn't there before." She crept toward it, ran her hand over the stones. There was no machinery for powering an obscureway, no sliding mass that could have been retracted. "It just wasn't here before," she said, mostly to herself, although the quiet servant stood beside her, and Sela could feel her doubtful gaze.

Another dragon howl reminded her why she was here. She darted forward, searching for the commotion as the source, and, as she passed an enormous flowering hydrangea bush, she found it. Near the center of the courtyard, a group of shouting men, wearing purple and black, were gathered around a black dragon. Its wings and legs and tail were chained and the men were trying to shove the creature into an iron cage. It strained and spat flame into the air.

She knew him. The dragon. He was young, his scales as black as onyx. The same mysterious dragon she'd seen from her secret place on the mountain. Vaya

Brownwing's secret.

Impulsively, she ran toward the men. "You're hurting him!"

One man turned to face her, and she pulled up short in astonishment. Bannon Raley, the soldier who had never murdered a living thing, now stood shoulder to shoulder with his cohorts to enslave a dragon precisely for the purpose of killing it. "What are you doing?"

His own expression shifted from surprise, to a deep furrowing of his eyebrows. "Me? What are *you* doing? Shouldn't you be at breakfast, charming your husband-to-be?" The thrashing of the dragon jerked him nearly off his feet, and he turned back to throw his arms around the Black's neck, forcing his head downward.

The dragon resisted, yanking his head upward to belch another stream of flame toward the sky. The men cried out and ducked, covering their head with their arms. The fire arched and dropped back toward them, spattering the ground with sparks that sizzled out on the grass.

"Get back before you're hurt," Bannon snapped. "This dragon belongs to the Venur, and will be turned loose soon enough." He leaped at the dragon's neck to pin it to the ground.

"Hurry, Muck," said Bannon to the guard beside him. Now, while I've got him."

Muck, thin and balding, stepped forward. He held a metal ring, and, judging by the trembling of his fingers, hadn't been a volunteer for this. "Got his chin tight, Bannon?" he asked.

"Got it." Bannon grunted, forcing the dragon's head against the grass. Other men joined him, pressing hard against the captive's skull.

"What are you doing?" Sela asked.

Muck released a lock inside the ring, and it snapped open. He crept toward the dragon's snout, holding it out.

"Come on, man, before you're a barbecue!" said Bannon through gritted teeth.

The dragon was staring, wide-eyed, at the metal ring, his claws digging trenches into the grass. Sela could hear his strangled voice in his throat, pleading "no…no…no…" She didn't know exactly what the men wanted to do, but the dragon obviously did. As Muck moved in, she cried out again. "Stop!"

She lunged at Muck to knock the ring from his hand.

Chaos broke out. She felt the ring come loose from Muck's hand, and she heard shouting, and felt a blast of searing heat. She hit the ground, knocking the breath from her lungs. She lay stunned on the wet grass, gasping.

Then she realized all had gone quiet.

She rolled over. Several men stared down in shock at her face. Some of them stared at her feet. Bannon pushed through them all, his muddy hands pulling at shoulders to make a path. "My God, what were you doing?" His face swerved into view. Then, he, too, gaped in surprise.

"I'm sorry, he was just so scared, and I didn't know

what you were doing to him, and…"

"Did you see that?" someone asked.

"Fire went right through her or something."

"No, she got *hit*. I was standing right there and saw it."

Sela finally followed the staring eyes to her feet. Embers glowed from the singed hem of her nightdress. Smoke lazily curled. So much of the cloth had been burned away that the bottoms of her knees showed, but somehow her skin was untouched. "What happened?" she asked.

Bannon knelt. "I lost grip of the beast, and it blasted fire right at you." He gripped her hand and pulled her to her feet. "I thought…" He didn't finish his sentence, but his pale face told her exactly what he'd thought.

"I'm fine."

"You should be crispy."

"I'm fine," she said again, and felt her face go hot. She glanced around herself, at the men still staring. "Really, I'm fine." Then her eyes found the dragon. He was staring, too. His nostrils, dark as midnight, were flared and trembling. His eyes glistened yellow-amber, and were so wide she could see the whites around them.

I am fine, she said for the fourth time, in her mind. In his.

The dragon's jaw snapped shut.

Others began to filter into the courtyard. Sleepy servants tucked shirts into their trousers, wandering closer. Guards crossed their arms and studied her. Gladdis appeared in the archway across the courtyard, shielding her eyes from the now-fierce morning glare.

And Venur Riddess strode toward her, his dark eyes puffy from sleep. He gripped the front of his fur-lined robe, thrown haphazardly around his shoulders. He came to stand in front of Sela, and Bannon, and the black dragon gone quiet and still, now that he was no longer being wrestled. "I haven't been roused from bed in years," he said to Bannon.

"I apologize, Venur." Bannon bowed his head.

"It's my fault," said Sela.

"So I've been told," said Riddess. He regarded Sela's face, and then the singed hem of her nightdress. "You're unharmed?"

"Yes," she said. She took a step toward him to explain, but she felt the eyes of the growing crowd, and became keenly aware of her thin nightdress. At that moment, the silent servant she'd met that morning came forward and slid a cloak onto her shoulders. As the woman tied it off at Sela's throat, Sela spoke her thank you with her eyes. The woman smiled.

"Thank you, Leesa," said Riddess. Leesa didn't smile at him.

The dragon suddenly tugged at his chains, clattering them, and gave a roar that made the crowd gasp. Leesa startled and hurried back toward the castle. Guards leapt at the dragon to subdue him again. Bannon watched Sela for a moment longer, and then joined his comrades in forcing the dragon's head to the ground.

"Please!" Sela heard herself say.

Riddess watched the chaos, wincing at the ear-splitting cries of the dragon. "Get that dangerous beast into that cage!" he called to Bannon above the din.

"He isn't dangerous," she said. "He's afraid!"

"As well he should be," said Riddess. "I have promised Esra a dragonchase today."

Mutters of amusement rippled through the watchers.

"Please," said Sela. "About that."

Riddess regarded her, his brows arched. He seemed patient, but something behind his sleepy eyes kept her tense, nervous.

"About the dragonchase," she said, working too hard to find her thoughts, her words.

"You wish to ask me something?" he said. "Esra has never had a woman on a hunt, but I would consider a first."

"No!" Sela shook her head, aghast and thrown off guard by the thought. "I don't want any part of what you're doing!"

The dragon's head was pressed to the ground, and Muck, the scrawny, nervous guard was again approaching him with that metal ring. Bannon and the others struggled while the dragon rolled one way, and the other, and screamed into Sela's mind.

Just then, Jastin Armitage broke through the crowd. He tugged his black leather vest into place. Beside him, an older woman, with her midnight hair drawn up into a high ponytail, and her pale blue ball gown rumpled, as though she'd slept in it, elbowed him forward. The woman wore clattering crystals around her neck, her wrists, her forehead. A wizard.

The wizard, Sela realized. The one meddling with Orman's magic.

"Vorham," called Jastin. Then he looked askance at the wizard. She lifted her chin, and gave him a flat glare. Jastin groaned quietly.

"Vorham," he called again, striding across the courtyard while the onlookers fell silent. "The Leland woman is right."

Sela saw Bannon in the corner of her eye. He turned, and stared openly. Riddess cocked his head in surprise. Sela nearly fell over where she stood.

"Jastin?" asked Riddess.

"Any child could hunt a dragon that's been caged, battered, and nose-ringed. I'm no child. Neither are the men that would join me." Jastin turned his gaze to the crowd. Guests in trousers and tunics, or trousers and robes, looked hesitantly at each other. "Turn it loose for a real chase," Jastin called. "The way of the old days in Leland."

Men groused. Then they mumbled. Then they nodded, and, one by one, began to shout, "Let it go!" and "For the sport!"

The other maidens had joined the crowd by now, and Sela caught sight of Emlee, with her silken robe and sleep-tumbled tresses askew against her back, and looking even lovelier for it. Riddess saw her too. He stared for a time at Emlee, and then regarded Sela.

If the man was comparing them just now—and Sela was certain he was—Sela would no doubt be on her way soon, kicked out without even time to pack. Not that she had much to pack. She only hoped she could help the dragon in some way before she left.

"So the hunters of Leland would call us children?" asked Riddess. "For chaining and ringing our dragons?"

Sela glanced to Jastin, who was regarding her darkly. She looked at the wizard, who nodded cautiously. She turned to regard the dragon, who still laid out, pressed to the ground, and returned her look with amber, pleading eyes.

"Very well," said Riddess. "Let no one say I deny my wife anything." He raised his arms. "Clear the courtyard, and the dragon will be released a distance from the castle."

Sela felt all of her senses trickle down into her legs, stiffening them. Threatening to topple her. "What did you say?" she asked Riddess.

"I said to release the dragon." And then he smiled. "At the behest of my chosen." He took her hand, and lifted it above her head. "My bride, and your Venuress-to-be!"

For a moment, all was silent. The dragon rattled a hot breath in his throat. And then, congratulatory bellows rippled through the crowd. Riddess bowed, and then waved the onlookers away. "Clear the courtyard." Guests and servants broke off and meandered back to their rooms, or to their stations.

The maidens lingered, stunned and silent. Gladdis gaped openly. Emlee pushed away tears, her eyes scorching. "And you are all invited to stay, of course,"

Riddess added, walking Sela toward them. "For the wedding ceremony. If you wish. Or, we will arrange transportation home."

Sela heard his voice, but could barely make out the garbled sounds. She saw faces before her, but they were fuzzy and disfigured. "What's happening?" she tried to ask, but her tongue was fat and sticky.

And then Bannon was beside her, his hazel eyes shadowed, his expression grim. Again she tried to speak.

The ground came up to slap her.

§

"It's perfect," said Vorham, pacing along the castle's outer wall, his hands clasped behind his back. His robe fluttered behind him; he'd been too eager to find Whitetail to change into day clothes. "It's just perfect," he said again.

Whitetail was hunkered in the trees, just a short distance away. With the milling guests, and the wandering, disappointed maidens, and the uncharacteristic hubbub of late, Vorham thought it prudent to keep the dragon away from the castle for now. But not out of touch. Not now, when things were beginning to fall into place.

"For someone who finds the situation perfect, you still seem quite nervous," said Whitetail.

"It's delicate," said Vorham. He leaned back against the stone wall and looked up to the sky. "It's a plan of strategy. I made my move this morning, entirely by opportunity. I had decided on Emlee. Only last night did I discover this other."

"Her name is Sela?"

Vorham nodded. "At first, I thought she was deceptive. Possibly sneaking out romantically with my guard Bannon. Or following me."

"Perhaps both."

"Yes, likely. And I believe she saw you leaving our meeting."

Whitetail rustled branches as he shifted position. "I was careful. As usual."

"I know. But she's observant and fairly bright." He pushed from the wall, and walked slowly toward the trees. Nearing Whitetail, he ducked a low branch and joined him in the foliage. "But she isn't deceptive or manipulative, or ambitious, like so many of them." He smiled, and patted Whitetail on the shoulder. "She's naïve."

"Naïve?" asked Whitetail.

"Beautifully so," said Vorham, remembering the look on her face when he waltzed with her, when she defended the dragon, when he announced their marriage.

"You are smitten."

Vorham shook his head. "Not by the girl, by the opportunity, Whitetail. Stay focused." He rounded the White, coming to stand near his back haunch, drawing his massive head to follow. "When I first met her last night, I suspected she came from nowhere. A servant girl dressed to look like a potential, maybe. But when she said her name, I remembered it. Before bed, I double checked the paperwork, and there it was. The burned scroll. With her name."

"I remember the scroll."

"What's more, she's not on the roll of the names chosen from Leland. Thirteen names were on the list, but we have fifteen women."

"So there is another infiltrator in our midst." Whitetail tipped his head. "Sela is working with someone."

Vorham smiled again, and held up his hands. "My first suspicion. Or..." He splayed his fingers dramatically. "She is working with no one, and is up to nothing."

Whitetail wrinkled up his snout. "If that is the case, she has stumbled into a situation she neither wants, nor orchestrated, and cannot possibly control." Whitetail slowly shook his head. "One might actually pity the girl, if one were the pitying type."

"Thankfully, one isn't," said Vorham. "Besides, I could be figuring her completely wrong, and she may be playing us all as fools."

"But you don't believe so."

Vorham drew in a deep, satisfying breath. He turned his gaze to the castle, his eyes probing the granite and marble structure as though he could see her now, in all her adolescent splendor. "I'll find out for certain," he said to Whitetail, "But no, I don't believe so."

"Naïve, you say," said Whitetail.

"Beautifully so," said Vorham.

Chapter Fourteen

Sela rolled to her side on a mattress as soft as a cloud, and so thick and receptive she thought it might swallow her, if she didn't resist. So she pushed up to sit, and forced open her bleary eyes. Velvet curtains covered the windows in the room, diverting the sunlight to dazzling strips on the floor and walls. Books were stacked in high towers that threatened to tumble, and were piled in mounds on the floor, and stashed sideways on the desk, the side table, and the chair of the room. Her eyes slowly adjusted, until she could see dust and cobwebs, and puddles of melted candle wax splotched erratically across what little bare floor there was.

Movement in a shadow startled her. A man stepped forward, and a ribbon of sunlight slashed his face. Jastin Armitage.

Sela pushed at bedcovers and lunged out of bed, away from him.

"You should stay," he said.

She threw herself against the door, fumbling for the

latch.

"It isn't locked. But you should stay. Layce will be back soon."

She paused. She looked over her shoulder. "Who?"

"Layce Phelcher. The crazy wizard."

"The woman in the blue dress?"

"The very one."

Sela looked down at herself to find she was still wearing her thin nightdress. Her borrowed cloak was draped over the foot of the bed, but she'd have to walk closer to Jastin to retrieve it.

He picked it up from the bed and held it out. When she hesitated, he tossed it to her.

She caught it, and wrapped it around her shoulders. "Where am I?"

"In Layce's chambers, in the belly of the castle."

"How did I get here?"

"I carried you."

"Where's Bannon?"

Jastin rubbed his hand over his face, dragged his fingertips through his beard. "Outside, I think. Dealing with the dragon mess you started."

"*I* started?"

"Look," said Jastin, and stepped closer.

Sela grabbed for the door again, and he halted. He held up his hands.

"I'm only here because somehow that woman gets me tangled up in all sorts of things I have no business being involved in. You fainted. I carried you here. She was watching over you, and then suddenly said she needed to leave, and would be right back, and would I please stay to keep you safe."

"You're the last person to make me feel safe."

He lowered his hands. He stared silently, his features softening in wonder. "Every time I convince myself I'm just imagining things, you crop up. With her eyes. With her voice. With her…" He opened his hands, pushed them toward her. "…with her way of hating me."

Sela wasn't sure what to say, so she didn't speak.

"I know you aren't her," he said. "You would be older. And you can't be her child, you would be younger." He stepped closer again, but this time, Sela allowed it. Although she did keep her hand on the door latch. "Are you a sister?"

"I have no sisters," she said.

Just then the door pushed open, nudging her backward. A smooth hand gripped the edge of the door near her cheek, and then the wizard, still in her blue dress, stepped into the room. "How is she?" she asked Jastin.

"Ask her yourself." He indicated his head toward Sela.

"Oh," said the wizard, smiling. "You're awake. I brought someone to see you."

Behind her, Orman emerged, his watery eyes casting about the room until they came to rest on Sela. "Sela!"

"Orman." She rushed to him and threw her arms around his neck. He smelled of leather and rain, and his bony, comforting embrace welled tears in her eyes. "Orman," she said again. "I've made a mess of everything."

"Now, now," he said, smoothing his hand over her back. "You had some help with that. Lots of meddling folks and mistakes being made."

"This is no mistake," said the wizard. "Already things are changing here. Unraveling. How else do you think I was able to bring you into the castle?"

Orman released Sela, but kept his arm around her shoulders while he studied the woman. "I felt enchantments dissolve away not ten minutes ago. But what that has to do with my niece—"

"Everything," said the woman.

Sela could see by the way Orman was watching the wizard he didn't believe her. Neither did Sela. Even Jastin called the woman crazy.

Then again, Sela wasn't too certain of Jastin's sanity, either.

"And what's your business in all this?" Orman asked Jastin.

Jastin shook his head. "None of this is any of my business. Layce just. She..." He shook his head again. "This is none of my business," he said again. Then he nudged between Layce and Orman, and stepped through the door.

Layce turned to watch him as his footsteps disappeared down the hallway. Then she closed the door, and faced them both. She smiled shyly. "Now that he's gone, we can talk."

"We have nothing to talk about," said Orman.

"Thank you for bringing me to my niece, we're getting out of here now."

"But you can't!"

"Indeed we can." He took Sela's hand, pausing at the sight of her singed nightdress, her mussed hair. Then he pulled the door open.

"Orman Thistleby," said Layce.

Orman and Sela both glanced at her. She stood with her hand outstretched, a glittering turquoise crystal pointed toward them. "Please don't go."

Orman upraised his fuzzy gray brows.

"I'm sorry to threaten you, but I will make you stay."

"Don't apologize," said Orman. "You're no threat. At all."

Layce waved the crystal. Sela felt her feet like boulders, growing heavier. She was suddenly tired, too, and couldn't help how her eyelids fluttered, trying to close.

Orman touched Sela's shoulder, and her heaviness evaporated. She became wide awake. He looked back to Layce and crossed his arms.

She lowered her crystal. Her thin shoulders sagged. "Well. That's embarrassing."

"I told you, you're wearing too many pendants and charms. And you don't seem to have real conviction behind your magic."

Layce stiffened. "I got her here, didn't I?"

"You used Armitage for that."

She lifted her chin. She pointed the crystal at him,

more to scold than to wield it, but she deflated before she had the chance to say anything.

"And why did you? You're not manipulating this for Riddess, as far as I can tell. You don't even like the man."

Layce shook her head. "No. I'm not doing it for him. Not exactly." She dropped the crystal onto the bed, and sat beside it. "And if I'd known you would be drawn into it, I'm not sure I'd have tried."

"Me?"

"Orman Thistleby. *The* Orman Thistleby."

Orman drew his wrinkled fingers down his beard. "Well now. I'm not so important as all that."

"Are you kidding?" Layce swiveled to regard him, her eyes shining. "My father hung your portrait in his study. He always told me one day wizards would be restored to their glory, with humans and dragons on either side. Respected. Useful." She smiled. "And your hands would make it happen."

"Me?" Orman asked again.

"When you were in school together, he thought you were a teacher, because you worked magic as though it was a part of you. A natural. Like the dragons themselves."

Orman laughed. Sela wasn't entirely sure she'd ever heard that sound from him before. "He thought I was a teacher because I was so old, you mean." Orman shuffled to the book-covered chair. He stacked the dusty tomes by size, largest to smallest, and neatly set them on the floor. He then sat in the chair, and rested his hands in his lap, watching Layce.

Layce tugged at a loose thread from her gown sleeve, and rubbed it between her fingers. "He did say you came into wizardry later than most."

"I did, indeed. I was a farmer before that. As was my father, my uncles, their fathers, and their uncles."

"A farmer? I love the outdoors. The best part of working for Riddess is his maple trees. I help tap them for syrup every season, and I don't even use magic for it."

"Something about being part of the cycle, I think," said Orman. "Watching seeds turn to greens, and then to beets. Or potatoes. Seeing how the earth provides. Just being involved in the process is magic enough."

Layce nodded. "I love that."

Orman's craggy face softened. "I miss that."

"You could help next season. It's only a few weeks away. I could show you how to hang the buckets, and I could make you hotcakes for the first batch of sap."

"Hotcakes?"

"It's my specialty!" Layce grinned, and lifted her shoulders in a deep shrug. "Well. It's the only thing I cook."

Orman laughed again.

Sela was actually becoming a little uncomfortable as their conversation continued. Not that she minded whatever was going on here—and what was going on here? Orman laughing? Grinning? He hadn't even cursed for five entire minutes. Whoever this Layce woman was, friend or foe, Orman seemed to have forgotten to find out. And he'd certainly forgotten about

Sela, hovering awkwardly near the door, feeling like an uninvited guest to a private party.

"I'm a friend," said Layce suddenly. She looked from Sela to Orman. "Definitely a friend."

"I'd like to believe that," said Orman.

"Please," said Layce. She reached across the space between she and Orman, and laid her hand on his knee. "You can believe me."

Orman blinked at her hand. He didn't withdraw, though. He tightened into a coil, like a rabbit prepared to run. But he stayed. And he arched his gray, scrubby brows, his eyes brightening.

Layce flared into a crimson blush, starting at her throat and suffusing upward into her cheeks. "I'm not used to others knowing my thoughts," she said.

"You think like this a lot?" asked Orman.

Layce shook her head. "Never about anyone else."

Orman smiled crookedly, his aged face unaccustomed to the expression. And Sela saw something else new to Orman. Her crusty old uncle blushed, too.

For a moment, impatience, or maybe anger, flashed through her limbs. Moments ago Orman was about to take her to safety, away from this castle and her—she shuddered to think it—fiancé. Now he was flirting with the wizard who entrapped her, kidnapped her, and dropped her into the middle of all this drama. What was he thinking?

But her frustration ebbed. Orman wasn't thinking, possibly for the first time ever. He was feeling. And she, no matter how desperate just now, was not going to take it away from him. "I'll, um. Be outside."

She stepped through the door, and pulled it closed. She stood for a while in the hallway, disconnected and alone. Dread hovered at the edge of her senses. She felt it like a vortex, swirling and pulling, and she knew if she didn't resist it, it would swallow her, drown her in its miserable depths. She didn't dare give in to it now. Not now. Or she'd be lost.

Instead, she tried to focus on a plan. Ultimately, she wanted out of this looming marriage. She needed Orman to help sneak her out of this castle. She might even be able to return to the little cottage in Simson, or she and Orman could settle somewhere new, and she could learn to be invisible all over again.

But she couldn't do anything more with her empty, growling stomach and her charred and immodest nightdress. She needed to find herself, feel herself again. Food would help.

Most of all, she wanted her trousers.

§

Drell was lost. He tried to fly through the suffocating woodlands, up and above the stabbing branches of hickory and red maple trees, but his wings ached from arrow wounds, and being pinned and twisted by the Esra guards. He couldn't power them. He slapped them into trunks, bruised their tips on tangled limbs. Finally, he resigned himself to walking, with his wings drawn in tightly to his back.

But in his fear and confusion, he'd lost his bearings. In this alien wood, with no sandy horizon or hot desert breath to orient, he was hopelessly and utterly lost.

He'd been felled and captured in these woods once already. Caught unaware and trapped by his bewilderment, he'd let himself be taken. At first, he'd thought the humans meant to help. In the desert, survival depended on community, and although Tay had warned him of human treachery, Drell had never before met a real human.

He understood now. The Esra humans shot at him, drugged him, chained him. And they tried to ring him, which would have devastating his sense of smell and direction, and would have made him easy prey for the hunt they kept referring to.

A dragon hunt.

Barbarians.

Except for that other. That girl, who had touched his mind like a Kind, and had fought to free him. And he *had* spat flame at her. It was an accident, but he'd seen the heat of it sizzle right against her skin, and her clothing, and yet she remained completely unharmed. He didn't know a kind of magic that could be responsible, and yet, he'd witnessed something magical. Hadn't he?

A rustling sound snapped him to awareness. No small creature scurried through the underbrush, the sound was too heavy and purposeful. He swung his head, his eyes narrowing to focus. He saw no movement, but sensed it, just beyond his vision. A shift in wind brought a spicy sting to his nostrils. Someone was following him. Some *dragon* was following him.

He relaxed, and opened his mouth to call, but suddenly seized with hesitation. Why hadn't they announced themselves?

"And so you have discovered me," said a voice from the trees. A voice with so lilting a timbre, Drell at first thought it female. "As I'd hoped, really."

"Who are you?"

A White emerged several feet away. His wings nestled gracefully against his spine. He drew closer, avoiding hickory trunks with serpentine steps. "A more fitting question might be, who are you?"

"I am Drell."

"Yes," said the White. "That does tell me your name, but it adroitly avoids telling me who, exactly, you are."

"Then I am as much mystery to you, as you are to me, White."

The White smiled, exposing his glimmering fangs. On any other dragon the expression might be seen as friendly, but with this dragon, Drell shivered. "I will tell you who I am," he said. "And why I am so curious about a Black fledgling in the woods of Esra, where there has been no Black Kind for generations."

The White seeped forward, his scales catching filtered sunlight, dazzling Drell's eyes so that he had to squint. But he didn't dare take his gaze from the dragon. The stranger circled, studying Drell as though searching for a tender place to sink his teeth. "I am Fane Whitetail, liaison to Venur Vorham Riddess."

"Do you mean Vassal?"

Whitetail's expression flattened. "I do not. I am no Vassal. I am companion, advisor, and ally."

"Ally," said Drell, shifting his weight, mirroring Whitetail's movements as the dragon continued to circle. "What could you possibly have to ally with concerning humans?"

"It is much to our Kind's benefit to befriend humans—"

"Vorham Riddess is the Venur of Esra. The man who had me captured for his dragon hunt."

Whitetail nodded. "That's the one."

"And you work for him."

Whitetail released a puff of breath. He ran his tongue over his scaled lips. Then he lowered delicately to his haunches. "For all intents and purposes, yes. It does appear that I work for the man." He lowered his chin. "But you and I know the truth, Drell. A dragon offers service by choice alone."

"You choose to cooperate with that barbarian?"

"As I was saying before, it is much to our Kind's benefit to befriend humans, in our world that is changing by their hands."

"I want no part of their world."

Whitetail slowly shook his head. "It is exactly that sentiment that has brought us to near extinction. We are a part of their world, as they are a part of ours. Humans and dragons have nowhere else to go, but toward each other."

Drell sat, too, wearied by the strain to his legs, and

the conversation. "None of this has anything to do with me."

"This has everything to do with you. With me. With all Kind." Whitetail stood, and slowly walked his loop again. "I maintain my allegiance to humans as long as it serves me to do so. But my first loyalty is to our Kind, as it always has been. And to the leaders who have seen fit to hold us together."

"Rage dragons govern ourselves."

Whitetail smiled, and again it brought a shudder to Drell's shoulder blades. "You are no desert dragon."

"They are my Kind. I am raised as one."

"But not born as one."

Drell didn't like the darkening tone of the conversation, and wished his wings would work. He tested them, stretching them toward the forest branches, but pain arced from base to tips, and he winced. "I have far to go if I am to walk home," he said. "I will be on my way."

"You won't reach home, and we both know it."

Drell paused.

"You weren't released to freedom," Whitetail continued. "You were released for the hunt, which will be upon you soon. Vorham chose not to ring you, but he knew your wings were wounded. And he had you followed."

"How do you know...?" Drell began, but realized the answer as soon as the words left his tongue. "You kept me here. Led him here."

"No one knows where you are, but we are running

out of time. I can help you."

"Help me? You are a traitor!"

Whitetail drew in a deep breath, and remained silent for a moment. His pale eyes weakened to nearly translucent as he gazed out into the trees. "I am a creature driven to survival, as any creature is." He blinked slowly. "You are not the first to distrust me." His eyes returned to Drell's face. "You may have good cause for your words. But I will say this. Despite my dubious fidelity to human or dragon, I have never made a promise I did not deliver."

Drell scuffed his feet forward, and straightened his tail behind him, trying to take up as much space as the crowded forest would allow. "You intend to promise me something?"

"Answers," said Whitetail.

"Answers," Drell repeated. "You think I have questions?"

"You are raised as a Rage dragon, but are not desert-born. You bear the distinct eye color of the Brownwing tribe, but you do not claim their name as your own. This means either you do not know your tribe name, or you do, and have been forbidden to speak it."

"I have been forbidden nothing."

"Then we have happened upon your first question." Whitetail turned his face, searching over his shoulder. "The hunters are coming." He looked back at Drell. "In your condition, you will fall quickly."

"And my death will be on your conscience."

"In more ways than one," said Whitetail. "I can't

imagine explaining to my longtime friend how I brought about the death of his only son."

The shudder Drell had felt before exploded into outright quaking, rattling him to his very toes. "You... You know my father?"

"I daresay I do."

Drell's brain stalled. He tried to think, but he could smell the hunters nearing, and could feel the moment compressing. He had barely enough time to process Whitetail's statement, let alone react. "How? Who?"

"That, my friend, would require an answer."

A twig snapped in the distance. Voices rumbled.

"What do you want?"

Whitetail gave his chilling smile. "Now we're making progress. First, I will distract them away. Then, we can further discuss the options." Whitetail unfurled his wings. "If the enthusiastic idiots don't shoot me."

The White sliced upward through the canopy, and Drell could hear his wings billow. Then human voices shouted, and arrows flung from crossbows. Horse hooves galloped away, farther and farther, until Drell was left to the quiet thrash of leaves against branches, and the muted crackle of rodents in the underbrush.

Alone, he realized he was waiting for the return of a liar, or a defector, or a villain. Possibly Whitetail was all three. The smartest choice he could make just now would be to turn, take advantage of the distraction, and put distance between he and the castle for good. But whatever the White's intentions, he did seem to have answers. For questions Drell had long given up on asking.

Despite himself, he stayed.

§

Sela pushed open the chamber door she shared with Gladdis, and peered into the room. Gladdis sat on the bed, her legs dangling. She held a candle sconce on her lap, staring into the steady flame. When the door creaked, she looked up sharply.

"It's me," said Sela.

"They took your things. I'm by myself now."

"Do you know where they took them?"

Gladdis shook her head, the tips of her golden hair brushing too close to the candle flame. Sela darted forward, gathered Gladdis's locks, and laid them against her back. "Careful," she said.

"I haven't seen you since the dance. I said something to make you angry, and I haven't seen you since."

Was that really only last night? Sela knelt before Gladdis, tucking her own dark strands behind her ear. "I wasn't angry."

"What did you do?" Gladdis asked, her brown eyes sad on Sela's face. "To make him choose you?"

"Gladdis!" She inched closer, and looked up into the girl's face. "I didn't do anything. I didn't *mean* to do anything. It's all happened so fast, I don't even know what's going on."

"You said you didn't want to be a Venuress."

"I don't. I'm not going to. My uncle is here, and he's going to get me out of this."

Gladdis blinked, rousing from her daze. "Your uncle?"

"My uncle Orman found me. He's here, in the castle. I've come to get my things so I can leave."

"You mean you really don't want to marry him?"

Sela pressed her fingertips to her eyes, pushing against a threatening headache. "No. I don't even know what happened."

In the next moment, Gladdis had her arms around Sela's shoulders, hugging her tightly. "Oh, I'm so relieved! I thought you became so angry that you flirted with him to spite me."

"Why would I do something like that?"

Gladdis released her, and sat back. "I don't know. You wouldn't, I guess. But I got to thinking how I don't really know you. And. Well, Emlee would do that sort of thing."

"I'm not Emlee." Sela pushed to her feet, anger tempting her to again give in to it. But she gazed down at Gladdis, and her tear-filled eyes, and the blotch of red embarrassment across her cheeks. And she realized she'd been wondering the same thing about Gladdis last night. Did she really know her?

"I did get upset about that disgusting dragon head in the Great Hall. And how everyone was just laughing and dancing as though it was a decoration, and..." Sela hugged her arms to herself, shivering with chill.

Gladdis stood. She'd already set the candle sconce

on the side table, and now she reached for a woven blanket from the bed. She wrapped it around Sela's shoulders. "And you wanted me to be upset, too, but I acted like everyone else."

Sela pulled the blanket tighter. "Yes." She felt embarrassment creeping into her own cheeks, although she wasn't sure why.

"After you left, I stared up at the thing, and tried to imagine it breathing, living. And I understood what you meant."

"You did?"

Gladdis nodded. "All creatures should be treated with respect, even in death. Even dragons."

Even dragons. Sela inwardly clenched. But Gladdis meant well, even if her words were tinged with ignorance. After a pause, Sela knelt to face her friend. "If I was going to try flirting, it wouldn't be for the Venur."

"What do you mean?"

"Do you remember one of the guards, with the light hair and hazel eyes?"

Gladdis frowned in thought. "I don't think so."

"His name is Bannon. I met him once when I turned in the census, and then I rode with him to Shornmar Castle. But he really works here, for Venur Riddess."

Gladdis grinned. "And?"

Sela lowered her voice, even though they were the only two in the room. "Last night, I accidentally found a chapel, and…" She decided to skip over the part about Jastin Armitage. "…well, he kissed me."

Gladdis's eyes widened, and she pressed her palm to her mouth. "He kissed you?"

Sela felt a thrill rise up from her belly and spread across her shoulders. She nodded.

"What was it like?"

"It was like…" She struggled to find the words for the sensation. The kiss had been warm and exciting, but comfortable, too. Familiar. Exhilarating. "It was like flying," she finally said.

"Oh," said Gladdis, her gaze going unfocused. "I'd like to fly."

Sela giggled, then, from the base of her belly, where her loneliness and homesickness mingled with this new longing. The sensation oozed up into her throat, spread a smile across her mouth, and spilled out as a strange mixture of joy and pain.

Gladdis barked a laugh, too. Then, startled by the sound of it, she pressed her hands to her face. Her shoulders arched forward, and she shuddered with giggling.

Sela flung herself backward, cackling. She laughed and laughed until her stomach ached, and tears spilled out to tickle in her ears. She slapped the floor. And each time she took a breath, she heard Gladdis howling, which made her go off again.

Finally, after long, exhausting moments, the sound ebbed. She heard Gladdis choke back another giggle, and cough lightly. Sela turned her head to find her friend had also flopped to the floor at some point, and was now staring at Sela.

At the eye contact, laughter erupted from both of them, and the whole thing started all over again.

Suddenly the door swung open. Both girls swallowed back their laughter, sitting to attention. Leesa, the servant, stood in the doorway, looking puzzled. Or annoyed. She pointed at Sela, and then swept her hand toward the hallway.

Sela pushed to her feet, and smoothed her nightdress. She lifted the blanket from the floor, and wrapped it around herself. "Come on, Gladdis," she said. "We're being summoned or something."

When they drew near to Leesa, the woman held out her hand toward Gladdis and shook her head.

"I'd like her to come with me," said Sela.

Leesa looked between them, and then shrugged one shoulder. She waved her hand toward Gladdis's bag on the floor near the bed. Gladdis retrieved it. And then she and Sela followed Leesa into the hallway, beside a long, overlooking balcony trimmed with a scrollwork railing, and around so many corners, Sela nearly lost track.

"Where are we going?"

Leesa remained silent, but came to a stop outside a door. Sela took a long look around herself. Another stairway descended into a large vestibule below, just a few feet past this door. To her right, a second door arched upward to scrape at the high ceiling. Bits of broken crystals—blue, green, mahogany, and amber—embedded mortar between slabs of stone and woodwork, decorated the painted gold door.

Leesa pushed open this nearest door, decorated in the same fashion, but with pink and lemon-yellow crystal nibs. Sela stepped into the room, and held her breath. The main chamber was enormous, the ceiling as high as the hallway outside. Plasterwork walls were painted a sky blue, and the pink and lemon crystals dotted across the walls as a sort of chair rail, lining the walls and coming to a diamond shape in the corners where they met. Near a window, a wardrobe was opened to expose Sela's red dress hanging inside, along with other pastel-perfect dresses, making the wardrobe seem filled with layered ice cream and a cherry.

"Are those for me?" Sela asked.

Leesa nodded.

Sela turned to Gladdis. "I think this is supposed to be my room."

"It's pretty," Gladdis said weakly.

Leesa withdrew a soft, drooping green dress from the wardrobe.

"No," said Sela. "I'd like my trousers. I can't even think in clothes like that."

Leesa frowned. She shook her head.

Sela regarded her. "Your name is Leesa, right?"

The woman nodded.

"You don't speak. Is it because you don't want to? Or because you can't?"

Leesa laid the dress over the back of a chair, and then touched her hand to her throat. She balled her hand into a fist.

"Was it an accident?"

Leesa's nodded. And then she lifted the dress and held it out.

"Please," said Sela. "I'd really like my trousers."

Leesa shrugged and again shook her head. Then she held up one finger. She carried out the dress. A moment later, a door opened and closed in the hallway.

"What are you going to do?" asked Gladdis.

"As soon as my uncle is ready, he'll get me out of here."

§

"She has to stay," said Layce Phelcher.

Orman crossed his arms and frowned at her, sitting beside her on her bed. "You'll have a doozy of a time convincing her of that."

"I was hoping you'd talk to her about it."

"Then you'll have a doozy of a time convincing me of that."

Layce stood, and paced a few steps back and forth. Orman watched the sway of blue fabric against her legs and hips, and then lifted his eyes to her anxious gaze. More blue. Her eyes matched the hue of her dress. He was beginning to develop a deep appreciation for the color blue.

She paused, and smiled over her shoulder. "I was hoping you'd like it."

Orman cleared his throat. "Uh, yes. You were saying?"

Her eyes darkened, turning anxious again. "This is

going to be difficult to explain."

"Not necessarily. You went to a lot of trouble to get Sela here. You manipulated events, wrestled her into a carriage, provided an attention-getting red dress, and even brewed a love potion."

Layce gasped softly. "How did you—?"

"You're not the only one who sees things, Layce."

She came to sit beside him again, pushing a stray pillow out of the way. "I didn't use the potion. Just so you know."

"You may as well have. Riddess has chosen her, hasn't he? If only one of your actions had been blocked, Sela wouldn't even *be* here to be chosen."

Layce sat back. She chewed the inside of her cheek.

Orman allowed her to wrestle with her thoughts, and he studied them as she did so. Her guilt was palpable, he didn't need to be a wizard to sense that. It was the only reason he'd managed to keep his head. Layce Phelcher had undeniably fiddled about in Sela's business, but at least the woman felt badly. She had a conscience.

"You have a lot invested in my niece. It would be an embarrassment to be wrong, now."

"I'm not wrong," said Layce.

"But you are," said Orman, standing. "And the longer Sela and I stay, the more she is in danger of being manipulated again."

Layce stood, too, and laid her hand on Orman's arm. "Please, as a fellow wizard, just allow me to—"

"You are no wizard."

Layce recoiled, removing her hand. She paled.

"You're no more a wizard than that oaf, Armitage. You've just had better training."

Layce turned, her hand pressed to her belly. "I should have better protected my thoughts. You're hurting me now, to push me away."

Orman circled around her, making his way to the door. He touched the latch. "I'm stating the truth. If it hurts you to hear it, I can't help that." When she didn't reply, he opened the door.

"Maybe you're right," she said. She began to peel off nuggets of crystals dangling from chains, or leather straps, or woven into twine bracelets. She tossed them, one by one, to the bed. She drew her hands over her eyes and down her face, and then lowered them to her sides, standing before him as unprotected and helpless as any human being ever was. Orman felt her fear, then. And her hope; flickering from her eyes as a fragile flame.

"Orman," she said, crossing to him. "If you can see things the way I can, search inside me now. Find my heart, and test it."

"Wizards aren't gods," he said. "No one can see into a heart."

"I can," said Layce. She reached to the bodice ties of her blue dress, and slowly loosened them. She worked the fabric against her collarbone to free it. And then she drew it open, exposing the soft indent of cleavage above the bodice. "I can see your heart, Orman. And now you can see mine."

He thought himself past this nonsense by now.

He knew a woman once, and thought he'd loved her, until he discovered she'd made all the same promises to several other gifted wizards at the university. At the same time. He couldn't say he suffered a real broken heart over it. He took it as a lesson, and simply chose to devote himself to the study of his life's pursuit without the distraction a woman could be.

Still, he found his wrinkled fingers twitching to touch the curve of her throat. His gaze lingered on her collarbone, and then lifted to take in her smile, and the pleasant crinkles at the edges of her eyes. "Why me?" he asked.

"Only you," said Layce. She leaned in. Her chest tickled against his beard, and he felt the zing of it through every whisker. "I won't keep you from leaving, but I'd rather you stay," she said.

"I...I don't..." he muttered. And then their lips were touching. And he was young again. Dashing. Confident. He pulled her close, and drew his fingertips over her throat.

He felt her hands against his spine. Her touch was a flutter, and he shivered. His knees trembled. He deepened the kiss, his mouth opening.

A sharp jab stung his tongue.

He reeled back, trying to spit out the crystal she'd wedged into his mouth, but it was glued in place. His knees trembled so deeply they gave out. He dropped hard, and she caught him, and directed his fall toward the bed.

"I did it," she said, smiling down into his face. "I

can't believe I did it. I mean. I'm awfully sorry, Orman. Really I am. I didn't want our first kiss to be like this." She grunted quietly, pushing him toward the center of the bed.

He tried to speak, but his voice was trapped. He tried to claw at his mouth, but his hands were stone.

She swung his taut legs onto the bed, and pulled a blanket over him. "When this is all over, you'll understand. Maybe you'll even be proud of me. Because, see? I am a wizard. It worked. Even on you."

He'd underestimated her, that much was true. But even a donkey could do magic with the right crystal and the right spell.

"Now you're calling me a donkey?" Layce tucked the blanket beneath his chin. "You're just about the most stubborn man I've ever met, and considering I know Jastin Armitage, that's saying a lot." She straightened, and looked down at him, shaking her head. "I can't believe I've been in love with you all this time, you old windbag."

If he could move, he'd show her just how much of a windbag he could be.

"But don't worry. I can see your heart, remember?" She smiled again. "You are going to forgive me. Eventually. And everything is going to be just fine."

He struggled to move his legs, or his feet, or at least his toes. But she'd solidified him well. Even his thoughts were getting muddy and tired.

She bent over him, and breathed across his mouth. "You're even going to kiss me again. Except I'll kiss back.

For real." She stroked his beard, and situated it neatly on top of the blanket, down his chest. "I'll be back as soon as I can. Just rest now."

He closed his eyes. Or, his eyes closed of their own accord. Either way, the darkness was a comfort to his senses, and for a moment, he had a clear and concise thought.

He used it to cuss.

§

Leesa returned to Sela's room with a pair of brown burlap knee-length pants, with buttons at the cuff. She held them out, her brows raised.

"These aren't mine," said Sela.

Leesa shook her head, but nudged them toward her.

"What happened to mine?"

Leesa shrugged, and shook her head again. Sela wasn't angry with the woman for her lack of answers, she couldn't help it. But she did have a sudden and panicky realization. "What happened to my knapsack?"

Leesa stepped to the wardrobe, and moved aside the long, wispy skirts to reveal Sela's pack shoved in behind them. Sela hurried to the pack, dropped to her knees, and frantically worked the drawstrings. Inside, her unfinished portrait of her father stared up at her with his distant, hollow eyes.

"What's that?" asked Gladdis, peering over her shoulder.

Sela quickly flipped the canvas. "Nothing. It isn't finished."

"You paint?" Gladdis reached for the work.

Sela resisted letting go. "I used to. I haven't in a long time."

Gladdis tugged it from her hands and turned it face-up. She blinked. "It's a dragon."

Leesa stood beside Gladdis, and studied the painting. She drew her finger over the dried pigments.

"You really have a fascination for them," said Gladdis.

Sela stood and snatched the canvas. "Do you have a problem with that?"

Gladdis held up her hands. "No. No, I just. I've never thought about them, talked about them, as much as I have since I met you. I even saw one, this morning! The first one ever."

"They are all around us, you know. Maybe all humans should give them more thought."

Leesa patted Sela's arm, and then tapped the canvas. She pressed two fingers to her closed eyes, and then laid her fingers on the painting.

"What do you mean, all humans?" Gladdis asked. "You're one, too, you know."

"That's what I'm saying," said Sela. "All of us humans."

Leesa tugged Sela's arm. She repeated the motion of touching her closed eyes, and then the canvas.

"Because it sounded for a minute as though you meant 'humans' as 'others.'"

"How could I mean that?" Sela asked, her voice tight. "I'm right here, being completely human."

Leesa grabbed Sela's chin, and forced her face toward her. She stared into Sela's eyes. Then she pointedly touched her fingers to her eyelids, and again touched them to the dragon painting.

"All right, all right," said Sela. "I'm sorry. Are you trying to say you've seen this portrait?"

Leesa shook her head. She traced the unfinished lines around her father's face.

"You've seen this dragon?" asked Gladdis.

Leesa shook her head again. She patted her palm against the portrait, and then smoothed her hand over the dark wood of the wardrobe.

"Oh. You mean the dark dragon from this morning. The one they'll be chasing," said Gladdis.

"I thought they let him go," said Sela, heat rising from her lungs. "The Venur promised to release him."

Leesa vehemently shook her head. She stuck out the burlap pants with her left hand, and tugged at the painting with her other.

"Right," said Sela. She took the short trousers, and stepped into them, sliding them up her legs. "Tunic?"

Leesa opened a drawer at the base of the wardrobe, and withdrew a tightly woven, burgundy tunic, that tied loosely at the throat. "Perfect," said Sela.

She pulled her nightdress over her head, and replaced it with the tunic. Leesa withdrew Sela's battered, familiar boots from the wardrobe and held them out.

"Old friends," Sela said to the boots, and tugged

them on.

"Are we going somewhere?" asked Gladdis.

Leesa took both their hands, and led them out of the chamber, back into the gaudy, crystal-decorated hall.

"Think of all the people these crystals could feed," said Gladdis absently as Leesa dragged them down the steps.

At the lower floor, Leesa paused. She peered around a tapestry-covered wall, and then hurried them all into a shadowed alcove.

"What are we doing?" asked Gladdis.

The back wall of the arching cubby suddenly shifted, and swung open, revealing narrow, winding stairs covered in dust and cobwebs. "I'm not going in there," said Gladdis.

"Yes you are!" Sela took Gladdis's hand, and stepped onto the stairs behind Leesa. "This castle is full of surprises. I knew it was playing tricks on me this morning."

"Playing tricks?" Gladdis gingerly crept alongside Sela, her eyes going wide in the dark, and studying the ceiling and dirt walls.

Sela had to keep Leesa's silhouette ahead of her, following closely, because as they descended deeper, the darkness grew in around them, pressing against shoulders and faces like a funeral shroud. "Is it far?"

Leesa either didn't bother to give an indication, or Sela couldn't see it.

"I don't like this," said Gladdis.

"You've never wanted to explore a secret passage?"

"No," said Gladdis. "Honestly, no."

Just then, warm, orange light filtered in from a distance, making the passage seem suddenly wider and full of fresh air.

"We're going to miss luncheon," said Gladdis. "And I'm hungry."

Sela's stomach rumbled quietly, but she'd rather be here in this winding, dank tunnel and starving than to have to sit at a table of food, staring across at Vorham Riddess, trying to chew and swallow as though nothing in the world was wrong.

Except, if the dragonchase was taking place, then he would be out there, tracking the poor dragon with all the others. Her stomach turned at the thought.

And her appetite vanished.

"I wonder if they'll miss us," Sela said.

"They'll miss you."

Eventually Leesa paused at a lattice-work door and pushed it, swinging, through a curtain of cobwebs. The girls emerged into a torchlit wine cellar.

"If you end up marrying him, Sela, you'll probably spend a lot of time getting to know this place," said Gladdis.

"I'm not going to marry him."

Leesa regarded Sela over her shoulder, her brows drawing in. But she didn't wait for Sela to elaborate. She just pressed on, continuing to walk silently past rack after rack of bottles, brushing her fingertips over dusty wood and glass, leaving raking prints in the dust. In the deeper recesses of the cave-like room, where dark bottles had been left undisturbed for, judging by the dust, years, many fingerprint marks had been made along both sides of the room.

Leesa did a lot of traveling through here.

"Where are we going?" asked Gladdis, her voice taut.

The far wall of the cellar loomed before them, draped in shadows. No windows. No torchlight to reach the chipped and moldy fieldstones. Leesa slid her fingers into a crack, maneuvered them, and, with a shudder and a tortured groan, the wall began to shift open.

"An obscureway," said Sela. "Just like the one in the chapel. Except this one works."

Leesa frowned, and shook her head.

"I mean the chapel near the kitchen. The one with the…" Then Sela remembered Bannon calling it the dragon chapel. The size. The shape. The golden effigy. She looked from Gladdis to Leesa. "Why would a province so calloused toward dragons that they hang a dead one in their festivity room, also have a chapel dedicated to them?"

"What are you talking about?" asked Gladdis.

By the perplexed look on Leesa's face, she must have been thinking the same question.

"The chapel I found last night. Bannon called it the dragon chapel."

"I don't know what that means," said Gladdis. "I just want to know where we are and what we're doing."

Leesa tapped Gladdis's arm and led her through the obscureway. Gladdis groaned. Even Sela was becoming more frustrated than curious, but she wasn't going to give up without discovering what Leesa wanted her to see.

One sharp curve in the damp passageway brought them to a choice. Before them loomed an immense wooden door, split down the middle, with a high, round latch on either side. To the right, the passageway disappeared into a black hole in the earth, so dense and impenetrable, Sela had to step toward it to focus on it. To see if her eyes were being fooled.

She was stopped by a wall as sturdy as brick, but she couldn't see it. All she saw was the black, black tunnel sucking air and light down its throat. "I guess not all the enchantments have been lifted," Sela said.

"Enchantments?" Gladdis asked.

"Orman said he felt some disappear. That's how he was able to come in."

"Who's Orman?"

"My uncle. He was talking with that wizard, Layce, and he said—"

"Wizard?"

"Look, don't you see that tunnel? Except we can't get to it, because an enchantment is blocking it."

Gladdis looked from Sela, to Leesa, who shrugged, and back to Sela. "I see a wall."

"Look harder. Past the wall."

"How can I look past a wall?"

Sela sighed. She turned to Leesa. "Is this what you brought us here to find? This tunnel?"

Leesa shook her head, and put her hands on the

wooden door. She rose up to tiptoes, and strained to reach one of the latches. Then her fingers caught, and the door swung wide, opening to the outside. Light flooded the space around them, making Sela's eyes squint.

Leesa pulled at their hands and drew them into the sunlight.

They stood on an open, grassy hillock, surrounded by undulating land swathed in waving fronds and yellow wildflowers. The nearest castle wall, from what Sela could see, was yards away and miniaturized by distance. Ahead and beyond the horizon, mounds sprouted elms and hickory trees that bunched together into a dry, sparse forest.

"How did we get so far away?" asked Gladdis.

"Underground tunnels," said Sela. She smiled. "There must be a network." All dragon-sized and familiar. Whatever the recent history of Riddess Castle, they had at least been interactive with dragons at some point. Maybe had even been allies. Friends. Like in the stories of those old scrolls her mother collected.

"What's that?" Gladdis asked, pointing to a blotchy thundercloud in the hazy afternoon sky.

The thundercloud shifted, and grew larger. It took shape, and swaying, flapping wings soared into view. Sela was just raising her hand to wave, when she was jerked violently, and nearly fell. She scrambled to keep her balance, but Leesa was running full sprint toward the trees and dragging Sela and Gladdis, and by the time Sela realized she was running, too, the three had reached a copse of hickory saplings. Leesa pushed them to the ground.

"Is that a dragon?" asked Gladdis, her wide eyes swirling with panic.

Leesa slapped her hand over Gladdis's mouth. Then, with her free hand, scraped up dried leaves from the ground and scattered them over her.

"This is ridicu" Sela started to say, but Leesa's forceful stare cut her words. Sela pressed to her belly, instead, and watched silently.

The dragon extended his paws as he lowered, and caught the ground. His onyx scales rippled with sunlight, until his wings gracefully folded against his back and snuffed them. He swung his massive head, rolling his shoulders, and then snapped open his mouth with a yawn.

His yawn squelched, though, when his black eyes found the door. The immense wooden door they'd left open.

The dragon spun, his nostrils flaring to scent them. His eyelids narrowed. He expelled a faint puff of breath, muddling the wildflowers beneath his chin with refractive heat.

Sela had never before been afraid of a dragon.

She was sure they hadn't been seen, or smelled, but she had to work very hard to empty her mind, lest she accidentally connect. After a moment, the dragon lifted his chin. Sela could see him pondering. Considering. Then he swiveled like a funnel cloud through the door, and it closed behind him.

No one spoke for several minutes.

Eventually, Leesa pulled her hand from Gladdis's mouth. Gladdis's cheeks were damp with tears. "Is that what you brought us here to see?" she asked. When Leesa nodded, she asked, "But why?"

"It's what she was trying to tell us. Why she was interested in my painting."

"I don't think that's the dragon we saw this morning," said Gladdis.

"No, he isn't," said Sela. As she pushed to sit up, she realized she was trembling. "But I think I know who he is." This dragon was older. Menacing. Dark from the inside out. Exactly as her father always described him.

Fordon Blackclaw.

§

Drell paced, as much as he was able in this confining web of forestry. He tested his wings, which were still weak and sore. He dug his claws into the earth, flexing them anxiously. Then he turned, serpentine, around an elm trunk, and paced again.

Scuffling feet approached, and he lifted his snout. That White was back, as he said he would be, but a second scent mingled, and Drell tightened in alarm. He was confused for a moment when he spotted only the dragon, who said quietly, "I don't risk flying with those hunter idiots about."

Then the dragon tipped his shoulders, and a limp human carcass slid from the White's back and crumpled against the ground. "I've done all the work," he said.

"The rest is up to you. But give me several minutes to work my way back."

"What do you mean?" asked Drell. "What do you want me to do?"

"Kill him," said the White. "I'll keep the hunters at bay for now."

"What about my father?"

"Well, don't kill *him*, of course." The White smiled, but when Drell didn't join him, he drew his long tongue over his snout.

"You said you would—"

"And I will. First do this for me. Then I will take you to the one I believe to be your father." He pivoted away, but Drell took a quick step toward him.

"Wait! How do I know you're telling me the truth?"

The White paused. He swung his head toward Drell, his milky-pale face wrinkled in impatience. "I have been his friend and adviser for many years. He is a Leland revolutionary, forced from his native lands." The White twisted moreso, facing Drell, his pale eyes steady. "And he has been waiting. Planning. Preparing. He has not been idle." The White smiled again, this time with a dusky edge that made Drell's spine tingle. "If you are unaware of his history, it is because you, too, have been forced from your native lands. Am I right?"

Drell knew little of Leland Province; only what Vaya shared during their flights together. He long suspected Leland was his birthplace. "What is his name?" he asked.

The White remained silent. Then he curved around to face the trail from where he'd come. "All will be revealed once you have done what I ask of you. Remember, give me some time."

Drell wanted to chase down the colorless swine and tackle the answers out of him. But he only sniffed at the unconscious man on the ground, and nudged him with a paw. "Who is this?" he asked.

"Does it matter?" the White said, before disappearing behind leafy trees.

It mattered to Drell. Maybe the White could be casual about death, but Drell had never even killed his own food. He poked at the man again, and rolled him to his back. The man's arms slapped the ground. A shining dabble of drool collected in the black whiskers of his beard. Drell didn't see, or smell, any injuries, but the man was so slack and comatose he already seemed dead.

Just how badly did Drell need information about his renegade father, anyway? He sat for a long time, wrestling his long-held questions, his driving need for identity, to the back of his mind.

Then he sniffed at the man again, and, just to test, opened his mouth and gently embraced the man's throat with his teeth. He squeezed until he felt the resistance of flesh.

He tasted salt, and curled back his tongue, trying to avoid it. He gripped again with his teeth, realizing it wouldn't take much force at all to crunch a human neck.

A sudden gasp startled him. He jerked back his head, accidentally scraping his teeth on the man's skin. He swung around to find a girl—*that* girl—staring wide-eyed.

"What are you doing?"

"I didn't hurt him," Drell sputtered.

"You were biting him!"

"I didn't! I was—"

"He's bleeding." She ran to the man and dropped to her knees. She dabbed her sleeve at his wound, just a scratch, really. His blood was already clotting. "What are you even doing here? You should have gotten away while you had the chance."

"I tried," he said. "My wings are injured. And I got lost."

"What have you done to this man?"

"Nothing," said Drell. "Do you know him?"

"His name is Jastin Armitage. The hunt is in honor of his birthday."

Only then did Drell realize he was having a conversation with a human stranger... in dragonspeak. He scuffled backward, looking around himself warily. Then he asked, "Who are you?"

The man made a garbled sort of noise, and rolled his head sideways. "He's coming to," said the girl, drawing her sleeve over his face to smear away the drool and black dirt smudged across his cheeks. "Jastin?"

"Who are you?" Drell asked again.

"My name is Sela." She stood, and spun to face a near blackberry bush. "It's all right," she called, changing languages. "He's not Blackclaw. He won't hurt you." She then turned a warning scowl to him. "Right?"

"Blackclaw?"

The man gurgled, and flailed one arm, striking

Drell in the toe. Some feet away, a human face peered from around the blackberry bush, her lips stained purple. She blinked. She placed a blackberry in her mouth, chewed slowly, and then whispered, "Are you sure?"

"Look," said the girl, Sela, and placed her hand on his throat. "Harmless, I promise."

"Now just a minute," said Drell. Of course he wouldn't hurt the puny human girls. But he wasn't exactly *harmless…*

"Hello!" said the second girl, stepping cautiously from behind the bush, speaking loudly as though Drell was deaf. "My name is Gladdis! I mean you no harm!"

"My name is Drell," he said, wincing from her volume.

The man at his feet groaned, and cursed, and pressed his hands to his face. Then a third girl rounded the blackberry bush and lingered distantly, twirling a blackberry leaf between her fingers.

Drell took another full step backward, feeling uneasy, himself. His second encounter with a live human being, and suddenly he was being encircled by them. Again.

Well, he realized. Not encircled. But at least outnumbered.

The man rolled to his side, and tried to wedge his arms beneath himself to push up. His biceps trembled against his sleeves, and he collapsed again. Then he spoke the sentence that was on Drell's mind.

"What is…happening…?"

Gladdis crossed the short expanse of undergrowth and knelt beside the man. She took his hand, smoothing her fingers over his knuckles. "We found you here with this dragon. His name is Drell. Sela says he's harmless, and he does seem polite, although I think he was trying to eat you."

"I was not eating him!"

The man flopped to his back. "Dragon!?" He slapped at his right thigh, where an empty scabbard dangled. Then he sat up forcefully, and crab-walked backward, until he bumped into a hickory stump. "Dragon!?" he said again, his bleary eyes squeezing closed and open, closed and open.

"Has Jastin been drugged or something?" asked Sela.

"I don't know. He was brought to me already unconscious." Drell looked from the man, to Sela. "The White wanted me to…to…but I didn't. I wasn't going to."

"What White?" asked Sela.

Drell shook his head, feeling foolish and guilty and somehow cornered. He didn't ask for this. Any of this. "I don't remember his name. He's advisor to the Venur."

"Whitetail?" asked Jastin. "That worthless piece of intestinal offal. He set me up." He pressed the heels of his hands to his eyes.

Voices erupted in the trees and echoed in the air around them. Boots crushed undergrowth, stomping closer. A dog yelped, and then another. "That's it, men! We're close now!"

Drell swung toward the sound, and then reared back. "He set us both up!" Drell thrust out his wings, smacking their tips against branches, causing a shower of leaves and broken twigs.

"Can you fly?" asked Sela.

Drell wasn't certain his wings would work for long, but he would fly, somehow. He crouched to lunge for the air.

"Wait!" Sela hurried to Jastin, and tried to help him stand. When the man collapsed, his eyes rolling about in his head, she waved Drell over. "If someone in the castle wants him dead, we can't leave him here. Take him with you."

"Me?"

"Just for now."

"I see him," shouted a voice. A dog's bark turned desperate, high-pitched. "Release Nock."

"Hurry!" Sela tried to hoist the man to his feet, but her boots slipped. Her face reddened with effort. "I'll go with you to help."

"You can't!" Gladdis swung the man's arm over her shoulders, straining to help. "If you go missing, they'll search for you. Maybe they'll blame the dragon."

Drell had completely forgotten about the third girl, until she scuffled between he and Sela, and she held up her hand. She tapped her fingers to her chest.

"Are you sure?" Sela asked.

"Wait a minute," said Drell.

The third girl touched her fingertips to her closed eyes, and then pointed them toward the woods.

"You'll be able to find your way back better than I could," said Sela.

A large dog broke through the treeline around them, and charged toward Drell. His pointed black ears flattened to his broad head, and he snarled so violently that spittle dropped a foamy trail behind him. Drell hoisted, wincing at the sting of pain in his joints. He could barely carry himself, let alone two passengers!

But the dog leapt to bite at Drell's tail, barely missing, and he knew the men weren't far behind. He swiped quickly at the girl, enclosing his right paw around her waist, and then he dove for the man, Jastin, and caught him by the shoulders.

He needed just enough distance to give him a chance to pause. To breathe. To think.

§

Sela watched the black dragon lift off over the trees, dangling the humans beneath him. His wings faltered twice, struggling to fully expand.

She had so much more to ask him. Now, she might never see him again.

"He spoke," said Gladdis, standing beside Sela, watching the dragon fade to a wisp of smoke below the clouds. "And I understood him."

The gray and blotchy black hound leapt, yelping at the sky, sounding off as though he'd treed the creature. Another round of barking joined in, as boots noisily pounded the ground, filling in behind.

Sela turned. Vorham Riddess, in a sage-and-brown hunting jacket and jodhpurs, stood out at the front of the crowd, seeming to command more space than the seven others all together. The second hound, brown but blotched about the ears and face like the first, strained at his leash. A man stepped out from the crowd, hooked a leash onto the frantic dog, and murmured to him, subduing him.

"Sela?" asked Vorham, his black brows arching against his dark forehead. His face twitched, from surprise to annoyance, to bewilderment.

"He's gone," she said.

"How did you…?" Vorham looked over his shoulder at a guard. The guard shifted his weight, and his face swerved into Sela's view. Bannon.

"What have you done?" asked Vorham, his voice strengthening. His facial features solidified into a threat.

"Me?"

"How did you know the beast would be here?"

"How could I?" Sela glanced at Gladdis, who was growing paler by the moment. She took Gladdis's hand, steadying her. "We don't even know where we are. We're lost!"

"But you saw him," said Vorham. "You said he's gone."

"We saw him." She pointed toward the gray and black hound. "But the dog leapt, and the dragon flew away."

"It's a wonder you weren't harmed," said Bannon, stepping forward. He wore the same sage hunting jacket, cut wide across his shoulders, but the short tails and bindings were tan, rather than russet, like Vorham's.

"He didn't frighten us," she said. "In the least."

"I was a little frightened," whispered Gladdis.

"And where is my brother-in-law?"

"Who?"

Vorham clenched his jaw. "Jastin Armitage."

"Oh." Sela shook her head. "I don't know," she said honestly. "I have no idea. I would have thought he was with you."

"He was." Vorham stiffened, and glanced toward his men. "We were separated. Which is why we thought him to be here."

"But if you haven't seen him," said Bannon, "Then he must still be hunting. He won't know the dragon is gone."

"Are we called off?" asked one of the men.

"I see no purpose in continuing," said Vorham, his heavy gaze on Sela.

"To the barrels!" shouted another man, joined by a third, and the excited dogs howled. "The better part of a hunt is that latter part of a hunt, eh?" The men elbowed one another, and laughed, and broke apart to seep between trees like a river carries away clumps of soil.

Vorham took Sela's arm, leering. "You had something to do with this."

She sucked in a breath, but tried to control her alarm. "You're hurting me."

"With all due respect, honorable Venur," said Bannon. "She is just a girl."

Vorham's grip loosened. He drew up. He pressed his lips together, and then they formed a precarious smile. "Of course. Just a girl. Who knows less about the woods than she does about dancing."

"We've missed lunch," said Gladdis.

Vorham seemed to have noticed her for the first time. "You shouldn't have wandered, unescorted. Bannon."

"Yes?"

"Please ensure these ladies be chaperoned at all times. See them safely to their quarters. And fed." He slid his hand down Sela's arm, until his fingers curled against her palm. He lifted the back of her hand to his mouth. "And rest, my bride. While you can."

It was all Sela could do not to recoil. She did pull her hand from his grasp, pointedly.

He smiled, and she got the distinct impression she'd pleased him, in some way. She watched Vorham follow off after the other men. And she burned.

Every minute she lingered, she came closer to a fate she couldn't bring herself to even think about. But she would be gone by tonight. As soon as she found Orman.

Gladdis could come, too, if she wanted. But Sela was definitely going to be gone by tonight.

§

Jastin pushed up to sit, and found himself staring at an orange slab of sandstone jutting out of the green earth. Hawthorne bushes interlaced with moss ferns, scattering the landscape with contrasting foliage and incongruent colorfill.

He'd never come so close to the Rage Desert, but he recognized the edge of changing land, nonetheless.

His eyeballs felt swollen twice their size, and throbbed within his skull. His tongue stuck to the roof of his mouth; when he lowered his jaw, his tongue released with a clicking sound.

Hands were beside him, offering him a cup of cool water. He eagerly drank.

He lowered the cup to find a pair of copper eyes regarding him from a face with the same gold and olive undertones as the terrain. The girl's head was enwrapped with the brown burlap of his brother-in-law's servant cap, and her shapeless shift dress and apron matched the simple weave. "I recognize you, I think," he said.

She nodded.

"How did we get here?"

"I brought you as far as I could," said a grumble of a voice. Only then did Jastin's flashes of memory suddenly collect into a realization.

"Dragon," he spat, as though he'd just tasted poison. He instinctively reached for his sword, but he was weaponless. He tried to stand, but he was weak. "What do you want with us?"

"I don't want anything," said the black creature, poised where he sat, regarding Jastin down his long snout. "Not from you, anyway."

Jastin glanced toward the woman, and shifted protectively toward her. The dragon pinched his digits to his eyes, and shook his head. "Not from either of you." He lowered his paw. "She came to help me help you."

"Help me?"

"The girl Sela thought you'd been drugged."

"Drugged?" Had he eaten something? Drank something? Thinking back, he could remember nothing after he'd left Sela in Layce's room…

But Layce wouldn't…would she? He and Layce weren't exactly friends, but she had no reason to take a side against him. Or so he thought. Hoped, maybe, even.

"I think the White had something to do with it," said the dragon.

More memories blinked on in his brain. The dragonhunt. Whitetail. Then this dragon. And three women. Sela was there. And her.

He looked back to his silent companion. "What is your name?"

She leaned to press her finger into a grainy patch of dirt. And she drew letters…L…E…E…S…A…

"Leesa," said Jastin. "From the castle?"

She nodded.

He touched his fingers to his throat, feeling them cold. "Are you injured?"

She nodded again, and reached out to brush mud from his throat where he'd smeared it. Then she combed her fingers gently through his whiskers, shedding dried nuggets of mud to his lap.

He caught her hand, stopping her. "Do you know who I am?"

She frowned, and looked from his hand on her

wrist, to his face. She nodded slowly.

"We both know who you are," said the dragon. "And I am Drell, not that you asked."

"I'm not interested in your name," said Jastin, trying to stand again. His legs trembled just as he put weight on his thighs, and he collapsed again, thudding hard to his hip. "If I had my sword, you wouldn't have had a chance to tell me!" Jastin pounded his fist on the ground, frustrated and humiliated at being helpless.

The dragon grumbled. Sparks lit the end of his tongue. "It wasn't my idea to bring you with me. I could barely fly as it is, all thanks to your cage, and your hunt, which would have seen me dead." He stalked one step toward Jastin, his onyx nostrils widening, breathing hot into Jastin's face. "I shouldn't have hesitated when I had the chance."

Jastin met the dragon's heat with his own. He rose to his knees. "The chance for what?"

The dragon's amber, glittering eyes narrowed. For a moment, Jastin thought his gaze might pierce right through his skin. But the dragon only snarled quietly, and spun, swiping his tail at the ground near Jastin's knees.

"The chance for what?" Jastin repeated.

Leesa stood, and touched the dragon on his shoulder. The creature snapped his head toward her, snarling again, and she startled, recoiling.

The dragon immediately shifted, holding out his paws, his growl choked back. "I'm sorry."

Leesa studied him. Then she tapped his leg, and

pointed to Jastin. When the dragon glared off across the landscape, she touched him a third time.

"What does she want you to tell me?" Jastin asked.

The dragon stretched out his neck, and slowly rolled his shoulders. Jastin found himself mimicking it, working to release the tension from his cranium to his tailbone. It helped clear his mind, too.

"You are the first humans I've ever met."

Jastin puzzled over why Leesa thought that was so important to share.

"Aside from the ones who captured me, wounded me, tried to put a ring in my nose, and shoved me in a cage," said the dragon. "My tribe warned me all my life about your viciousness. But it seems some of you are violent, and some of you are not. I'm not sure how to tell the difference."

"It's just degrees," said Jastin. "We are all violent, when pushed to no other choice." He tested his legs again, stretching them out across the ground, rotating his feet. "Some take more pushing. Some less."

The dragon regarded Leesa, searching her reaction. The girl chewed against her bottom lip, and then tipped her head. She nodded once, faintly, in hesitant assent.

The dragon looked again toward Jastin. "And you?"

"When it comes to your kind, I don't even need a nudge."

"Challenging words from a weaponless man," said the dragon.

"Hatred is my weapon. I'm never separated from it."

"Hatred for my Kind? Or for every kind?"

Jastin didn't have a reply for that. He caught in a thought loop, considering. Surprised. Unaccustomed to staring inside himself, he had no way to begin to unravel the tangle of anger and loathing enwrapping his spirit. For him, there were no discrete threads that began or ended with any particular moment; he only knew himself as a snarled, festering ball of knotted wrath.

"Is that why the White wants you dead? Because you're so dangerous?"

The dragon's question caught his attention, and closed off his uncomfortable search for insight. His brain engaged. And he laughed; a single, dry shout of sardonic amusement. "That's what this is? Vorham finally worked up the nerve to deal with me, and all he could come up with was to lure me, drug me, and have Whitetail drop me at the feet of a baby dragon?"

The dragon drew up his shoulders, and a flash glinted behind his golden eyes. He rose slowly to all fours. "I'm not a fledgling."

"I was unconscious and splayed out like a lamb. You had nothing but opportunity." Jastin leaned sideways to make a show of inspecting the dragon's nethers. "Have they even dropped yet?"

The dragon's nostrils seeped haze. His wings flexed against his back. "You're mocking me because I didn't kill you?"

"I've seen plenty of dragons claim compassion, but what they really display is cowardice."

From the corner of his eye, he detected Leesa coming closer, but he was too focused on holding the dragon's gaze to pay attention. Until a sting of pain erupted from his face, and he was knocked aside to his hip, again.

It took him a full five seconds to realize she'd slapped him. Then he rolled and landed on his knees, one arm cocked and ready to swing.

She drew up her fists and glared.

The dragon galloped to close distance, and swept his wing between them. "Do not dare," he said.

But he needn't have bothered. Jastin had never struck a woman, nor would he. And his fury was spent, leaving behind a weakness that overtook his legs, and worked its way into his arms. He couldn't even hold himself up on his knees. He drifted aside, and sprawled to the ground.

"What did they do to me?" he asked.

Leesa pushed at the dragon's wing, and walked around it to glare down at Jastin. She shook her head slowly, her hands on her hips. Then she motioned to the dragon, waving him away from Jastin and toward the horizon.

"Are we going to just leave him here?" the dragon asked.

Leesa gave a firm nod. She began walking away.

Let them go. Jastin despised every feeble moment he spent in front of them, and would rather be left to himself anyway. He could think better alone, survive better. Others just distracted him and slowed his reflexes. They talked when he wanted silence. They demanded attention, when he wanted concentration.

Let them go.

He tried to say as much, but even his jaw betrayed him. He couldn't speak, couldn't push to roll to his back. Whatever recovery he'd managed seeped into the ground beneath him. He was the baby now. Vulnerable. Wounded.

Foolish.

"Wait," he tried to say, gurgling.

Chapter Fifteen

Drell was unaccustomed to so much walking. The pads of his feet were sore, and his shoulder and haunch muscles cramped. But the woman, Leesa, stalked strong and tall beside him, keeping up his pace and even striding ahead, now and again.

She'd defended him, back there. Gotten angry at her fellow human on his behalf. He felt as though he should thank her, but the sentiment seemed inappropriate, somehow. He hadn't needed her involvement, of course. But she'd been offended. Hurt, even.

He opened his mouth to suggest they rest, when the sky above them darkened with shadows. They both looked up to find lofty shapes slicing back and forth across bedraggled treetops. The shapes drew together, and Drell caught sight of a snapping tail, with a bent angle near the tip. Tay Ambercrest.

"My tribe," he said to Leesa. Tears welled in his eyes with the relief of seeing them.

Tay glided to a landing beside them, followed by his

mate, Lena, and then Orus and Rasp Ruddyhock, twins from the dunes. Their clay-red, mottled scales stood vibrant against the wan setting of the dying forest edge. He dashed toward the four of them, his wings catching air and billowing gently. "You found me!"

"We have been searching day and night," said Tay, enveloping Drell with his sandy wings. "We feared the storm claimed you."

"Something as insidious," said Drell.

"You cannot fly?" asked Lena. "You are injured?"

"I flew a short way. But I carried others, and wearied quickly." When Tay released him, he turned to find Leesa, to introduce her.

She hung back, her eyes wide and intense, her mouth unhinged. "Don't be afraid," he said. But even as the words left him, he realized she didn't register fear, but something else he couldn't place. "This is my tribe," he said. "My family."

She looked from Tay, to Lena, her keen eyes taking in their shape and size, their earthen-colored scales. She studied Orus and Rasp, and even walked toward them, a half-smile blushing across her mouth. She reached a hand to touch Orus, and he flinched, but Drell's reproachful look steadied him.

Leesa drew the tip of Orus's membranous, terracotta wing toward Drell's black and leathery one, and pressed them together. She held them up, her eyes questioning.

"Yes, you noticed that," said Drell, matching her half-smile with one of his own.

She brightened, blooming into a full grin, and she threw her arms around Drell's neck.

Tay's brows arched high, and he looked to Lena, to the twins, and then to Drell. Drell lifted one shoulder in a bewildered shrug. And then he raised a paw to Leesa's slender back, and he patted.

§

By the time Sela reached the castle, she was sweaty, thirsty, and miserably tired. Neither Gladdis nor Bannon had spoken much the entire walk, and now that they sat at a table in the echoing Great Hall, sipping cold soup and warm water, moods had improved little.

"If I were to be Venuress," she said, scowling up at the dragon carcass she'd come to loathe entirely, "My first command would be to remove that once and for all."

"What do you mean, if?" asked Bannon.

"I'm not going to be here long enough to become anything," she said. "But I would enjoy seeing that torn down and properly honored."

"It's vile," said Gladdis.

Sela smiled, Gladdis's comment more curative than either the soup or the water. Sela stood, and dabbed a cloth napkin at the corner of her mouth. "Now is as good a time as any to get out of here."

"While the Venur is still celebrating," said Gladdis.

Sela nodded. "I just need to find my uncle. He should be downstairs."

"Wait," said Bannon. "What do you mean? You can't leave."

"What difference does it make to you?"

He rose, and walked around the end of the table to take her arm. "I never took you for someone who could be so cold."

"Cold? You're the one who has been angry with me. You've hardly spoken a word to me since this morning, even when I'm forced on you, and you can't avoid me."

"Since this morning," he said. "When the Venur announced you as his bride."

"So be angry with him!" She jerked her arm from his grasp, and turned to cross the expansive room. Gladdis joined her at her side, glancing behind them.

"I'm not angry, Sela," said Bannon, catching her above her elbow once more. "I'm…"

Sela paused. He tugged her around to face him, and he regarded her silently. He tucked a loose strand of her hair behind her ear.

"I'll wait over there," said Gladdis, retreating backward.

Bannon's gaze never left her face. "You probably think I'm more…experienced…than I am. Being a soldier of the world, as I seem to be. And, I have kissed girls," he said, pink splotches rising to the skin beneath his eyes.

Sela nearly blurted something about boasting, but at the sight of his discomfort, she decided to remain silent.

"But last night, in the chapel, I kissed you out of

real feelings. Whatever you might think, I am sincere toward you."

Sela had thought about it, of course. "I was hoping that to be so."

"Then...why? Why did you respond to his attentions?"

"Why did I *what?*"

"He noticed you. He chose you. What compelled you to—?"

"Now wait just a minute." She stepped back, pushing at his chest. And she looked at Gladdis, who stared intently at her own beribboned slippers. "Just exactly what kind of wizard do you people think I am that I can turn about others' feelings on a whim?" She looked back at Bannon. "What your Venur says or doesn't say has nothing to do with me. This isn't my province, and I don't want to be chosen for anything. I'm not even supposed to be here!"

"Then..." he began, reaching toward her again. But he stopped cold, and a haze passed behind his eyes.

"Bannon?"

He blinked. He stared at Sela for a moment as though she were a stranger. "I have to go."

"Go where?"

"I don't know how long I'll be gone." He continued his reach, and drew his fingertips along her arms, until their hands touched. He gently gripped her fingers. "You really don't wish to marry him?"

"I really don't."

"You can leave as soon as possible? Tonight?"

She nodded, feeling dread slide a clammy hand up her spine. "Why?"

"I don't know when I'll again see you."

"But…"

He kissed her.

Her eyes closed. His lips were soft, but desperate.

He pressed her tightly against him, and though she didn't resist, he released her quickly. Too soon.

Sela had little knowledge for this sort of thing, but even she recognized the kiss for what it was.

A goodbye.

He unlashed his scabbard from his left thigh, and offered it out, sword and all. She accepted it, for lack of knowing what else to do.

"I'll find you," he said. Then he sprinted into the hallway beyond the kitchen.

She followed, and she heard Gladdis's soft footfalls behind her, joining her. But when she reached the hallway, he was already gone, and the distant door swung on its hinges. She hurried to the creaking slab and pushed it open, searching the grounds outside for any sign of him.

There was none.

High above, an eagle released a sharp cry, drawing her eyes to the sky. It circled, flashing golden feathered legs. Then it veered up and over the castle spire.

Gladdis stepped out into the lower bailey, shielding her eyes and staring after it. "What's a golden eagle doing this far west?"

Sela leaned against the door jamb, hugging

Bannon's heavy scabbard to herself. "It's a long way from home," she said. "A long, long way from home."

§

Drell stood on an outcropping at the desert's edge, his dusted knuckles gripping the rock face. He'd only just stolen some rest at home, and here he was, back outside in the raw elements, urged there by the silent human, Leesa.

The reunion with his family was brief, but they'd braced him from beneath to help him fly across the sandy hem of Esra, into the rocky ledges of sandstone crags and precipices the desert dragons called home. In his cave, he'd slept well, but too short.

Still, Leesa seemed determined to communicate something, by the way she'd drawn pictures in the cave floor from the time he'd awoken. Finally, in frustration, she'd kicked dirt over her drawings and pulled at his wing, tugging him outside.

She'd learned too easily that his sensitive wings were good way to maneuver him.

Now, he regarded her. She was a petite silhouette against the brutal horizon, watching the sky, her breath seemed held; she barely moved. She'd pulled her head cap from her hair and wrapped it around her mouth, instead, blocking the cutting desert grains. Her inky black hair, almost the deep hue of Drell's own wings, was sleek and sheared straight at the shoulders.

"Am I the first dragon you've known?" he asked.

She peered at him over her shoulder. She smiled, and shook her head.

"You haven't seemed frightened of me. So I wondered."

She shook her head again, still smiling.

"You're one of the first humans for me. And my tribe, too. At least the twins. I know they've never ventured far enough from the north to even see a human, let alone speak to one."

She regarded him, patiently awaiting him to continue.

"They don't speak your language well. They haven't had much practice."

She pointed to Drell, and then touched her ears.

"You understand me well?"

She nodded.

"I've had a teacher. She makes me practice with her. I never really thought I would need it."

She indicated her hand toward him, then toward herself.

"Yes," he said. "But here we are." He smiled. And then he realized he sensed her thoughts as easily as did his tribe's. When, exactly, that had happened, he wasn't sure. To test, he tried again. "We're waiting for someone you want me to meet."

She nodded.

"A friend of yours. Named Bannon."

She smiled, less surprised than he'd expected. She nodded again. Then her features brightened with anticipation, and she looked up to the sky, shielding her eyes against the glare.

A brown spot appeared, washed out and wavering through ribbons of heat. The spot swelled into bird form, feathered wings gracefully pumping, raptor claws extending in preparation to land.

"And there he is now," said Drell.

§

Sela spotted Layce Phelcher near the entry door of the Keep, and waved. "I'm looking for Orman."

Layce returned the wave, smiling tensely. She drew near, and Sela could see weariness etched in the lines around her eyes. She wore a long tunic over beet-dyed leggings, and her dark hair smothered her shoulders, thick and tousled. "I'll take you," she said, taking Bannon's sword from Sela's hands. She nodded to Gladdis, and then to Sela. "Follow me."

"I'll take the sword with me when I go. Once I meet up with Orman."

Layce nodded again, leading Sela and Gladdis into a long, chilly hallway where they'd never been. "Where are we going?"

"Almost there."

Muffled warnings drummed at the base of Sela's skull. The wizard was subdued. She didn't meet Sela's gaze. And Orman…something felt amiss concerning Orman. But Gladdis was thoughtfully smiling, and Layce had claimed to be a friend, so Sela was still in the process of sorting out what to think when Layce extended her arm toward an arched doorway, lined with candles that winked friendliness and invitation. Surely nothing threatening could exist beyond a doorway so delightfully warm.

"Pretty," said Gladdis.

Sela agreed. She pushed open a heavy, squealing door, and giggled at the abrupt sound in the otherwise pleasant space.

She stepped into a chapel, much like the one she'd already visited. This one had a long, carved banister around a sturdy altar spilling with more glittery candles. Colored glass partitions rose up on either side of the altar, scattering the candlelight around the room into vibrant fairy flutters. Before the altar stood a lanky man in a golden robe. Beside him, Vorham Riddess. Beside Vorham crouched a White, his scales flickering with multicolor prisms.

"Oh. Hello," said Sela, recognizing the White in the back of her mind, although she couldn't place it. And she smiled at Vorham, who looked dashing in a midnight satin jacket over a red tunic and black leather breeches. His coffee-colored skin blended into the lit room like shadows.

"Hello, Bride," he said. "I hope you don't mind the surprise."

"Surprise?" she asked.

"I had intended to give you the traditional fanfare, with all the ladylike time to prepare, but Layce suggested we skip to the legal part."

"Legal?"

"Who needs a wedding?" asked Layce, who took Sela's hand and led her to stand beside Vorham. "When the marriage is the important part?"

"How romantic," said Gladdis.

Sela smiled, and smoothed her hands bashfully over her tunic and drawstring trousers. "I would have dressed for the occasion."

"You're perfect," said Vorham, taking her elbow and drawing her closer. "Perfectly perfect."

He was the most debonair man Sela had ever known.

The cleric in his golden robes outstretched his hands. "In the eyes of God and before all willing observers and parties, I honor this union and bless the future of Vorham Riddess, Venur of the Province of Esra with his life choice, Sela Thistleby, henceforth known as Sela Riddess, Venuress of the Province of Esra." He lowered his arms.

"And now you're my wife," said Vorham, lifting Sela's hand to his mouth.

Gladdis clapped her hands together against her chest. "What a beautiful ceremony!"

Sela met Vorham's eyes as his lips grazed her knuckles. Warmth infused her chest, her shoulders, and her face, and she gripped her bottom lip with her teeth, trying to hold back the swell of pride, and anticipation, for the coming hours.

"My advisor and I have some pesky paperwork to finalize," said Vorham. He stepped forward, and brushed his lips over her ear, whispering, "but I'll find you shortly in your suite, where you can undress appropriately for the occasion."

Sela giggled again. She glanced to Gladdis, who snickered behind her hand.

"Come, Bride," said Layce, taking Sela's hand.

"Goodbye," Sela said to the White.

Gladdis clutched Sela's sleeve. "I'm so jealous!" She hurried through the candlelit doorway into the hall. "I guess I won't be seeing you for…a while…"

She turned slowly to face Sela and Layce as they emerged, her smile evaporating, and her complexion turning to wax. Horror welled into her eyes.

"What's wrong?" asked Sela, wondering how Gladdis could seem so distraught on such a perfect…

A few steps into the hallway, Sela stopped. Inner joy wound into a knot in her belly and punched her there. Waking from a dream, she felt numbness in her fingers, nausea climbing her throat. She looked from the chapel candles to Layce, who hugged Bannon's sword and sheath against herself. Braced.

When Sela regarded the sword, Layce took a wide step back. But Sela was too appalled to think, too sickened to move. "Layce Phelcher," she said weakly, the gloomy hallway tilting, crooked. "What have you done?"

§

Sela's friend, Gladdis, caught Sela just as the girl wilted. Layce heard the rumbling voices of Vorham and Whitetail, felt their footsteps shuffle toward the door.

"Hurry," she said to Gladdis. "This way."

"Did you do this?" asked Gladdis.

Layce paused. She reached toward Sela's cheek, pressed against Gladdis's arm, and patted it gently. "How could I have anything to do with it?"

"I know what I felt. I know what I heard. Sela says you're a wizard."

"Yes, I'm a wizard," Layce said, glancing anxiously toward the chapel door. Vorham would be here any moment. "And you can bring Sela on your own, or I can force you."

An empty threat. Layce didn't have anywhere near the right crystals or incantations ready for that.

Gladdis didn't budge. Clever girl.

"I can protect her," said Layce.

"Protect her! You're the one who got her into this!"

"Yes." Layce pressed the sword and sheath against Sela's belly, and wrapped Sela's arms around it. "I did this, Sela," she whispered. "But you'll understand soon. You'll forgive me."

Sela's eyes slowly opened, but her color remained pale. For a flash of a moment, Layce wondered how Sela could begin to understand, when she didn't even understand, herself. But her vision was clear. Pure. Strong. And she walked where her visions led her. It was her way. Her calling.

Her only choice.

"Now get moving," Layce said to both girls, "...or things are going to start happening that even I can't control."

"Too late," said Gladdis, scowling. But she nudged Sela into balancing on her own feet, and then gently pushed her into walking.

"I married him, Gladdis," Sela moaned, scuffling. "I'm married."

"Hurry," said Layce, grasping both girls and dragging them forward. "Hurry."

The three of them turned a corner, spilled into a foyer, and stumbled down a back staircase. Behind them, Vorham and the cleric spoke, and Vorham chuckled with the white dragon. She heard them—felt them—close. Too close.

They collided to a stop, all three of them frozen, and staring up at the sound of voices.

Vorham spoke clearly. "And Armitage?"

"Done and done," said Whitetail.

"You'll deliver the parchments yourself?"

"Legal and binding," said the dragon.

"Well done," said Vorham, over the sound of his gloved hands slapping together. "Well done, indeed." His footsteps moved toward the stairs. "I have much to celebrate this evening. Well and good."

Gladdis and Sela both gaped, stricken, at the footfalls. Then Sela spun around, and laid her hands on the stone wall beside them. "In here," she said. "He's coming!"

"In where?" Layce passed her hand over the wall, feeling the rutted fieldstone scratch against her palm. Then Sela wrapped her hand around a latch, suddenly visible, imbedded in the mortar. "Where did you…?"

Like setting fire to a cobweb, the stone wall dazzled and shriveled away from Sela's hand, revealing a ruddy door. "A ward," Layce said, drawing back one step from Sela, staring at her, trying to see *through* her, to who the girl really was. She touched Sela's mind, but hesitated to explore it, nervous. Intimidated.

Sela unlatched the door and swung it open. She pulled Gladdis into the darkness with her, regarded Layce around the edge of the wood, and then slammed the door in Layce's face.

From that brief moment in Sela's mind, Layce reeled. She'd caressed against magic as solid and deliberate as Esra's maple grove. As earthen and wise as Leland's ancient mountains. The girl didn't discern magic as much as she *was* magic, fabricated from the same primordial elements that created their world. Ancient. Unfailing.

Except even Sela didn't seem to understand who she was, anymore than Layce could decipher. And Layce was struck by the realization that, had she better understood, she might have waited. Played this out differently.

Not might. Would. Layce would have protected Sela from Vorham and his greed, not betrayed her to it. Layce had stubbornly forced her vision into being, when, perhaps for the first time, she'd been wrong.

Wrong.

Layce drooped onto the bottom step and hugged her knees to her chest. What had she done?

"Ah, Layce," said Vorham, descending the stairs to

join her on the last step. He drew her to her feet, his eyes shining in way she'd never seen. He laid his hand on her shoulder. "You've supported me for so many years, and I've hardly thanked you. Tonight shows me how truly dedicated you are to me, and to my goals."

She must have really overdone the enchanted candles. Vorham was still drunk from them.

"I've wondered, at times, you know. Locked away in your little room, coming and going on a whim, with little to say. I'm glad to know you're still with me."

"Of course," she mumbled.

"Because you know what I do to people that are against me." His hand on her shoulder squeezed. "Especially to those that seem to want what I want, but are really setting traps. Manipulating my means for their own ends."

She touched her fingertips to a smooth crystal in her tunic pocket, sending a snap of electrical charge to Vorham's hand. He twitched, and removed his hand, flexing his fingers, his eyes darkening. "You can't intimidate everyone, Vorham," she said. "Choose your threats carefully."

"Threat?" he asked, slipping into an easy smile. "You misunderstand. I'm thanking you for arranging my wedding night so effortlessly. After all," he said, moving beyond the stairs and into the main hall toward his chambers, "We work for the same side."

Layce lingered, stung by his words. She'd clung to Riddess Castle with unrelenting devotion to her belief that one day, the elder Riddess's eyes would again open, and set Esra back on its true path. She'd let others misjudge her motives, distrust her character. She'd obediently played her part, hating as many moments in life as she'd relished. But never, ever, had she before doubted herself. Until tonight.

And now she began to wonder if she hadn't become so good at deception that she fooled even herself.

She lunged into the hallway, following after Vorham. She caught a flash of satin as he turned a corner, and she hurried to catch up. Just as he reached his chamber, he opened the door and peeked in, calling for Sela.

Layce's stomach turned.

He pulled the door, and for the second time tonight, wood closed shut in Layce's face. She stood fuming, thinking. Then she dug into a pocket on her tunic, searching for a sliver of ruby crystal. "Same side," she said under her breath. "Not for long."

She shoved the ruby shard into the keyhole of Vorham's chamber door.

§

When the door slammed behind Sela, she startled. Gladdis threw herself against the latch, thrashing it, but it wouldn't budge. "We're locked in!"

"Who are you? What are you doing here?"

The aged, watery voice made Sela turn around, and she blinked in the half-light, her eyes too slowly adjusting. "Who's there?"

A shadow rose up beside an enormous, curtained bed. The shape of a chair separated from the shadow. Sloping, slender shoulders illuminated in the cast flamelight of a melting candle. "I am Avara. Has Vorham sent you?"

Finally Sela's eyes allowed her to take in the full sight of the woman, her dilapidated chair and tattered gown, and her voluminous, silvering hair. She stood beside the pine timber bed, her pale hand lying atop another hand of brown fingers resting against the bed.

"I'm so sorry," she said immediately. "I hope we didn't wake him."

"I wish that were possible."

Gladdis slowly stalked toward the bed, her chin raised, trying to peer at the sleeping patient. "Who is he?"

"Ebouard Riddess," said Avara. "Venur of Esra."

"But he can't be," said Gladdis.

"Yes, he can," said Avara.

"Wait," said Sela. "Vorham Riddess is the Venur of Esra."

"She ought to know," said Gladdis. "She just married him."

Sela cringed.

"You married Vorham?" asked Avara. "Why?"

"I didn't mean to."

"I don't understand."

"Neither do we," said Gladdis. "Let's start all over again."

§

Layce made her way back to the remote hallway and staircase, hurrying quietly. When she reached the wall where Sela had found the chamber door, she knocked, and whispered with her face pressed against the stones, "Sela. Let me in."

A moment later, a door swung open where there wasn't one, and Sela pulled Layce into the room. "Do you know who this man is?" She pointed toward a large pine bed, carved with sprites and rustic leaves.

Layce closed the door, her gaze catching not on the man on the bed, but on the woman beside it. "Avara?"

The woman lifted a candlestick and held it up. "Layce?" Then she ran forward, and Layce captured the candlestick before it was dropped, and handed it off to Sela. She threw her arms around her sister.

Her sister. Her sad, quiet younger sister who she'd been searching for all these years. Here and now.

Layce could hardly believe it.

Avara stepped back, smiling, her once soft mouth now wrinkled and pale. "You look the same. Exactly the same. How are things at the university?"

"I wouldn't know," said Layce, confused by Avara's strange question. "I haven't come from the university," said Layce.

Avara's smile faded. "I don't understand."

"Avara, I haven't been to the university in years. Not since Father died. I've been here."

"You've been here?" Avara's eyes deadened, and she

sat onto her broken chair, drooping into faded creases. "All this time?"

Layce knelt, cupping her hands over her sister's knees, watching Avara's gray eyes while the past several years unwound and replayed themselves through her memories. Realization settled into the lines of her face, aging her even more sharply. "Vorham told me—"

"Vorham lied to you. He tried to convince me you were the one who left. To marry Tarmus."

"Tarmus?" Avara shook her head. "I barely remember him."

"I never believed him. I knew you had to be here, somewhere. I knew he hid you from me."

Avara blinked slowly, dazed. "I never really believed him, either, I suppose. A part of me hoped you'd moved on." Avara gazed at Layce then. "Another part of me wondered why you never visited. Never wrote."

"I didn't leave you," said Layce. "But a part of me wondered, too. Why he would hide you, and why you would let him."

Sela and Gladdis shifted, creaked the floor, reminding Layce they were still here. She glanced toward them, and she caught sight of Ebouard Riddess, lying in the immense pine bed, white blankets tucked around his waist. His dark skin was supple and bright, as though he was on the verge of opening his eyes and smiling at a fresh morning.

Layce stood. She touched the Venur's sleeve. "He's here? Alive?" There had been so many healers, and so many lies all jumbled together in everyone's heads, she hadn't known what to think.

Avara stood too, and stroked her fingers over the back of Ebouard's hand, where it laid over the coverings. "Not alive. Not dead. It's as though he was drawn to the shadows, but never stepped through them."

"And you've stayed with him?" asked Layce, stepping closer.

"Caring for him. Waiting for him to decide if he'll wake up, or slip away."

He didn't look any closer to slipping away than he'd ever looked. But Avara, with her gray, listless hair, and hunched shoulders, her tired eyes; she'd aged enough to be mistaken for Layce's mother.

"It's the linking stone," said Sela. "Isn't it?"

Layce studied her sister a moment longer before turning toward Sela. "The what?"

"The linking stone." Sela pointed to Ebouard's throat, where an amethyst shard peeked from beneath his bedcoverings.

Layce drew back the covers and stared down at the thing. The shard was affixed to a leather cord around his neck, and it pulsed faintly, glowing pale purple. Layce herself had made the bauble for her sister years ago—she recognized it.

"What are you looking at?" asked Avara. She touched Ebouard's chin.

Gladdis moved closer to see, too.

"The amethyst stone," said Layce, her voice weak. "You gave it to Ebouard?"

Avara withdrew her hand, regarding Layce with a

wrinkled brow, and she drew her lips together in that way she always did when she'd been caught in a lie. Avara was just about the only one who'd ever been able to lie to Layce. Her own sister could keep Layce out of her thoughts while nosing about in Layce's muddled mind.

Layce's father had been a better wizard than she. Avara had always been a better secret-keeper.

"You should have told me," said Layce.

"That he loved me?" Avara shook her head. "He asked me not to. He didn't trust his son."

With good reason. But, still. "I'm your sister," said Layce.

Avara regarded Layce for a time. Then she drew in a breath. "Yes," she finally said. "I should have told you." She took Layce's hand.

"What's a linking stone?" asked Gladdis.

"My mother and father..." Sela began, but her words faded, as well as the color in her cheeks. "I mean. They've told me about it. How the crystal's connection is love, even in death."

"I didn't understand exactly what I was doing at the time," Layce said. "I was just practicing with Father's leftovers."

"But I'm confused," said Avara. "I don't see any crystal."

"Me either," said Gladdis.

"It's there," said Layce. She pointed to the stone against his collarbone. "It's right there. And it's keeping him strong, while you fade away," she said to Avara.

Confusion lifted away from Avara's eyes, replaced by wonder. Then she looked back to Ebouard. Her profile hardened, and then released. She wilted into her chair. "I knew it was something," she said. "I couldn't leave his side. Couldn't bring myself to let him go."

"All these years," said Layce. "All these years. Surely he wouldn't have wanted you to—"

"I couldn't leave him," said Avara.

Layce smoothed her sister's gray hair over her shoulder. "I wish you would have asked for me. I would have helped. I could have kept you company."

"I did ask," she said. "Vorham told me you'd gone, and I wanted to believe you were happy somewhere in a new life." Her voice softened. "I barely convinced Vorham to let me stay. I told him I could tend to his father and keep watch for the minute he was finally gone." Avara stroked Ebouard's hand again. "But I had to promise to keep him a secret. I agreed to let Vorham lock me in." She passed her thumb over Ebouard's knuckles, and turned her wrinkled face to Layce. "I didn't know I would grow as dusty and forgotten as the Venur himself."

"Oh, Avara." Layce hugged her sister again, her heart wrenching. "I never forgot."

Avara wrapped her arms around Layce, returning the embrace. "We found each other today. Finally, today."

But it hadn't been Layce who'd found the secret room. It had been Sela. That mysterious girl with ancient magic in her blood.

Sela spoke. "How did Ebouard...get like this?"

"Vorham," said Avara, releasing Layce. Her upper lip curled in an angry sneer. "I don't know how, exactly, but I know a poisoned man when I see one. Vorham and that dragon have always whispered. Plotted. They're evil through and through, the both of them."

"The dragon?" asked Gladdis. "The black one in the tunnels?"

"What black one in the tunnels?" asked Layce.

"Fordon Blackclaw," said Sela. "Leesa showed us where she'd seen him. I think he's been living in the tunnels beneath the castle."

"Tunnels?" asked Layce.

"This castle is full of tricks," said Gladdis.

Layce knew all about that. She regarded her sister again.

Avara shook her head. "I don't know of any dragon except Fane Whitetail. If anyone is greedier and more conniving than Vorham himself, it's that sniveling, devious dragon. He's evil through and through, I tell you."

"Then we need to do something," Sela said to Layce. "Because that linking stone, and your sister, are the reason Ebouard is still here."

"The festering thorn in Vorham's side," said Layce.

"If he finds out—"

"He won't find out," said Avara, suddenly rising. "Not from me."

"Vorham won't find out from any of us," said Layce. "But Whitetail..." Layce already sensed the dragon at the edge of her awareness, causing ripples of commotion in the castle, in the hallways, outside the door.

"Can't you break the link?" Gladdis asked Avara.

"Break it?" Avara went pale. "Even if I knew how, I couldn't do that!"

"Then wake him up, Avara," said Sela. "You know how to do that."

"I do?" She looked from Sela to Layce, and back. "Could I really do that?"

"You can," said Sela.

Layce didn't have the first idea how to help Avara do such a thing, but if anyone could, it would be Sela of the Red Dress. Sela of the Ancient Magic.

"Hurry," said Layce, feeling Whitetail bearing toward the secret room.

Avara stroked Ebouard's hand, and leaned over to whisper in his ear. "Ebs," she said. "It's Avara. Can you hear me?"

"Try touching the stone," said Sela.

"But I can't even see it."

"Hurry," said Layce again, feeling Whitetail's presence as a hot coal against her neck.

"It's here," said Sela, lifting the purple crystal to offer it toward Avara.

Just then, the door burst open. But it wasn't Fane Whitetail who charged into the room.

All the women startled and turned, and met the equally startled stare of Vorham Riddess.

From the corner of her eye, she saw Sela snap the cord from Ebouard's neck, and quickly hide the crystal behind her back. The stone pulsed once, and then went dark.

Vorham drew a dagger from his belt. "Everyone stand exactly where you are." He moved the tip of his weapon toward Layce. "Especially you."

"How dare you," Layce growled, hoping she sounded more offended than terrified.

"They are here," Vorham called through the open door.

"As I suspected." Fane Whitetail's sinister voice drifted up from the hallway, and filtered into the room with an arcane stench.

"What exactly you are doing, though," said Vorham. "That is the curiosity."

"Vorham," began Avara.

"How you found the room is no mystery," he said, his hard eyes on Avara.

"She didn't—" said Sela.

"And you, my lovely bride," said Vorham, swinging his blade toward Sela. He stalked toward her, and she recoiled, until her back was against the wall and Vorham's dagger tip was pressed to her belly. "Just what are you doing in my father's sickroom, the very evening of our wedding?"

"I—"

Vorham shook his head. "Don't."

Then his eyes moved to Ebouard Riddess. His dagger lowered, a little. He blinked. But he couldn't suppress the flash of eagerness that lit his tiny eyes.

Even Layce could see what Vorham reacted to.

Ebouard's breath had stilled. His skin was fading. His jaw slacked, and he appeared as much the corpse as he should have already been.

Vorham pressed fingers to his father's throat, searching for a pulse. Then he turned a faint smile to Sela, and Layce couldn't tell if he was even bothering to try to hide it.

"Somehow, I knew you were the right choice," he said to Sela. Then he raised his voice, and called out into the hallway. "Whitetail, call me a guard or two." He glanced toward Layce. "Or three."

"Your Eminence?" Whitetail's voice crooned.

"I have uncovered the plot of these women to murder my father, Venur Ebouard Riddess. I've witnessed this with my own eyes."

Avara gasped. "I would never!"

"Unfortunately for my father, I was too late to save him."

Avara gasped again, and withered. Layce darted forward to support her. "What do you mean?" Avara asked.

"He's dead," said Vorham, his voice a sliver of concealed glee. "Ebouard Riddess is dead."

"No," moaned Avara.

"My condolences," said Whitetail. His shifting claws scraped against stone and wood in the hallway, causing as much irritation to Layce's ears as his over-acting. "My sincere condolences," he said again.

§

Kallon gazed down at the white-foam wrinkles of the endless sea beneath him. The air tasted of brine and fish, although Kallon had yet to see any sea creature break the surface in the day's travel. Evening filtered toward the edges of horizon and coated the sea with haze. He hadn't been looking forward to this part of the journey, over endless ocean for a full day and night, before he could even pause to rest on the only tree-filled island between eastern and western provinces. His wings were already tiring, but he had long to go. At least Riza was company, quiet as she'd been for the past few days.

He turned his head to ask her how her wings were holding up, but she wasn't beside him. He lowered his legs and braked mid-air, billowing his wings forward to turn about. He finally spotted her some distance away, a crimson sparkle above the writhing sea. She was going the wrong way.

He thrummed his wings to catch her, but her head was slanted, her legs drawn up tight, and her wings threw wind behind her so that they blurred like a hummingbird's. She flew with purpose.

"Riza!" he called, his legs running over the air, his wings scrambling to find rhythm. "What are you doing?"

"Something's wrong." He heard her words bounce off the water in delay, she'd traveled so far ahead. "Sela," said Riza's voice, splashing from the waves. "Something's wrong."

Kallon drew up his feet, too, slanted his head, and

dove to follow.

Chapter Sixteen

Jastin Armitage lay on the hard ground, pebbles digging into his hip and shoulder, and he dry-heaved. His legs spasmed again and again as his stomach turned inside out, trying to spew contents.

He had none left.

He'd lost track of the hours he'd lain alone on this arid frontier, shivering despite the heat, cramping, engulfed in pain, and too weak to even lift his cheek from the puddle of his own vomit. As dark closed in, he listened for rustling nightlife, tried to determine which creatures would emerge to sniff and explore him; which ones were dangerous. But as daylight failed, he also lost the shape of trees, the depth field of boulders and desert grasses. Even for a moonless night, the darkness was too consuming.

This wasn't night. He'd gone blind.

This must be what death felt like when the body had succumbed but the mind was still aware enough to understand.

He wasn't afraid to die; that's what made him such a strong warrior. And he always knew he'd die alone, just him against whatever elements surrounded him at the time. What he hadn't expected was to be taking it lying down. Slowly, miserably. Completely and utterly helpless.

A whuffle of air sounded somewhere to his left, and then feet shifted pebbles, grinding them against each other. The sound screamed in Jastin's head, echoing painfully.

He didn't bother to cry out. He didn't have the voice. And he took comfort in realizing that finally something had arrived that sounded large enough, and strong enough, to put him out of his misery.

But hands lifted him from his vomit puddle and leaned him back against smooth rock. A water bladder pressed to his mouth. He tried to drink, but more liquid splashed down his chest than made it to his swollen, cracked throat. It was mild relief, anyway, both to his throat and his clammy chest. More water dribbled over his face, and a soft cloth drew over his forehead, his cheek, and his beard.

He tried to mouth the words *thank you,* but his stomach clenched against the water and tried to send it back up. A cool hand pressed his abdomen, spreading warmth through his insides like the comfort from a belly of hot soup. The water stayed down. And Jastin reached out his hands, searching for the bladder. It pressed again to his lips, and this time, he swallowed and swallowed until his stomach sloshed.

"Thank you," he managed through his splintered throat.

"You are welcome," answered a voice that rippled with strength and the distant colliding of storm clouds.

A dragon.

Jastin wasn't so dead he didn't recognize that.

As much as he hated dying helplessly, being cared for by a dragon in the end was almost more than he could bear. "I'd rather you eat me than help me," Jastin growled.

"Because you have cleverly guessed you are poisoned. And if I eat you, I would be poisoned as well. And then your last act would be to kill one more dragon in the world."

"At least my death would count for something."

"That is one way of looking at it. I would rather see your life count for something."

Jastin wished he had his sword. Or the strength to grasp a rock. Or to make a fist. Anything to make the creature shut up. Or at least go away.

"You needn't resort to violence, Jastin Armitage, although I realize it is your way. But if you wish me to leave, you only need ask."

"How do you know my name? Are you Redheart?"

"To which Redheart do you refer? There are three in that tribe now."

Riza's face flashed into Jastin's mind, erupting as much pain as the sound of the dragon's heavy landing had. He squeezed closed his eyes, trying to force the memory behind his pounding headache. But if his eyes failed to see, his mind vibrantly remembered. "She's an abomination," he said. "A demon."

"Riza Redheart is no demon, Jastin Armitage." He could sense the dragon before him swelling in size, rising up to loom over him, breathe soot into his face. But the voice remained calm, although insistent. "If actions are the fruit of character, then your character is more demon than many."

"I would expect that, coming from a dragon. But I act for a higher authority."

"In these lands," said the dragon, "I *am* the higher authority."

Jastin wanted to laugh, but the effort was too much. He settled for a grim smile, and a faint cough. "In these lands, we each answer to ourselves."

"Which is the sightlessness you have lived with all these years," said the dragon. "Your physical blindness finally equals the condition of your soul."

For which he was grateful, just now. "To save me the torture of seeing you."

"To save yourself from the pain of knowing who you are and what you've done. Every death of my Kind at your hands has dimmed you, darkened you. The poison your body now fights is no less dangerous than the ignorance you have inflicted on those around you."

"Ignorance?" Jastin tried to move his legs, to test if he could walk away, since the dragon didn't seem eager to leave.

"You have yet to ask me to go," he said.

"Of course I want you to go. I would kill you if I

could."

"Yes, you would try," said the dragon. His footsteps retreated. "But you have no strength, and so I have come for the chance to speak while you must listen."

"I don't want to hear anything you have to say."

"Very well," said the dragon.

A breeze drifted into the silence between them, cooling Jastin's damp face, and scraping the tips of dried grass against sandstone boulders. He felt the air whisper across him, heard it whistle through the minute tunnels in the rock behind him. Soon he would be a part of the world in a way he hadn't imagined before. He would die, and fade into the earth, and become the earth.

If he could choose, though, he would rather become the wind.

"Why the air?" asked the dragon.

"It travels," said Jastin weakly. Tired from talking, weary from illness. "It shapes the sands."

"You wish to do in death what you have done in life."

"I've shaped nothing," he said. "I have survived. I have hunted. And in the end, I have failed at the one and only thing I ever promised."

"To avenge her," said the dragon.

Jastin rested his head back against the stone, trying to see through his blindness to find the dragon. "You know too much about me. Who are you?"

"I can tell you who I am, or I can show you, Jastin Armitage."

Jastin felt an oncoming trap. He shifted his

shoulders. He tried not to be curious, and worked to settle his thoughts.

"I have answers," said the dragon. "About your wife. Her death. Your life. And how your choices have indeed shaped the world around your anger and hatred, whether you admit that or not."

"My wife?" asked Jastin, his voice breaking, betraying him.

"Shall I show you?"

Ensnared, Jastin cursed himself. He cursed the dragon. He cursed the wind, and the desert, and his aching body. He railed against his own mind, and his need to know. He resisted bravely, sapping the last of his strength to fuel his stubbornness. But then his will betrayed him, too, and he felt himself seeping away into the ground beneath him, ebbing into nothingness.

And he didn't want to die still wondering.

"Show me," he finally said.

Dragon steps padded closer. "It will require you opening your eyes," he said. "Seeing things as they really are."

"Show me," Jastin said again.

A cool, scaly palm pressed against Jastin's eyes.

Instantly, Jastin was flying. Up and over bright evergreen treetops, he felt his arms as wings, soaring, pumping, sensing danger, and hurrying toward it.

Below, he heard a conversation. Voices drifted toward him, and he could hear them as clearly as though the people were standing beside him, although he was high in the sky and far from any humans.

"I'm not going with you," said a woman. Rimin. His wife.

Jastin's heart seized, but the vision in his mind was too powerful and consuming to be distracted from it.

"You promised," said the voice of a man Jastin didn't recognize.

"I promise a lot of things," said Rimin. "What makes you think I would keep mine to you?"

"We were to be a family," said the man. "I gave up my post. I left everything behind."

"You don't want to be a farmer," said Rimin. "And I don't want to be a farmer's wife."

"You are a soldier's wife," said the man.

"In name only. I am the daughter of a Venur, and in time the lands will be mine. Mine, to pass to the child I carry."

"*My* child," said the man. "The child of a lowly guard in the Venur's service. Do you really think your brother will allow you to claim the rights you released upon marriage, and to pass the lands to a child fathered by infidelity?"

"My brother has little choice. It is my father's decision, and I am still the elder. A grandchild is a perfect gift of repentance."

"*My* child!" the man said again. "Will you tell that to your father? Your husband?"

"No, Tarmus," said Rimin. "I'm not going to mention that. And neither are you."

"Rimin, what are you—?" The man grunted, and, within the vision, Jastin sensed the sliding of a knife into his gut. His backhand to Rimin's face, Rimin's scream, and a brief struggle that left his wife bleeding out onto the cold ground, with the man standing over her, his own blood dripping and mingling into hers.

"Well, now," said a third voice, joining the scene. Jastin knew it immediately to be Whitetail. "Isn't this a curious fix."

"She stabbed me," said the man. "She promised. But she stabbed me."

"Yes, I see," said Whitetail. "The foolish woman tried to kill a trained soldier. Pardon me, ex-soldier. Oh, don't look at me like a frightened rabbit, Tarmus, honestly. I was coming here to do much the same thing to her, only without so much blood."

Now the vision drew nearer to the scene, and Jastin could see them all, Tarmus hunkered and stunned, his wife lying askew on the grass, and Whitetail circling them both. Still from above, he also saw himself—which sent a distressing chill through him—running through the trees, pushing leaves and branches away from his face, alerted by his wife's scream.

"You've done me a bit of a favor," said Whitetail to Tarmus. "Now I'll do you one. Run."

The man didn't hesitate. He plunged into the trees.

Whitetail spat flames in a circle around Rimin's body with no more effort than a yawn. Then he turned toward the direction of Jastin's clumsy and noisy approach, and drew in a deep breath for another attack.

But the vision descended, and Jastin felt himself blast heat at Whitetail, singeing the dragon's scales.

Whitetail lurched skyward, and the vision arched up in pursuit.

"Enough," Jastin cried, trying to pry the dragon paw from his face. "Stop!"

The dragon slowly withdrew his touch. As he did, light filled in around Jastin's sight, stinging, speckling his brain with pinpricks like hot ash. He winced, and blinked, and as his eyes adjusted, he stared openly at the dragon that blinded him in a different way—by glowing golden-bright as the desert sun, and streaming the color of his scales across Jastin, and to the rock behind him, and the ground beneath him.

The Gold.

"But you killed her," Jastin said, sounding childish to his own ears.

"See the truth, Jastin Armitage."

The truth. That he'd believed all these years the Gold had killed Rimin, unprovoked. His wife, and his child. But what the Gold had really done was save Jastin.

Unprovoked.

Every death of every dragon after that day had been a substitute for the unreachable Gold. Every death was an innocent sacrifice to Jastin's hatred. Blues, Greens, Browns… he'd hacked them down and chopped them into trophies. And he'd relished it. As though bringing down one more monster would serve to rid the world of evil.

"The truth," said Jastin, arching forward to press his forehead to the ground at the Gold's feet. His hatred loosed like the vomit from his stomach. His anger unknotted, revealing shame and regret, which were the real monsters he'd been trying to kill. "What have I done?" he whispered. "What have I done?"

He lifted his head, staring up into the dragon's majestic, golden face. "You should have let me die that day. You shouldn't have saved me."

"But I did save you," said the dragon. "With good reason."

"What reason?" Jastin asked. "What possible good reason could there be?"

"That is what I have been hoping you would show me."

Jastin crumpled again to the ground.

And he wept.

Chapter Seventeen

Drell sat at the back of his sandstone cave, watching Bannon talk to Leesa while the girl gestured and nodded. Even wearing the burlap sackcloth his tribe had mustered for the shapeshifter, Drell remembered Bannon in a black and purple uniform, as one of the Esra men who'd pinched and battered his wings, tried to shove a ring in his nose before the hunt. He liked the man better as an eagle, a flying creature much smaller than himself. As a human, Drell disliked and distrusted him.

But Drell trusted Leesa. And so, for the moment, he would give them both some of his time.

"All right," said Bannon, lowering his arms to his sides. He regarded Drell as though Drell was the suspicious one. "Leesa believes she has found you, and she's not the capricious type."

"I didn't realize I was lost," said Drell.

Bannon smiled a little. "We need to explain ourselves."

"I would like that."

The man glanced at Leesa, who nodded, and opened her hands, signaling Bannon to continue. He finally did.

"We are from the forest. Murk Forest. To the far east of Leland."

"Leland?" asked Drell. "I believe that is my birth place."

"Is it? Does that explain why you are the only color of your kind here? After seeing your tribe, you seem to be an original."

Drell hadn't thought of himself in quite that way, but he liked it. It softened him toward the man. "I am a borrowed dragon," he said. "With ties to Leland that haven't really been explained to me. I only know what Vaya Brownwing has told me; that I am not to reveal myself in my homelands."

"But you don't know why?"

Drell shook his head. "But I…" He hesitated.

Leesa stepped forward, her dark eyes probing. Expectant. He knew she was reassuring him she could be trusted, but it wasn't Leesa he was hesitating over.

She looked at Bannon.

"I met a dragon in the Esra forest yesterday. During the hunt. You remember that, don't you Bannon?" Drell's voice was flat. "The hunt?"

Bannon turned away, and leaned one arm against the cave wall. He was silent for a long time. Then, "I remember. I'm sorry."

Drell had expected posturing, or excuses, or

something other than a heartfelt apology. Now Drell remained silent.

"For what it's worth," said the man, "I hated it. Hated myself for it. I've been a part of Esra for so long, I wondered if, when it came to it, I would have the guts to take a stand, and risk revealing myself."

"Someone else did."

"Yes. Sela made the move I should have made." Bannon turned to face Drell again, smiling gently. "She's very brave."

Leesa nudged Bannon with her elbow. Bannon sobered. "I'm relieved it worked out the way it did. Likely, it all came together for this reason, but the truth is, if fate brought us here, it has everything to do with Sela, and not me. So I don't blame you for not trusting me."

"I don't blame me either," said Drell. "So at least we have that in common." He studied them both for a time, and then settled onto his haunches, resigned to listen, for now. "So why are we here?"

Leesa stepped out behind them, and circled around Bannon to stand before Drell. She smiled, a deep, emanating smile, and then captured Drell's face, placing either hand on his jawline.

Drell felt heat and blood rush into his face, and was glad for his dark scales, and the obscuring night. Especially when Leesa pressed a kiss to the tip of his nose.

When she turned to embrace Bannon, Drell took the opportunity to shake the embarrassment from his face, and to redistribute the blood back into his chest and legs. Well, the best he could, anyway.

Leesa drew back from the embrace. Then she gave them both a light wave, and began climbing back over the rocky dunes, back toward the Esra forest.

"Where is she going?" asked Drell.

"Back to the castle."

"In the dark?"

Bannon's eyes tracked her climb over the sandstone crags, and then turned to Drell. "The wilds are her true home. She knows her way."

"I thought she would stay," said Drell.

"She'll go back for now. She brought me to you, and that's what's important now."

"Brought you?"

Bannon regarded Drell silently for a time, seeming to search for words. Then he spoke. "Murkeans have been searching for a dragon," he said.

Drell strained to remember what Vaya had told him of Murk Forest. Precious little. It was a place of danger and darkness, and even dragons respected it by keeping distant.

"We've been searching for a hidden dragon," said Bannon. "Born of the mountains, of a leader of the mountains. Taken from his kind and kept unaware of his own power and strength."

Drell shifted his weight on his haunches, prickling at the sound of where this was going. "And?" he asked.

"And Leesa thinks we're found him. She believes you're the one."

Drell had the impulse to laugh, but seeing the seriousness of Bannon's face, he kept his amusement to himself. "I suppose you're going to explain to me exactly what that means?"

"I am," said Bannon. "But get comfortable. It's a long story."

§

Jastin awoke slowly, his bones weary. His first thought was that he'd been dreaming, or hallucinating, and the conversation with the Gold hadn't been real. But then he shifted his weight, recognized the ground beneath him, and the lingering scent of peppered dragon musk, as well as his own stale scent of having been ill and out of doors for the past…days? He'd lost track.

But he didn't feel ill now. Only weak, and hungry. Plus, hollow. As though with his anger gone, he had nothing to replace it with.

He tested his arms, pushing up to sit. When he opened his eyes, he found darkness, and for a moment he panicked, thinking he was still blind. But then a fractal golden glow made its way into his awareness, and he rubbed his hands over his face. "I was just thinking if I'd dreamed you."

The reply was a crackle and hiss of burning sap. He lowered his hands.

He'd awoken to nighttime. The glow was a campfire. Maybe he *had* dreamed up the Gold.

The fire was forcing warmth into his skin and filling his nostrils with the scent of autumn. And sizzling meat. His mouth watered. He crawled toward the flames, spying a slab of rabbit skewered at the end of a stick. His gaze followed the stick to find a woman—he'd forgotten her name—holding the stick over the heat, watching him.

She offered it to him.

He took it, opening his mouth for a greedy bite. But she touched the stick, pausing it, frowning lightly.

"Oh," said Jastin. "I, uh. Thank you."

She smiled. Then she shook her head. She puckered her lips, very near to his face. He blinked at her mouth.

She blew over the searing meat.

"Oh," he said again. "Right." He cleared his throat, and then blew over the rabbit, too, and tested it with his fingers, before he ripped off a glistening piece and shoved it into his mouth.

She sat back and nibbled at her own rabbit-on-a-stick she'd already prepared. "Your name," he said around the food in his mouth. "It's Leesa?"

She nodded.

"I'm Jastin."

She nodded again.

"I'm supposed to be dead."

She lowered her food to regard him.

He shoved more rabbit into his mouth to keep it from babbling.

Leesa continued to watch him, campfire lighting her burnished brown eyes. Maybe it was her silence, or her patient expression, but Jastin felt awkward and conspicuous, and he wished she could speak. He opened his mouth to say something about how surprised he was at finding a woman who was too quiet, but what came out was, "Have you ever heard of a gold dragon?"

Her delicate eyebrows arched.

"I think I spoke to him. Or I hallucinated him." But the dragon had showed Jastin things about his life that Jastin didn't even know. Could he have dreamed up all of it?

Even as he thought it, he knew it had been real. The conversation. The vision. He knew it had happened, because he was he was strangely empty inside, and feeling set loose to drift. And Jastin had never drifted. Ever. All his life, even in his youth, he'd been driven.

Since Rimin's death, all his motives had melded into one single purpose, giving his determination a focus. Strength. But now, that purpose was gone. Vanished. In the blink of his opened eyes.

Without it, he didn't know what to do next.

He found her smiling the sweet, indulgent smile of a mother tucking her child into bed. Jastin bristled inwardly. "You think I'm still sick. That it's the poison making me a blithering idiot."

She shook her head. She set down her rabbit, pushed to her feet. Then she took Jastin's food away, and tugged at his arm, encouraging him to stand. He tilted, light-headed, but recovered enough to follow her a few steps away from the fire, and out of the warm circle of light. Then she took his hand, holding it up between them.

Jastin's skin faintly illuminated, as though he'd been dunked in starlight. "What is that?" he asked.

Leesa pointed to the small pocket on his leather vest. He patted it, and then he slipped in his fingers. They discovered an object, grooved but smooth, and he withdrew it. He held a scale, a golden, glowing dragon scale the size of a flat chestnut. "How did you…?"

She took the scale, pressed it into his hand, curled his fingers around it. Then she opened his hand again, lifted the scale, examined it, and slipped it back into his vest pocket. Then she tapped her chest.

"Did you know what it was when you found it in my hand?" he asked.

She hesitated. Then nodded slowly.

Jastin retrieved the scale and turned it over. Of all the dragon trophies he'd collected over the years, this was the only one given to him freely. Emotion choked his throat, but he was already too tired and disjointed to give in to it. Despite his many faults, his inner strength had always served him well, and he rallied it again.

This time, his focus rose up to fill in with a new purpose.

"Do you know where we are?" he asked her. "And how to get to Riddess village?"

She nodded.

"Then I need your help, if you're willing to give it. I need you to lead me to the village, where I can muster a horse. I need to go home."

CHAPTER EIGHTEEN

"**Y**ou killed him," Avara whispered, clutching Sela's tunic, wringing it as though she wished it was Sela's neck.

"He isn't dead," said Sela. "He isn't." She held up the purple linking stone, as dark and lifeless as Ebouard's face had been.

But Sela remembered the story of her parents. Her mother had called out the ancient words "May vita en dae" to save her father, and died in his place. Except she wasn't dead, exactly. Her father and mother had shared a linking stone.

"Take the stone," Sela said. "You'll feel him in there."

Avara held the amethyst crystal, her pale face damp with tears. Sela watched, hoping, praying, that she'd done the right thing. That Ebouard only seemed dead, but could somehow, some way, still be saved.

After a breathless moment, Avara blinked. Soft, purple light infused her weary features. "He's there," she said. Her eyes flicked upward to Sela's face, and a hopeful smile diminished the pain in her eyes. "He's there," she said again.

"Thank the stars above," said Layce. She wrapped her arms around them both.

"What do we do now?" asked Gladdis.

Sela turned. Gladdis huddled against the damp stone wall of the dungeon cell they'd been thrown into. She shivered in the gloom. Cobwebs clung to the ends of her marigold-yellow hair. A swipe of dirt stained her cheek.

"Oh, Gladdis," said Sela, dropping to her knees before her friend. "I'm so sorry you're mixed up in this."

"What about your uncle? Can he help us?"

Orman. Sela had been asking herself the same question, and had been searching in her mind, sending out messages, desperately hoping he'd respond. He didn't. And she was as worried about him as she was about Gladdis. And herself.

"It isn't his fault," said Layce. She knelt beside them.

Sela sat back. "What do you mean?"

Layce closed her eyes. "He was going to take you out of the castle. I had to stop him."

Sela was grateful to be kneeling, because she grew suddenly dizzy. "Did you hurt him? Layce, what did you do?"

"I didn't hurt him." Her blue eyes opened. "But he won't be coming to help us."

Gladdis spun around onto her knees, too. "You're a wizard. You got us into this, now get us out."

"Layce isn't a wizard," said Avara, her shoulders

stiffening. She joined the others on the floor, settling onto the damp cobblestone floor. "How could she have anything to do with this?"

"Why don't you ask her?" Sela said, crossing her arms.

"They're right," said Layce. "This is my doing."

Avara turned, and Sela studied her profile. The deep lines in her face had reduced. Her silvery gray hairs had faded. Avara seemed to be strengthening, while the rest of them were tired, rumpled, and weakened.

"Well?" Avara asked Layce.

"I needed a reason to stay so I could look for you, didn't I?"

"What are you saying?"

"I'm saying I took the position Father left open. I became the Venur's wizard."

"But, Layce!" She reached behind her neck, fastening the linking stone. Then she faced Sela. "She's no wizard," she said, looking from Sela to Gladdis. "You can't blame her for her mistakes."

"We can blame her for her choices," said Gladdis. "She used magic to trick Sela into getting married. I felt it."

"And she's done something to my uncle."

"Anyone can learn spells," said Avara. "Anyone can recite the words, wave a crystal."

"That's not true," said Layce. She stood, and paced toward the cell door. "Self-righteous wizards say that. But not just anyone can learn magic." She leaned back against the bars, and regarded Sela. "No one is more surprised than me when my magic works, but it does work. Most of the time." Then she wrinkled up her mouth. "Well, some of the time."

"You're no wizard, Layce," said Avara. She shook her head at her sister, and looked at Gladdis. "She's a Seer."

"A what?" asked Gladdis.

"A Seer," said Layce. "I know things. Things as they were. Things as they will be."

"Well, can you see a way out of this place?" asked Gladdis.

"It doesn't work like that."

"Of course not," said Gladdis. She crossed her arms, and stalked toward the iron bars of their cell, leaving footprints in the floor's dirt and dust.

"I can," said Sela.

Layce, Gladdis, and Avara all turned to stare at her.

"I see it," said Sela. At first, she'd been too distracted to look. But Layce walked away from the back of the cell, and then Gladdis, and then Sela spotted the tell-tale crack in the wall, and the felt the blackness of a dark passage just beyond it. She stepped to the stones, digging her fingers, searching.

Avara stood. She ran her hands over the crags, too. "What do you see?"

"An obscureway?" asked Gladdis.

"A what?" asked Layce.

"For a wizard, you don't know much about dragons," said Sela.

"Layce isn't a wizard," said Avara.

Layce just grumbled something quietly, and then joined Sela and Avara in touching the wall.

"I've discovered obscureways all over this place," said Sela. "I think they're part of a tunnel network, all dragon-sized and part of some kind of old Esra."

Her fingers found a latch. The floor rumbled. The wall shook, sending a shower of granite dust and cobwebs into their faces. "Come on," Sela urged the wall.

It shuddered and broke free, rocking them all on their feet. The wall thundered open to reveal a cavernous blackness.

"What did you call this?" Layce asked.

"An obscureway. Dragons create them."

"Where does it go?" asked Gladdis.

"Let's find out," said Layce. "But wait." She hurried back to the cell bars, reached her thin arm through them, wrestled a torch sconce from the dungeon hallway, and then carefully drew the flaming thing between the bars again. She carried it to them. "I'll go first."

"Be my guest," said Gladdis.

"Let's all get in there," said Sela. "The noise might send a guard coming in to check." She pulled Gladdis by the hand, and Avara stepped into the passage behind.

When Sela activated the latch again, the wall rattled and ground back into place, sealing them into the darkness.

Layce's torch brightened their faces, their feet, and the nearest dirt wall, but did little to find a path.

"I hate these things," said Gladdis.

"Come on," said Sela, taking Gladdis's hand. "I'm

sure there's a way out at the other end."

"Tell me again how you found this," said Avara, her hand gripping the stone around her neck, her eyes searching ahead through the blackness.

"I don't know," said Sela. "I just sense them. I see the wall for what it is. A doorway."

"That's a kind of talent we could all use," said Avara.

"It's not just talent," said Layce, carrying the torch forward. Her left hand dragged along the dirt tunnel, collecting grime around her fingertips, leaving a trail. "Sela has magic beyond any wizard."

"No, I don't." Sela followed Layce, pulling Gladdis. "I'm no good at anything, except getting in the way. Making trouble for the ones I care about. How do you all think you got here?"

Once, she'd thought she was something special. She'd indulged in believing she had a place in this world, and a calling. To be one with the sky, and one with her art. To create something where it had never before existed.

"What changed?" asked Layce. She disappeared around a turn, leaving only orange torchlight glowing just ahead of them.

"Layce?" called Avara from the back of the group.

"We have a choice to make," called Layce.

"What kind of choice?" asked Gladdis.

Then they stepped into a giant cavern. Crystalline stalactites absorbed Layce's flame and exhaled it back out, transforming the few light lumens into a thousand. The cavern shimmered nearly bright as day.

"We can see!" Gladdis, filthy and crumpled, smiled. She gazed up at the blades of translucent stone. "Look at that."

"Yes," said Avara, moving around them to join Layce. She turned in a slow circle, examining the choices Layce had meant.

Three tunnels sloped away from the cavern.

"Sela?" Avara asked. "What do you see now?"

"Me?" Sela asked. How did she become the guiding leader of the group?

"If you knew who you are, really understood, you wouldn't have to ask that question," said Layce. "You can choose. You know the way."

Sela was tired of being reminded how lost she was. She didn't need an underground maze and a wizard to keep pointing it out.

"That way," she said, pointing randomly. If she was going to get them *all* lost, she might as well do it really, really well.

"Let's go," said Layce. She trudged forward without hesitating. So did Avara.

"But I like this room," said Gladdis.

"You want to stay?" Sela asked.

Gladdis scowled.

Several yards into the tunnel, Sela stopped. "Wait," she whispered.

The others paused.

"I smell something."

Gladdis looked from Sela, to the unending blackness ahead of them. Avara sniffed. Layce narrowed her eyes.

"Yes," said Layce. "Me too."

A dragon. Spice, acid, musk. Sela tried to block the scent by pinching her nose, but her brain had already memorized it, and her throat stung. "I think it's him," she said.

"Blackclaw?" asked Layce.

"Let's go back and choose a different way," said Gladdis.

"Wait." Layce held up her hand. "Chances are this is the way out, if Blackclaw uses it. We can follow him."

"I don't think he's leaving."

"Then we'll settle down right where we are, and we'll wait," said Layce. She dropped to floor, and sat cross-legged. Avara sat beside her.

"What if he finds us?" Gladdis tugged on Sela's hand, the torchlight finding the fear in her eyes.

"Then we'll hide in one of the other passages."

Gladdis settled slowly beside Layce, unconvinced, but quiet.

Sela sat too, across from them all. She rested her spine against the cool dirt wall. After a time, in the silence and flickering light, with the smooth earth at her back and the musty smell of the tunnel, mixed with dragon scent, she was oddly comforted.

"So what changed?" asked Layce.

"Hm?"

"You once believed you had a calling. To create something where it never before existed."

Had Sela said that? Had she thought it? She didn't

quite remember.

"So what changed?" Layce asked again.

She regarded the women in the tunnel. They waited, expectantly, for her reply.

"I did," she told them.

She couldn't pinpoint the exact moment; the memory was too buried, too deeply disguised to be able to recall it. "One day I was happy and in love with my life. And then I was different." Small and weak. Plain and disappointing.

She'd looked up into the eyes of her father for answers, he'd looked back at her with confusion and distance. And she knew she'd failed him.

"You didn't fail him, Sela Redheart," said Layce. "You exceeded him."

At the sound of her name, her real name, tears rose. She was too drained to fight them. "I just want to go home."

Gladdis pushed away from tunnel wall and crawled to Sela. "I thought your name was Thistleby."

Sela shook her head. "I never said that."

"It was assumed," said Layce. "Smartly done. Brave." She tipped her head. "Dear girl, who you are has everything to do with all of this. But you're trapped. By the one moment when your fear won."

Sela dragged her fingers over her damp face, drying it. Layce and Avara held hands, sitting like bookends, each mimicking the same far-away depths in their eyes, the same slack jaw.

"What do you mean?" she asked.

The sisters spoke in unison. "You heard them coming. And you looked, and saw dragon teeth dangling from their pockets. Dragon claws strung around their necks."

Sela's memory unfolded in a rush, slamming against her skull so that it jarred her. It was true, she'd seen the human males, one of them on horseback, and the other two walking alongside. She'd been painting, hiding in her perfect place, but they were trudging up the mountainside and she was perched beneath an overhang, concealed from above, not below. For a moment, she almost flew, but she knew they would see her. And in that same moment, she knew for certain that once they saw her, they would kill her.

So she didn't fly. She didn't move. She wedged in and under the outcropping, tightening herself into the smallest, tiniest bundle she could manage. She wished and wished and wished to never be seen.

Then a man spoke. She opened her eyes to find him, not poised with a weapon, but smiling. "Well, hey there," he said. "You're a long way from home, little one. Are you lost?"

"No sir," she'd said with a voice she didn't recognize. She reached for her art satchel with hands, not claws. She fumbled to press the pack against her smooth, cold, too-tight skin.

"Hungry?" asked the man.

She shook her head.

"Let's go, Eustan," said the man on the horse. "You can't be a father to every little urchin." The men shared a jovial laugh.

"Be safe, little one," said Eustan. And they left, trudging up the mountain, scattering pebbles and pine needles.

And she was. Safe.

Until she ran all the way around the mountain, past the Leland arena, up the marble steps of the manor, and into the Great Hall. "Father, Father," she called, trembling, naked, and puny.

Human.

Just as quickly and harshly as the memory came, it faded. Sela was left trembling, and feeling naked and puny.

"We see you for who you really are, Sela Redheart." said the sisters. Then Layce blinked, coming to as though from a sleep.

"Now it's your turn," she said.

"I don't know how," said Sela.

"You do. The ability is within you."

Gladdis's cool hand touched Sela's arm.

For a time, they sat quietly, listening to the crackle of the fading torch, and spending moments in their own thoughts, their own weariness.

Then Avara spoke. "Is she really who we saw in the vision?" she whispered.

"She really is," Layce whispered back.

§

Kallon's wings slumped wearily against the air.

Morning had dawned, red-orange and suffused with the back-lit sparkle of salt air. The day promised to be warm and clear; the kind of day Kallon would normally indulge in hours of unfettered flight.

But he'd been airborne since early yesterday, and rather than being closer to their destination across the sea, Kallon and Riza were back to where they'd started, and still miles from the shore of Leland Province.

"If we don't take a break," said Kallon to Riza, who drooped heavily, like a soggy, red cloud, "...we'll be swimming soon."

She didn't reply, although she did seem to startle awake from some sort of hazy near-sleep. She blinked at him, and then swept her gaze along the horizon.

"We won't make Reacher's Pass for hours. We can catch the edge of Leland near the eastern jut. We need to land, to rest, and to hunt."

"She needs us."

"I know. But we can't help if we drown here."

"We know how to swim."

"It's not about knowing how." Kallon had just enough strength to pass her, and to curve around to block her path, to slow her. "We can barely push air, how will we manage water?"

She bumped her snout into his throat, her steering off kilter. "Very well," she said, her voice low and disappointed, and resonant with blame. As though Kallon's weariness was her burden.

"East, from here," he said.

"No. No, we'll push on to the mountain shore."

"But that's another several miles. The east jut is closer."

"I'm not going east," she said. "There is little cover, and the villagers near the shore will shoot us from the sky before we can even see the land."

"How do you know that?"

"I just do."

She'd never told him before about dangerous, mysterious villagers. Not in all the times she'd spent traveling this way, collecting scrolls for the library. Kallon swerved left, toward the east. "We either take our chances with the jut, or risk drowning before we reach the mountain shore."

He thumped his wings and stretched out, aiming toward the east without looking back. He often indulged Riza's stubbornness, but not this time. She avoided an obvious solution for no good reason that he could fathom. He only hoped she'd follow him. He wasn't sure what to do if she didn't.

But she did. Sensing her growing frustration, which seemed to be the only emotional mortar that connected them lately, he remained silent and allowed her to stew. At least she'd joined him. It felt a small victory.

And then he was struck by a thought. Maybe Riza wasn't resisting turning east because she didn't wish to go there, but because she didn't want Kallon to go. To find something Riza didn't wish him to see.

Maybe *he* was there. Somewhere near. The dragon, or, heavens forbid, the human, who had caught Riza's eye. Kallon's invisible rival. In the lands to the east. Or one of those dangerous villagers.

Now he wished he hadn't insisted.

But like it or not, it had been the right choice. Even as the coastline shimmered into view before them, seducing them closer as a mirage, Kallon's reserves gave out, and he dropped suddenly toward the ocean's foamy, ragged surface. He tried to pull up, but his wings brushed the water, and even the minute weight of dampness overcame him. He splashed hard, too fast, and tumbled forward, spraying water and sand and scratching his chest and neck across shards of pulverized seashells.

When the water settled, and Kallon had righted himself, he stood ankle deep. Riza was on shore, and twisted with a great shake that rippled from her head and neck, across her ribs, and through her sparkling, ruby tail, dislodging the seawater with which Kallon had inadvertently showered her.

By the time he'd loped onto the shore beside her, she'd already found a craggy boulder to lean against, and was curled up, mimicking its sloping shape, and seemed instantly asleep.

He perched beside her, regarding the landscape. The sea nudged his backside and played at his tail, covering and uncovering it as each wave swelled and retreated. He would have liked to walk farther inland, but Riza had been right about poor cover. From the shoreline to the lumpy ridges of village rooftops in the far distance, only a single, sparse ribbon of palmbushes and pompous grass snaked from the sand to the fat planks of fencing surrounding the village. The bushes outlined the village barrier in porcupine tufts and hedgerat spikes.

Boulders erupted here and there, offering the only camouflage, and Riza had found the largest. He hunkered down beside her, and with the ocean tickling against his ribs, he closed his eyes.

Moments later, splashing footsteps roused him. At least, it felt like moments, except when he opened his eyes, the sun had made its way deeply across the sky, and cast long, looming shadows of the rooftops and boulders, as stretching fingers reaching for his resting place.

And a pair of gray eyes, as dark as a winter sky, stared from a young, male, human face.

A boy stood frozen, a fishing stick in his hands, his trouser legs rolled up to his knees. A basket hung at his hip, dangling from a leather strap over his shoulder. He gaped at Kallon.

"I mean no harm," Kallon said.

The boy jolted when Kallon spoke. He regarded Riza, still sleeping, and then Kallon again. Then his hand moved slowly to the lid of his basket, and he pulled it open, his eyes still fixed on Kallon's face. He dipped his hand into the basket, and withdrew a weakly flailing spongefish, its jaundiced scales like a ray of sun in the boy's hand. He tossed the fish at Kallon's feet.

Kallon dipped his head and sucked the creature down his throat.

The boy's face crinkled in amusement. He threw

another fish. Kallon gobbled it, too.

With the third fish, Kallon nudged Riza. She lifted her snout, blinked dreary eyes, and spotted the treat near her paw. She pulled it between her teeth, just as she saw the boy. She went still, the spongefish tail dangling.

The boy laughed.

Riza swallowed the fish, and looked from the boy to Kallon.

Then a voice called out, "Armen! Don't move!"

Kallon swiveled toward the voice, discovered a hunched man running toward them, a bow drawn, and an arrow already nocked.

"No, Father," cried the boy.

"We mean no harm," said Kallon, fumbling to rise up on weary legs.

Riza emerged from behind the boulder, moving stiffly, her emerald gaze riveted on the approaching man. She stared without blinking, one paw curled against her chest, and Kallon could feel, and hear, the thrumming of her heartbeat, even over the surf and the hammer of his mind's warnings.

The man released the arrow, directly at Riza's chest. The tip bounced off with a hollow thud, and broke Riza from her stare.

"Go," she said, and leaped skyward.

Kallon didn't know where she found the strength to fly, but he followed her, up and away, his wings like stone, and flailing. He glanced down to find the man beside his son, aiming another arrow. The boy set his hand on the bow and lowered it. The two humans watched them escape.

"I told you," she said through her teeth, gritting to keep flying, keep moving.

"The boy fed us. Only the man was dangerous."

"That man was my father."

Riza's words nearly shook Kallon from the sky. "What?"

"That village is Cresvell. That man was my father."

Kallon looked behind himself, at the retreating hulk of village slapped in place between the sea and the flatlands, miles from the foothills of the mountains, existing wholly separate from any other Leland settlement. Lonely. Friendless.

"The boy who fed us. You never mentioned a brother."

"I didn't know I had one."

He looked forward, orienting himself, trying to find mountaintops and hints of home. "We've never really talked about your home village, Riza," he said.

She glanced toward him, her green eyes dark. Her face tight. If she was tired, he couldn't find evidence in her expression.

"Never ask me to come near it again," she said.

§

"He's moving," said Sela.

Gladdis jerked awake. Layce pushed to her feet. Avara stretched, and then shifted her weight. "Thank goodness," she said. "I'm all knots and cramps."

The tunnel, for a moment soothing, had turned cold, small, and stifling to Sela. She'd lost track of how long they'd waited, and Layce's torch was growing ever dimmer. Finally, the dragon scent she'd been keeping track of was pulling away, further into the warren. She only hoped Blackclaw, if it was indeed him, was moving toward an exit.

Chapter Nineteen

Jastin trudged through the woods, his heavy boots as noisy as his thoughts. He was too distracted and feeling hungover from the last couple of days to concentrate on a cautious prowl.

Leesa guided him well around sharp blackberry thorns and over smooth, battered underbrush. Bright summer still clung to green elm leaves and ruffled oak, but the trees were somber, scenting fall, or perhaps seeing it approach from their towering vantage point. He felt an impulse to climb one, to borrow their view, and to orient. But Leesa confidently led, and so he followed, and he used the silence to sift through his chaotic mind.

If Whitetail poisoned him, it would have been at the beck of Riddess. The dragon didn't relieve himself without permission from the man. Although Jastin had always wondered about the White, and how much subservience was an act. Pliant, directed, and coy, but there had been moments when Jastin caught a grim smirk here or there.

In the least, Whitetail was always thinking.

What would he be thinking now? That Jastin was dead? Or would he be looking for his body, and evidence?

The sound of scuffling feet sounded to his right. Too light to be Whitetail or Vorham, but too numerous for a single person. Leesa turned toward the sound, too, and then ducked, invisibly, behind a tree. Jastin had never in his life hidden from anyone. But, just this once, he took her lead, and stepped behind a fat oak.

"I'm starving," said a woman's voice. "And I've been wearing this dress for three days."

"We're all hungry," said another voice.

"We can eat later."

The third voice he recognized. He stepped out. "Layce?"

She startled, and drew a faintly younger and shorter version of herself closer. A third person, the young girl from the castle, busily disentangled her blonde hair from the tip of a scrawny pine branch.

Then Layce squinted. "Jastin? Thank heaven."

He never expected to hear those words from her mouth. "What are you doing here?"

"I'd ask you the same," she said. "You look like death warmed over."

"It's a long story."

"It always is."

He regarded her, a half-smile on his dry mouth. never expected to be glad to see her, either, but in fact, he was.

She smiled, too, slowly. "Well," she said. "I guess even a wizard can't predict everything."

"You're no wizard," whispered the short Layce look-alike.

"This is my sister, Avara," said Layce, removing her hands from the woman's shoulders.

"You have a sister?"

"Leesa!" The girl who managed to free herself from the pine tree rushed forward and nearly tackled his guide in an embrace. How long the silent woman had stood there, he didn't know, but she released a sort of breathy grunt beneath the crushing hug, and smiled.

"Gladdis," pointed Layce. "And now that we've been introduced, I'd like to keep moving, toward some possible food and a definite bath…" She sniffed toward Jastin, "…for *all* of us."

"Who are you running from?" asked Jastin. The women still hadn't explained themselves, but he knew by their condition, and the fear in their eyes, they were escaping.

"We're fugitives," said Avara. She touched a purple crystal that dangled around her neck. Amethyst. Jastin recognized something about it.

"Too much to explain," said Layce. "But we've just come from the dungeon."

"Dungeon?" Jastin stared from woman to woman.

The blonde girl, Gladdis, began quietly crying. "Me, Sela, Avara, and Layce."

"For murdering Ebouard Riddess," said Layce.

Jastin narrowed his eyes, trying to decide if Layce

was making some kind of sick joke. "Riddess has been dead for, what? Ten years?"

"He isn't dead!" Layce's sister gripped the amethyst even tighter.

"I told you it's too much to explain," said Layce. "And we're tired and hungry. And we need *bathing*," she said toward Jastin pointedly.

"Why isn't Sela with you?" Jastin asked.

Gladdis's crying turned decidedly louder. He was sorry he asked.

"She went back," said Layce.

"To the dungeon?"

"To the castle. Orman Thistleby is still there."

"She refused to come with us," said Gladdis. "After all that work to get us out of the tunnels, she wouldn't come with us!"

"She'll be all right, Gladdis," said Layce, patting the girl's shoulder, looking to be more annoyed than sympathetic. And there was something else behind Layce's expression. She was working very hard to hide something.

"She'll be all right," she said again.

"I was heading home," he said. "I have something to do." He regarded the women again, all of them with pale eyes, or blue eyes, or eyes as brown as metallic earth. Each of them watching him. Expecting something from him. But Jastin was no leader. No hero.

"You could come with me," he said. "But without horses, it's a long way."

"We have to walk?" moaned Gladdis, shriveling

into a husk.

"You heard him," said Avara. "Without a horse, what are we going to do? Fly?"

Just then, an eagle screamed, echoing against low clouds. Jastin turned to find the gold-feathered creature circle the treetops. And then a second form loomed over them, dousing them all in shadow.

A black dragon. A young one. He followed the eagle, circled once, and then dove for a landing in a sparse clearing.

Leesa waved, and hurried through the trees to meet him.

"You've got to be kidding me," said Jastin.

§

In his study, Vorham Riddess decanted a bottle of maple mead into his father's prized silver chalice. He leaned back in his chair, propped his feet onto his desk, and raised the chalice in salute to his father's portrait. "Good riddance," he said to the face. He drank deeply.

Fane Whitetail squeezed through the doorway. "Your eminence, the casket is being laid out for the viewing."

"Yes, yes," said Vorham, feeling so light and amiable this morning he didn't even mind the frivolous formalities. In fact, he'd been picturing this particular event in his mind for so long, now that it had finally come to pass, he was ready to celebrate. "Have a glass, Whitetail. Have two." He poured himself another.

"You might want to rethink your jolliness in front of the assembly and your citizens," said Whitetail.

"Why? What are they going to do? Fire me?" Vorham chuckled. "No one can touch me. Not now. Appearances don't matter anymore."

"Perhaps you're right. We have little need to hide behind them now. You should drink and celebrate your victory while you can."

Vorham tipped his chalice toward Whitetail, and nodded. Then he caught a flash behind the dragon's eyes. Vorham dropped his feet from the desk and sat forward. "What do you mean?"

Whitetail bowed low. "Before the tediousness of your leadership responsibilities take over once again," he said.

"Mm-hmm," murmured Vorham, knowing full well that isn't what the dragon meant.

"Well," said Whitetail. "And there is the business with the frozen wizard, Thistleby. And the escaped prisoners."

Vorham sighed in frustration, and then swallowed a mouthful of mead. The dragon did have a way of dampening spirits. "The wizard's been thrown into the dungeon?"

Whitetail nodded. "In a manner of speaking."

"And guards are tracking the women?"

Whitetail nodded again. "As many of your men as I could muster."

"Well," said Vorham. "We don't need Sela in person for the hearing, just the verdict on a piece of paper, so we'll gather the assembly while they're here for the viewing. And we can use the wizard as a stand-in, give the assembly the satisfaction of seeing *someone* pay."

"If we can't break the spell he's under?"

"Break it or don't." Vorham set his chalice on the desk. "He can still be thrown into the desert."

"And what about the women? They still know the truth."

"Knowing the truth and proving it are two separate things," said Vorham. "I can't be accused of a murder already committed by someone else."

"Very well," said Whitetail.

"Unless there's something about this that you know, and I don't."

Whitetail arched his scaly brows. "Such as?"

"You tell me."

For a moment, Whitetail remained silent, regarding Vorham with a steady gaze. Then he smiled. "I assure you, Your Eminence, that if I had any knowledge of developing events that you needed to be aware of, I would inform you."

"Of course you would," said Vorham, reading the lies in the dragon's eyes. But Whitetail had always been a flatterer, a sycophant, a deceiver. Pushing the issue would reveal nothing.

He poured himself a third cup of mead, and waved it beneath his nose, inhaling the malty scent. "Whitetail?" he asked. "How do you suppose she did it?"

"Your Eminence?"

"Sela. After healers and surgeons and wizards, all

these years. She steps into a room, and my father dies. He dies. Just like that."

"Perhaps she didn't kill him," said Whitetail. "Perhaps things are more complicated than they seem."

"If not her, then who?" Vorham shook his head. "No, there's something about that girl, Whitetail. I was drawn to her, compelled to marry her. I don't know how I knew, but I must have. I knew she would be my triumph."

"Or your undoing," said Whitetail. There was that flash behind his eyes again.

Vorham didn't bother to ask, he knew Whitetail would dodge a straight question. But he set down his mead, deciding against more drinking.

With that look in the dragon's eyes, Vorham couldn't risk losing his edge. No, no more mead. He needed to stay sharp.

Very sharp.

§

Sela crept through the trees, darting from one thick elm trunk to the next, closing in on Riddess Castle. She'd led her friends to the open air, and to safety, she hoped, but couldn't bring herself to go with them. Not when Uncle Orman still lay in the castle, abandoned and helpless.

He hadn't left her, not once, since this whole thing began. He'd followed her, fought for her, and risked for her. The least she could do for him was the same.

The problem was, she didn't know how to find him. Once she found him, she didn't know how she could help him. If she could help him, she didn't know how they would get back out.

If she kept thinking like that, she would talk herself right out of trying. So she just concentrated on the castle in the near distance, and made it her goal to reach it.

She was focusing so intently on the ruddy castle wall, she didn't even hear the batting of air above her, until a strong gust of it pushed against her face, and a spicy, musky scent stung her nostrils.

Blackclaw! She dove without thinking into a thicket of bramble bushes.

His landing was sudden, forceful. It rumbled the ground where she lay. "So we meet at last," said his reverberating voice.

Sela peeked up from the bushes to find his black eyes staring from a black gem face. He settled back, relaxing into a sitting pose, although his expression remained hard, focused.

She didn't speak.

"I've scented you in this castle. In my tunnels. I was expecting someone taller."

She was still crouching in the bushes, and so she pushed to stand. Brambles scratched her arms, raising blood, but she tried to ignore the sting. She disentangled from the branches and barbs, suddenly embarrassed on behalf of her Kind at her impulse to hide.

Blackclaw smiled. It carved eerily into his face, more menacing than friendly. "You cannot seem to keep yourself out of my way. I am not sure you even try. Now your wizard is stinking up my den, but do you know what I am going to do? I am going to let you go right in to fetch him."

"Orman?" asked Sela, trying to make sense of how her uncle managed it. "In the tunnel?"

"Orman Thistleby," said Blackclaw. "The harbinger of my coup." Blackclaw chuckled, but Sela didn't find humor in the sound of it. "I confess I did not expect that, of all things."

Sela pulled herself up, tried to stare at Blackclaw, undaunted. "I do not know what you—"

"And I might sooner snap your head from your shoulders than converse, on any other day," Blackclaw continued, "But you have turned out to be more than I first expected, as well."

The satisfaction in his tone made her cringe. She tried to sort out just what she'd done, or what she'd said, to make him so smug…and then it dawned on her their entire conversation had been in dragonspeak.

"Alas," he said. "I have neither the time nor the interest in delving into the mystery of this human girl with a dragon scent, who brings my old friend Thistleby to my home away from home. This insignificant speck of a life, who sets into motion the grandest scheme of a campaign even I had not before been able to initiate."

"I don't know what you're—", she tried to say again, this time in Common.

"No, of course you do not." Blackclaw billowed his wings, startling her. He shifted his weight, blocking the sunlight, enveloping her in shadow. "Suffice it to say I am delivering you as a gift to Whitetail, and I regret only that I lack a pretty ribbon with which to decorate you." He pumped his wings once, and bent his legs, preparing to leap. "Your wizard is in the dungeon cell. You know the way."

He lofted upward through the trees, drummed his wings, scattering leaves and broken twigs over Sela, and then swerved off and away from the castle. Sela watched him go, baffled at what, exactly, had just happened.

Tunnels? Whitetail? Pretty ribbon?

Orman in the dungeon cell.

She could figure out Blackclaw's threat later. First, she had to find Orman.

§

Vorham stood beside his father's stone casket in the chapel, nodding somberly to each citizen that filed through to pay their respects. There were few visitors now, but more would come as word spread. Eventually, his father's remains would need to be cleansed and ritualized, but for now, Vorham wanted the murder hearing done and finished with.

He could hardly think of anything else.

He counted his city's assemblage representatives; two from Meedes had arrived quickly. Three from South Morlan collected together, chatting quietly at the back of the room. Just one from Blaisvil would be enough to proceed.

Vorham caught the eye of Buce Vewel, his longtime representative from South Morlan. He nodded toward the exit. Then Buce stealthily gathered the four other men and women, and ushered them out of the chapel.

§

Sela found Orman. Even without a torch, she knew the tunnel, recognized the expansive cavern deep within it, and turned without doubt toward the obscureway that led her to the dungeon cell.

Now she shivered uncontrollably against the dank floor, holding Orman's cold and stiff body tightly, trying to warm him and not doing a good job of it.

When she'd first spotted Orman laid out, his eyes glazed, his skin like wax, she'd screeched, thinking him dead. But she hugged his chest, heard heartbeats. And so she tried to pry open his mouth to remove the solidifying crystal the way Layce had described, but his jaw was clenched tight. She couldn't wedge her fingers between his teeth. Couldn't pull his chin.

So she rubbed her hands against his cheeks, trying to warm them. She blew hot breath onto her fingers, massaged them together for friction, and pressed them against his mouth.

"I was just trying to give my parents what they wanted. A way to be together without worrying about me," she said to him. "If I'd stayed, you wouldn't have followed me." Tears welled, stinging her eyes, the back of her throat. "Help me help you, Uncle Orman! What do I do? What do I do?"

She shook his shoulders. She tugged at his arms. And then, in desperation, she screamed with as full a mind voice as she could muster into his sleeping brain. *Uncle Orman! Wake up!*

She closed her eyes. Waited. Listened to the *splat-splat* of moisture in the echoing cell.

"Now isn't this an interesting development," said a voice behind her. She spun to find Fane Whitetail, hunched against the dungeon ceiling, his pale eyes blinking in genuine surprise. "I've never heard of a prisoner breaking back into custody."

"Orman is sick," said Sela. "Please, you've got to help him."

"Have I?" Whitetail sauntered forward, and enwrapped his claws around the iron bars of the cell door. "Why would I do that? I was just coming to collect him for his hearing."

"Hearing? What do you mean?"

"The hearing for the murder of Venur Ebouard Riddess."

"Murder!? Orman didn't have anything to do with that!"

"Didn't he? What a travesty it would be that he stand in on your behalf, and face the justice due you," he said.

"What justice?" she asked.

"The desert," said Whitetail. "Esra justice has always been the desert." He dug a claw into the lock on the cell door, and clicked it open.

"Wait!" Sela stood. "I accept the justice. I'll go, instead. I'll say whatever you want me to say. If you promise to help him."

"You're a murderess, and you will meet the desert whether you say anything or not. Why should I make any promise to you?"

"Because I know," said Sela. She lifted her chin, and met Whitetail's gaze with as much courage as she could muster. She willed her voice to sound strong. "I know all about how you poisoned Ebouard Riddess."

Whitetail regarded her, his head tilting. He crossed his forelegs, his expression crinkling in faint amusement.

"And I know why he didn't die, no matter what you and Vorham tried. And I know he isn't dead now."

Whitetail's eyes went flat.

"I know who holds Ebouard's linking stone, and that he could be awakened to tell the truth."

Whitetail's face filled in with gray, like a cloud gathering itself into a thunderstorm.

"I even know about Blackclaw," she said, although she wasn't entirely sure what sort of threat it was.

Apparently, it was enough. A faint wisp of steam escaped Whitetail's snout. "You are meddling about in dark affairs," he said, his voice tight with warning.

"Take me, instead of Orman."

"Oh, I will," he said.

"And promise to help him. Free him. And I'll keep your secrets."

"You will die in the desert," he said.

She trembled then, and felt her façade slipping.

She looked back at Orman; at his ashen face, his death-haunted features. And she pulled in a deep, shaky breath. "Or I will talk. You decide."

"Done," said Whitetail. He surged into the cell and gripped her tunic.

"Wait," she cried. "I want to say goodbye!" She reached for Orman.

But Whitetail tugged her, and she only caught hold of Orman's beard. She dragged him along the floor with her, until Whitetail abruptly jerked her out of the cell.

Orman flopped forward, banging his face against the floor. She reached for him again, trying to right him, but she was lifted from her feet.

§

Orman Thistleby heard. From the moment his face slapped the dungeon floor, dislodging the stone behind his teeth, he began to awaken. His eyes began to focus. When Sela was taken, he knew what was happening, but all he could see was the dirt beneath his face. All he could feel was the crippling weight of the spell.

And then, his mouth open and his tongue askew, gravity found the stone. The crystal clung for a moment in the moisture of his mouth, as little as there was. And then it dropped. It hit the floor and bounced.

And Orman Thistleby could wiggle his fingers again.

§

Vorham stood in the center of the executive chamber behind a wooden podium. The podium creaked and threatened to disintegrate each time he rested his hand on it, so he tried not to touch it. But it looked official, felt official, and in this room that hadn't been used in years, the ritual helped validate the proceedings.

"As personal witness to the crime, I feel a swift action to justice is called for." He looked from face to face. The assembly members nodded.

"But one wizard does not account for all those of the plot," said Buce. "I demand the others pay for their crime when they're caught."

"No others were responsible," said Sela's voice from the doorway.

Vorham swiveled, so startled his heart actually skipped. He had to lay his fingers on his chest.

There she stood, his wife of twenty-four hours, her tunic and trousers stained with dirt, hems unraveling. Her braid dangled aside, half unwound, and she had streaks down her cheeks that must have been left by tears.

"You were captured?"

"She came of her own volition," said Whitetail's voice from the hallway.

The assembly members whispered together. Buce stood. "This is the murderess, then?"

"It is," said Vorham. This was going to be easier than he thought.

"I alone should be punished," said Sela. Her voice quavered, and her gaze stared at the floor. But her words were enough.

Self-convicting.

And perfect.

"She must face the desert before sundown," said Buce.

Each assembly member stood, one at a time, and voiced the same. "Before sundown."

"I will see to it myself," said Vorham. And he would bring along that mead, and that prized chalice, after all.

He'd drink one to Whitetail, for arranging this.

Despite his doubts about Whitetail's loyalties, that dragon came through again.

CHAPTER TWENTY

"Strange, how we keep meeting with bars between us, Wizard," oozed Fane Whitetail's voice through the dungeon door. Orman rolled to his side, covering the crystal that had dropped from his mouth. He hadn't recovered enough movement that he could talk, but he could glare, and he really put his effort behind it.

"Oh, come now, Thistleby," said Whitetail. "We have an established system, don't we? You get yourself imprisoned, and I show up to let you out. Save the day, and all that."

"Ah," Orman tried to vocalize. Direct contact with the solidifying crystal for so many hours on his tongue had rendered the organ no more useful than a slab of uncooked bacon.

Although bacon could be helpful, considering how hungry he was, now that his stomach was working again.

"Speechless, are we?" Whitetail slipped his claw into the lock on the iron bars. "Never mind, you can thank me later." He swung the bars open and stepped back, pointing one milky wing toward a torchlit hallway.

Orman moved his arms, testing them. He pushed up to sit. And since his arms worked, he crossed them. Now he really wished he had use of his tongue so he could stick it out.

Whitetail chuckled. "All right, I see we have an impasse, so I'll tell you something you'll want to know. Your niece, Sela, is on her way to the Rage Desert. She's confessed to murdering Venur Ebouard Riddess. You remember Ebouard, don't you?"

Orman stood on weakened, rickety legs. "Ah! Ah!"

"Please don't do that, it's very unbecoming of a wizard of your stature."

Orman shook his fist.

"As I was saying, about your Sela. She may be there already. If she lasts the afternoon, there's the frigid night temperatures…"

Orman rushed Whitetail, swinging the solidifying crystal, unable to mutter a spell, but he hoped for a good eye gouging, or at least an irritating paper cut.

Whitetail blocked him with a smooth poke of his scaly tail. "Should a man of your age exert himself?" He tsked. "Now, don't blame me. I was ready to feed you to the desert instead, and she up and made me promise to take her, instead. To save your scrawny hide."

Orman passed his hand over the crystal, warming it, causing a faint glow within it. Whitetail watched, distractedly, as he continued. "Odd thing that; her willingness to die for a murder she didn't even commit.

But humans are strange little things. In fact, this entire situation is the most curious situation I've had the pleasure of being involved in, and that's saying a lot, considering."

Orman slipped the warmed crystal behind his back.

"But what I'd really like to discuss with you is this linking stone she mentioned. The one keeping the senior Venur alive? I'm sure you heard my exchange earlier with your niece. She mentioned that the Venur isn't even dead, yet."

Whitetail stroked his claws along his jaw, dragging out a dramatic pause. Orman flipped his tongue around his mouth, trying to get the thing to form one word, any word, of a flame spout. Or a transformation spell. He did a mental check of all the crystals he had hidden on his person. Just one could at least shut the dragon's mouth, and buy himself enough time to get his legs working.

"It strikes me as an opportunity I'm willing to share with you, Thistleby. To both our advantages."

Orman didn't bother to vocalize. He stared flatly at the White.

"I'm thinking only of you, and the girl, of course. Because if, in fact, Ebouard Riddess could wake up, your Sela couldn't very well be blamed for his death, could she? I would see to it that Esra guards go find her at once, and set it all right again."

Orman held his stare.

"You see where I'm going with this."

Orman could see Whitetail's treachery, that's what

he could see. What he didn't know was whether or not Sela was in real danger. She'd been in the cell with him, and had been taken away. He'd heard the discussion about the desert. But Whitetail couldn't care less about Sela. What he cared about was his own agenda.

"I assure you Sela is in real danger," said Whitetail.

"Nee…me…for?" Orman struggled to say.

"Risky business, waking someone from a linking stone sleep," Whitetail said. He rested on paw on the edge of the wrought door. "But you know how it's done, don't you?"

Whitetail turned, then, and slinked into the dungeon hallway. "For the girl's sake, I hope you do. And now is as good a time as any, while the Esra assembly is gathered, and Vorham is away."

Whitetail paused, and turned his slender face over his shoulder to regard Orman. "To minimize distractions, of course."

§

"The sun is high," said Vorham. He dragged a cloth over his sweating forehead, and dropped it to the floor of the carriage. A bottle of mead rattled around on the seat beside him, and Sela watched it, hoping it would crash to the floor and splatter the man's legs.

During this carriage ride across the open fields and toward the west, the humidity thinned and the heat inflamed. She could feel them drawing closer to the desert even if she couldn't see the landscape through the windows, with its dried patches of grass aching for moisture, and thin, dehydrated trees that appeared as though a whisper of wind would disintegrate them.

Then the carriage stopped. Two guards clattered across the top of it, and then the carriage door swung open.

"This is as far as I go," said Vorham.

Sela felt glued to her seat. Not by any magic this time. By terror.

"You can say something on your behalf," said Vorham. "Last words, as it were."

Sela wanted to scream *I didn't do anything wrong!* But she was bound to her deal with Whitetail. She only hoped beyond hope that the dragon was holding up his end of the deal.

§

Whitetail paused in a deep hallway, outside a room. He offered his paw toward the open door, and when Orman stepped inside, he discovered it to be the castle chapel. Draping banners of purple and faded red hung from corner to corner. Candelabra lined the walls, and curled in waves toward an open casket seeping waterfalls of pink flowers.

He saw Ebouard Riddess's profile in the casket, as thin and dry as the paper hydrangeas decorating his coffin.

The Venur had no visitors, except for five men and women who sat on a bench against a side wall. They were trumped up in the official purple and black colors of Esra, and held themselves in the stiff way rich folks did that kind of thing when they were uncomfortable, but were trying to look like they weren't.

"Esra assembly representatives," said Whitetail. "Paying their respects. Shall I introduce?"

Orman scowled. He already hated what the dragon was pulling, and now he was being paraded around in front the upper crust as though he was some kind of trained hound.

"Bah," Orman said, and was relieved his frozen mouth could at least manage that.

§

A thousand different thoughts careened through Sela's mind. How her parents would wonder about her, worry about her. How she would never know if she helped save Orman. How she hoped her final decision in this world would be one her father could admire, even if he didn't understand. She even thought about Bannon, whether he would ever know what sort of light he'd turned on inside her.

But none of these things came out in words. She stared at Vorham, trying to come up with one phrase that would sum up her life, her feelings, and her ultimate reasons.

One phrase wasn't enough.

Vorham nodded to the guards outside the carriage, and she was pulled from her seat. Her feet touched ground as hot as a hellfire canyon.

The guards trudged her ever closer toward a rim of sand, blown scattered and parched, and Sela felt even herself dry up inside, eaten through from terror. "Wait," she whispered, although she'd promised herself she wouldn't.

Sela resisted the guards, pulling, unable to help herself. "Wait. Please wait."

The men didn't wait.

The dark-skinned one on the right squeezed her upper arm, trying to twist her forward. Sela suddenly recognized him. "You're Hamos, right?" she asked.

He didn't even look at her.

She felt her feet slide as though she was breaking through water, and then she tumbled. Hard. Her left elbow hit first, and then her face. She tasted blood and grit.

Time paused. She blinked away the sand working into her eyes, and turned her head, her movements awkward and stiff. Then she made it to her knees, and to her feet. She glanced around, finding the edge of the desert where it chewed toward the guards' feet.

The desert shifted and slithered beneath her feet like a living thing. The air sucked at her skin, dehydrating hit. The heat rippled against her face, scorching it. Hamos eyed her now, as he walked backward across the sand.

"I didn't kill anyone," she blurted.

Hamos paused. He frowned.

"He isn't even dead," she said.

She wasn't sure why she was confessing to this man, at this moment, but the relief of it welled inside her, and tried to release as tears, but the desert wouldn't let her have them.

Hamos glanced at the other guard, who was withdrawing his sword at his side. "Here," he said. He withdrew a pouch from beneath his sash. "When it gets real bad, put this on your tongue."

"Let's go," said the other. Then his arm rose up high, and Sela blinked up toward the hazy sky to watch it. Down came the handle of his sword, and, oddly, she took notice of the flash of green from a crystal imbedded near his knuckle. Then stars erupted behind her eyes, and everything went black.

§

Orman approached the casket already confounded, and already fearing. He did get a sense of magic, a weak, indefinable sort of pulsing that no dead man could give off; but Ebouard lay as still and lifeless as any corpse he'd ever seen. His coloring was mottled around the edges of his jaw, his throat. His eyelashes were pale with flecks of dust.

But what really sank Orman's hopes was the man's lack of a stone. Anywhere. Linking, or otherwise.

Orman passed his hands over the Venur slowly, searching. He even poked around the man's slippered feet. He felt inside his ears, peered into his nostrils.

"Not here," Orman said, his mouth finally

remembering speech.

"No stone?" asked Whitetail.

Orman turned toward the dragon. The assembly members had stood, and were looking from Orman to the dragon. One man, balding and round as a barrel, touched his hand to his belted dagger, questions in his eyes.

"Fear not, Buce," said Whitetail, offering his paw. "The wizard is trustworthy, and here at my request."

"What's going on?" the man asked.

"I have long suspected Ebouard's son to be involved in the deaths of his family members, including this one," said Whitetail. "And I've brought this wizard, Orman Thistleby, to examine the body in Vorham's absence."

"You're looking for proof?" asked a woman.

"I am."

"Well, what did you find?" Buce asked Orman.

Orman shook his head. "As dead as any living man. As alive as any dead man."

"What's that supposed to mean?" asked the woman.

"Yes, Wizard," said Whitetail, the lilting edge of his voice gone hard. "Make it clear to these people what exactly is going on here."

Except Orman didn't know, exactly, what was going on. He didn't know what Whitetail wanted out of this, and he certainly wasn't going to give it to the lout.

And then Whitetail's gaze tightened. "Help us save the girl, here, Wizard."

As though the dragon had any intention of helping Sela, or Orman, or anyone but himself.

Still. Orman already knew he had to try. If there was any chance at all to save Sela, he had to try.

"What's going on here," said Orman, with as authoritative a voice as he could muster, "Is that the girl, Sela, hasn't killed anyone. Because Ebouard Riddess isn't dead."

"What?" asked the woman.

"Isn't dead?" said Buce. "Fane, just what are you playing at? What's happening around here?"

"What's happening?" said Whitetail, without losing a beat. "Vorham Riddess believes himself above reproach. He has been stripping away every obstacle, year after year, eliminating whoever comes between him and absolute power. This day, his latest victim was Sela Riddess, his own newlywed wife."

At that, Orman felt his bones like powder, his breath like sandpaper. Sela *Riddess? Wife?* Had so much really happened in the hours he'd been solidified?

"What do we do?" asked Buce.

"We must act swiftly," said Whitetail. "Strike now, while the moment is upon us. I have paperwork for you each to sign, reverting temporary power to the assemblage, while Vorham's right to position is investigated."

Orman heard the dragon, heard the shuffling of hurried feet as the Esra men and women filed out of the chapel and into the hallway. He heard the opening of a second door, and the low talk and hushed fervor of people being bamboozled.

Yes, Vorham deserved to have his power taken

away. But the orchestrator was Fane Whitetail. A weasel being outthought by a cockroach. Not a better situation by any stretch of imagination.

The rotund man, Buce, paused in hallway, and looked backward to Orman, who watched from the chapel archway. "You're certain, old man? That the Venur isn't dead?"

Orman didn't have the foggiest notion how to rouse the Venur. If he could even be roused. Maybe the man would drift for years in the non-sleep of being almost dead, as much as an unlife as anyone could be cursed to. But technically? Had his soul departed to the great beyond?

"I'm certain," said Orman, the honesty of his statement giving him no comfort. "The Venur is not dead."

"Well and good," said Buce. "You've served Esra well."

Moments later, Whitetail emerged from the room, curling a parchment into a tube. "You've all done the right thing today," he said, bowing low in the doorway. "Please rest here now, knowing that egomaniac has been removed from causing any more harm to your province."

Then he drew in a deep breath, and blasted searing flame into the room.

Screams erupted. Whitetail slammed the door.

"Whitetail!" hollered Orman. He ran to the door, fumbling in his pockets for crystals. He had only the solidifying crystal left behind from Layce, although it didn't keep him from pounding the door, shouting

"Rain! Sky crying! Let loose your cloud water!"

A small, gray thundercloud collected over Orman's head, and crackled. Drops of water slapped to the hallway floor, and tapped against the iron door of the burning chamber.

The door that scorched Orman's fists. The door that suffocated the agonized screeching inside the room, but couldn't stifle the stench of burned meat.

§

Sela awoke, struggling to breathe. Scratchy wool was wedged in her throat. She clawed at it, trying to pull it free. But it wasn't fabric, it was her tongue. She rolled to her side and opened her mouth to let the swollen thing hang. She wanted to lie there and gather her senses, but the sand was an open flame, and her rough clothing did nothing to keep the heat from licking at her skin, roasting her. She pushed to her knees, and then to her feet. She tried to swallow, but her tongue was still broken, and her whole mouth felt dry as the sand beneath her boots.

She suddenly wondered if that's how the desert came to be so vast. Grown from the dehydrated bones of all those who came before.

The thought nudged her feet to motion.

She first rounded back, trying to find the shortest distance to where'd she been carried in. The relentless wind had long since erased her steps. She squinted into the distance, searching for flat, grassy lands, but everywhere the horizon looked the same. Orange dunes. Tan dunes. Mounds of shifting, breathing, angry sand.

She ripped her tunic cuff, stripping off a thin fabric slab. She knelt, partially burying it. She walked several feet, and repeated it. And she continued on, making a trail for herself, keeping track of where she'd already walked, so she would have something to follow if she needed it.

Follow it where, she didn't know. But rather than dwell on that, she kept her mind, and her fingers, busy.

Until she ran out of sleeves, and began tearing at her pant leg. She paused. She peered up at the sky, white-hot and dizzying.

Then she was on her back, and she didn't even know how it happened. Heat stung her bare arms, and she climbed once more to her knees.

Had she been wandering a full day? Or had it only seemed so long? Would her family realize she was dead, or would they only notice slowly that she hadn't come back in weeks, years? What would happen to Orman?

Would he awaken, relieved to be rid of her?

"Don't think like that," she tried to say, but her voice came out as a croak around her unmovable tongue. Her lips cracked, her chin peeled. Even her eyes felt dry, stretched like tanned leather, and they struggled to blink.

Somewhere nearby, heavy footsteps thudded rhythmically, shaking the ground around her and making her wince. But, no, it was a headache, rattling her from the inside out.

Could skin melt from bones? Or would it char and scrape away?

Sela had come as far as she would go. As far across this land, and this life, as she was able. Others before her had tried to survive these sands, others guilty or as innocent as she. They had suffered. Perished. Blown away. And nothing about Sela was any different, any more special, than anyone else.

If she had her wings, she could fly. But she'd stopped believing, long ago.

Was it the wind that sizzled like open flames? Or the sands themselves?

She'd lost faith she'd ever be the hope for her generation, the legendary dragon her father could be proud of. That her mother could brag on. She'd curled up one day into a smaller version of herself, and she'd settled there. Stayed there.

Because wings were too heavy a burden. Too frightening to keep.

Would she know she was dying, or would her death come first, before she fell?

What was it that soldier had given her? She patted at her tunic, and what was left of her trousers, searching. Something to put on her tongue if it got too bad. But she couldn't find it. Couldn't remember what happened to it.

She heard a growl, and paused, trying to decipher if the sound was some strange development to her headache. This time, when the sound came again, it was distinctly outside of her. Rumbling. Threatening.

The wind scraped at her tunic, tried to flay it from

her. It scratched her face, snapped angry fangs near her ears. She looked up to find a cloud, a whirling, snarling tangle of sand bearing down on her.

She leapt to her feet.

She veered left, pushing hard against the sand, dragging her legs. But she moved, to her own surprise, with the desert howling at her heels, clawing at her back.

Up, up, her own instincts screamed. But she had no 'up', only forward, and she gave in to it, willing her feet to be her wings. She tripped. She stood and kept going. She ran. And ran. And ran.

Into a barrier of carved stone, as firm and solid as any castle wall. She crashed right into it, seeing it only for a brief speck of time when the wind swallowed its own sand to reveal it. Too late for her to adjust.

Stunned by the impact, she dropped back. She stared up, trying to make sense of an ancient wall in the middle of a wasteland. But a swipe and growl reminded her she had no time to wonder.

She pressed her hands to the gritty surface and followed the structure, searching for a gap. Or a gate. Or a broken rock that offer shelter. But all she discovered was more wall.

Then her foot caught the edge of something, and her ankle twisted. She heard a snap. And she fell. She tumbled down, down, down, deep into the throat of the swallowing desert.

And found relief.

§

Orman was yanked from his feet and dragged across the hall. Then he was thrown. He landed in a heap at the base of the casket stand in the chapel.

"Now either figure out how to kill that damnable man," said Whitetail, "Or get him awake enough so I can do it."

Orman unfurled himself enough to push up on his bruised arms. "You killed them," he said. "You never meant to save Sela, you used her. And now you've done it, all on your own. You've started a war."

"Not entirely on my own," said Whitetail. "But I may as well have."

The dragon slammed the chapel doors, and Orman heard a bolt slide home, locking him inside.

He stood slowly, his hands gripping the casket wall for support. Then he stared down into the discolored face of Ebouard Riddess, a man whose sole purpose all these years, his only contribution to frazzling the plans of his son and that monster of a dragon, was to *not die.*

Orman, strangely, knew how he felt.

§

A glint of light appeared at the edge of Sela's senses. A firefly suffused sandstone walls covered with brown, withered ivy. The light bobbed closer, casting brilliance over a circle of water that was crusted over with algae.

She held out a bleeding hand, offering the light a place to land. But it wasn't light that set there, but a gleaming, golden paw. She lifted her dry eyes, up, up into the regal face of a dragon, his scales vivid and blazing as though carved from the surface of the sun.

She knew him from the stories in the scrolls. From her father's tales.

And she knew him, somehow, in the depths of her heart.

"Am I dead?" she tried to ask, her throat wrecked.

"You are not."

"Where am I?"

"In the desert," said the Gold.

"The desert?"

"This was a garden, once," he said. "Can you believe it?"

Sela had to admit that was difficult. She shook her head.

"A garden as lush as Wren Meadow. As deep as Murk Forest. The garden where all dragons were birthed." The Gold shifted his weight, and settled back, tipping his head.

Sela saw his features as plainly as if the room was open to the sky and drenched with sunlight. She finally recognized the wide, stone edge that encircled the festering water, and a carved arch just beyond it.

"Do you live here?" she asked.

He smiled. "I'm drawn to all places where magic survives. And toward those who seek it."

Sela remembered seeking shelter. But she would have searched for magic, if she'd known it was here.

"Most have forgotten this is here," said the Gold.

"Some still seek it. But you have found this garden, as no other could have. No human. No dragon."

Sela's throat ached too much to talk, her face throbbed too much to frown, so she just regarded the Gold, confused and silent.

"You will discover much in the coming days," he said, settling down to the stone floor, "As no other before you can do. You are the first of a new Kind."

"Me?"

"You are the first, but not the last. Generations of new Kind will look to your teachings, beginning with your own brother."

"I have a brother?"

"He, too, will be born into a new age. An age of magic unlike this land has ever seen, but one for which it has been forever preparing."

Sela tried to swallow, but her throat was too tight.

"Even this garden, as fragile and weak as it is, knows you. It knows the magic you have brought with you."

"Me?" asked Sela again. "What could I have possibly…?" Then she remembered again the pouch the soldier gave her, and she patted herself, searching.

"Sela Redheart," said the Gold, standing to his full height. He gleamed down at her, eyeing her firmly, but from a face softened by a smile. "This world knows you for who you are. And here, where dragons first stepped into the world, is the place for you to rediscover yourself."

Sela stood, her breath catching behind her dry

throat. Suddenly she trembled, and pressed her hands to her face, dreading what he meant.

"I know you fear," said the Gold. "It is the stone you wear. Even now you hide it from me, but I see it there, all the same."

"A stone?" she asked. She hadn't worn a stone in years. She opened her hands to show him she carried nothing.

"It's there," he said. He pointed at her neck. "It shines. It's beautiful, in its purpose."

"How could it be beautiful, if it makes me afraid?"

"It doesn't cause your fear," he said. "It holds it. Transforms it." He lifted his claw, and she felt the tug of a necklace against the back of her neck. And then, there, lying against the glitter of his paw, was a pale pink crystal, polished and gleaming.

It *was* beautiful. It was hers. She wanted to put it back on, to protect it. Keep it.

"And you can, if you so choose," said the Gold.

"Has it really been there all along?"

"Ever since you created it. Since you needed it."

She lowered her hands from her throat, and reached them impulsively toward the stone. As her fingertips drew near, the stone gave a throb a white light, and she startled. She gripped the edge of his paw, instead. "But I've never seen it. All this time."

"Our minds are as easily fooled as our eyes," said the Gold. "But you do recognize it."

She nodded. "I've felt it. I've tried to release it. To make it disappear, so I can fly."

"Is that what you want, then?"

She hesitated. Wings were a heavy burden to bear.

Then she inched her hand over his scales to touch the stone. It pulsed beneath her fingertips; familiar. Comfortable.

Suffocating.

"I want to be whole," she said.

He closed his fist around the crystal, dousing its light.

"Done," said the Gold.

Chapter Twenty-One

Sela flew. She rippled upward, slicing through the desert storm that grappled at her tail, trying to keep her. She closed her eyes against the fury of the wind and released her own pent rage, fueling her forward. Upward.

And then she was free. High, and beyond the storm's reach. She paused mid-air, glancing down at herself, holding her paws before her face, smoothing delicate claws over her long lash of a tail. Her skin fit again. Her scales flashed ruby, her muscles tensed and remembered their purpose.

And her wings; her wings were light, and strong, and had much flying to make up for.

She would start now, because though the storm was beneath her, the sun was still brutal. Waves of heat snarled at her scales, and revived her thirst. She circled, searching the distance for the nearest patch of green.

But first, with a risky dip toward the sand, and a yelp of sheer joy, she somersaulted.

Then she flattened out, pointed her snout toward the horizon, and soared on.

Reacher's Pass claimed the widest gap between Leland mountain peaks, and had been smoothed by generations of travel. The east had long been swallowed by dangerous Murk Forest, and the west ensnared by the Rage Desert. So the only way to reach lower Leland from upper Leland, or vice versa, was through the mountains.

Travelers chose, and inadvertently created, Reacher's Pass.

Sela chose it now, as well, because a shallow pond of mountain water seepage bubbled beside the trodden path. And she was desperately thirsty for water, and equally thirsty for a taste of home.

She landed, her tail scraping across a marbled spire on her way down. She flared out her claws, brought her wings to her sides, and captured the pebbled ground, hopping to slow her momentum.

Not her most graceful landing. She curled her tail around and inspected the damage from her mountain collision. All her scales were intact, but she could tell she was inwardly bruised. She was going to have to get used to her new size, since her last dragon days had been when she was a fledgling.

Finding the brook, she flopped her whole face into the water and sucked mouthful after mouthful of the cool, mineral-tinged flavor. Better than any water she'd had in Simson, or Riddess. Better than any water she'd had, ever.

Then she rolled over, splayed across the path and

half-submerged, and let her wings relax. She stared up at the Leland sky and drank some more; this time, of the view. She absorbed the scent and the scene of it. The feeling of it.

She was home.

It was real.

She was home.

§

Kallon and Riza flew together in tense silence. Now and again, Kallon would turn his head to regard his mate. He opened his mouth. But then he looked forward again, concentrating on making his tired wings keep moving, keep pumping. As much as he wished to break the silence, his attempts as words usually made things worse.

They were just cresting the lumpy northern ridges of the mountains, when Riza called out. She pointed toward Reacher's Pass.

A Red dozed comfortably, stretched out across the rocky path between peaks. Too comfortably. As though she belonged.

A Red!?

He beckoned to Riza with a nod, and then veered right to drop into a landing on the pass. He set down softly, but arched his wings, flaring them, to double his size and send a distinct territorial message. "Who are you?"

Riza sniffed the air, creeping closer, her wings

flattened toward the ground. Her expression lightened. Her head lifted. She began a hopeful smile.

The young Red rolled to her feet and sleepily fluttered her eyelids. Then she burst into a wide grin. "Father! It's me!" She opened her wings, and her forelegs.

"Sela?"

Kallon recoiled. A trick? A joke? Was it really possible that his fledgling, his child, was this Red come of age, and into her own? Finally, after all these long years?

At his reaction, the Red drew back. Her eyes, the green of Wren Meadow grasses, dimmed.

But Riza rushed headlong into the young Red's embrace. "Sela!" she cried, and nearly tackled her flat. "How? When? Oh, I've missed you!"

The two shot into the air, giggling, play-pouncing, and circling each other. Kallon watched Riza, her eyes bright, brighter than he'd seen them in so long. She flipped about, sky-writing, with the young Red beside her and mirroring her every twist. When they both faced him, for a breath of a moment, their eyes of emerald stunned him. Again. As they always did.

The eyes of two dragons he loved.

Riza backed onto the ground, landing firm and breathing heavily. "A wish come true," she said.

Sela set down, her front and back legs off-rhythm. She had practicing to do. "My wish, too," she said, nuzzling Riza's throat.

Over the top of Sela's head, Riza looked pointedly at Kallon.

Kallon rankled. He didn't know what to say! Or how to react. He was stunned. Unprepared.

He'd given up Sela to the hands, and the fate, of the humans she'd chosen to be. He'd let her go. Given up on her. Because he hadn't known how to protect her.

He hadn't known how to be a father.

He'd failed her.

And every time he looked into those eyes, the eyes like her mother's, whether in a human face or a dragon, he was reminded just what a disappointment he was.

"Your mother has been worried about you," was the best he could manage. "She was sure you were in danger."

"I was," Sela said, regarding him. No longer the fledgling he remembered.

"But you're safe now," said Riza, drawing her back to nuzzle her again. "You're home. Home to stay."

Sela smiled. But her smile faded, and she drew back from Riza, looking between both she and Kallon. "Not to stay. Not yet."

"Orman," said Kallon.

Sela nodded. "He's still there. He needs me."

"Where?" asked Riza.

"Riddess Castle." She turned to Riza. "I have a lot to explain. And much to apologize for."

"Nonsense," said Riza. "You're not the one who owes an apology." She looked around Sela at Kallon with *that* look again.

Kallon took it, and stacked it alongside all those looks he'd been collecting, there at the back of his mind.

"For one thing," said Sela. "I'm sort of married."

"What?" Riza's forelegs softened, as though she might droop.

"It's a twisted mess of magic and deception. The whole castle is full of liars and bullies. And Venur Riddess is the worst of them."

"Sela," said Riza, still lilting toward collapse. "What kind of world did we send you into?"

"And there's more," Sela said, turning this time to Kallon. "I know where Blackclaw is."

§

That evening, while candelabra cast long, shady fingers over the woven mat in Gore Manor, in the Great Hall, where dragon-woven tapestries decorated the space instead of dragon remains, Sela stretched out, her stomach comfortably full, and her bones sweetly weary. She watched candlelight paint sparkles on her father's crimson scales, and she was no longer envious. Or shameful.

She was whole.

Her mother, try as she did to stay awake, had dozed off in the middle of a mumbled sentence. She lay now in the corner, curled up and breathing so deeply tiny slivers of misty sulphur leaked from between her teeth.

Her father regarded her mother with an empty longing behind his eyes. She'd never known him to look at her any other way. Sometimes she wondered why her mother chose the way she did, to follow her love into a new body, a new world, when all Sela had ever witnessed was her parent's distance from each other.

Or had she? As a fledgling, hadn't the three been happy?

"We were half way across the ocean, when she sensed your trouble, and turned right around," said her father, still regarding her mother.

He'd mentioned it. Repeatedly. She'd already apologized so many times her tongue was tired from it. Still, he kept mentioning. She wasn't sure what he was trying to say, except he was still angry, resentful in some way. That much was obvious by his reaction to her homecoming. She wasn't sure what she'd been expecting from her father, but it hadn't been shock and dismay. And she certainly hadn't been prepared for more awkward detachment.

"I wouldn't have guessed the Gold would meet you in the desert," he said. "All those myths about where dragons began, I never believed it. In Esra? All we've ever known are the mountains."

"It's a big world, Father."

"Don't I know it. Your mother doesn't seem happy unless she's out in it, flying over it, exploring and searching."

"She's often said the same thing about you," said Sela.

Her father shook his head slowly. "Maybe once upon a time. When I was younger. When I had the freedom to do as I wanted, without letting anyone down."

Sela stretched out her claws, looked down at them and away from his eyes. "Before you had me, you mean."

"I don't mean that," he said. "My father left behind a legacy I've never lived up to. He led our tribes with pride and courage." He shook his head again. "I'm just a place marker until a real leader comes along."

"Have you talked to the Council about it?"

"No," he said. "We all realize it without having to speak."

"Maybe it's time to stop trying to lead the way your father did, and lead the way you are. He was a dragon for a different time. Leland has a changed nature."

He narrowed his eyes, considering.

"He isn't even looking, you know," she said.

"Isn't he?"

Her grandfather was in a world beyond the sky. She supposed he had better things to do than to keep watching over his shoulder, judging his offspring through the veil, taking notes on just how differently he would have done things if he was still in charge around here.

Her father smiled, his brown eyes soft. "When did you become so wise?" he asked.

When you weren't looking, she tried not to think. But there it was. Her father's smile dimmed.

"Anyway," she said, talking to chase away the sudden discomfort. "Now that I'm rested and recovered, I need to return to the castle."

"We need a plan," he said. "You can't just fly down and scoop up Orman."

"I've thought about it, though," said Sela. "But I'll walk in. I survived the desert. I'm still Venuress. I must have some power to release him."

"Walk?" asked her father.

"On two legs."

"Two?" he asked, blinking.

"I understand now," she said. "What happened to me. Why I changed the way I did, and how to change back. It works both ways. I'm dragon *and* human, Father. Without fear, I can choose."

He stared mutely. She didn't really expect him to understand, when it had been so difficult for her to grasp. She rose to her feet, stretched purposefully. "The important thing is I have to return. I'll figure it out as I go."

"You should at least wait until morning."

"I can't risk it. I don't know if Whitetail even kept his part of the deal." She strode her to father, feeling the weight of her dragon body, the strength of it. Remembering it. Then she nuzzled him beneath his chin. "I'll be back. With Orman. Back to stay," she said. "Tell Mother not to worry."

"She will anyway."

"Then tell her I love her and I'll do my best to make her proud."

"She is already proud of you, Sela."

Sela paused, and looked up into his sad, eternally solemn face. "Then I'll try to make you proud, Father."

She turned then, facing the immense archway at the manor stairs, and leapt into the night, throwing her wings at the air and chasing the scent of her destiny.

CHAPTER TWENTY-TWO

J astin watched the fire spit and crackle, tasting the edges of kindling, testing, before swelling orange to greedily feast on the seasoned wood. He tossed a thick log into the depths, and that, too, was gorged on. He faced the heat, feeding it, preparing it. The work he had planned for it would likely last deep into the night.

Gladdis sat on the warm grass in the yard behind his house, cradling a cup of spiced cider, her back against the low wall of his well. She'd bathed, and dressed in a pair of his old work trousers, so ridiculously large on her she had to tie a rope around them and fold them over twice to keep them from dropping. And she'd insisted on a brown tunic, now gone damp down her back from her long, yellow, freshly-washed hair.

She watched the fire, too, and sipped her cider. Flames lit her cheeks, deepening the worry lines of her young face.

Perched on the well stones, just at Gladdis' right shoulder, was the eagle. He watched the girl, or the campfire, or sometimes the stars. That bird had a look in his eyes Jastin had never seen on any raptor; he understood what was happening. He listened and reacted.

That eagle was aware.

Just like the other animal Jastin never thought his backyard would host. Drell, the black dragon who had recovered him in the woods, instead of ripping out his throat. The dragon who carried Jastin and four women on his back for miles across Esra without complaint. And who had waited for the others to eat cheese and dried meat to their fill before accepting any for himself.

Drell had been patient, sturdy, and, Jastin was forced to admit, benevolent. But the creature was about to witness the evidence of Jastin's atrocities, and he wasn't sure just how far Drell's compassion could go.

Strange thing was, Jastin cared. Hoped, even, that Drell could forgive.

Uncomfortable, this whole *feeling* experience. But even more unnerving was that whenever he looked into the golden eyes of that black dragon, he was convinced the creature knew things Jastin was only thinking. Drell seemed aware of them even before Jastin heard his own mind form them. Not quite in the infuriating way Layce Phelcher managed it, but he did, all the same.

That dragon *knew*.

"Of course he does," said Layce, behind him. She came around to his side, smelling of lavender and saddle soap. "Human magic is just a shabby version of what dragons live every day. Whatever we manage takes hard work, but dragons breathe magic like air."

"Some need more work than others," said Jastin.

"Some need more soap than others," she said, elbowing him. "And you're going to need to heat more water, too. We've gone through it all."

"Can't you just wave a stone or something?"

Layce wrinkled up one eye. "And who are you again? Riding a dragon instead of slaughtering it, and now asking me to do magic to save you some work?"

"I've got plenty of work to do tonight. It's just more important than woman chores."

Drell spit a laugh across the fire. When Jastin and Layce both looked his way, he cleared his throat. "Sorry."

"Go head and laugh," said Layce. "Saves me the trouble. Speaking of woman chores, who taught you to make a campfire? Most folks throw wood on one, they don't build it so high it finds its own trees."

"It needs to be hot," said Jastin.

"How long are we going to stay here?" asked Gladdis, who Jastin had nearly forgotten.

"You have somewhere to be?" he asked.

"She's worried about Sela," said Layce. "We all are."

"Well she can go wherever she wants, whenever she wants. All I offered was a bath and some food, and she's had that."

"Where are we going?" asked Avara, Layce's sister, who came to stand at Jastin's other side. She still gripped the purple stone around her neck.

He was suddenly nervous, between two Phelchers.

"We found some dresses in a trunk in your loft,"

said Avara.

He glanced at her, recognizing his wife's old brown, vested dress with black lace trim sagging on Avara's thin frame. Then he heard footsteps, and turned to find Leesa, her cropped black hair glossy with dampness, the tips pointed forward to trace her jaw line. Flamelight deepened the burnish of her olive skin. And she wore a jade green dress, the neckline low and ruffled, revealing curves he didn't know she had. The waistline wrapped around and flared toward her generous hips. He didn't know she had those, either.

It had been Rimin's wedding dress. On Leesa, the fabric moved like grasses brushed by wind. The silken material had softened, either by age and time, or by the gentle woman inside it. As she walked nearer, toward the fire, he watched her, watched the dress.

"I hope it's all right that we borrowed some things," said Avara.

"It's all right," Jastin said.

"So where are we going?" Avara asked again.

"Nowhere," said Jastin, finally dragging his gaze from Leesa. "I came here to do something." He hadn't expected an audience, especially the menagerie that collected in his yard, but he would go through with it, while they watched or not.

"Let's have it, then," Layce said. "You're stalling. But you needn't worry we'll be surprised by your brutality. We're very aware of it."

He impulsively glanced toward Leesa. She stared at the eagle, stroking her fingers over his tan-gold feathers.

So he began. He walked through the fire-lit darkness toward his shed, and there, just at the door, he paused. Then he hunched up and released his shoulders, displacing his threatening embarrassment, and he pulled open the door. Hand tools, a rake, and withered dragon parts spilled out into a tumbled mess at his feet.

He bent, and gathered as many toes, claws, and arrow-tip tails as he could manage. He walked back to the fire. And he threw them into the blaze, scattering sparks and interrupting the flames.

The fire gave off a bellow, as though in gratitude for fresh fuel, and raged on. Standing there in the funeral silence, as Drell and the others looked on, Jastin got the sense the dragons were grateful, too, released from their trophy prison. Dragon souls rode the smoke into the sky, where they belonged.

When he turned back for another armload from his shed, Leesa joined him. He dropped the knuckles of a Green, and she picked them up, cradled them in her arms. She stacked more trophies on top, and carried them toward the fire.

"I'll start inside," said Layce. Avara went with her. And then Gladdis.

Even Drell rose up, lumbered toward the shed, and collected strewn scales and claws. And the eagle swept up and over the fire, swooped down to pluck a dragon claw from Jastin's arms, and returned to drop it into the sizzling heat.

He'd been right about the work involved. Late into the night, he and the others retrieved grisly mementos from beneath stacks of weapons, from shelves, and inadvertent showcases. And with each toss into the fire, Jastin felt himself cleansed. Scrubbed clean from the dusty, morbid places in his soul.

Released to the world, where he belonged.

After the last of the keepsakes had been placed, they all rimmed the fire, watching it starve away to a dull flicker. Tired eyes grew heavy. Yawns caught like contagion. But everyone, including Jastin, seemed hesitant to go.

It was Layce who finally spoke. "Do you know what would be really ceremonial now?" she asked.

"Hm?" Jastin drew ash-streaked fingers over his eyes.

"Your bath."

Soft chuckles broke the somberness, and everyone moved away, fracturing into activity. Gladdis and Avara claimed the loft bed, Layce declared Jastin's. That left Jastin the wicker chaise in the living room.

"What will you two do?" he asked Drell and the eagle.

And realized he was talking to a bird.

"It's a nice night," said Drell. "I'll watch the fire until it dies."

Jastin nodded. He turned.

"It's a good thing you did here," said Drell. "A brave thing."

Jastin paused, regarded Drell over his shoulder. Whatever words Jastin wanted to express, he didn't have to say. That dragon *knew*.

In the bath, in the small room off the kitchen, Jastin sank into the freshly hot water of his iron tub. The water immediately clouded with soot. But Layce had been right about the ceremony of it; with a deep scrub and long soak, he felt renewed. He scratched his fingers into his beard. He could use a trim, too, but that would have to wait for now.

Several minutes later, after he'd submerged for so long the water was cool, he reached for the lump of clothing he'd dropped before he got in. It was gone.

He twisted, searching. His vest, his leather pants, his tunic, all vanished. He jumped from the tub, threw a cotton towel around his waist, and sloshed into the kitchen. If someone had taken his vest, they'd taken the Gold's scale, too, and he wanted it near. Safe and close.

The kitchen was dark, and he bumped his toe into a table leg. He bit a curse word behind his teeth. The living room wavered with yellow light, and he followed it to find a low fire at the hearth, and Leesa walking toward him with a bundled cloth in her hands.

"What happened to my clothes?" he asked.

Leesa regarded the drips of water around his feet, his thin towel, his chest hairs curled with moisture. The shade of her skin darkened around her eyes. She offered the cloth, which tumbled from her arms as a long, dangling, cotton nightshirt.

He pulled the nightshirt from her hand. "But my clothes."

She pointed toward the door, and outside.

"My vest is out there?" He moved toward the door

and simultaneously tugged the nightshirt over his head, which glued itself to his still-damp chest and back.

Leesa tapped his arm, stopping him. She offered her hand again, and this time, a trinket on a leather cord dangled from her fingers.

Not a trinket, a scale. The Gold's scale.

"You did this?" he asked.

She smiled, and stretched out her arms, rising to her tiptoes to wrap the leather around his neck. He tilted his face away to give her access, but his gaze remained on her face as she drew close, breathed against his throat. Her fingers fumbled against his hair, sending a shiver across his shoulders.

"Thank you," he said.

She stepped back, easing space between them again. It did little to calm his tight breathing, however. And when she gave a little wave, and swished across the room in that green dress, that delicately clinging dress, his pulse quickened. She stepped into his bedroom, and he knew she would soon be sliding into his bed, smoothing that dress and her scent over his sheets, closing her copper eyes, and resting her smooth cheek against his pillow. She would be sharing that intimate space with his own scent, his dreams, and…

…Layce Phelcher. Who also slept in the room. And in Jastin's bed.

That thought was exactly the splash of cold water he needed to get some sleep.

Chapter Twenty-Three

Sela's wings grew heavy, as well as her eyes. Fresh food and water had gone a long way to revive her, but she'd lost track of the last time she slept. Two nights ago? Three?

She flew into the deepest part of the night, and emerged from the other side, into a soft dawn that brought the rough and hulking shape of Riddess Castle onto the horizon. After all her time trying to escape the place, here she was, stepping back into the clutches of the beast. But she was drawn, not just to the people who needed her—Orman, for one—but to her own unfinished business with the man who had her killed.

Nearly killed. She couldn't wait to see the expression on his face when she greeted him.

But first, she had to transform again, and to do that, she had to land. She swooped as close to the castle as she dared, but dropped into forest trees for cover. She set down the tunic and skirt she'd brought along, looked about herself, feeling conspicuous, even though she was alone, and then closed her eyes, thought very small thoughts, and found the place inside herself where it was very cozy and just a little bit scary.

§

"I don't know how many times I have to tell you," said Orman to Whitetail, who hovered over him, the casket, and the silent Venur. "I can't give you what you want."

Whitetail swerved around, tapping his claws together. He glared across the room, silent.

A hiss of flame whispered at the colored glass chapel window. Outside, a huge and shadowed dragon figure dipped, circled, and spat orange fire toward the ground, and toward a growing blaze in the distance.

Orman didn't need to ask Whitetail who the dragon was.

Whitetail continued to stare for a time, and then he looked back at Orman, and the prone Venur. "As always, I'll have to do things myself. Surely the man can't survive if I burn him out of that human shell."

"Don't do it!" Orman stood between the dragon and casket.

Whitetail snorted. "Two with one flame," he said. He drew in a breath.

"Orman?"

A sudden, startled silence overcame the room. Even Whitetail leached alarm.

"Orman?" asked the voice, again.

It was Sela's voice.

"It can't be," breathed Whitetail.

"Sela, run!" hollered Orman. "Don't come any closer! Get out!"

Footsteps hurried near. And then Sela rushed into the room. She paused to look from dragon face to human face, and then she gasped, and threw her arms open.

"Orman!"

Orman pushed from the casket and limped his aching bones toward her. He pulled her into an embrace, keeping his eye on that White who seemed unable to gather himself. "Sela," he said. "I thought you were lost. I was afraid to think about it."

"I survived," she whispered. "I flew."

Orman drew back, pushed tears from her cheek with his fingertips. "You flew?"

She nodded, beaming.

Single, popping sounds of clapping erupted from the corner of the room. Whitetail was applauding, and smiling vacantly. "Well done, Sela Riddess, Venuress of Esra."

"Thank you for releasing my uncle," she said to the White. "I didn't think you'd keep your word."

"Don't thank him." Orman pushed Sela behind himself and glared up at Whitetail.

"He's right," said Whitetail. "I'm the one who should be thanking you, Sela Riddess." He began a slow circle around them. "You leave the castle, and you return. And leave again, and return again. You're compelled. Have you ever wondered why?"

"Don't listen to him," said Orman.

"You're meant to survive here. To rule here," said the White.

"Orman?" Sela asked into his ear. "What's going on?"

"He's a goner," he replied, turning a circle to keep Whitetail in his vision. He pulled Sela with him, his hands behind himself, guarding her. "I don't think even he knows what he's saying anymore."

"Allow me to explain," said Whitetail. He eased backward into the hall, and made an indication with his paw. Moments later, two guards wrestled a chained and bound Vorham Riddess into the chapel.

One of the guards, dark-skinned and craggy, released Vorham to stare openly at Sela.

"Hamos?" she asked.

Hamos gaped.

"Your husband is no longer in charge around here," said Whitetail. "As you can see."

"Sela?" asked Vorham. "How?"

"That's the mystery, isn't it?" Whitetail swept backward, easing toward the casket. "A man who can't die. A girl who won't die. Am I the only one beginning to realize the connection here?"

"I don't know what you're getting at…" Sela began.

"Of course you do, my dear." Whitetail clicked his claws over Ebouard's face. "I have this pesky problem. One formality before the castle can truly be mine." He spun gracefully, gesturing his paws toward Sela, and formed his wide mouth into a sort of, what was he doing? Pouting?

"But I'm willing to share," he said. "Sela Riddess. Unlike your husband, here, I'm willing to share."

"How could you share a castle that doesn't belong to you?"

"Oh, but it does. Nearly entirely." Whitetail smiled. "If you'll just release the Venur so he can awaken—"

"Me?" asked Sela.

"Or I can kill him now, where he lay. Your choice."

"But I can't! I don't have the stone. It isn't me you need."

"Very well," said Whitetail. "Can't say I didn't give you a chance." His nostrils flared with a deep inhale.

§

Jastin startled awake. He blinked up into Leesa's face. She shook him roughly, and pointed behind herself at Layce Phelcher, who clutched her hands together, and Avara Phelcher, who held out the purple stone from her neck.

The stone pulsed with light.

"It started a few minutes ago," said Avara.

Outside, the eagle screamed. Claws slammed into the closed cottage door, rattling it on its hinges. And then the bird called again. Desperate.

"Right about the time the eagle started in with that," said Layce.

"What am I supposed to do about it?" asked Jastin.

Leesa pulled at him, stood him on his feet.

"Am I going somewhere?" he asked.

A black dragon pressed his face to the wavy glass of Jastin's living room window. "We're all going," he rumbled.

A dragon at his home. Talking to him. Making plans with him, as though they were working together.

Would he ever get used to that kind of thing?

"Where, exactly?" Jastin asked.

"Riddess Castle," said Layce. "It's happening."

"What's happening?"

"Something I didn't see coming," she said.

§

Sela threw herself at the casket, and tried to make herself stretch as wide as she could go. A blast of flame hit her back.

"No!" she heard Orman yell. "Sela, no!"

The casket beneath her caught fire, licking at her shins. She smelled burned wood, burned hair. Then, when Whitetail's breath finally extinguished, she shoved her arms beneath Ebouard's back, hugging him tightly, and rolled. They both flopped out of the smoking casket and to the floor.

Her hip crunched beneath the weight of him.

"Sela," Orman said, and knelt beside her.

Whitetail, beyond them, let out a roar that shook the room, clattered the chains around Vorham's wrists, and caused one guard to slap his hands over his ears.

The other guard, Hamos, had drawn his sword. Now he lowered his weapon slowly, his eyes on Sela.

The clatter of heavy footsteps rang loudly down the hallway, echoed about in the chapel. And then more Esra guards spilled into the room, weapons drawn.

"Take them all," shouted Whitetail.

"What?" said Orman. "The guards are with him?" He stood.

Sela rose behind him staring at the scene.

Vorham tried to wrestle Hamos's sword from him. When that failed, he dove at the key ring on Hamos's waist. Hamos shoved him away with his shoulder. Vorham hit the ground.

The second guard blocked an oncoming thrust from a fellow soldier.

Chaos.

A dagger skittered across the floor and bumped into Orman's toes. Sela lunged at it.

"You're fighting?" asked Orman.

"What else can I do?" she called over the noise of rushing guards, defending soldiers, and Whitetail shouting orders.

In moments, the guard Hamos leapt toward the casket. He turned defensively, protecting them both behind him. "I'll do your fighting, Venuress."

"Help me, Hamos," she said. "Get us out of here. Outside."

"I will," he said. "Forgive me for the desert. I won't let you down this time."

"Forgiven," Sela shouted, as a soldier lunged a blade

toward her shoulder. Hamos blocked, spun, and thrust, knocking the soldier in the head. The soldier crumpled.

"Go!" shouted the second guard, and stepped into position behind them all.

"Save the Venur," Sela cried.

Hamos led, blocking and parrying. Blood seeped through his purple sleeve. The rear guard countered attacks from behind, a gash oozing in his cheek. Through the veil of swinging arms and angry faces, Sela saw a flash of movement. A third guard, wearing the purple-and-black colors of his Venur, scooped the death-scarred man from the floor and threw him over his shoulder.

Finally, the group reached the hallway, bursting through to knock soldiers and swords askew. Sela tripped over a prone soldier's arm, and he groaned. Orman steadied her. Huddled together, with fighting guards before and behind them, they inched toward the freedom of the castle's open spaces.

In the hallway, Whitetail screeched "Enough!" He reared up and swiped his forepaw at Hamos.

Hamos toppled.

A soldier rushed Hamos, his sword raised high.

Sela saw Orman yank at the soldier's black trousers, and drop a crystal into the man's loincloth. His legs froze in place, and he made a choked sound. Then his whole body went rigid. His eyes glazed.

Sela pulled Hamos to his feet and pushed him into the next hallway. "Go, go!" Sela glanced up at Whitetail, who was sucking in a breath. She gave the second guard a hearty shove, just as Whitetail wheezed a fan of flame. Sela threw herself into the fire.

"Not again!" Orman shouted.

Both guards, bloodied and soot-covered, staggered toward the landing that would lead them all to the arched entrance hall.

Then Whitetail sucked in another breath, and the flame disappeared. Sela's hands, her tunic sleeves smoking, pushed at Orman's shoulders. "Go. Go," she said again.

"How…?"

"Go, Orman, hurry!"

Orman turned. He hurried.

Sela's lungs seized, trying to breathe through panic from Whitetail's searing flames. She felt them at her back, flaring against her legs and charring her skirt away from her calves. If she could only reach outside, into a clearing, she would fly and take Orman and the others with her, home to Leland.

She was close. She could see the arched vestibule. Just beyond it, the door. Then she would be free.

Her guards ran ahead and leapt outside. Orman shuffled feebly, and Sela guided him, watching the wide entrance grow closer and closer.

Then her feet were swept out from beneath her, and she fell sideways, pulling Orman with her.

Vorham Riddess trampled over them both and flung himself at the doorway. Behind them, a soldier sliced at Orman's shoulder.

"No!" Sela dove forward, but Orman shrieked,

and his shoulder spilled blood. "Leave him alone!" She threw herself at the soldier's legs. She heard a pop and a crunch, and the soldier collapsed, writhing.

Sela grasped Orman's spindly legs, and dragged him toward the doorway. "Almost there," she said.

Orman pressed a hand to his shoulder, his beard staining red, his face pale. "It's my blasted arm, not my leg," he said. "Help me up."

She crossed the threshold. They were outside.

There, at the stairs, Sela released Orman's legs and rushed toward his arms. She wedged her hands into his armpits and tugged. Orman rose, scrambling, and then wavered on his feet.

"I'm getting us out of here," she said. She closed her eyes.

An eagle screech ruptured the sky, interrupting her thoughts. She looked up, just as a sword appeared in her vision. Then the weapon was knocked aside, and pulled from the wielding soldier's grasp.

The eagle swept skyward, the sword in his talons. The soldier, Orman, and Sela all gaped.

"Who is that?" Orman asked.

"I don't know."

The weapon dropped, careening downward, and the hilt clanged the soldier in the middle of his forehead. He slumped.

"Nice shot," called Orman to the eagle.

Flame erupted at the ground, a backlash of heat knocked Sela off her feet. She crumpled down the steps, slapping her face to the marble, woozied. She rolled to her back, spotting Whitetail's glittering tail. He was retreating into the sky. His tail seemed to split the clouds, drawing a black line between them, sending a rumble through them.

Raindrops drummed her face.

Then the black line swelled into a round lump. The round lump sprouted wings. And the shape arched up, joined Whitetail in the sky, and the pair rounded and dove, spitting fire.

Orman drew Sela to her feet, his gaze fastened upward. "Fordon Blackclaw," he whispered. "That evil snake is behind all this."

Orman lowered his chin, and his gaze, and leveled it on Sela. "Whatever you're going to do to get us out of here, do it now."

Sela nodded, her face throbbing in pain, and her head still buzzing. But she closed her eyes again. And she thought large, brave, ruby thoughts.

A headache sliced her brain. She gasped, her eyes flashing open.

And then flame sizzled through raindrops, steaming them, and she leapt at Orman, pushing him to the muddy ground, covering him.

Another eagle scream reverberated, and the flame spout abruptly vanished. She'd taken the dragonfire again. But her skin was reddened and stung. She didn't know if she could take it again.

She slid from Orman, who was spattered with mud from his legs to his belly. His beard wore handprints of it, mixed into dried blood. "Are you all right?"

He nodded. He seemed unburned, but he was not all right.

"I'm trying," she said.

"I know," he croaked.

Hamos and the second guard clanged swords with soldiers. Whitetail veered to concentrate his flames on them. Blackclaw chuckled low in the sky, and the sound of it rolled into a peal of thunder that shook the ground beneath her.

Just then, another black shadow of a dragon flew into view. It careened swiftly toward Whitetail, and slammed its snout into the White's ribs. Whitetail's mouthful of fire hit the castle, instead of Hamos.

Then the Black looped around, snapped its tail to thrust forward, and jutted his wings. He landed. "It's Drell," said Sela.

"Who?" asked Orman, sitting up, squinting through the rain.

From Drell's back scrambled three women; Gladdis, and Layce and Avara Phelcher.

"Gladdis!" As relieved as Sela was to see her, she was terrified at her timing. "Look out!"

Blackclaw swerved toward them all, but he slowly circled. Drell lifted his head, regarding the movement. Finally, Blackclaw dropped into a stance, and landed solidly. He swished the tip of his tail.

"You have golden eyes," he said to Drell. "I know them."

Drell didn't reply. He only stared, his chest heaving.

"You have the scales of the Blackclaw tribe, but you

ride in with women on your back, as a pack animal. A vassal."

Layce, Gladdis, and Avara huddled against Drell's ribs, hiding as much from the cold rain as from Blackclaw's hot breath. Drell moved his foreleg protectively in front of them.

"Rule with me," said Blackclaw. "And humans will be your vassals, not your masters. Claim your place beside me. My son."

Orman touched Sela's leg where he still sat on the ground. He whispered something Sela couldn't hear, but at the same moment, she sensed someone behind her, bearing down on her. She lifted her arm instinctively, and the tip of a sword brushed past it, stabbing toward Orman's face.

Then the swinging soldier grunted, dropped his arms—and the weapon—and fell forward. He landed on Orman's splayed beard, an arrow in his spine.

Sela followed the trail from where the arrow flew. She found Jastin Armitage, splashing through the mud on a chestnut mount. He lowered a crossbow.

Leesa sat behind him, her arms enwrapping his waist.

"Armitage," snarled Blackclaw, seeing Jastin, too. "You fight for the wizard?"

"Armitage?" asked Orman, twisting to see, but unable to move his head with a dead man on his beard.

Jastin didn't reply; he just nocked another arrow into the bow.

Blackclaw swiveled his head toward Drell, his wings

flaring. "Come with me."

"No," said Drell.

Blackclaw lofted upward. "I won't ask again."

Jastin's arrow chimed against Blackclaw's foot and bounced away.

In that moment, as Blackclaw mounted the sky, and Whitetail curled forward like mist to meet him, as rain pummeled the ground and soaked Sela through to her bones, as Drell turned to face her, and Jastin rode closer to join her; in that moment she felt the day close up and seal over. She became aware.

She'd reacted to the last few violent moments with instinct. She hadn't thought, she'd responded. Numbed by the surreal scene of it all, she'd gotten lost in it.

She was thinking now.

She watched humans tumble out of doorways from all angles of the burning castle. Vorham's servants shrieked and limped, or ran gasping into the rain. And from all visible sides of the castle, Esra soldiers descended on them, stopping escape with the points of their swords.

Hamos had collected his own small group of loyal Venur soldiers near the castle entrance, and fought to free captured servants. Blackclaw spat flame, singeing the resistors. "We can't fight this," she said to Jastin. "Not here. Not now."

"Fly," said Orman, his voice weak as a spiderweb.

A human scream crackled through the rain.

Avara raced toward the castle steps, her hands shielding rain and heat. Fire surged across the castle wall, shattering windows. "Ebouard!" Avara screamed again.

She disappeared into the castle, into a billow of black smoke.

"Avara!" Layce hiked up her skirts and galloped her long legs across the courtyard.

And then, just when Sela thought she might faint with frustration and fear, the gray and thundering clouds shifted with driving wind, and rumpled into speckled smears. The smears met, bled over into a leakage of colors; brown, yellow, pale orange and blue, spilling as a sunrise across the horizon.

It was no sunrise. "Dragons!" she cried.

"Here to help?" asked Gladdis.

The herd of dragons met Blackclaw and Whitetail, and encircled them. Sela tried to count them, but they moved too quickly, and were too far away. But they didn't attack Blackclaw or Whitetail. They dipped into formation.

"They aren't here to help," said both Drell and Jastin.

"Fly," said Orman again.

Sela wasted no more moments, not for explanation, not for warning. She simply closed her eyes, and remembered herself.

When she opened them, she unfurled her wings, shook from head to tail tip, and settled into her skin.

"Someone help Orman onto my back," she said.

Jastin stared, his dark eyes pools of surprise. Leesa, behind him, parted her lips. Sela was pretty sure she'd have made some kind of sound, if she was able.

Drell grunted, his nostrils wide. "What…?" The eagle swooped in for a landing on Drell's head, tucked in his wings, and blinked golden eyes.

She'd explain later. "Someone help Orman," she cried.

Jastin slid from his horse, and pulled the dead soldier off Orman's beard. "You *are* her daughter. Aren't you?" he asked Sela.

"I'm the daughter of Kallon and Riza Redheart," Sela said, for the first time she could remember.

Jastin pulled Orman to his feet, and Orman flailed like a ragdoll. He groaned.

Arrows mixed with raindrops, and scattered to the ground around them. The soldiers had foregone swords for bows. And the collected dragons over Riddess castle began, two by two, to peel away from the group and aim for them.

"Hurry," said Sela.

"Wait!" called Layce Phelcher. She emerged through smoke and mist, side by side with her sister, and with a feeble, shuffling Ebouard Riddess between them.

"She did it," said Sela. "She woke him!"

Drell launched and swept over Layce, Avara and Ebouard, and collected them in his paws, just as a barrage of arrows stabbed into the ground where they'd stood. He carried them to Sela, and gently set them down. Ebouard sank to the ground. Avara knelt beside him.

Layce ran to where Orman sprawled across Sela's

back.

"Oh dear," she said. "I should have grabbed my crystals while I was in there."

"Just get on, Layce!" Sela said.

She did. She clung to Sela's back like a crab, bracing for she and Orman both. Gladdis helped Avara to push Ebouard onto Drell's back, and both of them crawled into place, holding the Venur from both sides.

Sela looked toward Jastin, where he stood in the mud. He shook his head. "You go. Don't worry about me."

"Meet us," said Sela. "At Mount Gore. You remember it?"

"I remember it," he said. "I'm not welcome there."

Sela rose up, balancing the riders on her back, struggling to find equilibrium. "Meet us," she said again.

Leesa offered her hand to Jastin, to help pull him onto the horse.

"Go with them," he said to her.

Leesa shook her head.

"Please?" Jastin tried.

The woman shook her head again, and opened her hand. Jastin grasped it, hoisted himself into place in his saddle. When Leesa wrapped her arms around his waist, Jastin dimly smiled.

The golden eagle circled Leesa, and then swooped up and over to join Sela. Drell fell in behind.

"Fly," said Orman.

§

Kallon and Riza flew hard into the day, and then into the storm, as thunder crackled over Esra and spat furiously in the distance. They were silent, focused, knowing together that something had shifted violently in the structure of the province.

And that Sela was in the thick of it.

Rain battered his wings as he cut through the downpour. He squinted. Wind splashed water into his eyes.

"Do you see?" asked Riza.

He did. Dragon shapes, dulled and slick. Two dragons clamored ahead of a pack, appearing to race, but barely able to maintain the pace with burdens on their back.

"Sela!" Riza shot forward.

Kallon drew up. The dragon beside Sela was a Black.

Without thinking or hesitation, Kallon dove ahead. He bore down on the black dragon, his hot breath puffing steam through the rain. "Get back," he roared.

"Father! Behind us!"

Kallon was just reaching the black dragon when he heard Sela's shout. He realized the dragon was a youngling, and not Fordon Blackclaw, despite the polished coal of his scales. He also realized both the Black and Sela were running from the dragon herd behind them.

Three dragons, a Blue, a Brown, and a Yellow, were gaining on his daughter.

Riza bent her head and slammed her horns into the Yellow. Kallon veered up and dropped into a spiral descent, twisting his spikes into the Blue's spine. The blue howled and dropped.

The Brown, in the center, careened upward. Kallon clamped his jaw around the Brown's hind leg and jerked, ripping him from his ascent. Then Kallon rowed his wings back to front, pulling the Brown away from Sela. And he spiraled, twirling the Brown again and again, before he opened his jaws to let him go, sideways and tumbling out of control.

"I am Kallon Redheart," he bellowed. "Leader of the Reds of Leland, and of the Dragon Council. You have crossed into my territory, in pursuit of my offspring. You will turn around and respect our boundary, or your actions will be taken as an act of war."

The Yellow, who had dropped toward the trees, recovered his trajectory, but paused. He pumped his wings, regarding Redheart. "It *is* war, Kallon Redheart. And a long time coming."

Kallon flared his wings, and lifted his crest, prickling the horns around his head into a sharpened crown. He lowered himself before the Yellow, and breathed sparks into the Yellow's eyes. "You would provoke this war with me? Now?"

The Yellow shrank back. He glanced toward his companions; the Blue was sprawled out across treetops, whimpering. The Brown was nowhere to be seen.

"We have taken Riddess Castle," said the Yellow. But he fell back several yards. "We will move across the land. If Mount Gore does not stand with us, it, too, will fall." He twisted about, glared at the Blue, and slinked off through the rain.

The Blue glanced behind himself at Kallon, his tail tucked, and followed the Yellow.

Kallon watched them until they were pinpoints over distant trees. Then he slowly turned back, and found his family, his Riza, smiling at him.

"Is everyone all right?" he asked, his eyes traveling the drenched faces of pale and dark human strangers. Plus the black dragon who eyed Kallon with some trepidation.

"Orman is injured," said Sela. "Drell has an arrow in his wing. But we're all right, now," she said.

"Yes," said Riza, nuzzling close, her wing tip stroking Kallon's ribs. "We're all right."

"Good," said Kallon. "Very good. Let's go home."

The four dragons shook out their wings, and fought through the wind in silence and concentration.

A moment later, Kallon spoke. "Who is Drell?"

Chapter Twenty-Four

Sela awoke to her first morning in Mount Gore manor that felt like real home in years. She stared up in her same chamber, with a leaf-woven canopy over her sleeping mat, and a stack of unused painting canvases. But it felt different.

She felt different.

All was not settled. Her father described the Riddess takeover as a rip in the province fabric, and Sela understood. A connection had been severed between dragons, the sort of tie so natural and accustomed, that it isn't noticed until it's damaged. Unrest whispered through the land.

And it would be naïve to think of the violence as far away, and 'over there.' Gone unchecked, unchallenged, it would be spreading like mold, contaminating all it could touch.

Sela shivered at the thought, familiar with the scent of it. She'd come too close to it already.

But that was for yesterday's thoughts, and tomorrow's.

Today, she was home.

She crept quietly from her chamber to peer down the hallway, and to listen. Others were up, too, talking quietly in another room. She heard the scrape of wooden plates against a table, and smelled the cinnamon-smoky scent of mulled meat. Her mouth watered.

Her wing tips trailed along the floor beside her as she made her way to the Great Hall. There, Drell shot to his feet, his golden eyes wide, his expression stricken with shock, or fear, or something she didn't recognize. She actually looked behind herself, expecting to find Whitetail or Blackclaw leering toward her.

"Good morning," said her mother, smiling, drawing her into the room with both forepaws. "We're serving your favorite."

"Where are the others?"

"All the humans sleep," said her father from a corner, his claws shining with greasy spices. "Just as well, for now. We've sent word to the council to gather here."

"And Vaya Browning," said her mother, her eyes soft as she regarded Drell. Relieved, in some way. Her mother's smile was rich and heartfelt, and it lit her face as though her mouth sparks were escaping.

Her father noticed it too, judging by the way he gazed at her.

"What will I do when she arrives?" asked Drell.

"You will talk," said her mother. She looked at Sela's father, returning his gaze. "We'll all have a long talk."

"No more secrets," said Sela.

"We can't afford them," said her father. "Not now. Not when we harbor an Esra Venur and Venuress, and the dragon faction there is priming for a fight."

Sela nearly asked about the Venuress, but realized her father referred to her.

"I believe Shornmar castle will stand with us when we denounce the uprising," said her father. "We'll need to gather our allies, dragon and human."

"Whitetail had Esra soldiers with him," said Drell.

Her father shook his head. "It seems those intent on war will have it, one way or another." He looked from Drell to Sela. "We tried to keep it from the land, and from our offspring. But your generation will not be spared."

"Is any generation spared?" asked Sela.

Her mother laid her paw on Sela's head, and sighed deeply.

Sela played the tip of her tongue against her longest tooth. Then lifted her chin. "Father, there is one ally I asked to join us here. He saved Orman in the fight. He helped us escape."

"We need all the brave souls we can gather."

"He is Jastin Armitage," she said.

She watched darkness pass behind her father's eyes. Her mother's face tightened. They regarded each other in silence, but Sela knew they communicated rapidly, their anger shared.

"He is not welcome here," said her father.

"That's what Jastin said."

"Then it is perhaps the first time he has been right about something."

"I've already invited him."

"He is a changed man," offered Drell. "I've witnessed his remorse."

Her father swung his burning gaze to Drell, who shrank back toward the wall.

"He won't come," said her mother. "Especially if he is as changed as you say. Put it out of your mind, Kallon. The council will be here soon, and we'll discuss all our options, everything, then. We'll decide what next to do."

"How long until they arrive?" asked Sela.

"Some time yet."

"Then I'd like to ask something," said Sela, her voice soft, uncertain whether it was appropriate to be so looking forward to something when they were so surrounded with uncertainty and trouble.

"Our daughter is home, after all these long years away," said her mother, her smile returning. "Of course it is appropriate to celebrate."

"Then may we?" she asked, turning her question to her father.

"We may," he said, rising. "And a fine idea it is."

"What idea?" asked Orman, hobbling into the room. The bandage around his shoulder had leaked through and turned brown, but his pallor had improved, and his eyes were clear. "Mulled meat? My dear Riza, you know how to please a palate. Indeed." He lifted a plate from the table and dug it into the pile of pulled pork in a serving trench.

That was a good sign, too.

"The council will be arriving soon, Orman," said her father. "If they arrive before we return, entertain them for me."

"Why? Where are you going?"

"We have some remembering to do," said Riza.

"Oh." Orman shoveled in a mouthful of meat. "More for me."

Moments later, they were there. Over the mountains she loved, across the sky that hugged the lands she'd long for, and through the misty ringlets of morning fog that stroked evergreen pines and mantled secrets beneath the shivering elms, Sela celebrated with her family.

Kallon, Riza, and Sela flew.

MORE FROM BIG IMAGINE

Own Them All!

Redheart

Book One of the Leland Dragons Series

Make sure to read the first
entry in the Leland Dragons
Series, too!

*"Marvelous! Jackie Gamber has
created a wondrous, enthralling
world of adventure, mystery,
and richly crafted characters.
Dragons soar--and so do we!
This is high fantasy at its most
extraordinary."*

- T. A. Barron,
New York Times bestselling creator of
The Merlin Saga and *The Great Tree of Avalon*

Find *Redheart* online and everywhere you buy books!
Print and digital versions are available internationally.

More from Big Imagine

Science Fiction

Living Things

Short Tales of Science Fiction and Dystopia

"Living Things is about aching to be, striving to embody our best selves, and remaining optimistic in the face of adversity; success not guaranteed."

- Anthony Taylor
author of *Voyage to the Bottom of the Sea: The Complete Series - Volume 2*

Find *Living Things* in both print or digital versions online, and wherever you buy books!

Fantasy

Liminal Space

Fiction from the Slipstream

"Jackie Gamber's world and character building are astonishing. The stories are so vivid they leap off the page and transport you into the middle of the story with the characters."

- Robin Blankenship
Librarian, freelance editor,
and literary blogger of *Robin's Book Spot*

Find *Liminal Space* online, or print and digital versions are both available wherever you buy books!

www.ingramcontent.com/pod-product-compliance
Lightning Source LLC
Chambersburg PA
CBHW072038190726
48294CB00005B/1315